Please feel free to send n
publisher filters these en

Violet Samuels – <u>violet_samuels(a)awesomeauthors.org</u>

Sign up for my blog for updates and freebies!
<u>violet-samuels.awesomeauthors.org</u>

About the Publisher

BLVNP Incorporated, A Nevada Corporation, 340 S. Lemon #6200, Walnut CA 91789, info@blvnp.com / legal@blvnp.com

DISCLAIMER

Praise for Unique, Different, Found

Loved this book! Was different than any other werewolf romance I've read! Has some action! Some comedy which had my husband staring at me like I'm crazy!! Would recommend for young adult to adult!

-Sissy Brady, Amazon

This story is a great read. When I first read it on Wattpad, I was pulled in and held hostage, and now the edited version on here is even better. Don't miss out on an excellent story that is the first of the series.

-Lesley Collis, Amazon

The book is so amazing it was filled with so much emotion and I couldn't stop reading the book I had to keep reading and reading.

-Liliana, Goodreads

No words to explain the feelings I felt reading this book. It was a great read! Absolutely loved it!!

-Jennifer Sanchez, Goodreads

I love this book, certainly one of my favorites.

-Alicia Zamora, Goodreads

I was amazed by this book. I mean I know there are tons of werewolf, alpha stories but this one is a real page-turner. This reminds me so much of the *Matefinder* series. I love this book and would read the next one.

-Emily West, Goodreads

Nightfall Series

Unique, Different, Found

By: Violet Samuels

BLVNP

ISBN: 978-1-68030-849-5

Table of Contents

It would be my greatest honour to dedicate this book to my friends and family who pushed me to write this book when I thought I couldn't.

FREE DOWNLOAD

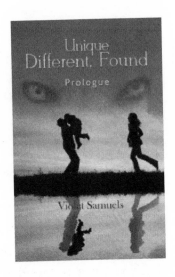 

Get these freebies and MORE when you
sign up for the author's mailing list!

violet-samuels.awesomeauthors.org

1

CELINA

Have you ever felt like you can never escape? Have you ever felt like there is no one there for you? Have you ever felt like the whole world is against you and you just want to get away and be free? Have you ever felt that you can never be loved or cherished?

That's my life.

I feel all of these things. You can't change what fate has in store for you. But sometimes, I wish I could just be free and live my own life. I haven't been able to do that for a total of nine years.

My mother and father died when I was seven. I was abandoned and left with my godforsaken pack. I had no regrets when my mother and father died. I spent every second of every day with them, and they never argued. We didn't have any major fights and we all loved each other so much. I didn't think my parents had any regrets either. I think they made the mistake of leaving me alone, though.

You're probably wondering why I'm blaming it on them, aren't you? Well, I don't. I blame my pack for being worthless, unfair, stupid and plain right mean. Childish I know, but true, down to the last detail. Every beating, every bruise, every broken bone and every possible evidence of them abusing me supports that horrid theory.

Ever since my parents died, I've been like a slave to the people I call my pack. I cook, wash, clean, organize and pretty much do everything for them. They throw away money like it's no big deal, and they don't spare a second glance to anyone who's 'lower' than them.

Someone like me.

All the wolves in my pack are gorgeous with either brown or blonde fur and have a mix of either blue, green, brown, or almost black eyes. Having plain blue or green eyes is rare. They have slim or muscular bodies and have the perfect height just to be much taller than humans. Unfortunately, that beauty is tainted by their bitter egos and cold hearts.

My parents were like the pack looks wise, but not personality wise. My parents were kind and thoughtful, always putting others before themselves. They never should've been in this pack in the first place.

The funny thing is, I look nothing like my parents or anyone in the pack for that matter.

Instead of blonde or brown hair, mine is pitch black, pin straight and comes down to just below my shoulders. My eyes are a shining gold that lost its shine many years ago, so now it looks like a light shade of mud. My lips are almost red and, strangely, my skin is pale. I'm not sure why... Most Werewolves have beautifully tanned skin. I'm also a bit shorter than everyone else, but I still have that slim body that anyone would die for. In my parents' opinion, being different is what makes you special. What makes you special, is what makes you unique.

I never believed it, though. All it has ever done was got me teased, and pushed around for being 'different' and 'unique'. It has always been like that. Even with my parents, they always said the pack was just jealous of my obvious beauty, one that I am oblivious to.

Another thing. When I turned sixteen, I made sure I was far away from the pack house, almost on the borders of our territory. The reason? I was shifting. I didn't want to give everyone the satisfaction of seeing my pain, and watching my every bone break after the other. I can honestly say that it is the most painful thing you will ever experience in your life.

When I shifted, I discovered that my wolf was snow white. Not one trace of colour other than white covered me. I was astounded. I had never seen a white wolf. Even my mother's and my father's wolves were brown and blonde, respectively. They told me that when I shifted, never to show to anyone my wolf unless they have my full trust. Nobody has.

I don't know what it means to have a pure white wolf, but I know that I'm different yet again. This time, in a way, I thought I could somehow fit into my pack. I thought wrong. When I came back, I got a beating because I was gone for most of the day, and everyone missed lunch and breakfast. That night, I had to make a three-course meal instead of the usual one, and I had to clean the house until it was spotless. Let's just say I stayed up way past midnight...

I haven't been for a run since. That was three weeks ago. My wolf has been howling in my head, and it feels like she's scratching my insides apart. I badly want to let her out, but I'm too scared. I don't want to get beaten up again.

My wolf has told me multiple times to get away, and I've been considering it for months now. Tonight's the night. I'm leaving. I'm ditching this stupid place and leaving for good. When I told my wolf, she was practically jumping with joy.

I'm making the dinner right now. Although this pack has treated me like nothing, I'm gonna give them something to remember me by, and if that means food, then so be it.

I decide to make one of my favourite courses. For entree, bruschetta with mini prawn cocktails. For main, lasagna with garlic bread. Then for dessert, my personal favourite, chocolate mud cake with whipped cream, ice cream and chocolate covered strawberries on top. If it were me, I would just skip the entree and main and go straight for the dessert.

I set the table for the pack, and as soon as I finish placing the last of the entrees on the table, they walk in through the door. As soon as they get a whiff, they come barging into the dining room, taking a seat and digging in. No 'thank you' or 'this is nice', just like the usual.

I always keep a spare bit of dessert for myself after I finish cooking, so while the rest of the pack eats, I tuck into my mud cake. At least, they let me eat, I guess.

When I hear the bell, I walk back out and collect the empty plates, taking them back to the kitchen. To let them digest a bit, I wash it all up and place it on the drying rack.

I come back out with the last of the mains and am about to walk out when Tina, the pack slut, calls my name.

"Celina!"

I slowly turn around, keeping my hands behind my back, and my head bowed. I'm wearing the correct uniform for serving dinner, and my hair is neatly pulled back into a high ponytail, so I'm not sure what she wants. Whenever someone in the pack calls my name, it's usually because I'm in trouble.

"Why the whole 'fancy-fancy' food? Is it a special occasion? Let me guess... Is it for Damon's birthday? A little present from you?" She snickers at me. I feel all eyes turn to me, but I obediently keep my head down. Damon is the soon to be the alpha of our pack and is turning eighteen in about four days. It's a big thing, and I'm supposed to cook for it...

"I guess you could consider it that. If the alpha is kind enough to accept my gift, of course," I answer in a small voice. I was told from the beginning to address Damon as alpha and nothing else, unlike the rest of the pack.

The room falls silent as every eye turns to Damon, who's sitting at the head of the very large dining table. I look through my long, black lashes to see his face. I'm met with a considering expression.

He nods his head once. "I accept your gift. I will expect a grander and more appropriate gift on my actual birthday, though. Do you understand?" His tone's filled with power and authority.

"Yes, Alpha, I understand," I say, returning to my former position with my head down.

"Good. Now, off you go." He shoos me off, and as soon as I enter the kitchen, I hear their laughs and snickers. I tried not to cry. I've shed too many tears over these heartless people.

They soon finish their meals, and it's time for dessert. I've finished mine by now, so I place theirs on the table with a blank face. They eat up and by the time everyone has finished and has stayed around talking, I've cleared the large table and washed up.

I enter back into the dining room and wait in my usual spot by the door of the kitchen. Every night before I go to bed, I either get hit or nothing for the meals I've cooked. It's the same with breakfast, lunch, and any other meals they eat. As each one walks out of the room, I either get shoved or ignored, which means they liked my cooking. Tina, on the other hand, slaps me across the face. You probably think that's harsh, but that's equivalent to someone else's shove. So just imagine what someone else's slap is to her. It's not a pretty sight.

Damon is the last to leave, and he stops in front of me. I cautiously lift my head and stare into his beautiful blue-green eyes. He has a blank face, as do I. We stare at each other for a moment before he walks out and leaves me alone in the dining room to fix up.

Damon has been my crush since I was about ten, even though he treats me like the worthless thing I am. His brown hair and blue-green eyes are the main aspects that draw me and many other female wolves in. He hasn't found his mate yet either, which means he's available. He wouldn't go for me, though. Not in a million years. I'm too different.

I head to bed in the early hours of the night. The pack no longer requires me after about 7:30 pm, so I am ordered to bed, which I quickly oblige, so as not to get beaten. I still have bruises from the worst ones.

The sad thing is, I believe everything my pack had said since my parents died. That I'm not beautiful, but ugly. That I'm not unique, but different. That I'm not a part of their family, but their slave.

I sigh as I enter my makeshift room. It's bare, except for a large window that lets the moonlight from the full moon flood into my room. My bed is pretty much a sheet on the hard, splintered, wooden floor, and my pillow is a pillow cover stuffed with newspaper.

I won't be sleeping there tonight, though. Not anymore. Not ever again.

I pack what little belongings I have inside a sack – A pair of worn out jeans, an oversized shirt with holes in it, a skirt, one other shirt that appears to be clean, and a pair of socks. I don't own any shoes.

I grab the only piece of jewellery I have, my mother's silver necklace with her and my father's names engraved into the heart-shaped pendant. The pendant has a yin and yang symbol in it, but it's made with little black and white crystals. I slip it into my shirt and proceed to the window.

I open it wide, and without a glance back, or second thought, I jump. I jump to my freedom and my new life.

I shift into my snow white wolf and take off with my sack in my mouth. I don't know where I'm going. I don't know if I can survive. I am only a newly shifted wolf at the age of sixteen.

What do I know? I'll never have to see my 'pack' again. That is enough to make me smile slightly in my wolf form. As I cross the border of the territory, my wolf lets out a howl, filled with happiness and joy.

We're free. I'm free.

Never again will we have to face the Moonlight pack.

2

CELINA

I pick up speed as I launch through the trees. I let my wolf instincts take over and let her guide me.

I've been running for a few hours now, and I'm just starting to feel the effects of it. For those few hours, I've been running in no man's land. I'm not sure if I'm going around in circles or if this land is really big. Maybe it's just me...

I finally cross a border in the early hours of the morning. I'm not sure if they have patrollers or not, but I sure hope they don't. I think this pack is the Greenwood Pack. They're not vicious or well known or anything really. They're just sort of there. I make it through their territory easily, which probably isn't the best for them if anybody plans to attack them.

This is the same for the next few territories. The Fire Pack had a few wolves chasing me down. Well, more like tracking my scent after I was long gone. Nobody's seen my wolf so far...

I'm once again on no man's land, but this is just a thin strip. About a kilometre wide, maybe? Anyway, I've been running for more than a good twelve hours. I think I deserve a rest after sprinting most of that.

I settle down by a nearby stream and shift back into my battered human form. I quickly pull on my old baggy top and worn out jeans. I sit down by the stream and let my feet flow with the water. I rest my head on my shoulder and lean on my arms as I soak up the heat of the sun.

I smile slightly. It has been so long since I could just relax, and not wait around fearful for the next beating to come.

I sit there for a few minutes before my stomach growls. I groan. Food! Why didn't I think of bringing food with me? I sigh and take my clothes off again, shifting into my wolf. Too late now. I'm not really one to hunt in wolf form... After all, yesterday was only the second time I shifted.

I continue on my run for freedom and reach the next pack's territory. I stop at the border and notice a few wolves lurking in the shadows, trying to be discreet. I look around for something to disguise myself in. What? I can't just waltz in there! What if they catch me and question me about the colour of my wolf?

I just roll in some mud after spotting it and make my fur look brownish. I wait for it to dry before hiding behind a bush, ready to run at any moment.

I watch the shadows and spot some of the same wolves as before. A few more minutes pass before they move on, maybe switching shifts. I take the opportunity.

I break out into a full-blown sprint, right through the middle of their territory. I don't stop when I hear howls of alarm from the new wolves that have taken over the section of the border I just crossed, probably smelling my scent. No, I keep running.

What I definitely don't expect is to be nearly tackled to the ground by a sandy coloured wolf. It growls at me with its teeth bared, and makes a move to lunge for me, but I jump out of the way and take off sprinting again. The wolf lets out a howl and I hear the heavy fall of paws close behind me. I think about four or five wolves are trailing behind me at the moment.

I pick up speed, begging my wolf to go faster. She whimpers, but increases her speed.

'Come on! We need to get out of here!' I scream at her as I make a sharp right and then left, trying to lose the wolves behind me. It doesn't work.

'I'm trying! I don't think I can go any faster!' she screams back in panic. As her panic overtakes her, my panic overtakes me as well. What if they catch us? What if I don't make it? What if they kill us?

That thought strikes home, and my wolf pushes to go faster and faster. I hear the fall of paws getting softer and softer in the distance.

'We're gonna make it!' I cry in relief, and we did.

Just as we burst through the border, I see that wolves line in it, for as far as the eye can see. The sandy one stands tall and proud in the middle of the line. Its light brown eyes penetrate my gold ones.

Its head cocks to the side as it observes me. My earlier relief washes away as he takes a cautious step over the border. I take an equal two steps backward, and he stops immediately. I stare at him with fear in my eyes, and he stares back at me with confusion.

He backs up into the border and ducks behind a tree. He emerges again with a pair of shorts on and in human form.

He has the usual blonde hair, more sandy-ish though like his wolf's, and light brown eyes. He's fairly tanned and looks about 19 or 20, I'm not sure. He has a built body, but not really the bulky or lean type. Just right, some people would say. Overall, I would class him as cute.

He steps over the border once again, approaching me. I take another step back, and he freezes.

"I won't hurt you. All I want to do is talk," he says, his voice calm and not seeming to hold a lie. I snicker, though. I've learned not to trust anyone, so I don't.

"Shift back," he orders. This is when I realize he's probably in a much higher place than I ever was. Maybe third in command or beta? Either way, I am at the bottom of the pack, so he immediately outdoes me. I'm no longer in his territory, though, so why should I listen? I can sprint off any moment, and he can do nothing about it.

I shake my oversized wolf head at him and growls erupt from the defense line. Well, they obviously don't like people disobeying their superiors.

Another wolf steps forward, and I cower away in fear. The guy looks him straight in the eye, and the wolf obediently backs down. I relax a little, but still stay tensed.

'Can't we just run? They can't follow us, we're not on their territory,' I ask my wolf desperately.

'We could, but they would still send others after us. Plus, you're only new to this and don't know how to harness all your power yet,' she answers back. Power? What power?

Before I can ask, the guy speaks up again. "My name's Callum. I'm the beta of the Nightfall Pack."

Well, that answers my earlier assumptions. I make no move to shift, and he doesn't make a move to, well, move.

Hold on a second... Nightfall Pack? I've never heard of them. Maybe Damon kept that little bit of information from me like he's done for other packs I've asked about. I only know the Greenwood and Fire pack. That's all I've learned.

It's silent for a few minutes. I guess he is waiting if I'll shift. Callum's face falls for a second before he puts on a blank face.

"It's either shift or see our alpha. Your choice," he says, and my eyes widen.

I back up behind a tree and shift. I yank on the same clothes as before but make no move to come out.

"You done?" Callum calls from his earlier spot. I nod before mentally hitting myself. He can't see you, Celina...

"Yes," I say quietly, but I know he and everyone else hear me. I can't help it. I just can't talk loud to someone I haven't met.

"I'm not coming out, though," I state a bit more firmly. I hear a chuckle and a few snickers at my statement.

"Why would that be?" he asks me with amusement in his voice.

I take a deep breath and answer him, "I'm no longer in your territory, and you have no rights to a rogue."

My wolf growls at the word 'rouge', but it gets everyone to shut up.

"You ran through our territory, and any rogue who trespasses must be punished. There is no exception to that rule," he answers in a business like tone.

I sighed before answering one last time, "You're right, there isn't, but according to werewolf law, there is. If a rogue is to trespass through a territory and is captured, they will be punished. If they trespass and make it through without being captured, they are free to leave without any questions. The only exception to the rule is if the rogue is a criminal, wanted, or psycho that needs to be locked away and captured. I am neither of those three. I have never committed a crime in my life, I am not wanted for any reason, and by no means am I a psycho. If you don't believe me, look up section D, paragraph 14.5.2, to see if I'm wrong, in the werewolf laws."

I take a breath once I finish and wait for an answer. Silence. That's what I'm met with.

I sigh once again and strip, turning back into my wolf. I make sure I'm still covered in mud and step out into the open. I'm met with the shocked faces of wolves and Callum. I nod my head in a sign of respect and trot away. Surely, they can't stop me now.

"Wait!" someone suddenly shouts when I am about fifty metres away from the border. I come to an abrupt stop and slowly turn to see a young teenager with brown hair and dark, almost black, eyes staring at me. He also has shorts on, thankfully. He's a bit lean but has muscle as well.

He slowly approaches me, and as he gets closer, I can see he's about my age. What is he doing protecting the borders and hunting down rogues at such a young age? That should be illegal.

He stops about two metres away from me and kneels down, staring into my eyes.

"Comrade! What do you think you're doing?" An angry and distressed-looking Callum calls. He doesn't move, though, and neither does the boy. Comrade, I guess that is his name.

"You're a long way from home, aren't you?" he asks, voice soft, and quiet, soothing almost. Flashes of my old pack run through my head, and I feel a single tear run from my eye and into my fur. I slowly nod my head, my eyes filled with sorrow and pain.

"Do you miss it?" he asks again, voice still the same as before. I shake my head this time and surprise flitters through his eyes. He obviously isn't expecting that answer. His eyes turn sorrowful.

"I think all you need is a friend. Someone who will listen to you and make you feel happy. Am I right?" he asks gently as he moves forward and strokes my mud covered fur. My wolf purrs with delight at the touch. I must admit, it feels nice.

I flop down onto my belly and lay my head on my paws, half closing my eyes.

"You want a home, a place you can be safe and comfortable. Not somewhere where you're constantly stressed and afraid. Tell me, am I right?" Comrade asks again, seeming to know everything about me without even knowing me. Another tear slips down my fur as I nod.

"Why don't you come with us?" he suggests. My head snaps up, and I stare at him with wide eyes. Stay?

"You'll have a home; you'll be happy. All those wolves standing along the border will be your family and will care for you. Just like they did to me," he whispers the last part, and a smile takes over his face.

I stare at him, contemplating. Sooner or later I'm gonna be killed or captured, and I have a feeling it's gonna be sooner rather than later. I slowly stand up and make my way to a tree, shifting and pulling on some clothes. I take my time and ask myself a question.

Do I really want this?

A home. A family. Love. Care. Everything I've always wanted. I guess the question shouldn't be hard to answer, but it is. I've been beaten, bashed, cut, whipped, spat on, pushed down stairs, the list is endless. Will this pack really show me kindness and compassion? Or will they be just like my old pack? Now understand this, why would I just give myself to a pack... when I just became free?

On the other hand, this pack seems nice. The beta seems to be a kind man, Comrade seems to have taken a friendly liking to me, and every one of those wolves on the border will protect their pack no matter what. You could tell by their worried faces when Comrade came up to me, and by the fierce expression that took over them when I questioned their beta.

Two valuable points. Only one answer.

Taking risks is what builds character and never in my life have I taken a risk. I've never stood up to anyone. Never questioned anyone. Never put my trust in anyone who's not my parents.

Taking a risk for once won't kill me.

I take a deep breath and step out from behind the tree. My hair is matted with mud; my clothes are old and worn; my face and body are bruised and scarred, yet... Comrade smiles at me. A full blown smile crosses his face, and I can't help the ghost of mine to cross my face.

Then I do something unexpected. I launch myself at him and hug him. I haven't hugged someone since I was seven. It's a nice feeling. He gladly hugs me back as I whisper in his ear, "Thank you."

I release him and back away, suddenly realizing what I've done. I drop my head and chew my lip nervously.

"Sorry," I apologize quietly. My old pack would've hit me and beaten me for touching them, so I brace myself for the hit. It never comes, though. Instead, I hear a small and quiet chuckle.

I look through my lashes to see Comrade smiling at me and shaking his head.

"No need to apologize. I take that as a yes then?" he asks hopefully, eyes shining with happiness. I don't know why, but I feel like I can trust Comrade, and that's the reason why I'm doing this.

I nod my head slightly, and his fist pumps the air while screaming, "Yes!"

I giggle at his dramatics and shake my head. He's certainly childish...

"May I have the honor, my lady?" he asks in a horrible British accent while bowing. I giggle again and nod my head, putting my hand in his outstretched one. He takes a firm hold of it and leads me back to the border where a grinning Callum and all the wolves are waiting.

I look back down and let my hair cover my face, nervousness suddenly overtaking me.

"They won't hurt you, you know? They're quite friendly," Comrade mentions with a chuckle and a shake of his head. I give him a small smile but look down again as we approach Callum and the others.

"Beta," Comrade addresses with great respect and loyalty, that it surprises me a little. Nobody even spoke to my alpha like that. Well, old alpha.

"I believe this little lady here would like to join the pack and, if I'm not mistaken, that needs the alpha's and beta's consent," Comrade says, still with a slight joking manner.

At the word alpha, I tense up. Comrade seems to notice and shoots me a worried look before turning back to a grinning Callum.

"It would be an honor to have such a lovely lady join the pack. All we need to do now is convince the alpha," he says with a shrug. I blink. I guess their alpha is pretty laid back if he has that kind of reaction to his pack mates.

A large number of the wolves spread back out along the border of their territory, and only a selected few stay behind.

"Right! Let's get you to the alpha, shall we?" Callum exclaims while clapping his hands together and grinning wickedly, making me a bit nervous.

As he walks off, Comrade and I trail behind, as the last wolves form a protective circle around us. Now is when I realize that Comrade still has a hold of my hand. I hurriedly drop it and cup my elbows instead. Comrade shoots me a questioning look, but I just hide behind my hair.

The trip is silent as we make our way through the territory. I didn't realize when I was running, but wow! This place is huge!

It has to be the largest territory I've come across!

After a very, very long walk and I almost collapsed multiple times from feeling faint, we arrive at the pack house. All I'm gonna say is that I'm glad I don't have to clean it.

It's huge! At least three times the size of my old pack's.

The whole of the outside is painted dark brown, and there's a patio going all around the house. Dark columns hold up the balcony that also runs around the whole second floor. In total, it appears to have about three floors in it and a very large backyard.

I hear Callum and Comrade chuckle at me, but I'm not sure why. That's until Comrade gently closes my jaw that is hanging wide open. I readjust myself and quickly put up my hair as a shield once again. They both chuckle and lead me inside. The wolves that were in a circle around us break off and disperse back into the shadows of the trees.

I gulp as I look at the large wooden door. Comrade slightly bumps me and whispers in my ear, "Relax. No one here will hurt you."

I nod my head but don't relax. Not even a little. I don't know these people, and I'm willingly walking into their very intimidating home. Now that I think about it, the dark colours really support that assumption.

As Callum opens and enters through the door, I take one more deep breath and trail inside with Comrade behind me.

The inside is just as magnificent as the outside. Instead of dark, intimidating colours, though, the walls are a cream colour and the floor tiles are a midnight black with white spots here and there. It's a beautiful contrast.

The first room you enter through the door is the foyer. It has a large, diamond chandelier that provides light in the room. Judging by the darkness from the outside by now, I would say it's about five or six o'clock.

As we walk through the rest of the house, the living room and dining room come into view, which are connected, the games room, which have a few younger pack members in it, and the cinema room. A cinema room!

The living room has a red, fluffy carpet spread across the whole floor and all the furniture is black leather. There is a massive flat screen TV spread across pretty much a whole wall and a fairly large cabinet underneath holding massive amounts of DVDs.

The dining room has the same tiles as the foyer, and I've realized that the tiles go right through the house, unless the room needs to be carpeted. It has a large dining table, which is much bigger than my old pack's that is placed as a kind of divider between the dining and living room. The countertops are all white granite with black spots here and there where an industrial-sized fridge and stove top are placed.

The games room is pretty much a room packed to the rim with game consoles, Wiis, controls, and about five TVs for all of the games to be viewed on. That room also has a carpet which is black. A good choice, in my opinion, because black carpet can hide stains and other things you don't want to know about.

The cinema room is basically like the games room, but with one massive flat screen and theatre seats instead of couches.

Callum and Comrade lead me down a long hallway and to a door with wooden carvings engraved into it. The carvings show two wolves, one black, one white. They are standing proudly next to each other with a whole army of black and white wolves behind them. There must be thousands! On the black wolf's left shoulder, there's half a yin and yang symbol. The half that's white. The white wolf bears the other half of the symbol. The black side. The way they're standing next to each other, it looks as though the symbol is one. It's the exact same symbol in my necklace.

I run my hand over the carvings of the symbol, and I'm suddenly knocked back onto the opposite wall with an invisible bolt of energy. It courses straight through me as I shake against the wall.

I see Comrade and Callum yelling at me, but I can't hear them. I'm sucked into a vision of black and white, and I'm suddenly on a full blown battlefield.

Standing on the outskirts of the battlefield, I watch as blacks, whites, browns and blondes muse together. It's clear to see that the blacks and whites are going against the browns and blondes.

Wolf after wolf drops down dead or injured, howling in pain. I want to look away, but I just can't. It captivates and intrigues me to see what's going on. I've never experienced this before, and it's reeling me in.

Two particular wolves catch my attention. One black. One white. Both working together to fight off oncoming wolves. They both have the yin and yang symbol that seems to join together even while they're apart.

Without thinking, I walk straight through the battlefield. Not caring if I got hit or attacked, all I want is to get to these wolves.

A wolf comes barreling at me, baring its teeth and getting ready to rip me apart, but it goes straight through me and attacks another wolf. Like I'm a puff of smoke. I don't pay much mind to it as I continue walking.

The wolves are smack bang in the middle of the fight, and when I reach them, everything seems to go into slow mo. The wolves turn around to face me at a normal speed, and as soon as their eyes land on me, recognition, disbelief, and love shine in them.

I stare into their eyes, both gold like mine. The only difference is that theirs are shining an alluring gold while mine looks like gold that's getting old.

They approach me, and I don't flinch or step back, which I'm guessing I probably should if I enter a full-on battlefield.

The white one bumps my hand with her snout. I rest my smoke like a hand on top of her head and pet it. The black one nuzzles its nose in the crook of my neck, having to bend down a little. Yes, werewolves are about as tall as a fully grown human male.

Time seems to speed up too quickly as the white wolf's snout and the black wolf's nuzzle go straight through me. I try to scream at them to come back when they jump back into the fight, but it's like my voice is taken from me.

I can't move. I can't speak.

I feel myself getting a bit lightheaded and fall to the ground. I grip my head as voices start to fill it, and I'm swept out of the battle.

3

CELINA

I drop to the floor in agony, gripping my head and holding back tears. What the hell? What just happened? One second I'm looking at the carvings on the door and the next I'm on a battlefield! What is this crazy and harsh world coming to? I don't even want to think about it right now...

"Hey, are you alright? We lost you for a sec there."

I can't tell who said it, but I look up to see Comrade and Callum staring at me with worried and confused expressions. I blink a few times and shake my head.

"Um, yeah. I have a bit of a headache, though," I tell them, grimacing. Relief takes over their expressions and Comrade pulls me up into a standing position. I wobble a bit and grip the wall for support.

"You sure you're ok?" Callum asks me. I close my eyes tightly and wait for the sensation to leave my body. I open them to find Callum in front of me and staring at me with an unknown expression. I take a deep breath and nod.

"Good. Let's get you to see the alpha then, shall we?" he asks, and cheekiness takes over his voice.

I stiffen once again when he says alpha and gulp. Comrade looks at me and smiles reassuringly. I take calming breaths as Callum opens the door, and we walk in. I notice Comrade doesn't move and shoot him a questioning look.

"I can't come in unless summoned. Only alphas and betas are allowed in there," he explains. All my calmness wash away when he said that. I nod stiffly and bite my lip. Here we go.

As soon as we enter the office, I'm engulfed by the most amazing scent. I breathe in deeply, closing my eyes for a moment. It's a mix of the forest and flowers, and my god! It's so amazing that's it's making my knees go weak!

What's with the crazy occurrences today?

I quickly control myself, having no idea what's going on. I duck my head and put my hands behind my back, still standing near the doorway uncomfortably and not knowing what to do.

"Alpha, this here is... Um, what's your name again? I don't think I've asked you yet," Callum starts, looking a bit nervous. Why is he nervous? I thought the alpha is laid back, isn't he? Getting back to Callum's question, I don't even realize I haven't given him my name.

I clear my throat before answering. "Celina," I say quietly. I hear a slight groan come from where Callum's standing, but I refuse to look up. I don't think I really want to know...

"Right. Alpha, this here is Celina. We found her on the outskirts of the border. She would like to join the pack. I've already given my consent, all that's needed is yours," Callum says respectfully, and still nervously. Well then, I guess the alpha is scary as hell... Even to the beta.

There's a long silence before a beautiful, deep, and husky voice speaks up. Again, making my knees go weak. "Callum, would you give us a moment? I'm going to have a... chat, with our possible future member of the pack."

Callum nods and shoots me a knowing a look, to which I reply with a pleading look. Help!

Callum exits and I'm left standing there. In an office. With an alpha. By myself. What's wrong with this picture? Fear courses through me and I start to shake. I can't do this! What will he do to me? Is he anything like my old alpha? Oh god, that's it! I'm outta here! Stuff joining a new pack, I'll just stay as free as a rogue!

As I reach for the door handle, a large warm hand grips it gently and entwines our fingers together. Sparks shoot from my hand and up my arm, making me gasp and jump. I still keep my head down, though. I don't think I want to look into the eyes of an alpha. They're so challenging and scary. Call me weak, I don't care, but they usually are.

"Look at me, Celina," he orders me in a soft voice. I whimper. God, that voice is amazing! I don't look up, though; too scared to see what beautiful eyes that voice holds. "Celina, look at me."

A finger tucks itself under my chin and lifts my head up, just enough for our eyes to meet. My gold eyes lock with his silver ones. They shine as they stare into mine, and a small smile comes to my face. His eyes seem to shine with happiness that I've never seen before. We hold the stare, and it's like I'm staring into his soul or something. Happiness radiates from him in waves as he continues to stare at me. I can't help but drop the guard I've been trying so hard to keep up, ever so slightly.

I let my eyes wander as he breaks the stare and examines me with a smile on his face. His natural white hair looks beautiful with his silver eyes and ever so slightly tanned skin. It's cut short on the sides, but a little longer on the top.

I've never seen a wolf with white hair before. It's unusual, like me. Even Comrade and Callum has brown and blonde hair. I wonder what his wolf is like. With my black hair and white wolf, I wonder if with his white hair comes a black wolf.

My eyes trail to his face. His pale pink lips and high cheek bones suit him well. The smile that lights up his face is even better.

As my eyes trail further southward, I see he has an amazing build. The dark blue button down shirt, with the sleeves rolled up to just above his elbows, clearly shows off the muscles in his arms and his amazing eight pack. The washed out, light blue jeans he's wearing also helps to compliment his over six-foot height. He looks to be around the same age as Callum, 19 or 20.

I run my nails over the exposed skin of his arms and he shivers at my touch. He grips my waist firmly and gently pushes me against the wall next to the door.

What am I doing? I never let anyone touch me! Sure, Comrade did, but I didn't realize I was doing it! This man's touch feels... nice. Comfortable, safe and secure.

"Well, aren't you a beauty to witness? A definite sight for sore eyes," he whispers in my ear. I shiver as his breath fans over my ear and neck, sucking in a sharp breath.

Once I realize what he's saying, I blush a slight pink and look down. His finger comes under my chin once again and wills me to stare into his eyes. His beautiful, totally strange, silver eyes. "Don't look away from me, Celina."

I gulp and nod. "W-what's your name?" I ask a bit curiously. I haven't really asked him yet, and Callum didn't help with just calling him alpha.

He chuckles at me before answering in a husky voice, "Axel."

He places a soft kiss on my neck, and I moan a little at the feel of it. It sends electricity pulsating through my veins and butterflies erupting in my stomach.

Axel chuckles. "You like that?" he asks as he places more and more feather-like kisses up and down my neck and across my jawline. My answers are more soft moans and silent whimpers. When he gets to just above my collar bone, I lose it. A loud moan escapes without my permission, and Axel returns it with a grunt.

He suddenly pulls away and backs up, leaving me to whimper and immediately think the worst. Doesn't he want me?

He looks pained as he stares at me. "Celina," he starts off and takes my hand in his, leading me to the couch on one side of his office. "Do you know what we are? Do you understand why you feel an attraction towards me?"

I stare at him blankly, and that seems to answer his question. He sighs and takes both my hands and entwines them together with his. He looks at them for a moment and smiles.

"Celina, do you know about mates?" he asks curiously, looking into my eyes. I nod silently, and he continues. "Do you know how to tell if someone's your mate?"

At that question, I shake my head. Where is this conversation going?

Axel lifts me effortlessly, making me squeal in surprise, before resting me in his lap. I stare at him in shock for a moment. He just smiles softly at me. I sigh and rest my head on his chest, counting his heartbeats as he strokes his fingers through my muddy hair. I should really wash that...

"You can tell who your mate is by looking into their eyes and everything around you stops. It's only them and no one else," he says as he grips me tighter to his chest. "Their touch to you is like a drug; you always want it. Sparks fly, and you feel butterflies in your stomach," he murmurs. He moves my hair to the side and draws little patterns on my neck, making me shiver with delight. "They can also make you feel a strong desire and need for them that you can't help but give in. You need them, as much as they need you." He lightly growls. His hands travel further downward to my hips, adjusting me, so I'm straddling his lap, and his hands are on my upper thighs. I blush at the position and look down.

He moves my black hair to the side and lifts my head, making me stare into his eyes. "So beautiful," he murmurs, before going for my neck. Instead of the nice feather-like kisses before, these are more demanding and lust filled. I tilt my head back to give him better access, moaning loudly as he nips my skin.

I run my hands through his gloriously soft, white hair and tug slightly, making him groan and a stirring in his pants draws my attention.

I gasp as I feel it push into my thigh. "Oh god," I moan as he pulls me tighter to him.

"You're my mate, Celina," he whispers against my neck.

I freeze, reality rushing back to me. I snap out of my lust-driven state and push against Axel's chest. It seems to catch him off guard as I push him away from me and jump off his lap.

Me? An alpha's mate? No way! How the hell is that possible? I'm too scared of alphas to have an alpha mate! Someone up there must really not like me.

I stare at him in shock, disbelief and... fear. Fear that I'm an alpha's mate. Fear of what Damon will do if he finds out. Fear about what might become of me.

"Celina, calm down. I'm not going to hurt you," Axel says calmly yet painfully while standing and taking a few steps toward me. My wolf's screaming at me to run to him and kiss him senseless, but I won't give in.

As he steps forward, I step back. I see the hurt and pain cross his face, and it brings me to a stop. I don't want to hurt him. I just want to be away from him.

"Please, j-just leave me a-alone," I beg with tears in my eyes. Flashes of Damon beating me run through my head like a DVD. I don't want that to happen again. I don't care if he's my mate; I'm getting out of here.

Before Axel can say a word, I hurry out of the room and sprint down the hallway. Ignoring the calls of Comrade and Callum, I burst through the door and shift, not caring about my battered clothes.

I run.

Like I always do, I run. Thunder up above tells me it's gonna rain soon, so I hurry up. Rain starts to fall lightly, and in a few seconds, it turns into a full downpour. I don't stop. I keep running and running until I reach the border.

I skid to a halt and look out into the forest. All I have to do is take one step, and I'm free again. My wolf's howling at me to go back to our mate, but I can't. I can't cross the border either. That would bring, not only me but Axel pain. I can't do that to him, as much as I don't want to admit.

I lay down on the forest floor that smells so much like him and put my head in my paws. Why is my life so hard? Is it too much to ask to be normal for once? No complications? Apparently so.

As the rain continues to fall, the mud covering my fur starts to wash away, leaving me with nothing but my white coat. I can care less if anyone sees me right now, though. All I want is for my mother to cuddle me, and my father to tell me everything will be alright. But no! The fate hates me, so my mother and father are dead and are never coming back. On top of that, I have an alpha as a mate! Yep, fate totally hates me.

As I sit there, I hear howls in the distance. One particular making me shiver. It's Axel. He's calling for us to come back, sending some type of message saying we're out here somewhere. As much as my wolf would love to howl out to him, I don't let her. I need peace right now and having him around isn't going to let me have it.

Hours pass before the rain finally stops. I can still hear the calls of the wolves in the pack. I don't believe they're still looking for me. A few more hours pass and the sun starts to rise over the trees, making the beautiful colours stand out that you couldn't see at night.

The falling of paws grabs my attention, and my ears perk up. From the corner of my eye, I see a chocolate brown wolf heading toward me slowly. I mentally sigh and stand up. The wolf freezes. Before I can make another move, two more wolves emerge. One I recognize as Callum, with his sandy fur and all. Now that I think about it, the brown one reminds me of Comrade. He has the same chocolate brown colour and almost black eyes.

Knowing they won't hurt me, I lay back down and close my eyes. I hear shuffling for a few moments before I hear two pairs of feet making their way toward me.

I open my eyes to see Callum and Comrade, wearing shorts. I just stare up at them as they look at each other uncertainly. The third wolf that had come is long gone. I guess he's getting Axel. Great.

"Celina, is that you?" Comrade asks as he sits down next to me, petting my fur and scratching behind my ear. I purr in response to his question. Callum silently joins him in petting me, sitting on the opposite side of Comrade.

"Why didn't you tell us you were a white wolf, Celina? We could've helped you," Callum says softly. I don't acknowledge him at all and continue staring out across the border. Nobody can help me. Not anymore.

I'll never be free again. I'll be forced to stay here with Axel because he's my mate and if I don't... I don't even want to think about it.

Don't get me wrong; I would rather be here than with Damon and my old pack. At least, the people here are kind and generous and actually listen to me when I talk. My old pack never did that. If I talked, I would either have a minor beating or be forced to work through the night. I'm glad things aren't that way anymore.

Without my permission, my mind wanders back to Axel. His beautiful face and hypnotizing eyes, their glorious silver colour flashing through my memory. I can stare into them all day.

I scold myself lightly for that thought. No, I will not give in to him. He's just like everyone else, an alpha who thinks he's higher and greater than anyone else in the world. He can be the alpha of the most powerful and well-known pack in the world or the weakest and almost invisible pack, but that still won't change the fact that he's just like every other alpha. Controlling and possessive.

With my mind coming to a conclusion, that I'm not sure I agree with, I stand up, knocking Comrade and Callum away in the process. I don't care, though; my body has gone completely numb. There is nothing left for me here.

I'm leaving... and never coming back.

"Celina? Celina, what are you doing? You can't just leave! You agreed to join the pack!" Comrade screams at me when his brain clicks onto what I'm about to do.

"Beta, do something! Anything!" he pleads desperately. I feel a bit guilty when I see the hurt in his eyes, but my decision stays the same.

Callum's standing there in shock. He merely shakes his head. He has no power over me, and he knows it.

"I can't do anything. She's made her choice. I have no power over her," he mutters to Comrade. My eyes are locked with his at the end of his sentence, and I nod my head in respect.

I take a deep breath and close my eyes for a second. 'I want this' I keep on telling myself, 'I want this.' I won't be forced to stay or do what I'm told. I'll be free once again and this time, I won't make any mistakes.

I step over the border, for the third time in one day, and look back at Comrade and Callum one last time. Callum's looking at me with what seems like pride and respect. He bows his head slightly to me, and I do the same.

I turn my head to Comrade and do a double-take. He's looking at me with so much sadness and sorrow that I feel sorry for him. I've only known him for less than a day, but even that short time can cause friendships. I walk over to him and nudge his shoulder. He hugs my neck and squeezes gently.

"You know, I thought I finally found someone like me. Someone who's gone through so much heartache and sadness, who could understand me," he whispers. I pull my head back to look at him and whimper out loud when I see the tears in his eyes. What has he been through? I'll probably never know.

"I thought I finally found someone who went through the same thing as me. I could see it in your eyes and still can. Please don't leave, please. Where will you go? You'll get yourself killed out there and you know it. Is that what you're trying to accomplish? Getting killed?" he asks harshly.

I back away from him completely, letting his arms drop to his sides. I look into his sad filled eyes and nod. That's my plan exactly. Getting killed means no pain. Having no pain means no heartache. Having no heartache means numbness, something I want so badly.

Comrade shuts his eyes for a few seconds, taking deep breaths. He finally opens them and looks at me. "I understand," he whispers, and I know he does. I nod at him and at a shocked Callum one last time, before turning around and walking away.

Sadly, I don't get very far. Out of nowhere, a beautiful pitch black wolf tackles me to the ground. Familiar tingles shoot up my spine as its paws make contact with my fur. I immediately know it's Axel.

He stands over me, growling in my ear. This is exactly what I'm afraid of. He's not gonna let me leave, ever. I am his and only his, and I'm gonna have to accept that fact. I know escaping is hopeless.

I stare out into the forest longingly, now knowing that I won't ever get to explore it. I'm limited to the borders of the territory, and I'm probably never gonna be allowed out of

Axel's sight. My freedom is snatched out of my hands like a lollipop taken from a baby. It's something I'm never gonna get back.

Axel nudges me in the side, willing me to get up. I slowly do as he wants and follow him closely back to the border, where Callum and Comrade are standing with only one emotion: sympathy. I don't want their sympathy, though. I want freedom.

I keep my head down as we trail back to the pack house. I wait outside as Axel shifts back to get clothes for myself and him. He leaves Callum and Comrade to 'guard' me outside, but all they're doing is sitting next to me and not saying a word.

Axel walks back out, throwing a simple, white sleeveless dress at me. I stare at it for a moment. Really? Out of everything in that place they call a house, he chose that.

He growls at me warningly, and I sigh lightly, lifting the dress up with my teeth and heading for a tree. I shift and slip it on. It hugs my small frame perfectly and shows off all the right curves. It complements my pale skin and contrasts immensely with my black hair and red lips. I now see why he chose it... Pervert.

I step back out, keeping my head down, and go back to stand in between Callum and Comrade. I feel safe with them, don't ask me why, I just do. Axel's a different story. I don't know what I feel for him now.

We all trail inside and head back to where I first started, Axel's office. As we near it, I remember the door and what happened when I touched it. When Axel opens the door and walks in, I turn to where the door turns. I stare back at the same two wolves I saw before, and silently think: "What's so special about them?"

A hand on my back brings me back from my little world. I stare back into Callum's eyes and silently ask him. He just shakes his head and leads me into the office. He soon exits, once again leaving me with Axel.

Axel hasn't spoken a word yet, neither have I. It's been at least 20 minutes. I just want to get my punishment over and done with; there's no point waiting.

I keep my head down and my arms behind my back, standing in the middle of Axel's very large office. I close my eyes and will myself not to cry. I know a punishment's coming, I just don't know how he does his punishments. Damon always chose the harshest ones. It either ended in me getting beaten, cut, or pushed. One time, they even shaved my hair. That's why it's just below my shoulders. It used to run down to my hips.

Axel stops what he's doing, which is pacing the room, and leans on his desk, putting his head in his hands.

"You were going to leave me," he whispers, his voice filled with so much hurt it makes a single tear slip down my cheek. "Why?"

I don't answer at first, not knowing what to say. I know why, because I can't stand to be around an alpha that I know will be just like my old one, but I can't say that to his face. I'm weak and a coward in some ways, thinking but never saying.

When he hears no response from me, he moves forward, coming toward me slowly. I close my eyes and will myself not to move back as he keeps taking more and more steps.

"Answer me," he demands.

I whimper in response as another few traitor tears slip down my cheeks. I slowly shake my head. I can't tell him.

"Why not?" he demands again. My knees shake from the intensity of his words. "Why can't you tell me why you left? Why can't you tell me why you ran out of here crying? Why can't you tell me! Why!" He's screaming by the end of it and this time, I drop to my knees. They give in.

I've never heard someone speak so fiercely, not even Damon, and it was all directed to me. Fear strikes me hard, and all I can wish for is that he won't hit me, or worse...

I stare at Axel's shoes and release a sob. "I don't want to hurt you," I choke out as another sob escapes me.

Next thing I know, one of the chairs in front of Axel's desk goes flying across the room, smashing into the wall, and breaking it into tiny bits. I whimper and bite my lip, trying not to release another sob.

"Hurt me?! You're telling me, that you won't tell me why you left because you don't want to hurt me?" He screams again. I just merely nod, silent tears running down my face as I continue to bite my lip so hard that I split it, and it starts to bleed. "You should've thought about not hurting me before you ran out of here," he whispers, a big downturn from his screaming.

"P-please, I n-never meant to h-hurt you," I choke through my sobs. He makes no move to acknowledge me. "Y-you don't k-know what I've b-been t-through," I whisper before I break down into sobs at his feet. He doesn't know, though, and with the way we're going, I don't think he'll ever know.

He doesn't move. He doesn't comfort me. He doesn't care.

"I just can't look at you right now," he whispers before leaving me in a crying heap. Seconds later, the door bursts open and I'm engulfed in a hug by none other than Comrade.

"Shh, Snow, shh. Everything's gonna be ok, calm down. Shh," he soothes while rocking me in his lap.

I cry into his lap for who knows how long. My mate, the one who's supposed to love, care and comfort me, walked out and left me. He just walked out.

When I have no more tears, I lift my head from Comrade's shoulder. I look into his pain-filled eyes and suddenly wish that he is my mate instead of Axel. Comrade's sweet, caring and is actually here for me when I'm crying. Why can't Axel be like him?

"I'm sorry," I mumble into his now wet shoulder. He must think I'm the weakest and the most stupid wolf of the century.

He surprises me by laughing lightly. "For what, Snow?" he asks, stroking my hair tenderly.

I lift my head up and look at him. He's so handsome. Brown hair, almost black eyes, tanned skin, and he's my age. He's normal.

"For wetting your shirt," I say sheepishly. He smiles at me.

"No problem, Snow. It's only water after all," he tells me, pushing my head back into his shoulder gently. He continues to rock me soothingly while humming in my ear and stroking my hair when something occurs to me. Snow?

"Did you just call me Snow?" I mumble into his shoulder. I feel them vibrate from his silent laughter, and I lightly slap his stomach, my head still tucked away in his shoulder. "I'm serious."

He sighs. "Yeah, I did. I think it suits you, with your white coat and all. I also think that your black hair, red lips, and pale skin remind me of Snow White. All you need now is the bright blue eyes," he jokes, making me laugh lightly as my eyes start to get droopy.

"Tired?" he asks and I hum in response. I start to doze off as he continues to rock me. Maybe staying here won't be so bad if Comrade's here with me, I think before I fall into a blissful sleep. Something I haven't done for a long time.

4

CELINA

As I run through the park in my seven-year-old self, I squeal in delight. Daddy's chasing me and mummy's laughing at us.

"Rah!" Roars daddy.

"Ahh!" I squeal in return. Soon mummy joins in and we all drop to the floor in exhaustion.

We stare up into the clear blue sky, not a cloud in sight, and soak up the glorious sun's rays. I close my eyes for a few brief seconds, only to open them and see that I'm in a dark room. I look around and notice that the room's bare. Where has the park gone?

The door in front of me gingerly squeaks open and in steps alpha Damon. I bow my head in respect. Next thing I know, I'm being thrown across the room into the opposite wall. I slump down and groan in pain. Then I dare to ask the question, "Where's my mummy and daddy?"

Damon's face breaks out into a wicked smirk, while I sprout a frown, as he slowly makes his way toward me. I cower back as he squats down in front of me.

"Mummy and daddy..." He pauses for a second, making suspense on what he's about to say next. "...are dead."

I bolt upright and scream bloody murder. Beads of sweat cover my forehead, my hands are shaking, my heart is racing way too fast, and my cheeks are wet from the tears I don't even know I've shed.

I hug my knees to my chest and cry. I haven't had that dream in years. That dream is the exact replica of how I found out my parents died. I didn't leave that room for a week. No food. No water. Nothing. I didn't know back then that it was part of my torture. I cried for weeks after that. I loved my mother and father so much; I can't even bear the thought of losing them.

I cry harder at the thought. The problem is, I've already lost them.

Seconds after my outburst, my door slams open. I don't look up from my knees, too scared for someone to see me like this.

Moments later, I'm engulfed in a hug and rested in the person's lap. "Shh, Snow, shh. Everything's ok, I'm here. Shh, calm down. Come on, deep breaths." Comrade's soothing words ripple through me, and minutes later, I actually calm down. I guess he has that effect on me.

We just sit there on my bed, me still in his lap, not saying anything, but I'm shaking slightly.

What can you say when a person you've known for two days comes in and hugs you after you've just had a nightmare that you haven't had in years? See, it's a bit hard. What would you say? Thanks?

Comrade pulls back from me to look at my face. It's probably red, puffy, and tear-stained.

"Oh, Snow..." he whispers, using my nickname. "What happened to you?"

He wipes the remainder of my tears away while gazing into my eyes. I'm not sure if he's asking about my face or my past...

I answer back in a whisper anyway. "Something that you can never even begin to imagine."

Comrade stares at me for a second until he nods his head, accepting my answer.

I lay my head on his chest and that's when I take in my surroundings. I'm in a fairly large room that has the walls painted a blinding white and has a carpet that's a midnight black. It has a grey dresser off to one side, a walk in closet next to it, and another door that's adjacent to the actual bedroom door. I'm guessing that's the bathroom. The king-sized bed I'm lying on is decorated with grey pillows, white sheets, and a black comforter. The bed is opposite the bedroom door. The wall which the bed is backed up against is pretty much a big window but has the exception of a wall for the bed to rest against. All in all, the room is a mixture of blacks, whites, and greys. I must say, it's pretty well designed.

"What's with this place?" I curiously ask Comrade. He stares at me confused and I stare back at him expectantly.

"What do you mean?" He finally asks, voice full of confusion, and trying to understand me.

"You know, how everything in this house is either black, white or grey? Sometimes red? I mean, pretty much all the walls I've seen are white, the tiles that go through the whole house are black, you got some grey and red here and there, and now there's this room that doesn't even have a splash of colour! Look at it! There's not even red in here!" I cry, horrified. Sure, when I was with my old pack I never had colour, but my old pack decorated beautifully with all the colours of the rainbow. Excuse the baby talk... They can, at least, put some effort in it.

Understanding dawns on Comrade's face after my little explanation. He shakes his head, making his brown hair fall into his eyes slightly, and he chuckles.

"Oh, Snow... You'll know in good time," he says mysteriously with a knowing glint in his eyes. I stare at him confused. All I asked was why is everything so plain, why do I have to wait for that answer?

I wonder if Axel will tell me... No! Don't even go there! 'Go there, go there!' My wolf screams at me. 'Ask where he is!' I hesitate for a second, do I want to know where he is? Or is it just my wolf? 'Now!' She screams when I don't talk. Maybe I should, I mean he could answer my question and now that he's in my head, I won't be able to stop thinking of him.

I sigh. Might as well make my wolf happy. "Comrade..." I start, a little nervous.

"Yes?" he asks, amused at my obvious nervousness. Stupid boy...

"Do you know where alpha Axel is?" I rush out. Disappointment crosses Comrade's face before he puts on a fake smile.

Gosh, I've known this guy for what? Two or three days and I can already tell if he's doing a fake smile or a real one? Wow, this place is having an effect on me. I think I've made a friend for life, though, something I've never had before.

"Yeah, he's in his office. He should be in here in a few minutes," he mutters in a small voice. Wait a second, in here? What does that mean? That he forgives me for running away or something? My wolf yips in joy, but I feel sick to the stomach. Does that mean he'll want me? Because I don't know if I want him. 'Of course, you want him! Who wouldn't? I can feel his wolf now.' My wolf sighs dreamily. Wow, she is so bipolar.

If I do accept him, does that mean we'll have to... to mate? Oh god! I can't handle that. I start to hyperventilate and shake a bit more violently.

"Snow? Snow, are you ok? What's wrong?" I vaguely hear Comrade speak before I jump up and sprint to the bathroom. I head straight to the toilet and puke my guts out.

I feel my hair being pulled back and silently thank that it's Comrade and no one else. This is so embarrassing! I can't believe I'm that scared of an alpha mate that I'm puking. What's wrong with me?

I finish up and flush the toilet. Well, that was disgusting...

"You ok?" A very concerned Comrade asks when I slump on the cool tiled wall of the bathroom. I close my eyes and nod my head. He brushes away the excess hair in my face and slowly lifts me up bridal style. He places me back on the bed and kisses my forehead.

"I gotta go. The alpha will be here soon, and I don't want to be caught with his mate. He'll rip me to shreds!" He jokes lightly. I smile weakly at him.

"Thanks, Comrade. I think the only reason I'll like it here is because of you," I mutter to him, and he laughs.

"Thanks. I'll be sure to not let that one slip. I don't think the pack will appreciate it," he jokes again and lets me have a laugh before he leaves. Leaving me all alone.

I get up off the bed and make my way to the window. There's no balcony, so this must be the third level of the pack house. The view is beautiful. It's a forest as far as the eye can see and a gorgeous blue sky with the few odd clouds above.

I sigh. I wonder what's going on at my old pack right now. Are they starving? After all, not many of them can cook. I wonder if the pack house is a mess. I smile slightly. I can just imagine Damon wearing an apron and holding a duster. That is a sight I will pay much to see.

"Beautiful, isn't it?" A deep voice says behind me, making me jump. I spin around and slightly relax knowing that it's just Axel. Why am I relaxing around him?

I turn back to the window before answering. "It is. I'll never get sick of this view. Some people just take the beautiful things for granted."

He doesn't answer for a while, and I think he's left. That's until I feel a set of very large and very warm hands rest on my waist. I jump at first and stiffen on the spot.

I hear Axel sigh. "You need to relax. I won't hurt you," he whispers before placing a lingering kiss behind my ear, making me shiver. Oh god, I can't handle this.

I step out of his hold and slump against the wall, putting my head in my hands so I can't see his hurt face. "I'm sorry, I'm so so sorry. I just... I can't do this right now," I say into my hands. I fight back the tears that are threatening to break loose and take calming breaths. This is going to tear humans apart.

"What can't you do? I don't understand. First, you try to run away from me, now you say you can't do this? What can't you do? What? Please, talk to me," he begs.

I nod my head and take another deep breath. Here it goes, complete honesty. I gulp and answer.

"I have trust issues, Axel. I don't just let people in. I just don't think the world is perfect and dandy. I don't just think that a mate will make me happy." I bite my lip hard to keep the tears from falling. "I can't cope with a relationship right now. I can't cope with anything. I don't know what to think. I've rocked up at this place and found someone else who's like me, who's different. It even turns out they're my mate, you're my mate. Just give me time and I'll let you in. Just please, don't come on to me, and think I'll let you mate with me straight away because I won't. I'm sorry. I'm so so sorry you got me as a mate. You deserve better. This pack deserves a better Luna than me. I'm a disgrace to all werewolf kind."

With absolutely no warning, I'm being thrown on the bed with a furious-looking Axel on top of me. I whimper and shrink into the covers, closing my eyes. He growls at me, and I start to wriggle. His whole body is pressed against mine, and I can feel every inch of him, especially his very noticeable erection. I continue to wriggle when he suddenly moans and buries his face in my neck, making me freeze. What did I do?

"If I were you, I would stop wriggling so that you're not rubbing against my very excited member," he mumbles into my neck. I shiver at the feel of his breath on my exposed neck. After all, I'm still in that white dress he gave me.

"I'm sorry," I whisper to him, still slightly scared, and he groans.

"Please don't be scared of me. I won't hurt you, I promise," he mutters before starting to nibble my ear lobe.

I don't talk anymore and focus on the feeling of his body against mine. If I'm gonna get through having a mate, then I've got to let him in, don't I?

He slowly moves from my ear lobe down to my neck with light feathery kisses. I bite my lip and will myself to focus on the feel of Axel's touch and not on how much I want to sprint out of the room screaming like a mad woman.

Come on, focus on the tingles and sparks, come on!

He travels with his hands down my body to my hips and grips them softly.

"Relax, Celina," he whispers while nibbling my collar bone.

He's gonna hate me for the next words that will come out of my mouth. I take a deep breath and whisper, "I can't."

He immediately stops and lifts all of his weight off me and off the bed. I sit up and hug my knees. My wolf's growling at me and howling for her mate in my head. I grip a pillow tightly and whimper at the amount of noise that is going through my head. Can't I ever catch a break?

A pair of hands takes my hands away from my head and takes them in his. I open my eyes to see Axel kneeling down in front of me with a pained look on his face. "Wolf giving you trouble?" he quietly asks.

I nod and whimper again at the headache I feel coming on.

He sighs before placing a hand on my forehead while closing his eyes. His eyebrows scrunch together in concentration and, slowly, the pain subsides, and I'm left feeling sleepy.

"Go to sleep, Celina. You've just had some energy drained out of you." I faintly hear Axel's voice say. I do exactly as he says, not even bothering to ponder on the fact that he just sucked energy straight out of me.

"Celina? Celina, you need to wake up to eat. Come on, sweetheart, wake up," the heavenly voice continues to say while lightly shaking me. I groan and roll over, hearing a chuckle soon after.

"Get up or have water poured over you," the voice threatens. I bolt upright at the voice's words and quickly jump out of the bed.

Standing there in all his glory, in new clothes and looking fresh, is Axel with an amused smile on his face. The sight of it makes me want to melt. Gosh, if this is after the first few days, what am I gonna be like in the next few weeks?

He's changed into a pair of blue board shorts and a plain black shirt. My god! I'm not sure if I'll last for a few weeks...

"How long have I been asleep?" I softly question, bowing my head and cupping one elbow with my hand. I hear a sigh come from Axel's direction

"A few hours. You took the energy drain a lot better than most wolves do. They would be out for days," he speaks with amusement and a light laugh. I stare at him in shock. Energy drain? What the...

"I'll explain that to you later, though. Right now, you need to eat," he concludes.

He walks into the closet and comes back out with a light blue skirt and a white sleeveless top. I stare at it for a second before looking at Axel. "Is that for me?" I mutter, walking up to the clothes and taking them delicately between my fingers. They're so soft...

"Of course, they are! Who else would they be for?" he questions. Strangely, all sorts of conclusions for whose clothes these are start popping up in my head. Jealousy consumes me, but I push it away. I don't think Axel is that low. After all, he is about 20. He can't be a player, can he?

I just shrug as an answer to his question and head to the bathroom. It's beautiful with mixed black and white tiles on the walls and large white tiles on the floor. A big mirror sits on one wall, and opposite to it is a shower that is absolutely massive! Next to the shower is a bath that could much resemble a spa. That's pretty much it... Oh! Also, the toilet I puked in earlier. It also has a window sitting above the bath, and guessing from the sunlight, I'm pretty sure I slept through the night.

I quickly have a shower and change into the outfit that Axel picked out. I look into the mirror and examine myself. The skirt hugs my hips and flows down, ending about mid-thigh, too short for my liking honestly. The shirt also hugs my curves and shows a bit of cleavage, not too much to be slutty, though. My hair is just sort of hanging, looking like a total mess.

I search through the cupboards trying to find a brush but fail miserably. I huff and run my fingers through it a few times. I never really worry about my appearance before, but I never had to. I guess if I was woken up to eat at this hour, then I suppose I'm meeting part of the pack. This thought takes my mind into an alarmed state. I'm meeting the pack? I'm meeting the pack! I can't do this, not now. I'll just make up an excuse. Yeah, that works.

I take a breath and cautiously step out of the bathroom. Waiting for me is the same looking Axel. But when he sees me, his face lights up, and his eyes shine with adoration. I look down and curl my toes into the carpet.

"Do I look ok?" I nervously ask, not that I'll be on show.

He walks toward me and tucks a strand of my hair behind my ear. "You look perfect, but here," he says as he walks to a drawer and pulls out a hairbrush. I smile slightly when he hands it to me.

I walk back into the bathroom, with Axel following me, and proceed to brush my hair. Five minutes later, knots are still going through it. I groan in frustration and roughly put the hairbrush down. Stupid thing doesn't work.

Axel chuckles from behind me. "Here, let me," he says as he takes the hairbrush and leads me back to the room. He directs me toward the bed, and I sit down on the edge. He copies my action but sits behind me with legs either side of me. He's careful not to touch me entirely, though, only letting our thighs brush together.

I close my eyes and focus on the feeling of him brushing my hair. It feels nice... Just like my mum used to do it. I quickly shake that thought from my mind, not really wanting to feel depressed.

What annoys me is that in less than two minutes, my whole hair is untangled and flowing down my back in its usual pin straight way. All because of Axel.

I take the brush back to the bathroom and set it down. Now I just have to come up with an excuse to not leave this room...

5

CELINA

"You ready to go now that you've brushed your hair?" Axel asks me with slight amusement in his voice. I start to panic as I walk back into the bedroom. I don't want to meet the pack who literally hunted me down to kill me! It just doesn't seem right.

"Um, do we have to do it now? I mean, we have plenty of time you know," I say as my lame excuse for not wanting to leave the room. I chew my lip nervously and twist a lock of my hair between my fingers. Please don't let me go!

"Celina, you don't have to go if you don't want to. I'll just tell the pack you're not ready," he says lovingly. I smile at him softly and nod my head.

"That would be great. I'm sorry about this, I don't mean to hurt their feelings," I mumble. I really don't. I'm just not ready to meet a new pack that seems really caring and loving and then might suddenly have them turn on me.

"Ok, well, I'll be back in a few minutes. Let me break the news to the pack. We can organize a date later, I guess," he tells me before walking out of the room and closing the door behind him.

I sigh and walk over to the glass wall, looking out over the forest. I really want to go for a run right now. I really want to be free. 'Why don't you?' My wolf asks.

'That will mean asking Axel for a favour and probably having a run in with some of the pack. I don't think I can handle that,' I admit to her. She growls a bit at my decision, wanting to be let out, but she accepts it anyway.

A soft knock diverts my attention away from the beautiful scenery and toward the door.

"Who is it?" I ask softly, knowing the person will hear me because of their wolf hearing.

"It's Callum," the voice calls back, and my eyes widen. I sprint to the door and yank it open, enveloping him in a hug. I must admit, I think Callum, Comrade, and Axel are the only people I've touched for a long time. I guess they just have that caring nature about them.

"Wow, hi to you, too," Callum chuckles, hugging me back. "How are you feeling?" His voice suddenly fills with worry and concern. I pull back from him and stare at him for a moment.

"I feel fine, honestly. A little tired and hungry, but fine," I mutter, looking down.

Callum leads me into the room and sets me down on the bed. He hands me a plate full of pancakes covered in maple syrup, whipped cream, and a strawberry on top. I stare at it in disbelief.

"Lucky I brought this for you then, hey? Oh yeah! Axel also asked me to tell you that something unexpected turned up, and he had to attend to his alpha duties. So, Comrade and I will be spending the day with you." He beams at me, but I'm still stuck on the fact he brought me pancakes. He actually brought them to me. I didn't have to cook them, help with cooking them, or even give them away!

"Is this really for me?" I whisper and Callum nods. I cautiously poke my finger into the whipped cream and lick it off my finger. I close my eyes at the scrumptious taste.

"This is amazing!" I exclaim in pure ecstasy. Pancakes... I haven't had pancakes for so long, I've almost forgotten how they taste.

Callum laughs. I look at him in question. What's he laughing about? What's so funny?

"It's like you don't get these sorts of things often. I imagine a beautiful and special lady like you would be treated like a queen!" he exclaims.

My smile fades as memories of how my old pack used to treat me appear in my mind. The beatings, the hateful comments, not being allowed out of the house. A single tear slips out of my eye, and I quickly wipe it away before Callum sees it. I softly put the plate of pancakes on the bedside table, suddenly not having an appetite anymore.

"Hey, you ok?" He asks as another tear slips out my eye. Damn it! Why do people always see me cry? Why do people always see how weak I am? Why?

"What did I do? Did I say something to offend you? Shit! I didn't mean to, I'm sorry!" He quickly apologizes. I sniff as he engulfs me in a hug. "You want to talk about it?" he asks quietly. I shake my head and try to find comfort in Callum's arms.

"Can you please not swear around me? I don't really like it that much; it brings back memories," I mutter quietly. In all truth, my old pack used to yell profanities at me when I did something wrong or something they didn't like. I always hated swearing, but now I loathe it with a vengeance.

"Yeah, sorry. I just thought I upset you, that's all," Callum says in an equally quiet voice. I pull out of his grip and look at him with a small smile on my face. "What?" He asks with a glint in his eye and a small grin. He's so... cheeky.

"I just find it funny that I've known you for three days, and I already find comfort in you. I feel safe around you, and I really like you as a friend. I haven't felt this way for a long time." I look into his brown eyes the whole time, so he knows I'm not messing around.

He smiles a breathtaking smile at me and jumps off the bed, doing a little bow. The smirk on his face is as clear as the sky.

"I'm honored, M'lady," he says in a horrible British accent, causing me to giggle a bit.

"What's that noise I hear?" A bogie calls from the door. Both our heads snap toward the door and standing there with slightly damp hair is Comrade. "I believe it is my job to make the lady laugh," he also says in a horrid accent while puffing his chest out at Callum jokingly. Callum's eyebrows raise, and he too puffs out his chest. I giggle at the two boys and they both grin.

"I believe a competition is in order!" Callum exclaims. "The first one to make the lady laugh wins!"

"I accept!" Comrade also exclaims. I giggle again because they are still doing horrible British accents, and this whole situation is quite funny.

First up is Comrade.

"M'lady," he says, doing a little bow to me. I nod my head and bite my lip to keep myself from giggling again. "I shall be juggling these oranges!" he tells me in an excited voice, revealing three oranges. I have no clue where he got the oranges from, but I really don't want to know. He grins at me, and I cautiously watch him. Can he juggle?

To my surprise, he can actually juggle. He's going really well, he's even singing his own circus music in the background! This is until an unexpected hair brush comes flying at him. Comrade drops the oranges and glares at an innocent-looking Callum.

"You ruined my performance!" Comrade whines like a little kid. I roll my eyes at him when Callum comes and takes his place in front of me.

"Today, I shall be doing a magic trick! One of pure amazement!" Callum says, trying to sound mysterious, but it just comes off as weird. I stare at him with raised eyebrows, which causes him to wink at me. "I am going to make this handkerchief," he says, pulling out a handkerchief, "disappear!"

I snort very unladylike and wait for Callum to do his 'amazing' magic trick.

"Right, on three," he tells me, and I nod, waiting to be utterly amazed. "One... Two... Three!" he yells. Just like that, he turns around and tucks the handkerchief into his sleeve. I purse my lips to keep in my laugh and shake my head. This man, who is supposed to be a feared beta throughout all packs, is standing here in front of me doing a magic trick.

"No, nothing?" He questions my red face. I shake my head, and he sighs. "Next time, M'lady, next time."

That's how the day continues to go on, Comrade and Callum taking turns in trying to make me laugh. All they get are giggles and very unladylike snorts. They laugh at me a few times when I snort or when I get red in the face, but they failed. Poor little boys.

"That's it! I give up! It's impossible to make you laugh! What are you? Laugh proof?" Comrade questions while lying on the floor, exhausted. Just before, they both did a horrible folk dance together, and they are now lying on the floor.

"Yeah, do you laugh at anything? When was the last time you laughed, woman?" Callum jokingly yells at me. I close my eyes and envision the last time I laughed. The last time I saw my parents, the day in the park.

"Nine years ago," I whisper, my eyes still closed, but I have a faint smile on my face. "It's been nine years since I laughed. Not even a giggle, so trust me, that's an improvement."

I open my eyes, and I'm greeted with shocked faces. I shrug it off and look away. They probably think I'm a freak. Haven't laughed in nine years, who'd believe that?

"I can believe that," Comrade mutters like he read my mind. My head snaps up, and I stare at him. Callum does too and sighs.

"I guess I can too. When we found you, you weren't the happiest munchkin out there," he teases, and everyone smiles slightly. I'm happy the tense atmosphere is gone.

Then I realize he just insulted my height. "I'm not short," I mumble, and he gets up to ruffle my hair.

"Oh yes! You are," he speaks like he's talking to a dog. I squeal and duck away from him, bolting to the other side of the room.

He holds his hands up in surrender and looks at me like I've grown two heads. "What did I do?"

I stare at him with wide eyes and a straight face. He gulps slightly and backs away next to a now standing Comrade, who looks just as equally scared.

"No one, and I mean no one, touches my hair," I let out calmly, my voice like stone. They flinch slightly and nod their heads. I smile again. "Don't look so scared." My voice back to normal. "All you have to do is avoid my hair at all costs or... Well, you don't want to find out."

Their eyes widen and as if on cue, Axel walks in the door that very moment. Comrade and Callum look scared and out of their minds while staring at my innocent face. This should be interesting...

Axel looks from me to the guys and then smirks. "Well, I see you've managed to scare your babysitters for the day. You're dismissed," Axel tells Callum and Comrade, and without needing to be told twice, they both sprint out of the room. I chuckle at their retreating backs.

Axel closes the door and sits at the foot of the bed. I join him, but I sit on the other end against the headboard. A look of hurt washes over his face before he smirks again. "What did you do?" he asks mischievously.

I shrug. "They got a warning not to touch my hair again or else."

Axel raises an eyebrow, but I don't elaborate. I'm sure Callum or Comrade will tell him.

"So how was the pack? Were they upset I didn't meet them?" I question nervously. I really hope I didn't.

Axel sighs and runs a hand through his beautiful and already messed up white hair. I follow the movement and can't help but see how his arm muscles flex or how hot he looks when he does that.

I look away before he can see me blush. Did I just perv on my mate? Oh god, I don't know how long I can hold out.

"I tell ya what, a lot of people wanted to meet the future Luna. Pretty much the whole pack turned up," he says, and I feel my face fall. Did I upset them? "No, it's okay, sweetheart, you didn't upset them," Axel explains quickly, pulling me into his arms and I let him. I feel the need to be comforted right now and who else is better than your mate? "I explained to them that you weren't ready to meet them, and they were fine with that. I'm giving it about a week, two weeks tops, until they want to meet you, though. They really feel guilty about almost killing their future Luna, and they want to apologize," he says, sounding sincere. I smile; well, at least, they don't hate me.

"Did you ask them to apologize?" I suddenly wonder out loud because if he did, I'm not sure what I'll say or feel.

He chuckles. "No, I didn't ask them. In fact, they asked if I could give you this. It's from the children of the pack, saying sorry about what their mummies and daddies did," he says with amusement in his voice.

I take the messily made card from his hands. The actual card is light blue, and the decorations on the cover definitely look like a bunch of kids did it. It's covered in glitter and ribbons and a big messy word saying 'Luna.' I slowly open it, and in it is a bunch of little messages from all the children in the pack. I read every single one, even though I can't read some very well because of their handwriting. On the back of the card is in big letters, 'Sorry!' I feel my eyes fill with tears. They made this... for me?

"Oh my gosh," I whisper as I lean back into Axel's chest. He wraps an arm around my waist and pulls me closer to him. "No one's ever done something so thoughtful for me before," I mumble as I trace my fingers over the messages and smile as a happy tear slips from my eye. "I love it."

"I thought you would. You seem like the person to love little kids," he mutters into my ear, burying his head in the crook of my neck, and breathing in my scent. It feels nice.

I sigh and read over the messages again until I've memorized every one. I gently set the card down and close my eyes. It must be at least eight by now, and I'm super tired. A big yawn escapes my mouth, proving my point.

"Tired?" Axel questions quietly.

"Mm-hmm..." I hum back. I soon feel myself slowly being lifted by a set of strong arms. I'm set softly down on the bed, and the covers are pulled over me. I feel someone lightly kiss my forehead.

"Goodnight, Celina. Sweet dreams," I hear Axel whisper before I fall into a blissful sleep.

6

AXEL

"Ok, well, I'll be back in a few minutes. Let me break the news to the pack. We can organize a date later, I guess," I shrug and walk out the door, closing it behind me.

I sigh when I'm out in the hallway. I know that Celina isn't ready, but what bugs me is that she doesn't just tell me; she has to come up with an excuse. Of course, I caught on, but I thought she'd tell me if she wasn't ready. I guess not...

I must admit, I wasn't the most accepting person when I first met her. She just ran away from me, and I was so mad! I just couldn't stand to be around her when I knew she didn't want me. Then I bloody forced myself on her! Not only that but right after she told me not to! What's wrong with me? Her scent, though, god! It's amazing, and when I'm around her like that, it's so hard not to just... Ugh!

I know she isn't ready for that yet, let alone consider it. I can wait forever to be with her, though. As long as she doesn't run away again or resist me, I'm good.

I step into the backyard, and I'm instantly met with eager stares and whispers. Wow, they're going to take this really badly. At least, Celina can't see the backyard from our room...

I step up onto the podium in front, and everyone quiets down almost immediately. I see the eagerness and hopefulness in their eyes for meeting their future Luna.

"I am aware that you have all been very eager and excited to meet your new Luna, but unfortunately, she will not be meeting you today," I announce in my formal alpha voice. Objections start being yelled off and growls coming from the crowd.

I growl loudly, and that seems to catch their attention. They will not disrespect her. "You will not disrespect your Luna in such a way! You do not know her position! You do not know where she came from! You do not understand what is going through her head! So if I hear a disrespectful word or even thought, you will be punished! Is that understood?" I boom as I watch all their heads bow and mumble words of agreement.

Callum comes walking up to me with a smirk on his face. "Well then, I'll take that you've forgiven your little mate?" He asks mischievously. I growl in response, and he laughs.

"Oh yeah, a pack a few territories over called in when you were with Celina. They asked me if I could tell you to ring them. Apparently they're in a bit of strife and need some help," he says in full beta mode. That's the good thing about Callum, when in a serious situation, he'll go into beta mode and get the job done. That's why he's my beta.

I nod my head and begin to walk back through the doors to the house. "Oh, can you keep Celina company?" I question.

He nods but adds into my statement. "Sure thing, I'll get Comrade to help too. She seems comfortable around him."

I resist the growl trying to erupt out of my chest, and nod stiffly. I know that Celina finds comfort in Comrade, so I can't really complain, but seriously! He annoys me so much because I know he got closer to Celina in less than two days, and I'm still trying to get her to hug me! It's bloody ridiculous!

I guess Comrade knows what she's going through. He's been through a lot, but it's not my story to tell. Comrade will confess when he feels it is appropriate. It's his secret and no one else's.

I should be able to connect with her, though. I am her mate. I may not know what she's gone through, but I know the pain she feels, if it's anything like that.

Let's just say, I have a very... special mother. She's one of a kind, literally. I only get to see her every once in a while, though. No, not like once every year. It's more like... once every few years and that's if I'm lucky. I'll openly admit I miss my mother, but I can live without her. I've lived without her my whole life.

I sit down on my chair inside my office and look at the little sticky note stuck next to the phone. Time for business, I guess... I pick it up and dial the number. It rings three times before someone picks it up.

"Alpha Damon," a gruff voice says down the phone. He sounds very young, maybe eighteen or nineteen. A reasonable age to take over a pack in the werewolf world, so I'm guessing, I'm correct.

I relax back into my chair and answer back. "Alpha Axel here. It has come to my attention that you rang my beta not too long ago and wanted to speak to me." I'm in a full alpha mode and put on a business-like tone.

I hear the shuffling of papers before alpha Damon speaks again. "Um, yeah. Our pack is in a bit of strife, and it would be highly appreciated if you could support us in some way."

I rub my chin and sigh. "What kind of strife? Financial?" I question.

There's a moment of pause before he speaks up. "I guess you could say my pack is falling apart. One of our former... pack members left us a little while ago, and she seemed to be the base of the pack. She kept us together and made sure we were fed, had clean clothes, etc. I guess you could say she was like a maid."

"Or a Luna," I state. He's quiet on the other end, and I take that he won't comment. "Let me ask you a question. Is your pack starving? Is your pack house looking like a mess? Are close relationships now falling apart because of this one person?" I ask, building up to support my theory of their Luna running away.

Again, silence. A few minutes of silence actually.

"Yes," he mumbles down the phone in defeat. I smirk at his answer. Wow, I didn't know one wolf could do that to a pack.

"All I'm asking for is a little help to get us back on our feet. Maybe a tip or two for keeping a close-knit and organized pack," he continues to say.

I think about it for a bit. To me, this just sounds like a pup who has lost his way and doesn't know where to start. In other words, a weak alpha.

"I will think about your offer and get back to you soon. Until next time, alpha Damon." I don't wait for his reply as I hang up on him.

I lean my elbows on my desk and run my hands through my hair. 'Fred, my office, now.' I mind link to my third in command. Not even five minutes later, Fred is walking through the door.

"You wanted to see me, alpha?" he asks, and I nod, indicating for him to take a seat. Everyone knows to address me as alpha in my office, except Callum of course. I think he just likes to get on my nerves... "A pack of few territories over has asked me for help to get their pack up and running again. Seeing that Callum is busy at the moment, I only have you to console with. Input?" I question. I may have sounded rude, but Fred knows that I'll go to Callum first before anyone, and he has accepted that.

"What type of help, financial?"

I shake my head at his question, and he looks at me confused.

"The alpha is young and weak, by the sound of things. He lost a former pack member, and the whole pack is separating, and apparently, the place looks like a mess. In all honesty, I just think they need a kind of motherly figure. A Luna. I don't think they need me at all," I comment and Fred nods.

"What about the Luna, alpha? I don't know her at all and hardly know her nature, but I think any Luna would be a good motherly figure to any pack. That's my opinion," he tells me with a small smile, probably thinking about his Luna. Of course, in a nonsexual way. I will personally take care of anyone who thinks about Celina that way, into shreds.

Celina does seem caring, kind, and gentle. She's also strong-minded, though and can put up a fight. I think she'll be perfect for the job, but first, I need to get her to accept me and for her to meet the pack.

"I agree, but she's not ready. In due time, she will be, but until then, the pack will just have to wait out."

Fred nods at my decision and exits soon after.

For the rest of the day, I busy myself with alpha work, but all my mind can focus on is Celina. I feel guilty for leaving her cooped up in her room all day, with nothing but the entertainment of Callum and Comrade. I can't even imagine that...

The day goes by slowly. I deal with pack issues, phone calls and make sure we're stocked up on food. By the time everything's done, it's about 7:30 pm and I can't wait to get back to my mate.

I step out of my office and shut the door. I turn around, about to make my way to my room. What meets my eyes, though, is certainly something I don't expect to see. About five of the pack children are standing there looking guilty and looking at the floor. One of them is holding a big blue card with ribbon and glitters all over it.

"Alpha..." the one holding the card trails off. His name's Henry, and he's one of the minor pack member's children. Not that it matters, everyone is an equal in my pack, whether they like it or not.

"What is it, Henry?" I ask gently as I crouch down to their level. You can't be too tough on the pack children, then they'll fear you. You want them to trust you.

"This is for the Luna. We thought that if our mummies and daddies didn't apologize for what they said, we would," he tells me while handing the card. I smile slightly. Well, what do ya know?

"Thank you, Henry. I'm sure the Luna will be very happy to have this," I say gratefully and smile at him. He beams back at me, along with the other children.

I stand back up and ruffle his hair. "Shouldn't you guys be in bed?" I ask them curiously in a joking tone. They all giggle and run off down the hall. I shake my head and head upstairs to my beautiful mate, Celina.

I reach the door and witness a sight I never thought I would see. Callum is standing next to Comrade, and staring wide-eyed at Celina, scared. Callum is scared. Wow.

"Well, I see you have managed to scare your babysitters for the day. You're dismissed," I say to Callum and Comrade.

Without any prodding, they both sprint out of the room. I hear a chuckle come from a certain someone, and I have the sudden urge to know what she did.

"What did you do?" I ask as I grin mischievously at her. Celina just shrugs.

"They got a warning not to touch my hair again or else," she tells me innocently. I raise an eyebrow at her, but she doesn't elaborate. "So, how was the pack? Were they upset I didn't meet them?" she questions nervously.

I sigh and run a hand through my hair. "I tell ya what, a lot of people wanted to meet the future Luna. Pretty much the whole pack turned up," I say and watch her face fall. I instantly know that she thinks she upsets them. "No, it's okay, sweetheart, you didn't upset them," I explain, pulling her into my arms. I'm glad she let me hold her for once, it feels nice to have my mate in my arms. "I explained to them you weren't ready to meet them, and they were fine with that. I'm giving it about a week, two weeks tops, until they want to meet you, though. They really feel guilty about almost killing their future Luna, and they want to apologize." Also for how they disrespected her, but she doesn't need to know that.

She smiles, then something dawns on her pretty little face, and she looks at me suspiciously. "Did you ask them to apologize?"

I chuckle in amusement. I actually didn't ask them, they came up to me. "No, I didn't ask them. In fact, they asked if I could give you this. It's from the children of the pack, saying sorry about what their mummies and daddies did," I say with amusement in my voice.

She takes the card from my hands and just stares at it for a bit. She runs her finger over the words, and I just watch her. I can't believe this beautiful person is all mine. A sudden look of adoration crosses her face.

"Oh my gosh," she whispers as she leans back into my chest. I wrap an arm around her waist and pull her closer to me.

"No one's ever done something so thoughtful for me before," she mumbles as she traces her fingers over the messages. She smiles while a happy tear slips from her eye. I wipe it away gently with my thumb. "I love it."

"I thought you would. You seem like the person to love little kids," I honestly admit as I bury my head in the crook of her neck, breathing in her scent. She smells like spring morning with newly blossomed flowers. Girly, I know, but so true.

She sighs and reads the messages over again. She reads them for a while before she gently sets the card down and closes her eyes. It must be at least eight by now and, knowing how idiotic Callum and Comrade are, she's had a tiring day. A big yawn escapes her mouth, proving my point.

"Tired?" I question quietly.

"Mm-hmm," she hums back, and I lift her slowly from my lap and place her on the bed, pulling the covers over her.

I lightly kiss her forehead. "Goodnight, Celina. Sweet dreams," I whisper, then she's out like a light.

She looks like a beautiful angel sleeping, like an angel from the Moon Goddess herself. I lightly brush some stray hair away from her delicate face. Maybe in a few weeks' time, she'll grow to understand what it really means to have a mate, and to be a Luna.

I head over to the couch in the corner and get myself as comfy as possible. That's not very much. My legs hang over the end, my body is cramped to fit into the small space, and my head sort of falls off the side.

I don't know what time it is before I fall asleep, but I'm met with the images of my beautiful mate in my dreams.

7

CELINA

I wake up the next morning tangled up in the sheets and hugging the pillow next to me. I groggily open my eyes, and I'm instantly met with the morning light. I groan and roll over, and guess what? I fall off the bed with a loud thud.

"Ow..." I mutter to myself as I hear stirring from my right. I look in the direction and notice a very asleep Axel on the couch. Why is he on the couch?

I crawl over to him and look at his peaceful face. He doesn't look stressed or worried, just peaceful. I wonder if he can be like this when he's awake. I stroke some hair off his forehead and lean in to kiss it, bringing a small smile to my face.

I stand up and back away, not wanting to disturb him. I check the clock and notice it's about six in the morning. I sigh and head to the bathroom to wash up. I usually wake up at five at my old pack, so I guess you can consider this a sleep in.

I splash my face with cool water and wash away all the sleep. I brush my black hair with the comb on the bench and head back into the room.

Taking a chance, I walk to Axel's wardrobe and peek in to see if there are any clothes that will actually fit me. To my surprise, half of the wardrobe is girl's clothing. I blink as I take in all the outfits. They're sorted by colour, with shoes on the floor and accessories on the top of the shelf.

I walk in and run my hands over the clothes. I've never really had a choice in what to wear before. I just wear what I'm told to. I have a choice now.

As my fingers skim over all the materials, they land on something lacy and soft. I stop and peer at the deep purple fabric carefully. I pull it out from the rack of clothes and gasp softly. It's a deep purple top that would come to just below my belly button. The chest area is covered in lace, and the whole of the back is just lace and no fabric.

I find a nice high waist black skirt and slip it on. I look in the mirror inside the wardrobe and smile. I actually look nice. The colour contrasts that of my hair and eyes as well and actually matches.

I walk out of the wardrobe smiling and head to the door. I take one last look at Axel's sleeping body and instantly know that when he wakes up, he's gonna run around looking for me. I giggle at the picture in my head and close the door behind me.

I must say, on my way to the kitchen, I do get lost. Since I was asleep when Comrade brought me up to the room, I have no clue where to go. By the time I get down to the kitchen, it is half past six.

It's a Saturday, so I doubt that the pack will be up before 10, so that gives me about three and a half hours to have some me time. Or until Comrade, Callum or Axel wakes up.

I make myself coffee on the very expensive looking and very complicated machine, and set myself down on a bar stool near the kitchen counter.

I take a sip of the strong goodness, and I'm awake in an instant. I don't really like my coffee sweet, so I have a straight black every morning. For some it's gross, but to me, it's absolute heaven.

Without my permission, my thoughts drift somewhere else other than my coffee.

I wonder what my old pack's doing right now. Knowing them, they'll all be sleeping with vodka bottles around them. It takes a lot to get a wolf drunk, so I'm guessing a lot of vodka bottles.

On the other hand, if my absence has affected them at all, they'll be up and running around trying to sort out the pack house. It probably looks like a bomb hit it right now. I don't even want to think about the dirty dishes.

"Oh, I didn't realize you were up. I would've guessed that you were asleep at this time of the day."

I jump at the unexpected voice and turn to see Callum smiling at me.

I relax a bit knowing that it's not someone who will harm me. From what I've gathered, Callum is a friendly guy who likes to joke around. I decided that, when he and Comrade ran out of my room looking scared, I could trust him. Just like that.

"Yeah, well, I'm an early riser," I mutter in reply, going back to my coffee.

He makes his own coffee and takes a seat beside me. We sit in silence for a bit, and I can see he wants to ask me something, but he seems scared. He keeps fidgeting with his coffee mug, not actually drinking the coffee.

"What?" I question. If he has something to ask, he can ask.

"Hmm? Oh, nothing, nothing," he mumbles. I stare at him blankly until he sighs. "Why don't you give Axel a chance?" he blurts in a rush. I blink at his question and choke while sipping my coffee.

"What?" I repeat my last question as Callum looks at me sympathetically.

"Sorry. I don't usually ask things that aren't my business, but I'm just curious. I mean, you give Comrade and me a chance, so why can't you give Axel a chance?" His voice is soft and gentle as he asks me the question. Almost instantly, the memory of Axel walking out of his office and leaving me behind in a crying heap comes to my mind.

"I'll give my trust to him when I know he won't leave me," I say bluntly, and Callum looks at me, confused. I'm not sure why, but that's the simplest way to put it.

"Leave you? What do you mean?" he questions, voicing his confusion. I sigh, no me time then...

"I really don't want to talk about this right now. I'm sorry Callum, it's just a touchy subject," I tell him, and he nods in understanding.

"Can I ask one more question?" I nod, and he continues. "Why do you trust Comrade and me then? I mean, what's so special about us? You hardly know us, and you trust us? That just seems weird to me, that's all."

I actually stop and think about his question. Why do I trust these people that I hardly know anything about and be ok with it?

"I don't know really, never thought about it. I just feel safe around you guys, and I'm almost positive you guys will never hurt me. Axel, on the other hand, I'm not so sure... He can be sweet, but can also be... well, mean in a way. How would you react to that?" I ask, telling him what's on my mind. He stays silent, and that just proves my point.

Without another word, I get up, put my cup in the dishwasher, and walk out. It's about quarter past seven now, and I have no clue what to do. Without Comrade and Callum entertaining me, I'm at a loss.

I wander aimlessly up the stairs, planning to go back to the bedroom. When I hit the top of the stairs, though, I get rammed into a very hard body and stumble back, effectively making me fall down the stairs.

Each step I land with a thud and another groan. My sides take most of the impact, but on the last step, the back of my head hits it hard. I land on the floor and hear someone curse loudly. I look up through blurry, unfocused eyes, to see Axel taking the stairs three at a time and Callum running toward me.

"What the hell! What happened? Why is she on the floor?" Callum asks, panicked. He slowly rolls me onto my back, and I tilt my head to the side so I don't put pressure on it.

"I don't know. I woke up, and she wasn't there, so I freaked out and ran to the stairs and accidentally rammed into her. Oh god, Celina? Are you ok? Can you hear me?" Axel's panicked voice fills my ears.

I look at him and nod slightly, making me wince from the pain in my head. I slowly move my hand to grip it and use the other one to push myself off the floor.

I feel blood seep through my fingers, and I grip my head harder. I slowly get to a standing position with Axel and Callum helping me on the way.

With all the times I've been pushed down the stairs, this is a minor injury for me. I've had broken arms, broken legs, sprained ankles and blows to the head. I actually had one of each, one time I blacked out because of the pain.

They lead me over to the couch and just get me to sit there. I stare in front of me blankly as Axel and Callum talk quietly to each other. I feel myself numbing out the pain like I usually do, and make a move to get up and go to the kitchen to clean myself up.

"Whoa there, Celina, you're not going anywhere. We called the pack doctor, and she should be here about... now," Callum says as the doorbell goes off. I thought the pack doctor stayed at the pack house. The one in my old pack always did, not that she helped me with my injuries or anything...

"Lola, thank you for coming. We had a bit of an accident," Axel says as he leads her into the room. She takes one look at my head and scurries over to me. While she is taking out her medical supplies, I move slightly away from her. I do not want this woman touching me, whether it's for medical reasons or not. Axel picks up on my movement and makes his way over to me.

He sits down next to me and leans in to whisper in my ear, "It's ok, Lola won't hurt you. She's helped us a lot with pack injuries. You can trust her."

I look at him and see the honesty in his eyes. I nod, and he backs up as Lola takes his place. My heart rate spikes at the closeness of this new person that I have never met before getting so close to me. It makes me wonder why it didn't happen with Callum and Comrade...

"Right, all I'm going to do is clean your head up, take a look, and then see if you need to get stitches or not. Easy enough?"

I nod silently at her gentle words but stay rigid and completely still.

She quickly cleans up my head with a soft cloth thing, then dabs around while inspecting it. I don't relax one bit while she's touching me. When she's out of the house, I will.

"Well, it's nothing serious. A bandage and you should be good. You're lucky you weren't knocked out cold." She chuckles a bit as Callum and Axel breathe a sigh of relief.

"I'm used to it," I subconsciously mumble, and everyone looks at me with puzzled looks. I realize my mistake and my eyes widen.

"What did you say?" Axel asks, stepping forward. Without my permission, I shoot up from the couch and sprint to the stairs, my legs acting before my brain can fathom.

"Celina!" I hear Axel shout after me, but I don't stop until I get to my room and firmly close and lock the door behind me. I don't believe I just did that! I lean against the doorway and wait till the dizziness fades. Note to self, don't go running and jumping right after you've fallen down the stairs. Lola didn't even get a chance to put a bandage on it.

I groan, gripping my head, and fall onto the bed. I briefly close my eyes before a knock comes from the door.

"Celina? Celina, are you in here? Come on, sweetheart, open up." I recognize the voice as Axel's, but I don't move from my spot. He doesn't take no for an answer, though.

"Celina, open up right now, or I'm breaking this door down," He states firmly, but I still don't move. He won't break the door down... Will he?

"Alright, you asked for it," I hear him faintly say before an almighty crash surrounds the room.

I gasp loudly and shoot up from the bed, gripping the headboard so I don't fall over from the sudden dizziness. I stare wide-eyed at a very angry looking Axel and gulp slightly.

"A-Axel..." I stutter, but I really have no clue as to what to say. He raises his eyebrows at me, crosses his arms over his chest, and spreads his legs into a defensive position.

With every movement he makes, all I can focus on is the way his arm muscles flex and how his very bare chest is showing off his amazing eight pack. I only notice that he's bare-chested now? Wow, I must've really been out of it. All he's wearing is low slung jeans and wow! I just want to run toward him right now and jump into his arms, wrapping my legs around his waist.

"Well? What was that back there?" he booms, making me shrink away from him. Seeing my reaction to him, he sighs and makes his way over to me. I stay where I am, not wanting to upset him more.

He stops about a metre away from me before softly saying, "Celina, look at me." He put his forefinger under my chin and gently lifts my head up. My gold eyes meet with his silver ones, and I instantly get entranced by them. They're so beautiful, like a shining star in the night sky. "What happened downstairs, Celina?" he asks again in that beautiful, deep, and husky voice of his.

My wolf screams at me to answer him and then kiss him senseless, but I don't let myself. What happened to me is in the past. It may be haunting me and maybe it will for the rest of my life, but I will not have Axel, Callum, Comrade, or the pack share that burden. So to answer his question, I shake my head.

Suddenly, his silver eyes shine with a new intensity, and everything else around me melts away. My sole focus is on Axel and nothing else.

"Celina, tell me the truth. What happened downstairs?" he pushes, his voice intense. This time, I can't fight the power that comes from his question and my wolf's loyalty to obey her mate's every need.

"The injury I have is one of many. To some, it was hardly a scratch," I begin and all I can comprehend is Axel's beautiful shining eyes. "I hardly feel the pain anymore. I numb myself, and that just blocks it out. Nothing else to it."

I slowly start to get some common sense back into my brain as I realize what I just said.

"What do you mean some? Has this happened to you before?" he questions, stepping closer, the same intensity in his voice.

"Ye-" Before I can finish that sentence, someone whistles, and catches both our attention. We look toward the door and see Callum standing there looking at what once was the door.

He looks at us with a cheeky smile, before it drops when he sees Axel's eyes. I look at them too, only to see they are still shining brightly. I start to get lost in them again, but will myself to look away.

"Axel, can I talk to you outside for a moment?" Callum asks, all cheekiness gone. Axel stiffly nods as Callum makes his way out to the hall.

Axel looks back at me, and his eyes are back to their normal grayish silver colour. I gulp as I look back at him. He sighs once again and grips my shoulders lightly, pulling me to him so he can kiss my forehead.

"I'll be back soon, just give me a moment to speak to Callum," he gently says, and I nod... again.

"Axel!" I hear Callum shout, and I giggle a bit. Axel groans but leaves the room anyway. I head to the bed before hearing Axel's faint footsteps stop a few metres from the door.

Being a wolf and having excellent hearing, I hear their whole conversation, and it leaves me very confused...

8

CELINA

"What the hell did you think you were doing?" Callum whispers but really yells to Axel. I hear a low growl, then Callum's voice again.

"Don't you dare growl at me after what you just did."

What did Axel do? I don't understand...

"She wasn't telling me what was wrong! What else was I supposed to do?" Axel also whispers yells. I'm a tad confused right now. I'm pretty sure they're talking about me, but I'm not sure why.

"You're supposed to wait for her to tell you, you moron! You can't just go pulling out one of your powers from your ass!" Callum seethes, and now I'm beyond confused.

Power? I know Axel briefly spoke to me about it once, but this is the second time he's used it on me. Whatever it is...

"She looked sad and hurt. I couldn't just let it go," Axel mutters quietly now. It's silent for a few seconds, and I wonder if they've walked away.

"I know you care about her," Callum's voice suddenly breaks the silence. "She'll find out eventually, though, and you know it. You can't just keep pulling these tricks on her. This is the second time, the first when you drained part of her energy. Just let her grow on you and give her time. Maybe then she'll learn to trust you, and you, her. Then you can tell her, just stop with the powers."

I'd never guess that Callum has this sincere, yet gentle side to him, some sternness mixed in there.

Silence falls once again at Callum's words. A heavy sigh is soon heard and a groan of annoyance. "I know. She just frustrates me sometimes," Axel says in frustration, and I'm slightly offended. I frustrate him? Does he ever think how frustrating he is?

"I think you'll be experiencing that a lot now. Good luck, buddy," Callum says with a laugh then I hear his footsteps walk off. That's the Callum I know.

Before Axel can walk back in the room, I launch myself on the bed and quickly lay down on it, staring at the ceiling. Act natural...

Axel walks back in, and I smile at him. He looks at me warily. Ok, smiling isn't natural then...

"What are you smiling about?" he asks, and the smile drops from my face.

"Oh, um, nothing?" I try to sound convincing, but it comes out more as a question than a statement. Axel frowns at me, and I look away. He walks over to the bed and sits down next to me, grabbing my hands.

"It doesn't sound like nothing," he pushes. Would it be wise to ask him about his powers? Right after he just had a conversation about them? No, probably not, but I do anyway, out of pure curiosity.

"What did you do to me?" I question in a rush, but as soon as the question leaves my mouth, I know it sounds totally ridiculous. "I mean like..." I trail off for a second, then decide to just blurt it out. "What are your powers?"

Axel looks shocked by my question, staying silent. I knew I shouldn't have asked...

"What?" he questions idiotically, and I smile sheepishly. I guess I should confess about overhearing their conversation. Before I can get a word out, though, realization shows on Axel's face.

"You heard the conversation," he mumbles, and I nod. He curses under his breath and drops my hands, getting off the bed. He's silent for what feels like forever, just pacing the room. Back and forth, back and forth, back and forth...

"Please talk to me," I beg. "I just want to know what's going on."

Axel stops his pacing of the room and stares at me, long and hard. I look at him with wide golden eyes and he sighs, his silver ones showing defeat.

He comes back to sit on the bed and pulls me onto his lap, my chest against his back. It feels a little weird to me to be in a guy's lap, but it also feels right. This is what mates do, isn't it? Comfort each other?

Axel buries his face in the side of my neck and breathes in. I just sit there awkwardly. What is he doing?

"God, you smell amazing," he mumbles into my neck, and that's when I realize what he is doing.

"Are you sniffing me?" The question comes out without my permission, and I blush crimson. Axel chuckles and lifts his head from my neck.

"Yes, I am 'sniffing you,' as you like to put it. It's a sign of affection mates show to each other," he explains, and my mouth forms an O shape. Axel chuckles again, then buries his face back in my neck, planting a soft kiss where my collar bone meets my neck. My soft spot. I hold in my moan and focus back onto the situation at hand.

"Axel, don't change the subject. I asked you a question, and I want it answered," I sternly state, but it sort of loses its effect when Axel bites the same spot he kissed before. I can't hold back the moan that escapes my throat, it feels so good.

"Calm down, Celina, everything will be answered in due time. For now, I'm just going to let your little imagination run wild," he teases as I lean my head back onto his shoulder and close my eyes. He is still working on my soft spot.

"Axel, why can't you just tell me?" I try to say, but it comes out as more of a muffled moan. Axel ignores me this time and continues on with what he's doing. It feels different from the first time he did this. It feels... pleasurable instead of forced.

He leaves my soft spot and kisses his way up my neck slowly and tortuously, working his way to my ear.

He nibbles on my ear lobe then whispers in my ear, "Looks like you're warming up to me, sweetheart."

As soon as the words leave his mouth, he jumps up from the bed and walks casually to what once was the door. I stare at him in shock, and he looks over his shoulder and smirks at me.

"You're dealing with the alpha, sweetheart. Time to step up your game," he challenges, then walks out, leaving me dumbfounded.

He wants a challenge? I'll show him a challenge.

I jump up off the bed and sprint to the stairs. Just as he's about to take the first step, I launch myself onto his back while screaming, "Axel!"

He obviously isn't prepared for the weight of me suddenly on his back, so he stumbles forward a bit, gripping the stair railing. He growls lowly and somehow switches me from his back to his front, so my legs are wrapped around his torso.

He opens his mouth to say something, but I put my finger to his lips. He raises an eyebrow.

"Uh uh uh, no talking," I tell him sternly, and he obliges. "You—" I stick my finger to his chest, "will not do that ever again, do you hear me? You can't just go and seduce a girl like that and then just get up and walk away!" I scream in his face. I have no clue where this newly found confidence has come from, but I think I like it.

"Did you go—" He tries to say, but I cut him off.

"If you want a game, you're going to get a game. It just might not be in the way you think." I smile sweetly and then jump down from his torso and onto the step below him. "My move, alpha." I giggle and then I skip down the stairs. I hear a low growl behind me, and large hands are suddenly gripping my waist, pushing me up against his hard chest.

He drags his nose up my neck, and I take in a staggered breath. "Do you know how hot it sounds when you say that?" Axel questions huskily and I feel something hard and large press against my upper thigh.

I moan and drop my head forward. "Whatever do you mean, alpha?" I question innocently, and another growl erupts from his throat.

"Don't test me, little Celina. I can take you right here, right now, without a regret in the world," he whispers in my ear, tangling his hand in my black hair and pulling my head gently back. "I can guarantee you'll enjoy it," he whispers again, his voice a lot deeper and huskier than before.

He plants a soft kiss behind my ear and works his way down. I moan as my knees go weak, leaving Axel to support all my weight. His lips leave my neck way too soon, and I whimper quietly while Axel chuckles.

"Don't worry, sweetheart, all in due time," he repeats the words he said earlier and, yep, he walks away again. Déjà vu.

I groan and follow closely behind him into the kitchen. As soon as we walk through the door, about four pairs of eyes land on us. My eyes widen. Oh, I did not think this through. Of course, the pack would be up by now. It's at least a little past midday.

"Alpha," they all say with great honor as they bow their heads in respect to their alpha

"You will address your Luna as well when in her presence," Axel states firmly, and my eyes widen. I hit his back lightly, and he turns to look at me. I look at him with wide eyes and shake my head furiously.

"You'll be fine," he whispers in my ear. "It's the weekend, these are about the only people left in the pack house."

He gently wraps an arm around my waist and drags me forward to be in eye view of the four pairs of curious eyes.

"Luna," they all say the same way they addressed Axel. I bury my face in Axel's chest, trying to find comfort and hide myself at the same time.

I hear Axel chuckle. "She's a bit shy with people she doesn't know," he mentions and out of the corner of my eye, I see all their heads nod in acceptance.

"Celina?" Axel questions, but I don't move. "Do you want to meet some of the pack?"

I take a deep breath, do I want to? Of course, I want to, just maybe not right now...

"What if I say please?" he bribes. I giggle a bit and take my head away from his chest and look at the floor.

"Celina, this is Jasper." Axel points to the first person, and I look through my lashes to see him. He would be about my age, in fact, all of them seem to be. He has gentle brown eyes and matching brown hair.

He bows his head to me. "It's a pleasure to meet you in person, Luna, a true honor," he compliments, causing me to blush.

"Those are the twins, Chloe and Declan," he continues to say while pointing to a blonde haired girl with bright blue eyes and a very small petite frame. The boy standing next to her must be her twin, but they certainly don't look like it. Declan has brown hair and the same blue eyes as Chloe, but his frame is a lot bigger and buffer than hers.

"Luna," they both say simultaneously and also bow their heads.

Before I can stop myself, I ask a question that is totally uncalled for. "Are you guys really twins? You look nothing alike." I gasp and cover my mouth with my hand, turning bright red all over again.

The twins crack up laughing and once again say together, "We get that a lot." The boy next to them rolls his eyes and Jasper whacks Declan over the head.

"Everyone asks that question, don't be embarrassed," the guy next to them speaks up and smiles at me. He has messy blonde hair and almost black eyes. A weird match actually, it's usually brown hair and brown eyes.

"Finally, that is Matthew," Axel says last. Matthew smiles at me and does a little bow like thing, similar to what they did in the medieval days.

"M'lady. Please call me Matt."

I giggle at his horrid accent and turn to see Axel subtly roll his eyes.

He does remind me of someone, though, but I can't put my finger on it. The looks remind me of that someone too.

"If you haven't figured it out yet, Matthew is Callum's brother," Axel whispers in my ear, and I look at him in shock. Of course! The joking and the looks are exactly like Callum's! I can be really slow at times.

"That makes sense" I mumble and Axel chuckles at me. I look back up to the faces of Jasper, Chloe, Declan, and Matt.

"Well, it was nice meeting you all. I think I'm going to go back upstairs now," I say politely and make a move to leave.

"Wait!" A sweet voice shouts and I turn to see it's Chloe. She's stepped slightly forward from the others, and Declan is eyeing her in case he needs to jump in and save her or something. I wish I had an overprotective brother like that...

I wait for Chloe to say what she wants to say, moving back to Axel's side. She bites her pink lip and shifts her eyes to Axel's, looking very unsure.

"Won't you stay for lunch? There are heaps here," she suggests hopefully, and I blink a couple of times. I look to Axel for guidance, but he just shrugs. I look back at Chloe's hopeful face and the eager faces of the three boys. I guess a Luna has to get to know her pack, right?

"Sure," I agree with a small smile. We all head over to the kitchen table that is stacked with pancakes, pizza, and party pies. I stare at it in disbelief.

"This is lunch?" I ask, shocked, and everyone nods. "Whoa..."

Everyone immediately tucks in, and Axel does the honors of putting a pancake, a slice of pizza and two party pies on my plate for me. Jasper goes straight for the pizza, as does Matt. Declan takes half of everything and Axel takes what's left. Chloe just has two pancakes.

I look down at the food on my plate and eye it warily. I've never had these foods before, and I'm too scared to admit it.

"I'm not too hungry actually," I say, pushing the plate away. I guess it's better not to eat what you're unfamiliar with than take a chance, right?

Axel pushes it back. "At least eat the pancake then. You missed out on breakfast this morning because of your little... accident," he mutters as a guilty look overtakes his face.

"It wasn't your fault," I say before pulling a piece of the pancake off.

"Oh, wait!" Declan exclaims, and I freeze. He grabs the maple syrup and whipped cream, covering my pancake with it. "Ok, now eat it."

I gulp and take a bite out of it. Immediately, the wonderful taste of syrup, whipped cream, sugar, and pure heaven explode on my tongue. My eyes widen on their own accord.

"These are amazing!" I exclaim and devour the pancake in seconds. Everyone laughs at me, and we just make a little chit chat amongst ourselves. Everyone's actually really easy to get along with, and it makes me a little less nervous about meeting the rest of the pack.

"Well, thank you for the amazing pancakes," I say to the four of them, and they smile at me.

"Welcome, Luna," they say at once. I smile back, then proceed to walk out of the kitchen. When I make it to the stairs, an arm wraps around my waist.

"That wasn't so hard, was it?" Axel asks me, and I shake my head, smiling. Once I get used to it, I think it's actually quite fun.

"No, it wasn't. I'm not sure how I'll react to the rest of the pack, though," I admit nervously. Axel pulls me to him and kisses my temple.

"You'll be fine," he reassures me as we head toward our room. I go straight to the window wall and look out over the trees.

'I wonder what it would be like to run for the pleasure of it,' I wonder to my wolf.

She sighs. 'I'm sure it would be a wonderful feeling, but we've just never had the chance.'

I sigh as well. 'I know.'

"Do you want to go for a run tomorrow?" Axel suddenly questions, and I whip around to look at him.

"I'm sorry?" I question, and he looks at me amused.

"You do know what a run is, right?"

I whack his chest, and he chuckles.

"I would love to go for a run tomorrow," I tell him and kiss his cheek. He smiles widely.

"Can Callum and Comrade come too?" I question him, and his face slightly falls.

"Sure, I'll just tell them," he mumbles. He's quiet for a few minutes before looking back down at me and smiling. "Done," he says. He must've used the mind link.

"Well then, I guess we're going for a run tomorrow," I say excitedly.

For the rest of the day, we just hang out in our room and muck around. I doubt anyone apart from Callum and Axel's family has ever seen him like this before, and I feel honoured to be able to witness it first-hand.

As we get ready for bed, I think over what happened today. I think mine and Axel's relationship has taken a step forward today. I'm getting more comfortable around him, and I'm actually giving him a chance. I don't know if he's gonna walk out on me or not. But I want a chance at love, and who else is better to try it with than your mate? It may take some time, but I think we'll eventually get there.

"Goodnight, sweetheart," Axel whispers while kissing my forehead. I close my eyes and cuddle up in the sheets.

"Goodnight, Axel," I murmur. I fall asleep knowing that tomorrow will bring something new.

9

CELINA

I wake up early again the next morning, and once again, I'm met with the sight of Axel sleeping on the couch. I really should ask him about that...

I get up and do exactly what I did yesterday: brush my hair, wash my face then head to the wardrobe. Today I choose a white satin dress with red roses on it. It reaches just above my knees, and it's strapless. I love flowy stuff. It makes me feel free when I never was. I guess I am now, though.

I walk out and check the time, about seven this morning. Today I'm expecting answers, about Axel's powers to be exact. Also to see if they're related to me in any way, and why I had that vision when I touched the door. I expect answers, and I want them now.

I walk over to Axel and shake him lightly. I really don't want to disturb his rest, but he needs to get up to get us breakfast. I am not, I repeat not, having another run in with pack members.

"Axel, come on, wake up," I murmur. He just groans and rolls over. I sigh. Heavy sleeper, I see.

An idea then comes to mind, my first move of his little game. I head to the bathroom and look for a jug of some sort. I eventually find one in the cabinet below the sink and fill it up with ice cold water. This is how I'm going to play the game. He can seduce me all he wants for all I care, but I'm just going to pour ice cold water over his head.

"Axel, this is your last chance. Get up," I warn. I'm met with silence, causing me to sigh. "You asked for it," I mumble before I tip the whole jug of water over his head.

He jumps up with a fright and looks ready to murder whoever just did that to him. I hide the jug behind my back and put on an innocent smile. Axel looks at me

"Celina..." he growls, and my smile grows bigger. "Did you just tip water over my head?"

I giggle and nod my head.

He takes a step toward me, and I take a step back, dropping the now empty jug. He stops and runs his fingers through his now drenched hair. My smile falters slightly when I notice that the water is running agonizingly slow down his bare chest and into his boxers, the only thing he's wearing. Axel notices this and gets a devious look on his face.

I gulp.

"Celina, why don't you come here for a second? I want to give you a big hug!" he exclaims and then runs to me. I squeal and run to the bed. I jump over it and see that he stops on the other side.

"Come on Celina, you know you want to," he teases.

Yeah, I want to! I can just imagine sucking every little droplet off his perfect body... Whoa! Where did that come from? I never think like that.

In my little moment of inner shock, Axel effortlessly jumps over the bed and takes me in his arms.

"Axel!" I squeal. He laughs at me, and it's hard not to join in.

"You tipped water over my head! Ice cold water at that!" he exclaims and starts spinning me around. I can't stop the continuous giggles that escape my lips, and I make sure to imprint this moment in my mind. When Axel's laid back, fun and laughing along with me.

He sets me down after a bit, but I'm still giggling slightly. He kisses my forehead.

"Good morning," he whispers, his lips still on my forehead.

"Good morning," I mumble, releasing a content sigh. I push him away after that and point to the bathroom. "Go dry yourself off. I don't want any more hugs," I say seriously, but he can see the amusement in my eyes.

"Of course, sweetheart." He mimics my seriousness, but bursts out laughing when in the bathroom. I giggle and shake my head. Men.

After Axel's fully dry and clothed, he heads downstairs to get us some breakfast. He wanted me to come, but I refused. He turns back up with two plates on a tray. One filled with crumpets that had strawberry jam on them, and the other a bowl of cereal.

"Take your pick," Axel tells me, and I take the cereal. I'm not that hungry anyway. Axel takes the crumpets and digs in straight away. I'm gonna have to remember he likes strawberry jam.

"I have an idea," Axel suddenly says after about two minutes of silence. I look at him, waiting for him to continue. "I want to know more about you, you want to know more about me. Why don't we play twenty questions? Cliche, I know, but we'll get to know each other better."

I agree with the idea and Axel tells me to start off. Like he said, it may be cliche, but it'll help us get to know each other better than we do now.

"Ok, um..." I mutter as I think for a second. It's good to start off with simple questions, right?

"What's your favorite food? Can be entree, main, or dessert," I ask. Axel looks at me weird, and I just stare back at him.

"That's a wise choice, um... I think my all-time favorite food would be a thick, juicy, steak," he admits. I laugh through my nose. Should've guessed that one.

"What about you?" Axel questions and I grin. He will not see this one coming.

"My favorite? Well, that would be chocolate mud cake covered in whipped cream with strawberries on top." Axel looks at me with wide eyes. I smile at him. "Don't knock it till you try it."

"It's not that. I just don't see a small girl like you actually eating something like that. I thought you'd be a salad type of girl," he mutters the last, and I playfully glare at him.

"Looks can be deceiving," I mutter, an image of Damon popping into my mind. I quickly push it away and refocus back on what Axel is asking me.

"Okay then, what about your favorite colour?" he asks, and I think for a second. Do I have a favorite colour?

"Um, I actually don't have one" I tell him honestly, and he looks at me stunned.

"Everyone has a favorite colour!" he exclaims, and I just shrug. He shakes his head but continues to tell me his. "Well, mine is yellow."

"Why yellow?" I ask out of pure curiosity. It's not a very common favorite colour from what I've gathered. It's usually blue or pink or something like that.

He shrugs. "It's the colour of happiness," he informs me. My mouth forms an 'O' shape, and I proceed to ask the next question.

"What do you like to do?" I question in an innocent manner. Axel suddenly gets a devilish smirk on his face.

"There's a lot of things I would love to do, sweetheart," he purrs, and my eyebrows pull together in confusion.

"What?"

Axel chuckles at my expression. "You're really innocent, sweetheart."

I shake off his comment, and he continues to say what he likes to do. "I like playing football, soccer, cricket, any sport really. You?"

"I like cooking, sewing and a little cleaning every now and then," I tell him shyly. He chuckles at me, and I look up to see him shaking his head. "What?"

"I've never met someone who actually enjoys cleaning. It's usually a forced thing, you know?" He questions offhandedly. The question strikes home for me, though.

"Oh yeah, I know," I mutter. I'm not sure if Axel heard me or not, but we continue on with the game.

In the end, I learn that Axel is twenty years old, he likes to play sports, his favourite colour is yellow, his favourite food is steak, he hates reading, and that he has a lot of dirty thoughts in that head of his.

What he has learned about me is that I'm 16, hate sports of any kind, don't have any siblings, don't have a favourite colour, my favourite food is chocolate cake, and that both my parents have died. I don't say how they died, we don't really dig into each other's pasts.

"I have one more question," I say nervously, and Axel looks at me expectantly. I fiddle with my black hair nervously and look into his greyish silver eyes. "What are your powers?" I rush out and Axel freezes. Please answer me, please answer me, I beg in my head.

"I really don't think—" Axel begins, but I cut him off before he says what I know he's going to say. "I know you don't think I'm ready, but I need to know what's happening. I need to know if I'm somehow connected, and you keeping it from me isn't helping," I beg as he looks into my golden eyes.

He sighs and gets up from the bed and heads to the still broken door. That's the last thing on my mind, though.

"Follow me," is all he says before he walks out of the room with me following close behind.

We walk down the stairs, through the hallway, and out the front door. He doesn't stop, though. He keeps going until we're at the edge of the woods. He pauses for a second, then keeps walking forward.

I follow without a second thought.

We step over outgrown roots, duck under low hanging branches and eventually come to a clearing after twenty minutes of walking. Axel sits down in the center, and I follow suit.

"Do know where you're sitting right now, Celina?" he questions, and I shake my head silently. "You're sitting on what once was the birthplace of the first Shade Wolf and battlegrounds of the Shaded Wolves against the Coloured wolves." His tone was full of seriousness, no humor present.

I gulp as I absorb this information. What have I gotten myself into?

"Long ago, back in the sixteen hundreds, there were thousands of Shaded and Coloured Wolves. They all lived in harmony for hundreds of years and disputes never arose," he begins like he's telling a story. "In the mid-seventeen hundreds, one Coloured Wolf named Alastair decided that he was jealous of the Shaded Wolves. They had special powers and gifts that no Coloured Wolf possessed. He worked up an army for the rest of the seventeen hundreds and in the eighteen hundreds he attacked. The Shaded Wolves had no idea and were unprepared for the attack." He stops when he sees the look on my face, probably horror.

"Why did he do it?" I question in a whisper. I don't think I can speak any louder.

"Well, you see, Alastair used to work for the King and Queen of wolves. We don't have one anymore because of this certain dispute. The royals were both Shaded Wolves, one white and one black. They were kind and fair, but when they exiled a Coloured Wolf for a crime that Alastair believed the wolf didn't commit, he took action. He fled from the palace and took his followers with him. He trained them to perfection in order to be the best killers of all wolf kind," he tells me then pauses for a moment, to let all this new information sink in.

"What happened to the other Coloured Wolves that didn't follow?" I question confused. Surely not all of them followed him, some would have seen his intentions.

Axel just shakes his head. "Let's just say that if they refused the offer Alastair submitted to them, they wouldn't have very long to run," Axel says darkly. I shudder at the thought of him killing children, and inexperienced women, as well as their husbands, came to mind.

"Tell me more," I push and Axel doesn't waste another second before continuing on.

"As I said before, he attacked. The Shaded Wolves were totally unprepared, but the King and Queen knew it was coming. The Queen had the Moon Goddess herself speak to her and tell her to not fight back, but to bear a child," he explains, and my mouth hangs agape. A child? Why would you bring a child into this mess?

"Of course, the Queen had her doubts, but she and the King did bear a child a few years later. A beautiful baby girl was born with hair the colour of night and eyes as bright as gold. She was destined for greatness. The night after she was born, the Moon Goddess confronted the King and Queen in person. She explained that the baby girl was not safe there, and she was going to take her away. The Queen instantly objected, but her husband soon convinced her to let her baby go. It was hard for both of them to see their baby fade away with the moon goddess, but they knew she was safe with her," he says with a smile.

He takes a deep breath, as if about to reveal the most important part of all this.

"They hadn't named the baby yet, they didn't know if it was going to be a boy or girl. Before the Moon Goddess took their precious child away, the King called out to her. The Moon Goddess came back, and the King took his baby girl in his arms. A name just fell out of his mouth, and the Queen agreed. After that, they let their baby go, and they never saw her again," Axel finishes and leans back on his hands. So many questions are swirling around in my head, though.

"What was the baby's name?" I question, and Axel looks hesitant. What comes out of his mouth next shocks me to the bone and millions of questions erupt in my head.

"Celina."

10

CELINA

Frozen. That is me at this moment, frozen in shock. The daughter of this King and Queen that was taken away from them by the Moon Goddess has the same name as me. Oh my god...

"Celina? Are you ok?" Axel questions, once he takes in my shocked expression. I stare at him, and it suddenly hits me. That's why he was so hesitant! That little girl was me. Is me.

"The little girl, Celina, that was me, wasn't it?" I whisper and Axel nods.

"Oh my god," I whisper again and put a hand to my mouth. This can't be happening, this just can't be happening.

That would mean I'm hundreds of years old, though! How could that be? If the King and Queen were my real mum and dad, then who were my recent mum and dad that died? Why was I put in the Moonlight pack if the Moon Goddess knew they would treat me badly? These and many more questions swirl around in my head.

"I know you'll have a lot of questions that you want me to answer," Axel starts, and I'm still in so much shock that I just nod. "Probably starting with how you can be hundreds of years old?" I nod again. "No one knows where the Moon Goddess took you after that night. She never returned, and neither did you. Rumors spread that she handed you over to Alastair, she trained you to be the next Moon Goddess, or even that she planned to kill you. No one could confirm them, though, not even your mother and father," he explains while a crease forms on his forehead.

A sudden thought strikes me. "That carving on your office door, that's the war that occurred, isn't it?" I question and Axel nods. "That means when I touched it and saw that vision, that I saw the battle and my... Oh my god," I mutter to myself and Axel looks at me curiously.

"Vision? What are you talking about?" he questions, sounding totally and utterly confused. At this moment, I would usually giggle because of the look on his face, but not today.

"When I touched that carving on your door, because I was curious, I was sucked into this vision like thing. It was a battlefield with black, white, brown, all sorts of coloured wolves. Two wolves caught my attention, though. One was bigger than the other and black, while the other had a more petite frame and was white. I was so confused and didn't have time to register anything before I was back in this time frame," I explain and Axel stares at me in shock. I look at him expectantly and wait patiently for him to answer.

"Celina, you do realize you met your real mother and father?" he questions inquisitively. I freeze for the second time in less than five minutes.

"What? That's impossible," I tell him. He shakes his head, and that's when I know he's serious. "B-but..." I'm at a loss for words and it seems as though Axel is too. "I don't understand," I finally mutter after what seems like hours of silence, when in reality it was only a few minutes.

"Let's move on from that question and back to the one with how you're hundreds of years old, shall we?" Axel decides, and I agree. "Well, it is believed that the Moon Goddess has the power to stop life as we know it. Whether it's on the whole werewolf race or just one special person. For example, you."

My eyebrows scrunch together, and I'm about to ask how before Axel continues again. "She could do this by harnessing her power and focusing it on that sole person. She must've done this to you, to keep you in a state of frozen life, until it was your time to rise again."

"Why was I given to my... fake mum and dad? Why was I given to the pack I came from? Why did all this happen to me?" I fire off questions, and each one seems to be a blow to the heart.

"I don't know the answer to those questions, your old pack might, though," Axel suggests and I hurriedly shake my head.

"No, that is not happening," I say sternly, leaving no room for comments. Axel looks at me blankly, but I don't elaborate on it.

"I want to know what happened, with the battle I mean. What happened to the Shaded and Coloured Wolves?" I ask, changing the subject. Axel quickly turns back onto the original path of the conversation.

"Well, when the battle began, the Shaded Wolves were succeeding and effectively killing off the Coloured Wolves that betrayed them," he begins, but a dark look crosses his face that sends shivers down my spine. "But as the fight progressed, the Shaded Wolves fell one by one. The Coloured Wolves advanced, they highly outnumbered them now. The King and Queen stood proud at the front of the Shaded Wolves, with their heads held high and their followers loyally behind them. All of them knew they were going to die that day, there was no escaping it. When the Coloured Wolves launched their final attack, the Shaded Wolves did put up a fight, but it wasn't enough. They fell, and the Coloured Wolves conquered," he finishes there, and I look at him, expecting more.

"That's it?" I question astonishingly. He looks at me like I'm crazy.

"Yes, that's it. You've just learned in hours what I've been learning over years and years. What else could you want?" He questions exhaustingly, and it's only now that I realize how tired he looks from searching his brain for all of that information.

I push on, though, wanting to know more. "What happened to Alastair? What happened to the other Shaded Wolves of that time that didn't fight? What happened?" I beg to know more and Axel answers each question.

"Alastair went on to be the ruler of all werewolves. He was ruthless and didn't listen to reason. He's the reason why wolves are in packs instead of having one ruler, apart from the Moon Goddess, of course." I absorb this information then motion for Axel to continue. "After the war, there were no Shaded Wolves left. They all fought alongside their royals, and no one knew of you. The only ones who knew were your parents and the Moon Goddess," he answers my second question, but that only brings up a new question.

"How did no one know about me if everyone respected their King and Queen so much? That seems a little strange," I mutter, and Axel nods his head in agreement.

"That's true, but the King just announced that the Queen was ill. This led everyone away from her. However, it did bring grief to the kingdom, knowing that their Queen was sick," he informs me, and I nod my head. "Any other questions?"

I think for a moment. I think I know everything I want to know... Except one thing.

"What's my destiny?" I innocently ask. It's a three-word question, but it's a complicated answer.

Axel shrugs and looks me straight in the eye. "I don't know," he concludes, leaving even more questions whirling around my head.

For the rest of the day, Axel and I sit out in the clearing and talk about how my parents used to be amazing and fair rulers. My mother was kind and had a heart of gold, always cared for others and only looked on the bright side of things. My father was a proud and honourable man; he was respected by all and had the mind of a true King. This is all from what Axel says of course, but you couldn't help but wonder.

According to the books, he's studied about them, I look exactly like my father with pitch black hair and gold eyes, but have the frame and structure of my mother, small and petite.

When it hits sunset, I look up into the now red, pink, and purple sky. I sigh and close my eyes. I began to wonder what it would be like to have met my mother and father in person. I would've loved them to bits.

"We should probably head inside. You haven't eaten anything all day, I can hear your stomach growling from here," Axel tells me amused, and I giggle a bit. Even with everything that Axel just told me, we can still joke around a bit and have fun. Something I rather enjoy.

As we take the long walk back to the pack house, Axel asks me an unexpected question.

"Why do you talk so lowly of your old pack? I mean, when you asked me that question about being given to them, you sounded so hostile towards them." He sounds concerned, probably expecting some confession out of me.

We reach the pack house door, and I turn to look him straight in the eye, something I don't do much.

"That's another story that should be left for another day," I tell him boldly. With that, I open the door and head straight to the stairs. I ignore the curious looks from the pack members that seem to be occupying the pack house, and go straight to my room.

When I get there, I notice someone has fixed the door. I smile slightly, remembering why Axel actually broke it down in the first place. I guess when I look back on it now, I realize he was only caring and worrying about me, something he tends to do a lot.

I head to the bathroom and take a nice, long, hot shower, letting everything that was told to me today sink in and be stored somewhere in my brain.

I walk back out into the bedroom with a fluffy towel on. I head to the wardrobe and pull out a red silk nightgown that will probably reach just below my butt. I can really care less right now, though, so I pull it on and chuck on a matching pair of red lacy underwear.

As I slip into bed, my mind goes back to the image of my mother and father, the way I saw them in my vision. They looked so happy and contented to finally see me after all these years. They finally saw the daughter they never got to know, and I never even got to say goodbye.

As I slip into dreamland, a single tear escapes my eye. The reason? For not knowing my mother and father and never being able to say I love them.

I run through the fields of lavender with the bright blue sky up above. The sun's shining and the birds are chirping. I've never been happier.

I laugh as I run through the field and come to a lake. I gently put my feet in and giggle at the feel of it on my bare feet. It's perfect.

"Celina, darling?" A feminine voice calls out. I look up to see two figures standing on the crystal clear water. One lady, who's probably the one that called out to me, with snow white hair and bright golden eyes like mine. She has a small frame, and a kind smile plastered on her face. The other is a man with pitch black hair and also golden eyes. He has a large build and is way over six feet tall.

It suddenly hits me. These people are my parents. The parents I never got to really love or care for.

"My little princess is all grown up," my father whispers in a soft voice. I beam at them.

They slowly make their way over to me, moving gracefully on the water, not even creating a ripple.

"Look how beautiful you are," my mother gushes and brings her hand up to stroke my cheek. I want to say something, but it's as if my voice has been stolen from me. My mother giggles at me.

"You can't speak in this dimension, darling. You're not strong enough yet. Only the dead and well trained can speak here," she whispers, and my smile drops.

They're dead.

A single tear slips out of the corner of my eye, causing my father to gently wipe it away.

"Don't cry, princess. We're still here with you. We love you no matter what and we will never leave you or let you go," he comforts and rests a hand on my shoulder.

I look at these two strangers in front of me. That's what they are to me, strangers. They're strangers with a heart, though, and love for the daughter they will never know and never knew.

'I love you, guys,' I whisper in my mind, but of course, they can't hear.

"You grew to be a beautiful young lady, darling, definitely something to admire," my mother praises and it's such a good feeling to know that my mother accepts me.

"A true beauty," my father adds, and I beam at them again. "Never let anyone tell you otherwise."

They both engulf me in a hug, and I gladly hug them back. This is what I'm missing, the family moments that can never be erased from your mind.

As time passes on, their bodies turn into ghosts. Their arms go straight through me, making me feel cold and alone.

"We must go now, darling. Be safe and never forget us," my mother whispers as her body starts to fade.

"Always know we're with you and that we love you," my father also whispers and with that, they disappear.

Tears stream down my cheeks. 'No! Don't go, please don't go. Come back!' I scream in my head, but yet again, they can't hear or even see me. They're gone, they're truly gone.

I wake up with a scream, bolting upright. Axel jolts from his sleep on the couch and falls to the floor with a thud. He rushes over to my hyperventilating form and pulls me into a hug. I cry into his bare chest and hold onto him for dear life.

"They love me, Axel. They said they love me," I whisper once I calmed down and Axel pulls away to look into my eyes.

"Who did, Celina?" he questions, making me smile a bit.

"My mother and father. I saw them, Axel, in my dream," I whisper, and Axel pulls me into another hug.

We just sit there hugging each other until I feel my eyelids getting heavy, and a yawn escapes my mouth. It must be at least early in the morning.

"Come on, sweetheart, let's get you back to bed," Axel whispers in my ear. After he lays me down on the bed, he makes a move to go back to the couch, but I grab onto his arm before he can.

"Stay with me," I whisper to him with my eyes closed, and sure enough, I feel a dip in the bed and strong arms wrap around my waist. I sigh contently at the feeling.

"Good night, Axel," I murmur.

"Good night, Celina. Sweet dreams," he mutters back and with that, I fall into a peaceful sleep with no more dreams of my mother and father.

11

CELINA

I wake up the next morning wrapped tightly in Axel's strong arms. As I slowly open my eyes, I see he's still asleep. I smile slightly at the sight of him. He seems so relaxed and at peace with himself. I don't know how long I lay there, but I just stare at him until I see his eyes flutter a bit.

I brush some stray hair from his forehead and stare into his greyish silver eyes that seem to captivate me no matter what.

"Good morning," I whisper as I stare up at him. He's definitely a sight for sore eyes.

"It certainly is," he mutters, grinning in his sleepy state. Most people will consider this cliché, but I just think it's sweet.

I never really had someone who can honestly say that to me before.

"How did you sleep?" he quietly asks, tightening his arms around me.

"I've actually had the best sleep in years," I tell him truthfully, and he grins again. I smile back and kiss him on the cheek before slipping out of the bed and onto the plush carpet.

A growl rumbles from behind me, and I turn, confused to see the lust-filled eyes of Axel roaming down my body. I look down at myself and gulp. I'm still wearing the nightgown from last night with the matching underwear. Oh boy...

Axel slowly lifts himself from the bed, exposing his boxers, and slowly advances towards me. My eyes travel down his body despite the situation, and my breath hastens once I see his very prominent erection through his boxers.

"Axel..." I warn. "Control yourself."

Of course, he doesn't listen.

With every step he takes forward, I take two steps back. This continues until my back is against the wall. Axel closes the gap between us in a second making me breathless, not even an inch is left between us. I release a shaky breath.

"Axel, don't-" I'm cut off by my own moan when Axel starts to expertly kiss the soft spot on my neck.

He guides my hands to his shoulders and around his neck, locking them there while he places his hands on my hips.

"Axel," I breathlessly moan as he starts to massage my hips with his thumbs, the little action slightly lifting the nightgown up.

He continues to ravage my neck and collar bone, making me throw my head back against the wall in ecstasy.

"Do you know how sexy you look?" Axel whispers in my ear, and I bite my lip to keep me from moaning. Axel picks up on the movement and slowly leans forward. I stare at his full lips, and he stares at mine. All we have to do is lean a little bit more forward.

And we do.

Axel makes the final move and roughly puts his mouth to mine. Sparks shoot from my lips down to my toes and back up, that's how amazing it is. I moan into his mouth as he works his lips on mine. This is my first kiss so I just let Axel take control; my first kiss with my mate, just like a fairytale.

He licks my bottom lip asking for entrance, but I keep it tightly closed. He growls at me as his hands start to travel southward. They slowly slip under the nightgown and up my back. I bite Axel's bottom lip to keep myself from moaning, but I hear a grunt from Axel instead.

"You can't win this," he tells me before tucking his hands into my underpants and cupping my butt. I gasp, and Axel takes advantage of the moment. He pushes his tongue into my mouth and immediately claims it as his own.

He explores every inch of my mouth and me in his. By the time we pull away, we're gasping for breath then Axel starts kissing my neck again. I moan when he softly bites my soft spot, and he forcefully lifts me up by my butt, making me wrap my legs around his waist.

He pushes me up against the wall, closing any space between us. He removes his hands from my butt and travels to my very wet core. He strokes it through the fabric, and I let my head fall to his shoulder as a loud moan escapes my lips. Oh god, that feels so good!

His strokes are long and teasing as he continues to massage me through the fabric. Just as he is about to push my underpants sideways, someone knocks at the door. That breaks me out of my trance, and I push Axel while jumping from the wall and run for the door. Wait! I should probably change first.

I race to the wardrobe and pull out a random dress, throwing the nightgown off and pulling the dress on. It turns out to be a sleeveless, bright red dress that's just above my knees.

I yank open the door to see a very impatient Callum standing there, ready to knock again.

"Callum! Hi, how are you? That's good. Let's go get some breakfast," I rush out and pull him away from the door, leaving a smirking Axel in his boxers. I'll get back to him later...

"I can't believe he did that to me! That's so embarrassing! I don't even know what he did! I'm just an innocent 16-year-old..."

"Um, do I want to know?" Callum asks, confused, then takes a whiff of the air. Pulling me to an abrupt stop, he sniffs down my neck and pulls away with a smirk.

"He didn't," he says astonished, and I nod, blushing red to match my dress. Callum bursts out laughing, and I lightly shake him to stop.

"Callum, stop, please. This is embarrassing enough," I grumble and Callum sobers up eventually. I cross my arms against my chest and decide to ignore him while walking ahead.

"Oh, Celina. Come on, it's funny! You gotta admit," he exclaims as he jogs after me. I just ignore him and head to the kitchen. Luckily, it's a Monday, which means all pack teenagers are at school, and the older members are at work.

"Celina, talk to me," Callum pleads, but I just ignore him again and proceed to get some cereal from a cupboard. This is his punishment for laughing at me.

I think it can be Axel's punishment, too. Not a word to them for the rest of the day!

For the rest of breakfast, Callum tries to get me to talk, and I just ignore him and pretend he isn't there. He even tries a horrible magic trick just to get me to laugh, it doesn't work. At this point, Axel saunters down the stairs, fully clothed. I keep my face neutral.

"Axel! Help me! She isn't talking to me because I laughed at her!" Callum explains, and Axel looks from Callum to me and chuckles.

"You're in your own boat, man. She's still very satisfied with me," he says with a smirk, sending a wink to Callum. I set my jaw to keep myself from bursting.

Axel heads over to me and pulls me to his lap. *Oh no!* I get up and move to the couch in the living room, still sipping my coffee.

"See! She ignores you too, and you can't do anything about it! I even tried to make her laugh!" Callum burst out while I suppress a giggle.

"Please, she can't resist talking. She'll crack eventually, won't you, sweetheart?" Axel says confidently, and I raise an eyebrow at my coffee.

'They're in for a shock,' my wolf mumbles to herself. How is it that she shows up in the most ridiculous moments and not the important ones? I swear I have the laziest wolf in the world.

'I know,' I tell her, making us laugh silently to each other. I put my coffee cup in the dishwasher and head out to the backyard. It must be a bit past nine now, and the clock on the wall confirms that it's 9:03 am.

"Um, Celina? You know there'll be people in the backyard, right?"

I stop and turn to look at Callum, raising an eyebrow and putting my hands on my hips. They can't fool me, everyone's either at school or work.

"It's true, you know," Axel adds and shrugs, looking away. I smirk. He's lying. I turn back around and push open the back door to find that a few children are running around playing.

I smile and take a rest on a wooden rocking chair that is set on the back veranda. A soft breeze whips some hair onto my face, and I delicately brush them away. Callum and Axel join me and soon Comrade finds us. I beam at him.

"Hey, Comrade," I greet him cheerfully, and he smiles down at me while Callum and Axel huff in annoyance. He doesn't laugh at me like you do, I think to myself.

"Hey, Snow," he greets back just as cheerfully. Axel growls at him then stares at me confused. Why is he growling?

"Snow? What's that, a nickname?" Axel mocks and Comrade nods his head while I run my tongue over my teeth and stare straight into Axel's eyes. We have a bit of a staring contest, but Axel backs down first. I grin in triumph.

I'm actually not sure why Comrade calls me Snow. I mean, I know my wolf is Snow White, but my appearance isn't. I have black hair, slightly tanned skin, and gold eyes. I guess for anyone who doesn't know me, it'll confuse them.

"Miss Luna, will you come play with us?" a little girl about six asks while pulling on my dress. I beam at her as the other children behind her stare at me hopefully.

I giggle, "Of course!" I reply cheerfully. They all laugh as I stand and start skipping towards them. I laugh with them as they tell me that I'm the 'it' for the tag. I race after them, but I'm actually only jogging to keep up with their pace.

"You can't catch me!" Rose, the same little girl who asked me to play with them, laughs over her shoulder at me. I increase my speed a bit more and pick her up in my arms, spinning her around. She squeals and the rest of the children, Lily, Jack, Rachel, and George, run towards me, clinging to me in some way. I end up falling to the grass with all of them on top of me. I laugh, and they join in.

I spend the rest of the afternoon just playing around with them, not even remembering Axel, Comrade, or Callum who are still sitting in the veranda. They're just talking quietly amongst themselves, with all of them sneaking glances at me from time to time.

"Miss Luna, can we play again tomorrow?" Rachel asks, and I pick her up.

"Maybe, we'll see what the alpha wants," I whisper the last part to her and grin evilly. "Hey!" I exclaim, and all the children look at me. I motion them over, and we all huddle together. "Ok, you see alpha Axel over there?" I ask them, and they nod. "Well, we're going to go jump on him."

I giggle when all the children cheer. I shush them and watch as Axel makes his way over to us from the veranda.

"Ready?" I ask mischievously. They all nod. This is extra payback for this morning. I love my payback methods. "Go!" I scream when Axel's a few metres away from us. We all launch ourselves at him, tackling Axel to the ground in a big heap. I laugh at his shocked face, stupid alpha.

"Sorry, alpha Axel, but Miss Luna told us to jump at you." Jack giggles and Axel growls playfully at all of them, earning a few squeals.

"Ok, guys. Let's get off the alpha. You should probably go inside," I say, making them pout at me.

"You're it!" Rachael suddenly yells, poking Jack on the shoulder. They all squeal as they run away from Jack and into the house.

I laugh silently at them as I offer Axel a hand. He gladly takes it and hauls himself up, brushing the dirt off himself.

"Well, that was fun," Axel mutters sarcastically. I roll my eyes at him and make my way back to Callum and Comrade. They both have soft smiles on their faces, causing me to stare at them questioningly.

"You'll make a great mother one day," Comrade says, and I blush and shake my head.

"He's right. And a fine Luna too," Callum joins the conversation, and I blush even harder. An arm wraps around my waist, and I look up to see Axel staring at me admiringly. I look down and shrug off his arm, stepping towards the back door.

"I don't know. I haven't really thought about having children. I never thought I would get the chance," I whisper and race back inside and up to our room. I can hear the heavy footsteps of Axel as he follows close behind.

Knowing it's useless to shut or lock the door, I just head towards the window and stare out over the forest.

"We never got to go for a run," I mumble as Axel enters the room.

He comes up and wraps an arm around my waist, resting his chin on my shoulder. The gesture is nice. It brings warmth to my body.

"Would you still like to?" he asks, placing a soft kiss on my neck. Images of this morning flash through my head, and I blush furiously. Axel chuckles when he sees my change in colour. "Thinking about this morning, are we, sweetheart?" he whispers in my ear, nibbling on my ear lobe.

I turn my head to the side and capture his lips with mine in a soft kiss. The sparks still course through my body, but this kiss is soft and gentle, not filled with lust. I pull away with my eyes closed and lips still slightly apart.

"I'd like that very much," I whisper, deciding to ignore his last question, and within no time, we're back down in the backyard. I wonder where Comrade and Callum go, but I don't ponder on it for long, though, just focusing on the forest in front of me that's waiting for me to run into it.

I strip behind a tree and shift into my pure white wolf while Axel shifts into his midnight black one. I marvel at his beautiful colour and slowly trot up to him and nuzzle his neck. He returns the gesture, and we just stay like that for a while. It's comforting in a way.

His size is slightly bigger than mine, and he's more muscular while I'm sort of skin and bones. I have some muscles, just not a lot.

I turn my head towards the forest, and Axel gets the point. Since I'm not part of the pack yet, and Axel hasn't marked me, we can't communicate through the pack link. We'll just have to use head gestures.

We start off at a small trot but soon progress into a full sprint. I don't know how long we run, but we soon stop in a clearing that's a bit away from the pack house.

Axel goes and shifts behind a tree and walks out with just a pair of boxers. He throws a shirt at me on the ground, and I scoop it up with my teeth. I go and shift behind a tree as well and pull the overly large shirt on. It reaches just to my knees, which I'm thankful for.

I've always wondered where my old pack got random clothes in the forest, and now, Axel's pack is doing it too. Where do all these clothes come from?

I step back out and make my way to where Axel is sitting, in the middle of the clearing. He motions me to sit on his lap, and I comply. I rest my head on his chest and think over how we've improved our relationship. A few days ago, I would've been hesitant to even come close to him, but now? Well now, I'm willingly sitting on his lap.

"Are you gonna tell me what you were talking about back there?" Axel softly questions, and I sigh. I knew this would come up eventually.

"Axel, I really don't think—"

He cuts me off with a small kiss on the lips, original.

He looks me straight in the eye as he says, "I want to know your background, Celina. I want to know where you came from. I want to know what kind of life you've had before here because, frankly, it doesn't seem like a good one. All I want to do is help."

My breath hitches in my throat. Am I ready to tell him?

12

AXEL

Celina looks at me doubtfully, and I smile to encourage her. She seems to be having an internal battle with herself, deciding whether to tell me or not. She eventually sighs and looks me in the eye.

"You really want to know?" she asks in a strange tone. I nod. At that, she gets off my lap and sits about a metre away from me. My body feels cold without her, but I shake it off.

"I want to understand what you've been through. You hadn't been a rogue for long when we found you, so, to put it bluntly, I'm curious," I admit and stare at her intently. She gulps and seems to be having another internal battle with herself. Then she comes to a conclusion, straightening herself and begins to speak...

"When I turned seven, my parents died. I was never told how or why. I was just told by my alpha that they were dead. Well, I guess they were my fake parents, but they still cared for me and loved me. After that day, I cried and cried not believing it. By the time I found myself out of my room, the pack had shown me no sympathy," Celina says as her eyes start to look glassy. I make a move to go to her, but she shakes her head at me, so I stay put.

"What happened?" I ask softly. I hate seeing her like this, like when we first found her.

"The pack has never liked me, probably still to this day. When I came out of my room, I expected gazes of sympathy, but that's not what I got. The first bad thing that happened to me was that night. I was making myself dinner since everyone else already had theirs, when suddenly I was slapped across the face," she continues, fear lurking in her eyes. My body goes rigid at her words, and a protective growl escapes my chest. No one, and I mean no one, touches my mate.

"Who slapped you?" I growl out. I'll kill the bastard who's done this to her.

"My Alpha," she whispers, and my wolf howls in pain inside me while I stare at her in shock, *her Alpha?* "He told me that nobody wanted me and that I was to become the pack slave and do as everyone says. Of course, he was a lot older and bigger than me at the time, so I had no choice but to obey. It also didn't help that he used his alpha voice."

Another growl escapes me, and my breathing becomes labored. I'll kill him.

"Since then, I cooked, sew, cleaned, and pretty much did everything a mother would do for her children, but 30 times worse. On top of that, I was repeatedly beaten, thrown down stairs, slapped, and hit. I was rewarded with light beatings when I did a good job but was almost beaten to death when I didn't do something I was told to do or I did something wrong.

That happened to me three times in my life. It seemed that no matter what I did, I would be beaten," she whispers again. I don't think she can speak any louder.

She stops to take a breath and regain her control. Tears fall from her eyes, and she gently wipes them away. I hate seeing her so broken and vulnerable.

"On top of that, I wasn't allowed to leave the pack house. Meaning, I couldn't shift or even go to school. I haven't been to school since I was seven, Axel," she explains, as tears continuously escape from her eyes.

"You don't have to keep going if you don't want to," I tell her gently as I subtly move closer to her.

"No, no, you have to hear this," she mutters, and her eyes suddenly become distant. I stare at her in alarm, thinking she's gonna faint or something, but she continues on.

"Back then, I hadn't shifted since I hadn't turned 16 yet. Before my parents died, they told me not to show anyone else my wolf because I was special and unique... Different, that's what I thought of myself. The pack constantly teased me about how I couldn't shift when I turned 16. Little did they know that my alpha, who has then taken over his Dad, had told me I'm worthless, waste of space and that I should go kill myself. I did try a few times, but I never had the guts to do it. I always thought that out of everything that's happened to me, something good must come out of it eventually, and look where I am now. I have you, Comrade, Callum, and a pack who loves me, even those who haven't met me yet. What more could I ask for?"

Silent tears fall down her cheeks, and I wrap her in my arms. "Shh, sweetheart, shh. It's ok now. I have you, and nothing's gonna take you away," I coo in her ear, and she just breaks down in my arms.

She burst out crying, shaking uncontrollably, and keeps whispering about the things they did to her. I don't believe my little mate, my innocent little mate, had to go through all those things alone. She didn't have anyone there for her, not even her alpha supported her.

A growl erupts from my throat once again when I think of the horrible people that did this to her. I'll kill them, especially that alpha. I'll kill him slowly, and make him pay for what he did to Celina. He doesn't deserve to live.

"Celina?" I whisper when she settles down a bit. She lifts her head from my chest and looks at me through wet eyelashes and glassy eyes. It breaks my heart to see her like this. She shouldn't even be thinking about half the things she just said.

"Who did that to you? Can you tell me the pack name?" I ask softly, and Celina shakes her head, choking on another sob.

"I can't tell you," she chokes out. I look at her with pleading eyes, but she doesn't break. This is their fault. That pack has made my mate broken and vulnerable.

"You'll hunt them down and kill them. I can't handle that, knowing that you might not come back, and the people who I haven't met yet may never return. Think about those who will lose their mates and children. I can't handle that," she whispers and breaks down crying again.

"Shh, sweetheart, it's ok. I understand," I tell her as I rub her back soothingly. She's showing such consideration and love for our pack, I just know she's gonna be a wonderful Luna.

"If it helps, you can meet the pack soon," I offer, and she seems to brighten up a bit at that. She lifts her head up and stares at me with hopeful eyes, a few more tears escaping.

"Really?" she asks quietly, and I nod. Whatever makes her happy, makes me happy. I'll do anything for this girl, no matter what it takes.

"Thank you," she whispers then soon falls asleep in my arms. All of that crying must've worn her out.

I gently pick her up, bridal style, and she instinctively cuddles closer to me, even in her sleep. She buries her head in my chest and sniffles quietly. I smile down at her peaceful, tear-stained face and sigh. She didn't deserve to go through that.

I wonder what pack it is... It seems like the pack depended on Celina a lot and won't survive without her. A thought strikes me. Maybe it's alpha Damon's pack. I mean, when he lost the pack 'slave,' I gained a Luna. He didn't let out anything, though. He only said that the abilities of a Luna should be shared by the pack women.

I set Celina on the bed in our room and tuck her under the covers. I push some hair off her face and kiss her cheek.

"Sweet dreams, sweetheart," I mumble and close the door silently.

I head to the kitchen to get coffee. All this new information about Celina is making my brain work to the extreme. Walking into the kitchen, I see Comrade sitting on a bar stool near the bench.

"Alpha," he says respectfully while I roll my eyes. Celina will probably go off on him for calling me that, and go off on me for letting him call me that.

"Call me Axel, for both our sakes." I chuckle as the image of Celina going on a rampage runs through my head. She probably won't, but I'll rather choose a rampage instead of a silent treatment. That is pure torture, and probably, my punishment for earlier this morning.

"Ok, then, Axel," Comrade says, testing my name on his tongue. I make myself a coffee and sit on one of the bar stools that face the kitchen counters.

"Where's Celina?" he asks, and I growl.

"Why do you want to know?" I retort menacingly. Comrade just shrugs. "If you must know, she's asleep in our room."

I emphasize the word 'our' to him so he doesn't get any ideas.

I've always thought that Comrade had a thing for Celina. I mean, he's the one that got her to change back and actually came and talked to me.

"Those little kiddies tire her out, huh?" Comrade laughs, and I crack a smile. Ever since Comrade joined the pack, I thought of him as someone I'd babysit, but he will not touch my mate or else...

"Yeah, they sure know how to play," I mutter, remembering when they all tackled me. We both share a chuckle before Comrade gets a soft smile on his face.

"What are you smiling about, pup?" I tease, and he growls lowly. I smirk. He can't do anything to me. It always riles people up when I call them pups. It's like an insult to any males of our kind.

He shakes his head and answers my question. "I was just thinking about how Celina will really be a great mother. She has a way with kids," he says honestly, and I stare at him. I can just imagine little Celinas running around. I will make sure boys won't even look at my little angels, though.

"Yeah, I guess she will be," I say distractingly. I've never really thought about it until today. When they mentioned it in the backyard, I thought that Celina wouldn't want kids for a long time. "I don't think we'll be having pups for a while, though," I admit to him, and he nods his head understandably. Celina's still young. I don't think she wants to deal with a newborn.

Our little heart-to-heart talk is interrupted by Callum sauntering in.

"Hey, man. What's up?" he asks in a horrible gangster impression. I roll my eyes at him while Comrade chuckles.

"The sky, dumbass," I tell him, and he puts his hand to his chest faking hurt. Sometimes I forget that we're twenty and no longer in our teens.

"That hurt, man," he says and his bottom lip trembles. I roll my eyes again and finish my coffee.

"Whatever you say, Callum, whatever you say," I chuckle and slap his back. He doubles over laughing, and Comrade soon joins in. After their little laughing fit, we all head to sit on the couch.

"So, what are you going to do about that pack in 'distress'?" Callum asks, putting air quotes on the word distress. I shrug, and Comrade looks confused.

"What pack in distress?" he asks, and I motion for Callum to explain. I can't be bothered.

"A pack called in a few days ago asking if we could help them get back on track and before you ask, no. Not financially. They seem to have lost a pack member that did all the 'chores' for them, and now, their pack house is a mess. Most of them are starving because none of them can cook," Callum wraps up in a neat package, and I nod my head in agreement.

Comrade seems shocked for a moment before a grin breaks out on his face.

"Lazy bastards," he says and we all have a laugh about it. Sometimes I forget that Comrade is only sixteen.

Callum suddenly grips a hand to his chest.

"Hey, you all right?" I ask as he goes into a coughing fit. "Callum, hey!" I push, trying to get his attention. Before I can register, Comrade clutches his wrist in pain and cries out. "What the hell!" I yell at them. Both their eyes widen as they look at each other.

They bolt up, ignoring their coughing and pain, and go upstairs to my room. I race after them into my room to find them trying to wake a stirring Celina.

"Celina! Wake up, woman!" Callum yells at her as he groans in pain, now also gripping his wrist. What the...

Celina tosses and turns in her sleep. She's trying to wake up, but can't.

"Celina!" Callum screams and she wakes up with an ear-piercing scream. I block my ears to keep my eardrums from bursting. Comrade and Callum relax as their pain ceased and they drop to the floor next to the bed, resting their heads on the side of it. I race over to them, taking a shaking Celina in my arms.

"What the hell was that?" I boom at them. Celina pulls back but stays cuddled in my arms.

"I-I had a dream about my old p-pack," she stutters, and I growl, telling her not to explain anymore.

"What were those pains, though?" I ask Callum and Comrade. They both shrug and rest against the bed, looking like their energy was drained out of them.

"What pains?" Celina asks with worry. I smile at her. I can't believe she could still worry about others when she just had a nightmare about her old pack that did unimaginable things to her.

"Huh? Oh, we just went into coughing fits, and our wrists suddenly felt broken. No biggy," Comrade shrugs and lays his head back on the side of the bed, acting like everything is cool.

"Coughing? Broken wrists? When did this start?" she questions while putting the back of her hand on both Callum and Comrade's foreheads.

"A few minutes before they came racing here to wake you," I explain and she gasp. Her eyes grow wide, and I'm almost positive she stops breathing.

"Celina, sweetheart, breathe," I coach her, and she takes in a deep, laboured breath. What's going on with everyone today? First, Celina's history, next Callum and Comrade breaking into coughing fits and having sore wrists, then Celina waking with a scream and recognition on her face! What is going on?

"I think you guys got the impact of my nightmare," Celina whispers, and we all stare at her in confusion.

"What?" we all ask at once, and I would've chuckled if it wasn't serious, given the situation.

"In my dream, I was being kicked in the ribs, and my wrists were being twisted. I was having a memory of a beating I once had," she explains quietly with guilty eyes looking down. Why would she feel guilty about this? It isn't her fault those monsters did that to her.

I pull her into a hug as she continues, "You guys must've picked up on it somehow. I'm not sure how, though..." she trails off, and an idea springs into my mind.

"Wait here," I tell them, then sprint out of the room. I open my office door and search the bookcases until I find what I'm looking for. I pull out the old leather book and race back to my room. I get back on the bed, with Celina on my lap, and show them all, the book.

"What is it?" Celina asks, and I smirk at them. I slowly open the front cover and there, in neat cursive writing, is the name of the book: *History of Shaded Wolves*.

13

CELINA

History of Shaded Wolves. That's the title of the book in front of me and my curiosity spikes to a level I never think possible.

"This book tells you everything recorded about the Shaded Wolves. It can tell you myths, legends, facts, pretty much anything," Axel explains, and I reach for the very thick and very heavy book.

"Is this how you knew about me?" I ask and Axel nods as I turn to the first page.

Written by: King Ronald Heart and Queen Rosemary Heart

Dedicated to their beloved daughter, Princess Celina Heart.

For her future to be filled with adventure, hope, and love.

I gently run my fingers over the names of the authors. Axel wraps an arm around my waist and rests his head on my shoulder.

"Are those my parents?" I say softly, and Axel kisses my forehead while silently nodding his head.

Tears prick my eyes and I sniff. I've never actually cried over my real parents' death before, and I don't plan to. They deserve to be remembered, not mourned, even if I don't remember them myself.

"Well, if my parents wrote it, then I'm sure that this stuff is valid," I mumble, and everyone chuckles as the once thick atmosphere evaporates.

I turn the page and see the contents. Wow, I guess my parents were smart like that. Seeing as not many people used contents back then... I think.

Contents

1. Introduction to Shaded Wolves
2. The Facts and Myths of Shaded Wolves
3. The legend of Shaded Wolves
4. How the Shaded Wolves lived
5. The Royal family
6. Guardians of the Royal family
7. What Powers the Shaded Wolves Possessed
8. How the Shaded Wolves Came to Be
9. How the Shaded Wolves Came to an End
10. The Prophecy

As I read through the contents, I can't help thinking that all of this happened to my parents and their people while

I'm happily living my life with my mate and the family that I never knew I could have.

I let those thoughts leave my mind as I turn the page over and begin to read the *Introduction to Shaded Wolves*.

The Shaded Wolves were one of the most highly respected races of wolves. There were three types of wolves: the Shaded Wolves, the Coloured Wolves, and the Rogues. Each of these groups made up the society of wolves across the world.

The Shaded Wolves were respected by all, even by the Rogues. They, in a way, ruled the wolf society. They made sure everyone was well and happy, as well as safe and secure. Not one little thing got past them, and not one wolf could do wrong without them knowing.

The Shaded Wolves had a royal family, consisting of the kind Queen and the brave King. All the different wolves lived in harmony, and there were hardly any disagreements.

The book continues to talk about how all the wolves lived in harmony and how the wolf society worked. As I near the next section, I start to feel giddy.

The Facts and Myths of Shaded Wolves.

Facts:
- Shaded Wolves possessed powers
- They practically ruled the wolf society
- They only had white, black, or grey fur, never mixed
- Only the royal family had the gift of gold eyes

- Non-royals had silver, black, or grey eyes
- Shaded Wolves were preferably larger than other wolves

Myths:
- Shaded Wolves were vicious creatures. They actually had the same instincts as any other wolf
- Shaded Wolves craved for dominance. They strived to be always on top of all wolf kind
- Shaded Wolves had more than one mate (that's definitely not true) Shaded Wolves only had one mate, unless those mates were twins, then yes, they had two
- Shaded Wolves used their powers for evil. Only the very, very rare ones did, and they were usually grey

That's all that part of the book says, but I know that my parents left a few things out. I can feel it.

Then the legend follows. This part is less than a page long.

The legend of the Shaded Wolves was that the Moon Goddess magically made them and had every wolf follow them no matter what.

That's pretty much the summary although it's not what I'm looking for...

"Did anyone else know about this book in my parents' time?" I turn to Axel and lock my gaze on his greyish silver eyes.

"No, nobody knew about it. Archaeologists found the book when they were searching the battlefield, that clearing we went to earlier. They reprinted it twice, and the actual copy is in a wolf museum," Axel explains, and I nod my head. That must be why it has contents... As that realization comes to me, I look back at the book.

How the Shaded Wolves Lived

Back in the early 1600s, the Shaded Wolves lived in huts made out of grass and mud. During the 1700s, they made more suitable houses out of clay and twigs. When the 1800s came, they had made more suitable houses, but they never got any further.

The royal family had always lived in a castle, ever since the dawn of time. As the centuries passed, the castle had renovations, and new sections were added to it, until it became large, majestic, and beautiful, that everyone adored. Only the royals, the royal advisors, and the castle servants were allowed to stay there. Others could enter but with permission.

The non-royals lived in the above-mentioned houses and planted crops for themselves and the royals. These wolves were what held the kingdom together, with the guidance of the royals.

Huh, I guess they had a very simple lifestyle. Why didn't they get to advance any further, though? My mind suddenly goes back to Axel's story, a while ago, and I feel my heart break. They never had the chance because they were betrayed.

The Royal Family

The royal family consisted of the beautiful and smart Queen Rosemary Heart, and the strong and wise King Ronald Heart. They had been the rulers since the Shaded Wolves first came to be. Only the Moon Goddess knew how they lived for such a long period of time and still stayed looking the same age while everyone else aged around them.

The royal family had no sons, only a daughter. This daughter was named Princess Celina Goddess Heart. Princess because of her title, Celina meaning moon, Goddess meaning the Moon Goddess, and Heart as the last name of the royals. Nobody knew what happened to this baby, for nobody knew about this baby. The King and Queen kept it a secret from their kingdom, for a war was brewing.

The royal family had a loyal and trustworthy advisor named Alastair. The King and Queen told him everything even if he wasn't fit to know. The only thing he didn't know about was Celina Heart, and the King and Queen made sure to keep it that way.

The royal family was a kind and caring one, always putting others before themselves. They didn't think of themselves as higher than other wolves, but more of a role model that the other wolves could follow.

Guardians of the Royal Family

Each member of the royal family had a guardian. The King's guardian was called Leo. Leo was a brave knight with much honor and loyalty towards his King. He was known throughout the three types of wolves, and no one dared to get in his way.

The Queen had two guardians. This was normal for a female royal to have two guardians because they were more important to the wolf society and needed extra protection. Only female wolves could have offspring, so extra protection was required. The Queen's two guardians were called Luis and

Paul. They were both gentle and kind towards the Queen, but were in immediate protection mode when danger ever arose.

If worse comes to worse and the guardians failed, then the King and Queen would protect each other with their lives. This was, of course, an instinct between mates. But since they already had guardians, that instinct was slightly brought down.

If these guardians were killed in any way, they would not be replaced and the royals' survival instinct of protecting each other would double or triple, depending on how much devotion they had for each other.

The guardians also felt the pain of the ones they were protecting. This could happen either the pain was real or just a dream. They would also experience headache when a vision occurred. These were the main aspects of the royal guardians. Furthermore, these guardians felt a connection and an instant trust to the one they were guarding. The one who was being guarded would also feel the same way.

As I finish reading the chapter, I sneak a glance at Axel. I wonder if he will protect me with his life. Then I look at Callum and Comrade. The book states that every female royal has two guardians. Can they be my guardians? They felt the pain on my chest and wrist when I dreamt about my beating. That also has to be the reason why I feel so safe around them... trust them. I look at Axel for confirmation.

"Axel, are Callum and Comrade my guardians?" I whisper, and Axel's eyes go distant for a few moments. Callum and Comrade stare at me wide-eyed while I wait for Axel to answer.

"Yes, I think they are. They felt your pain, and you seemed to trust them before you even knew them. So yes, I believe they are your guardians," Axel states proudly, knowing that two of his pack members whom he appreciates and trusts are protecting his mate.

I smile softly at the shock on Callum and Comrade's faces. I will be too if I find out I'm protecting a Princess.

"G-guardians?" Comrade stutters and I nod my head. Then they both look and smile at each other. They jump up and do a happy dance while I giggle at them, and Axel rolls his eyes.

"We're royal guardians! We're royal guardians!" they chant in sync, and I throw a pillow at them to stop. They both settle back down after a minute or two, and I continue to read.

What Powers the Shaded Wolves Possessed. This is the one I've been looking for...

Shaded wolves possessed many powers. Some came naturally while others required training. There were some powers the Shaded Wolves did not have at all. The main three are listed below:

1) Hypnotism - to influence someone or something by staring into their eyes.

2) Energy Drainage - to suck the energy out of someone and transfer it elsewhere.

3) Invisibility – to be not seen by others around.

Some used these powers for evil, though it was rare. There were some cases about the evil usage of the Shaded Wolves' powers.

The royal family may have also possessed the following powers, but not all:

1) Flying - when one can fly like a bird without wings. They can reach speeds of 80 kilometres per hour.

2) Vision - when one can see the past and the future. This is a very rare trait and has only been gifted to Queen Rosemary.

3) Manipulating the Weather - when one changes the weather from hot to cold, sunny to rainy, etc.

4) Super Senses - when one has heightened senses than the normal wolf: sight, smell, hearing, taste, etc.

5) Absorbing energy - when one can not only take the energy from others but the energy from nature itself. Only King Ronald had this power.

All of the powers listed above required training and great concentration. They were not something to fool around with and should be taken seriously. A royal Shaded Wolf did not possess all of these powers, but definitely some. It depended on the strength of that wolf.

I should really see if I can do any of those things. I'll ask Axel later if he can help me.

How Shaded Wolves Came to Be

For some, this may sound complicated, but it was actually quite a simple process.

The Moon Goddess caught the brightest star in the sky and whispered some words to it which remained unknown to this day. She then pushed the star into her heart and transported herself to earth. She came to a clearing and sat there for many days and nights. On the twenty-first night of her stay there without moving, light beams erupted from her fingers and all over her body, causing her eyes to shine. At that moment, the tiniest baby wolf was born. It was black, just like the night. The Moon Goddess declared it to be the first Shaded Wolf, and that little wolf went on to build the Shaded Wolves' society.

When the Moon Goddess decided that the society was well built and to her liking, she took the midnight black wolf away with her. The wolf only returned when the Shaded Wolves were dying or were in serious trouble. When it left, though, all its memory was erased except for the fact that its mother was the Moon Goddess. This had never happened before, but Queen Rosemary had seen it later in the future when the Shaded Wolves were on the brink of extinction.

The midnight black wolf's name was Axel Moon Night. Axel meaning source of all life, Moon meaning the Moon Goddess, and Night meaning the time he was brought to life.

That was how the Shaded Wolves came to be.

My eyes are wide and my mouth agape as I finish reading the chapter and turn my head to Axel. He stares at me with knowing eyes, telling me he already knew about this and never told me.

"Y-you..." I start, but can't finish. I'm in shock right now.

"Shh, sweetheart. I'm sorry I didn't tell you, but I thought that would just raise more questions, so I let you read it for yourself. If it helps, I can't remember any of that. All I can remember is that the Moon Goddess is my mother," he explains as he takes me in his arms and buries his head in the crook of my neck.

I stay silent as I absorb all of this and let it sink in. Axel, my mate who just so happens to be a Shaded Wolf like me, is actually the son of the Moon Goddess and was made from a star. Whoa...

"So, you're telling me, that you're the Moon Goddess' son and that you were made from a star... but you can't remember any of it?" I say to Axel, and he nods against my neck. I take a deep breath through my nose and let it out through my mouth.

"Right, I can deal with that... I think. After all, I am royalty," I mutter to myself, but three snickers are heard around the room. I just roll my eyes and return them back to the book.

How the Shaded Wolves Came to an End

The Shaded Wolves came to an end by an act of betrayal. Alastair, the trusted advisor, thought that he could overthrow and bring the Shaded Wolves to the brink of extinction.

As the 1800s went on, Alastair devised a foolproof plan that would bring down the Shaded Wolves for good. He rounded up all the Coloured Wolves that were willing to help him and got rid of those who wouldn't.

When the time came, Queen Rosemary had already seen this happening and knew when the plan of attack was. She shared it with King Ronald, and they agreed to wait for what the Moon Goddess said about the matter. That night, Queen Rosemary got a message from the Moon Goddess telling her to let her people fall. She said that a bright future was coming for her child and that she would be safe. At that time, Queen Rosemary did not know she was pregnant, but she followed the Moon Goddess' orders and indeed, she gave birth to a beautiful baby girl.

The night Princess Celina Heart was born, the Moon Goddess appeared to Queen Rosemary and King Ronald. She told them that in order to keep their baby safe, they had to give her up to the Moon Goddess. The Queen didn't want to let go of her baby, but the King convinced her to, for the sake of the future of his baby girl.

The day after Celina Heart was born, the battle commenced and went on for three days and three nights. On the third night, Alastair stood over the wounded King and Queen and killed them with a silver dagger. Alastair and his followers killed every single Shaded Wolf... Except one, that one being Princess Celina Goddess Heart, the last surviving Shaded Wolf in existence.

I gulp as I finish reading. The last surviving Shaded Wolf in existence. Me. I don't believe it... Just as I'm about to close the book, Axel gently grabs my hand.

"There's more," he whispers and turns the page to reveal the last chapter...

The Prophecy

It is believed that Celina Heart would be the mate of Axel Night. When the Moon Goddess deemed it to be the right time, she would bring the two together and fate would take its course.

They would face many struggles, and another war would start. No. Not between Shaded and Coloured Wolves, but between dominance, revenge, greed, and power.

The lives of Princess Celina Goddess Heart and Axel Moon Night would not be a road once travelled.

14

CELINA

After reading all of that, my mind feels numb, and my eyes feel heavy. The prophecy about Axel and me being mates is obviously true, so that means another war is coming... and I can't do anything about it. I feel so useless.

"Tired?" Axel asks, and I sigh while resting my head on his shoulder.

"My whole life has been a guessing game of what will happen and where I will go," I explain while looking at Axel, Comrade, and Callum. "I guess my life was already planned out for me from the start, though. I just never knew it."

I smile at all of them, and they smile back. If it isn't for my past, I may have never met these people, whom I now call family.

My eyes close of their own accord, and I faintly feel Axel kiss my temple before falling asleep.

I wake up to the sun's rays falling into the room and lighting it up. I turn and bury my head into something cozy, not a pillow, though. Without opening my eyes, I feel it around with my hand to see what it is. When I come in contact with something hard, my eyes shoot open and I bolt up straight. My eyes lock with grayish silver ones and I relax back down.

"Axel, you gave me a fright," I tell him and rest my head back on his chest, releasing a small yawn.

Axel chuckles at me. "Sorry, sweetheart. Have a good sleep?" he says and I nod. He leans to kiss my lips and I gladly respond to him. A thought suddenly strikes me. This is only the second time I've kissed my mate. The first was the other morning.

He nibbles on my bottom lip asking for entrance and I happily open. The kiss isn't heated or lustful; it's soft and loving.

We break apart and I smile widely at him. He returns it with a goofy grin.

"Well, that's a good wake-up call," he says and I playfully slap his chest.

"Shut up," I mumble when he laughs at me. We spend the rest of the morning talking about random things while Axel continuously runs his fingers up and down my back, leaving little goose bumps and a trail of fire.

"So, ready to meet the pack yet?" Axel asks while kissing down my neck. His question doesn't register as I focus on his magic lips.

"Mmm-hmm..." I mumble and I feel him smirk against my neck. He starts to suck where he'll mark me, causing a loud moan to escape my lips. I feel his hard erection pressing into my stomach, making me moan again.

"Would this afternoon be ok? I'm sure they would all love to meet you," Alex mumbles against my skin. Again, his question doesn't register and I happily agree without knowing.

He slowly pushes me down onto the bed and presses his body against mine, but not letting any of his weight on me. He leaves my neck and makes his way to my jawline then my lips. I moan into his mouth as he massages my tongue with his. He lets his hands travel up and down the side of my body, lifting my shirt up every time.

I wrap my arms around his neck as his hands dive under my shirt without any warning. I gasp loudly as he starts to massage my stomach with his thumbs. In a flash, my shirt's gone.

My arms fly up as I try to cover myself. Since I didn't get dressed this morning, I have no bra on. Axel pulls his mouth away from mine and growls. I stare into his black eyes and know that mine probably looks the same.

"Don't hide yourself from me," he growls before pinning my arms above my head.

I gasp as he stares down at me. A feral growl leaves his mouth and I blush bright red. He trails one finger across my jaw line while the other still holds my hands.

"I love it when you blush," he mutters huskily. Butterflies erupt in my stomach at the sound of his voice.

Before I can respond, his mouth connects with one of my nipples. I moan loudly and thrash my head from side to side from the pleasure.

"Oh god!" I yell when he sucks hard. He moves to the other nipple and the pleasure doesn't cease.

He kisses down from my cleavage to the waistband of my shorts. He releases my wrists to massage my breasts. I take that as an advantage and trail my fingers down his toned back. He looks up at me with black, lust-filled eyes.

"A bit eager, are we?" he teases with a smirk. I growl at him and trail my fingers along his boxers' waistband.

"Axel, please," I beg and he immediately complies. I'm filled with so much pleasure, I could burst! I don't know how he does it, but Axel always seems to get me worked up.

He slowly, torturously slides my shorts and underwear down my legs. He pulls them all the way off, leaving me bare to him. He kisses back up my legs and sucks on my inner thighs. I moan again and Axel grunts.

His hands slowly make their way to my butt and he cups it, squeezing it slightly, making me squirm. Without warning, his mouth goes straight to my very wet core.

"Axel!" I moan out as his tongue circles before he thrusts it into me. I arch my back at the pleasure, and my eyes close with another moan. God, this feels so good!

He continues to explore my core while pushing me up to his mouth with the help of his hands on my butt. I don't know how long he does it, but I feel this sudden pleasure rise in me, begging to be released.

"Come for me, sweetheart. I want to taste you." Axel growls before I explode in his mouth and he licks up every bit of it while I moan.

He leaves my core and kisses me gently on the mouth as I try to catch my breath. If that's what it feels like to have an orgasm, I can't wait till we mate.

Axel's hands continue to rub my breasts as I still try to catch my breath.

"You liked that, huh? Just imagine what mating will be like," Axel whispers to me what I'm just thinking.

With new confidence suddenly bursting in me, I straddle Axel's waist. He looks at me curiously, and it seems his eyes grow darker.

"What are you doing, sweetheart?" he asks huskily, but I don't answer as I slowly trail my hands down his bare chest and over his abs.

I bend my head and lick his delicious-looking abs and get a grunt from Axel as he tangles his hands in my already messed up hair.

"What are you doing, sweetheart?" he repeats, but more distractingly. Ignoring him, I pull his boxers down and marvel at the sight of his very hard, very long, erection.

I gulp as I shakily bring my hands to it and grip it tightly. A groan comes from Axel, and I begin to slowly work it.

"Faster, sweetheart, oh god, faster!" he pants and I do as he says, working my hands faster and faster.

I get this strange urge in me to taste him, so I immediately do what my wolf is begging me to. The taste of him explodes on my tongue and I moan. He has a sweet, but spicy taste. I just take him whole in my mouth. I gag slightly, but that seems to just excite him more.

"Celina!" he groans before exploding in my mouth after a few minutes. I moan along with him as the taste and feel of him runs through my body. I slowly take him out of my mouth but leave a lingering kiss on his head. I collapse next to him and he takes me in his arms.

"Well, who could've known that my little, innocent mate isn't so innocent at all?" he says, playfully pulling on my earlobe with his teeth. "I like it," he whispers in my ear and I find myself trying to control my excitement.

I can't wait till we mate.

After our... alone time, Axel explains to me that we have to get ready to meet the pack because, apparently, I agreed to it. In my defense, he seduced me and he knows it. So here I am, standing at the back door leading to the backyard with Axel by my side and all his pack members outside in the backyard. Let's just say I'm a little nervous.

I'm wearing a beautiful red dress that flows gracefully down to my ankles. It's got one sleeve and the back is like a corset type of thing. It has white swirls starting from the sleeve and fading down until they are hardly recognizable at the bottom. My hair has been kept down with two thin strips tied back to keep the hair off my face. On my feet, I have white stiletto heels on. I argued with Axel that I'll fall over, but he didn't budge. I just know I'm gonna fall over...

Axel is wearing a nice black suit with a matching tie, and his hair is in its normal messed up state. He grips my hand tightly when the opening music starts to play.

"It's now or never, sweetheart," he mutters before opening the door and leading us out.

15

CELINA

The pack goes silent as they see us walk out the door. I spot the children I played with a few days ago, as they all smile and wave at me. I wink at them with a smile, and they all giggle. That little moment kinda takes away some of the nerves I'm feeling.

As we make our way onto the stage, Axel walks up to the microphone and clears his throat loudly. Hundreds of eyes focus solely on him, and I take a deep breath, waiting for what Axel will say and the reaction from the pack members.

"Today, we are gathered here to celebrate a new arrival to our pack," Axel begins with a loud and clear voice. He smiles and graces the pack members' faces. "I have found my mate and your new Luna. She's smart, kind, caring, and loves children, so I'm sure everyone will get along just fine," he jokes, and everyone laughs. I feel my heart swell at his words. Knowing that's how he sees me is a wonderful feeling.

"Welcome your Luna with open arms and big smiles, for she is something this pack has been waiting for, for a long time!" he finishes, and everyone erupts into cheers and whistles.

I smile broadly at everyone and feel a sudden wave of acceptance wash over me. I've been accepted. I've been accepted as their new Luna.

Axel's face turns into a warm smile as he gazes at me, and I return it with my broad one. Axel's eyes light up suddenly, and that's when I realize that I haven't smiled like this around him before. In fact, I haven't smiled like this since I was seven.

"I'm accepted," I whisper to myself as Axel engulfs me in his arms.

We make our way down the stage, and I'm immediately swarmed by the teenagers of the pack, and Axel's been dragged away by all his buddies. I shoot him a worried look, but he just smiles reassuringly at me.

I turn back to all the girls who have wide smiles on their faces and shyly look down.

"Hi," I softly say, and they all giggle. What's so funny?

"Hi, I'm Kayla!" a blonde haired girl says, and she continues with introductions. All the girls surrounding her seem to have the same dyed blonde hair and pink dresses on. As they continue to chat, I spot a small group of four people off to the side near the edge.

"Excuse me," I say to them, but I don't think they notice. As I move closer to the group, I realize it's Jasper, Chloe, Declan, and Matt. My rescuers!

I tap Matt on the shoulder, interrupting him mid-sentence. He turns around, slightly surprised, but a smile graces his face when he notices it's me.

"Well, hello there, Luna. How are you today?" he asks teasingly, and I giggle.

"I'm very happy, thank you," I reply, and he motions me into the little circle.

"I see you got away from the Barbie dolls over there," Chloe says while motioning to Kayla and the other girls I was with.

I shake my head as I mutter, "Too much pink for my liking."

Everyone laughs, and we fall easily into a carefree conversation. It's hard to believe that I've only met these people, and it seems I talk more now than I've done in the last nine years! I like this, though. Just talking. I've never really been able to just talk to people, and knowing that these four new friends of mine won't judge me, it's a good feeling.

A woman that looks a lot like Chloe suddenly races up to us. I stare at her with worried eyes. What's wrong?

"Chloe! Thank the Goddess I found you!" the woman exclaims with a frantic look in her eyes. Chloe looks at her with the same worry I'm showing.

"What is it, Mum?" Chloe quickly asks. That answers the question why she looks so much like Chloe.

"The Alpha didn't organize food for the party and people are starting to complain. I need help!" she cries as she grips her daughter's shoulders.

"Mum, calm down. I'll go help, ok?" she says, and her Mum visibly relaxes.

"Well, come on!" she exclaims while dragging her smiling daughter away. Declan chuckles at his Mum, and everyone soon joins in.

"I think I'll go help out, she seems a bit stressed out," I tell the guys as I make a move to leave. I enter the kitchen and see about four women, including Chloe, slaving away in the kitchen.

"Do you guys want some help?" I ask, and all heads snap up in my direction.

"Yes!" Chloe's Mum exclaims before Chloe gives her a stern look, and she clears her throat. "I mean, yes, Luna. That would be highly appreciated," she says in a much calmer voice while Chloe rolls her eyes. I just chuckle at them and get to work.

"So, what are we making?" I ask again as I take out the hair tie that was holding my hair back and tie my hair up in a ponytail. All the women look at me uncertainly.

"What can you cook?" Chloe's Mum asks me, and I shrug. "Can you make desserts?" A smile lights up my face. I eagerly nod as some of the women who were making salads clear a place in the kitchen.

"Well, choose what you want to make and get to work," she orders me. My wolf growls lowly at the order, but I ignore her and set to work. She hasn't spoken to me lately, so why should I pay mind to her?

Of course, I choose to make a chocolate mud cake with whipped cream and chocolate shavings. Surprisingly, they have all the ingredients. Chloe looks to me curiously as I begin to mix stuff without taking measurements or anything. I always do this with all my meals.

"Whatcha making?" she asks suspiciously, quickly getting the attention of everyone else.

I shrug without looking away from the bowl I'm mixing stuff in. "Surprise," I say, and that seems to satisfy them as they all go back to their stations and continue working.

Twenty minutes later, I've made up at least five separate mud cakes that are ready to go in the oven. I place each one in and get to work with the whipped cream.

Another few minutes pass before Axel bursts through the door. His eyes look frantic and worried as his eyes lock onto Chloe's Mum.

"Nancy! Have you seen—" he stops mid-sentence as his eyes land on me. I stare at him with wide eyes as he takes two long strides towards me and engulfs me in his arms.

He buries his head in the crook of my neck, and I run my fingers through his silky white hair.

"Axel, what's wrong?" I softly ask as he breathes in my scent deeply before pulling back and looking me in the eyes.

"I couldn't find you anywhere outside, so I panicked. Please don't do that again," he whispers, and he actually looks vulnerable. I kiss him softly on the lips and hug him close to me.

"I'm sorry. I didn't know I would cause you to worry. I'm here now, though, I'm safe," I coo to him, and he eventually calms down.

"Aww, that's so sweet. I wish I'll have a mate like that," Chloe mumbles to herself, and I giggle at her antics. She'll get her mate soon.

"So..." Axel says after clearing his throat. He's back into the big bad alpha mode, I guess. "What are you making, since I forgot to organize food?" he rolls his eyes as he looks at a frowning Nancy.

"Pardon me, alpha, but you usually organize these things with food for all the pack," Chloe's Mum bravely speaks up, but before Axel could reply or growl, I step into the conversation.

"That's all right. He didn't mean to. He was a bit distracted this morning." I giggle, and Axel growls lowly.

"Just make sure everyone gets their food ok, Nancy?" Axel growls and Chloe's Mum nods her head. I guess her name's Nancy then... Axel walks out with an annoyed look on his face, but I just smile at him. He's cute when annoyed.

"Don't worry about him," I assure her as she seems frozen in place. "He seemed to be distracted lately, don't worry about it."

Nancy nods her head at me, and everyone returns to what they're doing.

An hour later and the pack is sitting at tables and wolfing down their food. I don't know how we managed to sit 300+ wolves, but we did. I have no clue how we managed to cook for them, too.

I'm sitting beside Axel at the head of the pack. Comrade is sitting across from me while Callum is sitting on my other side, so I'm pretty much surrounded by my mate and guardians. It's a nice feeling, to be safe, I mean.

"So, how have you gotten along with the pack so far?" Comrade asks as he stuffs half a burger in his mouth. I roll my face up in slight disgust at his manners. I silently put another bit of salad in my mouth before I answer.

"Everyone seems really nice. I think I'm gonna like it here," I say with a slight grin. They all return it as the pack members that heard also seem to grin.

"Well, I'm glad you like it here. Everyone seems to like you very much. You seem to have won the hearts of many," Comrade wisely says, and I raise an eyebrow at him. He just shrugs and swallows the other half of his burger.

I pick at the food on my plate. I'm honestly not hungry. I'm used to being fed so little that I'm just used to hardly eating anything.

Axel looks at me worriedly while saying, "You should eat more, Celina. You look a bit thin."

I look at his worried eyes and contemplate it. I could eat more for him...

I slowly take a bite of my meat, and he smiles at me. I smile back, and we continue to talk aimlessly. Well, more like me listening while they talk.

A little while later, I watch as Nancy gets up, excusing herself and heading to the kitchen.

"Excuse me," I say distractedly to Axel and not waiting for a reply as I get up.

As I followed Nancy to the kitchen, I feel blisters forming on my feet, and I slightly stumble in my ridiculously high heels. I'm surprised I haven't fallen over yet...

I enter the kitchen and see Nancy holding an armful of chocolate mud cake with whipped cream and chocolate flakes.

"Here, let me help with that," I tell her, and she looks at me in shock. Am I not supposed to say that?

"You'll actually help serve people?" she asks in disbelief. I look at her strangely before slowly nodding my head.

She clears her throat before saying, "Well, ok then."

Then she hands me six or seven plates and rushes me out the door with her behind me.

We go to my table first, and Axel looks up at me with a smile. I place a plate of mud cake down in front of him and peck him on the lips.

"Enjoy," I whisper before walking off, hearing a low growl behind me as I place a plate in front of another pack member. Oh, Axel...

By the time everyone has a plate, they're all looking at me in awe and amazement. I smile at them and walk back inside as a tired Nancy takes a seat next to a man, who I am presuming is her mate. I take the last two plates in my hands and place one down in front of her.

"Thank you, Luna. Not just for this, but for cooking and helping. You're certainly one of a kind," Nancy tells me, and I feel my insides blossom.

"It's very welcome, Nancy," I reply back, and her eyes widen slightly before she bows her head respectfully. I quickly head back over to Axel after that.

"That was very nice, what you did," he whispers in my ear when I'm sitting down. I look at him confused. What did I do? I don't understand why these people think of it as strange for me to serve them. Axel seems to read my mind and answers the question for me.

"Not many Lunas help in cooking and serving for her pack members. You really are one of a kind, Celina Heart. One of a kind," Axel mutters the last part as I beam at him. I bite my lip to try and keep the smile, but it doesn't work.

When everyone's finished eating, Axel once again gets back on stage and pulls me along with him. Everyone looks at me with acceptance, awe, happiness, and kindness in their eyes. I don't think I can be happier than right now, at this moment.

"My fellow pack members, to finally accept your new Luna, we must make the bond final!" Axel booms as some people whistle.

Callum suddenly appears onstage and takes my hand. Axel does too, with my other hand.

"On this day, a new Luna will lead by my side and lead the pack to greatness!" Axel announces. With a final cheer from the crowd, a sharp pain strikes through my head.

I wince slightly and close my eyes against the pain. It doesn't last long, though, as I soon feel the thoughts and feelings of the pack members. I open my eyes and see everyone looking at me.

"Thank you," I whisper, and they once again erupt into cheers and whistles.

"You did great," Callum tells me and pulls me into a bone-crushing hug. Axel possessively snatches me from him and pushes me up against his hard chest while nuzzling my neck. I giggle at him and hear laughs from the pack members.

"Mine," Axel whispers in my ear as he places a gentle kiss on my soft spot, making me shiver with delight.

I look back over all the smiling and joyous faces of my new family and wonder how I ever got this lucky.

16

CELINA

I smile at all the happy faces and softly kiss Axel on the cheek. He smiles at me, and we make our way down the little stairs that lead up to the stage. Callum goes first, then Axel, then me.

My heels are absolutely killing me by now, and I just can't wait to get them off! I'm gonna have blisters galore!

As I make my way down the three small steps, my heel suddenly gets caught on the edge of one, and before I can even react, I'm sent plummeting towards the floor. I let out a squeal and the next second, I'm on the floor face first.

Everyone goes silent. I don't even bother to lift my head and see the shocked expression on everyone's faces. I sigh softly and slowly push myself up, taking my heels off. Axel stares at me, shocked as Callum and Comrade seem to do the same with a little disappointment on their faces. I'm not sure if that's because of me, but I take it is.

I don't bother to look at the pack members and just race inside, forgetting the heels. I knew I would fall over!

"Celina!" I hear someone call behind me, and I instantly know it's Axel. I don't stop, though. I keep running until I'm in our room. I close the door and lock it, slowly sliding down to the floor. How embarrassing...

I bury my face in my hands and growl. "I can't believe I just did that..." I mutter to myself.

'Well, you should be more graceful,' my wolf butts in and I internally glare at her.

She's finally making an appearance. 'Why do you only come out when I'm angry or embarrassed?' I question her before she runs away again.

She's silent for a moment, and I think she's left, that's before I hear her quietly say, 'Moon Goddess' orders.' Then she's gone again.

I sigh. Of course, the Moon Goddess told her that. A soft knock interrupts my thoughts.

"Celina? You in there?" Axel says through the door, and I know I have to get up otherwise he'll break it down. I slowly get up and open the door. Axel takes one look at me and engulfs me in a hug.

"Shh, sweetheart, shh. It's ok, you don't need to be upset," he coos softly. I push my head away from his chest and look into his greyish silver eyes.

"Why do you always seem to comfort me?" I suddenly question, but he only smiles. He does, though. Whenever I'm the slightest bit upset, Axel will be there first and foremost to comfort and hold me. Is that a mate thing?

"Well, sweetheart, that's just what mates do. They want their mate to be happy and smiling all the time, so when they're upset, we try to make them smile. I guess it's like an instinct," Axel explains, and I smile softly. It's nice to know that Axel will always care.

"Thank you," I say, then bury my head in his chest again. We stand there like that for what seems like forever. I'm wrapped up in his warm and comforting arms while his head rests in the crook of my neck. His hot breath teasingly hits my neck, and for the whole time he's comforting me, I have to keep myself from losing control.

"We should probably head to bed," Axel mumbles into my neck. Without waiting for my answer, he swiftly lifts me up bridal style and carries me to the bed. I squeal when he does that, but he just chuckles at me. He places me gently on the bed and sleep consumes me almost instantly.

"Celina. Come on, sweetheart, wake up. It's time to get up now," a soft voice says in my ear. I snuggle closer to Axel's chest and sigh contentedly. Man, I slept well.

"Come on, sweetheart, wake up," the soft voice continues to speak, and I groan, not wanting to get up just yet.

"Five more minutes," I mumble. I hear a chuckle before I'm being lifted off the bed. My eyes snap open, and I come face to face with a smirking Axel. Why, that little...

"Axel!" I groan, and he laughs again. I slightly slap his chest as my eyes start to drift close.

"Ah ah ah, don't you dare go back to sleep, Missy. We have a big day ahead of us. I'm planning something that I need your approval on," Axel tells me and I glance up at him sleepily. Why does he need my opinion? He's the alpha after all.

He gently places me down when we enter the bathroom, and I head to the sink. I wash my face, and that's when I notice that I'm not wearing the dress from last night. Instead, I'm in a pretty white nightgown with lace around the bottom.

I look at Axel with a raised eyebrow, and he grins at me. I blush furiously, and he laughs while I walk past him.

"I don't believe you," I mutter, and he laughs even harder. I love that laugh...

I ignore him as I head to the wardrobe and pull on a random dress. It's a plain, blue sundress and I just match it with white flats. After last night's events, I don't think I'll be wearing heels for a long time. That was way too embarrassing.

Passing a still laughing Axel, I reach for the doorknob and silently walk out the door with a small smile on my face. Axel has a beautiful laugh, deep and straight from the chest. I would do anything to hear it...

"Morning, Luna," I hear someone say, and I turn to see one of the women from last night. I smile at her, and she smiles back shyly.

"I'm Eva. I didn't get to introduce myself last night, we were far too busy," she explains. She has a slight British accent and has dimples when she smiles.

"Well, it's lovely to meet you, Eva. Want some coffee?" I ask casually, and a momentary shock passes across her face before she smiles again.

"Sure, that would be lovely."

I nod my head and quickly make us coffee. She seems really nice, but I know better than to judge a book by its cover.

"If you don't mind me asking, Luna, but how old are you? You seem very mature. Alpha mates are usually a few years apart..." she trails off, and I smile at her. I like how she doesn't beat around the bush a lot.

"Actually, Eva, I'm sixteen. No more, no less," I tell her, and she goes into shock again. I stare at her, concerned and place a hand gently on her shoulder.

"Eva?" I ask, slightly shaking her when she doesn't answer, "Eva, you there?"

She seems to snap out of it and looks at me. Shock once again appears on her face, and I can't help but wonder why everyone keeps on staring at me like that. Am I not supposed to do what I'm doing?

"You're only sixteen? You can cook for more than 300 wolves in just over an hour, though! I can't even get my seventeen-year-old daughter to cook a meal for herself. You must've had a very devoted mother to teach you," Eva explains. I push back the tears that are threatening to fall. I will not think about both the mothers I lost, one without even knowing her.

Not wanting to be asked any more questions, I quietly mutter a response that is partly a lie, "She was the best mother I could ever ask for."

It's partly a lie because my fake mother didn't actually teach me to cook. I learned on my own, yet it's still true because I couldn't ask for a better fake Mum than my own.

We're silent for a few minutes, just sipping our coffee. When we finish, I take our cups to the sink and rinse them out. Axel chooses that time to strut into the kitchen. He's wearing low-slung, dark blue jeans and a plain black shirt that sticks to his abs like glue. I grip the bench to keep myself from running over to him. God, he looks so amazing...

"Good morning, Eva. How are you today?" he asks Eva politely, and she blushes under his gaze. I guess Axel will always have that effect on the woman, even though I don't really like it.

"I'm very well, alpha Axel. Just heading to work actually," Eva says before turning to me with a warm smile on her face.

"Thank you for the coffee, Luna. I hope we can do it again sometime," she tells me. I smile at her as she leaves. What a nice lady, I guess she is what her cover tells me.

My attention is turned back to Axel when I see him moving out of the corner of my eye. I turn to face him.

"So, what important business are we going to talk about today?" I ask as I wrap my arms around his neck when he's close enough. He grips my waist and pulls me to him, but it's not something sexual. It's more like a loving move. Love? Where does that come from?

"Well, that is classified and can only be discussed in my office," he mumbles as we stare into each other's eyes. They're so hypnotizing...

"Let's go then," I say as I break eye contact and move away from him. We make our way to his office, and he opens the door for me like the gentleman he is. I go to take a seat in the chair opposite his desk, but he's having none of that. Before I can even sit down, he lifts me up and pulls me to his lap as he sits on his chair.

I don't bother arguing as I rest my legs on either side of him and lay my head on his shoulder.

"So, what are we gonna talk about?" I inquire again, and Axel sighs.

"Celina..." he starts off very business-like, so I lift my head to look at him. He means business, and I must say this is quite a turn on.

"I've recently been called by a pack which has a major need for a Luna figure. Their pack house is a mess, half of them are starving, and I'm guessing there's a lot of washing to be done. They called for my help when I first found you. My third in command suggested that you go and help out, with me accompanying you, of course, as well as a few other pack members. I agreed that it was a good idea, but only when you are ready, and I think you're ready to face some of your Luna responsibilities. You've come a long way. I want others to see that." As Axel explains all this to me, all that's running through my head is what a state that pack must be in. Those poor people...

Axel looks at me intently as I think about what he said. If a pack's in need, then I want to help. The problem is that I don't think I'm ready yet. Honestly, I was nervous about meeting my pack, so how can I cope with someone else's pack? Will they even accept me as their temporary Luna figure? Doesn't the alpha have a mate?

I look at Axel. He thinks the total opposite. He thinks that I'm ready to take control and step up to my Luna duties, but can I really do them? Can I really step into my role?

Maybe if I know what pack it is, I can have a better understanding of it.

"Axel, if you don't mind me asking, what pack is it that needs help?"

He looks at me for a moment. "Will that help with your judgment?" he asks. I nod, and he answers my original question, "The Moonlight Pack."

I freeze, my breath getting caught in my throat. The Moonlight Pack? They're the ones who need help? My old pack?

"I-I'm sorry, who?" I stutter, and Axel looks at me with concern. I feel all the blood drain from my face as dread sets deep in my stomach.

Ignoring my question, he lightly touches my cheek with the back of his hand.

"Celina, are you ok? You look a little pale? Do you want me to get the pack doctor?" Axel hastily asks, but I'm frozen.

Before Axel can process what I'm doing, I fling myself out of his grasp and push myself up against the wall. The Moonlight Pack is my old pack, and now because I've left, they're falling apart? I can hardly believe it! How can little old me affect a pack as big as that? All I did was run away.

This is a question, though: Will I, or will I not help?

If I help, then they will all realize that it's me and that I can shift. They will recognize the real me. They will realize that I'm not just another maid or servant they can order around. I'm a real human being that deserves respect.

On the other hand, if I don't help, then my old pack will fall, and they will probably disperse into other packs or be killed. Can I really let that happen? They're still sort of my family. Will I not regret helping them?

What if they get angry at me, though? What if they take action and try to take me away from Axel? I can't let that happen! I can't let them all die, though. No matter how horribly they treated me, they're still living, breathing people, and they deserve to live no matter what they've done. With that mindset, I bring myself to my feet with new determination.

"I'll go," I say bluntly. Axel stares at me with mixed emotions, confusion coming out on top. He doesn't know what pack tortured me and made me their maid because I never told him, and he still won't know.

"Are you sure, Celina?" Axel asks, and I nod. No matter what happened in the past, I'll leave it behind me and help the pack in need because that's what Lunas are supposed to do. I only hope that they won't react to my new title badly.

17

CELINA

Over the last month, Axel and I have been talking about how to help out the Moonlight pack. He's constantly asking me why I reacted like I did, but I just can't bring myself to tell him and permanently seal the fate of my old pack. That would just be mean...

Axel and I have also grown a lot closer. We were too close for comfort sometimes when it comes to fully mating, but when we go too far, Axel always steps back and stops himself. Back then, I was actually grateful, but now? Well, I'm thinking that maybe we should complete the mating. It's gonna happen anyway, so why delay it? My wolf is ecstatic when she hears my news.

Axel is spoiling me rotten with new clothes, jewelry, shoes, and tons of other stuff that I will probably never use. He's been really caring and loving to me. He's very patient with me and answers all questions that I suddenly shoot out. One of which is, very embarrassing...

I was walking through the pack house's backyard when I heard two teenage girls talking. One of them looked really nervous, so I walked up to her and asked her what's wrong. She told me that she's scared of going into heat because she met her mate. I didn't know what going into heat meant, so I just told her to trust her mate to look after her. She and her friend smiled at me while running off and giggling like school girls. The funny thing was, they were probably older than me but didn't know it.

That night, I asked Axel what going into heat meant. He seemed uncomfortable at first but answered anyway.

"Um, well, going into heat is like... a girl's period, I guess. They get really horny and can't control their wolf or their needs. That's the time mates usually fully mate, and the male claims what's his. The only problem with this is that any unmated wolf will also try to get in your pants. I won't let that happen, though, sweetheart," he said with a slight growl.

I blushed furiously at his explanation, and he chuckled.

I asked him when I would go into heat, but he just shrugged. "When your wolf feels you're ready, then she'll welcome the heat, and the male will immediately sense it. I doubt when you get it that we'll leave the bedroom at all," he said with a smirk.

That's when he took me in his arms and kissed the sense out of me. When we finished our little make-out session, he also explained that only alpha mate wolves decide when their human goes into heat. Non-alpha mates go into heat after a week or two of meeting their mate.

I blush at the memory, and Axel chooses that moment to walk into the backyard where I'm sitting. He smirks at me, already knowing what I am thinking because my mind wall isn't up. Oh, that's another thing. I found out a few days after meeting the pack that the pain in my head was my brain linking with everyone else's. Since then, Axel is always in my head, and I can't do a thing about it. I've figured out how to block everyone else, but not him, and it's annoying me to no end.

"Thinking about the other day, are we, sweetheart?" Axel teases as he squeezes in behind me on the sun lounger I'm currently sitting on. He pulls me to his chest, and I immediately feel his hard erection press into my lower back.

I bite my lip to keep from moaning as Axel runs his hands up and down my thighs. I'm wearing a skirt that reaches just mid-thigh, so Axel has free access to my legs.

"Maybe..." I answer his earlier question, but it comes out as more of a moan. Damn him and his effect on me.

He chuckles at me but doesn't stop. He rests his head on my shoulder and lightly kisses my soft spot. I sigh and lean my head on his shoulder.

"We're leaving tomorrow, so make sure you're packed. I don't know how long we're going to be there, so pack the essentials," he lightly says into my ear, and I sigh again.

No, he still doesn't know that the Moonlight Pack is my old pack, and I intend to keep it that way. It will cause me pain, knowing that he and my old pack might get hurt, because although what they did is in the past, Axel won't think of it that way. It will be a lose-lose situation.

"Ok, what time are we leaving?" I ask as I close my eyes and breathe in Axel's heavenly scent.

"We need to be gone by five in the morning so I would suggest waking up at about four if you haven't packed yet," he tells me and my eyes shoot wide open while I push my head off his shoulder and stare at him in shock.

"Five in the morning!" I scream in his face, and he blocks his ears slightly. I breathe in and out to calm myself down. "Five in the morning?" I ask in a much calmer and quieter voice. He nods his head. "Why are we leaving at five in the morning, Axel?"

Axel smirks at me before answering, "The former Luna of the pack has decided she wants to make us breakfast and insists on having it at exactly seven o'clock. That gives you, and a few other mates, time to get ready and have a one hour snooze."

"Who else is coming along?" I ask as I look at him inquiringly. Axel continues to tell me that both Chloe and Declan's parents are coming, Callum and Matthew, and a few more pack fighters in case trouble arises.

"Oh," is all I mutter before I get up and make my way up to our room.

As I start to pack, I think over Axel's choices of who to bring along. I guess he chose to bring Nancy, Chloe's Mum, because he sees I find comfort in her, and she has to bring her mate too, who I still haven't met. I'm glad that Callum's coming because he is my guardian and all, and it's nice to know that he'll have some family with him. I guess the fighters are just for extra precaution.

Who's going to run the pack while we're away, though? If Callum and Axel are coming, then who's left to see to the pack?

What about Comrade? He's my guardian too, and he should be coming with us, although Axel doesn't really seem to favour him. I let that one drop and push it to the back of my mind.

As I finish packing, Axel walks into the room with a set of papers in hand. His brows scrunch together as he reads over them, but I don't question it. Last time I did that, I was ignored. I pushed it, and he snapped at me. He apologized but after that, I don't interfere with pack business anymore unless he asks me to.

"Axel?" I ask to get his attention. He lifts his head from the papers, and his eyes are filled with adoration as they land on me.

"Who's going to look after the pack while we're gone? I mean, you and Callum are both coming, so who's left to see to the pack?" I voice my earlier thoughts and Axel smiles knowingly at me.

"Are you caring about the pack you didn't want to meet?" he asks with a smirk. His voice is filled with smugness as he speaks, but I keep a straight face, raising an eyebrow.

"If you must know, Callum's Dad is actually looking after the pack. He's the former beta before Callum took over. He still has it, though," he informs me and my mouth forms an 'O' shape.

I zip up my bag and is about to take it, but Axel grabs it and carries it downstairs with me following in tow.

"Where's your bag?" I ask him, and he just shrugs.

"I already packed earlier this morning while you were in the backyard," he tells me, and I nod, even though he can't see me.

He puts all the bags that are sitting out front into three separate cars. I don't bother to question him about who goes in what car because I'll probably find out tomorrow. There's a good amount of bags, though...

He wraps his arms around my waist possessively as we re-enter the house. He guides me to his office and pulls me onto his lap once he shuts the door.

"The pack is holding a going away barbecue tonight," he informs me softly.

"Is there food this time?" I ask cheekily and Axel chuckles.

"Yes, sweetheart, there is food there. Although, a lot have been asking for your desserts to be there, and I don't just think of the mud cake," he admits. I smile at his words. I'm glad the pack likes my desserts. It's very rare that a werewolf will lie about liking their food because, frankly, we eat way too much.

I've been eating just above the normal intake for a wolf my size, and Axel's happy with me.

"I'll be sure to make something then," I tell him as I make a move to get off his lap. His arms tighten around my waist, and he buries his head in my neck.

"Don't go," he whispers. I'm taken back by the sudden sweetness in his voice, but I obey and stay in his lap. I run my fingers through his soft white hair and lightly massage his scalp. He groans at the friction, and I smile, pleased that I've satisfied my mate.

"What's wrong?" I quietly ask. Axel doesn't move from his position. All he does is move his hands up and down my thighs. I bite my lip as I try to stay on track. Dammit! He knows I love it when he does that.

"Axel, I can't help you if you don't—" I'm abruptly cut off with my own moan when Axel bites down hard on my soft spot. "Axel..." I warn, but it loses its power when I focus more on the feel of his touch.

"Relax, Celina. All I want right now is you before we have to go away tomorrow. Please," he begs as he continues to torture my neck. I silently nod, and he slowly pushes me up onto the desk.

For the rest of the afternoon, we just tease each other and satisfy our mate's desires. By the time we're done, I'm breathless and pressed against the wall in my underwear, no bra, and Axel just in his boxers.

"You're getting better at this," he whispers in my ear as he playfully nips it. I laugh breathlessly and push him away.

I walk over to where my bra was carelessly discarded, but as I bend over to pick it up, I hear a growl across the room. Before I can process it, Axel has me up against his chest again with his hands tightly holding my breasts.

"Don't do that, sweetheart," he warns and gently sucks the back of my neck. I let my head fall forward with a moan, and I feel Axel smirk against me triumphantly.

That's when I realize, he's playing me.

I slowly turn around in his arms and run my hands through his hair, down his chest and trace the waistband of his boxers, gripping it slightly. Axel groans, and it's my turn to smirk. With all the time I've spent with Axel, I've become more confident around him and what he does to me.

I slowly stand on my toes to whisper in his ear, "Nice try, sweetheart."

I then jump away from him and quickly pull on my bra and shirt, which are conveniently placed next to each other.

"Better luck next time, Axel," I tell him while pulling on my skirt.

I walk out of the study as I glance at Axel's shocked face one last time. When the doors shut, I giggle slightly and skip my way to the kitchen to start making dessert.

About two hours later, I'm able to make three massive cheesecakes that will definitely feed the pack. I wipe the sweat from my forehead as I place the last heavy cheesecake in the fridge. I hope everyone likes it...

With desserts done, I make my way to our room to get ready for tonight. I shower quickly, washing my black hair. I wrap it in a towel and pull on the clothes I brought before. Since I really don't like wearing jeans or shorts, I choose to wear multi-coloured galaxy tights, a plain yellow tank top, and one of Axel's Camo hoodies over the top. I smile at my reflection. I actually look my age.

"Celina? You in there? It's time to go," I hear Axel say on the other side of the door. I quickly open the door, and I'm met by a casually dressed Axel in jeans and a shirt. He looks me up and down then smirks.

"I don't think I've ever seen you wear pants before. You actually look your age," he tells me as he wraps his arms around my waist. I smile at him, and he kisses me lightly on the lips.

"I need to get some shoes," I tell him, and he reluctantly releases me. I chuckle at him and pull on flat, yes flat, ankle boots. It's been getting colder, and I always catch colds easily.

"Ready," I say as I walk back to Axel. He takes me in his arms again, and we make our way down to the barbecue.

Everyone has a blast, and they love my cheesecake. All night, I got compliment after compliment. It feels nice to know people like my cooking.

I yawn as I lean onto Axel's side. It must be at least ten o'clock by now. Axel stops talking to his buddies, some of whom are the fighters that are coming with us and looks at me.

"Tired?" he asks quietly. I nod my head, and I'm suddenly being lifted into the air by warm, comforting arms.

"See you tomorrow morning, guys. Bright and early," he reminds them and they all groan. I smile slightly. They probably haven't even packed.

'You're right, sweetheart, they haven't,' I suddenly hear Axel's voice in my head and smile at how it sounds. It sounds like it belongs there.

'Too bad for them then,' I mutter back through the mind link tiredly. In less than a minute, I completely zone out and fall asleep.

18

CELINA

"Celina!" Someone shouts really loud in my ear. I scream as I jump out of bed and push myself against the wall, gripping where my heart is. I look up, only to see Comrade rolling on the floor laughing. I glare at him as Axel bursts through the door with Callum in tow.

"What the hell was that?" Axel booms and Comrade immediately sobers up, but his shoulders are still shaking with silent laughter.

"Do you know what time it is?" I screech at him, and he nods innocently. Callum watches the scene with a smirk while Axel looks a bit confused. He's a bit slow sometimes...

"It's exactly 4:30 in the morning. You're actually half an hour late, Snow. Tsk tsk," Comrade scolds me. I growl lowly at him. He just shakes his head while walking out the door with Callum following him.

"Stupid, immature teenagers, boys these days..." I keep muttering to myself as Axel watches me with a smile. He chuckles a bit then wraps me in his arms. I sigh contentedly and lean into his touch.

"Don't worry, sweetheart. I'll get back at him for it," he promises, and I smile. I turn my head and kiss him gently on the lips.

"You always do," I tell him, then wriggle out of his arms and head towards the wardrobe.

I pick out a long-sleeved, deep purple shirt and a matching black skirt with purple swirls. I pull on some flat ankle boots and make my way to the bathroom. I splash some water on my face and brush my hair.

"Celina! Time to go!" I hear Comrade yell from downstairs, so I quickly tie my hair into a low ponytail and dash down the stairs. When I get there, everyone's finishing last minute things and mates are saying goodbye to one another.

I look at Comrade and see him staring off into space with a sad expression. I glance at Axel, who's preoccupied with helping out some fighters.

'I'm gonna talk to Comrade quickly. I'll meet you in the car,' I tell him through the mind link. He averts his eyes to me and nods slightly before going back to helping.

I gently place my hand on Comrade's shoulder when I reach him. He jerks at the sudden touch but smiles at me nonetheless.

"Hey, what's bothering you?" I softly question. He chuckles at me before answering.

"Always the caring one, aren't you?" I give him a pointed look before he sighs and tells me what's bothering him.

"I don't want you to leave me," he admits in a small voice. "I'm your guardian, yet I still can't be with you 24/7 like Callum and Axel can. I guess I just feel left out. I really want to protect you, but I can't do that if I don't have access to you, right?"

My eyes glaze over as I pull Comrade into a hug. He hugs me back as he rests his head on my shoulder.

"Comrade, I'll always have you and you, me. When I come home, you can spend all the time you want with me, and I'll make sure we won't be interrupted," I tell him as a single tear slip from the corner of my eye. Comrade pulls back and gently wipes it away.

"I know," he tells me and then frowns. "Do you know when you're getting back?" I shake my head at his question. "Of course not," he sighs. "Just be careful, ok?" I nod then hug him one last time.

A horn honks, and that's when I realize that everyone is already in their designated car with Axel leaning on the side of one, waiting for me.

"I better go," I tell him then kiss him on the cheek.

"Good luck," he says before I run off to Axel. He takes me in his arms as he gently places me in the passenger seat of the car. He runs around to the other side and jumps in.

We drive off down the driveway as I silently say to myself, you'll be coming back.

I groan as I slowly peel my eyes open and move my stiff neck. "Did I fall asleep?" I ask Axel, and he chuckles at me.

"Yes, sweetheart, you did," he tells me, and I groan again. I massage my neck with my fingers, but that hardly helps. It's so stiff...

"A bit stiff there, are you?" Callum asks from the back. I mutter to him under my breath and next thing I know, the head console is being unclipped and pulled away.

"Hey!" I object as I whip my head around, but instantly regret it as my neck cracks. I hiss in pain as Axel looks at me worriedly. I move my head around a bit to get the after effect of the crack out. A warm hand suddenly stops my head from moving.

"Relax, Celina. Prepare to get a massage," Callum tells me cheekily. I don't bother saying anything as his magic fingers do their work. A good hour later and my neck's as good as new.

"Thanks, Callum," I tell him gratefully, and he grins at me.

"Anything for thy majesty's daughter," he makes a fake bow in his seat as he does a horrid English accent. I giggle at him and see Axel roll his eyes out of the corner of my eye.

"How much longer, Axel?" I whine. I can wait forever actually, but I want to get out of this car. I'm not too keen to meet my old pack again... I'm not too keen to know what Axel's reaction will be either.

"Well, it's just past noon now, and we still need to get lunch, so I'll say... a good five to six hours."

I sigh, but don't argue. I hope time slows.

We stopped for lunch at a service station, and everyone ordered pies, sausage rolls, or spring rolls. I didn't have anything since I wasn't hungry. Axel wasn't happy with that. He convinced me to eat at least one spring roll, and I did to make him happy.

That was about three hours ago. I'm still not hungry.

Axel, Callum, and I sit in silence as I just enjoy the scenery. I need to figure out how I'm gonna handle this situation.

My first option will be to tell Axel before we enter their territory. That will jeopardize what we've come for, though... Even if my old pack has mistreated me, I don't want them to die. Those people are someone's mates, children, aunts, uncles. I can't just take it away from them and not care. That will be inhuman.

My other option, though, will be to not tell Axel and let him figure it out himself while giving my old pack the heads up. Then, Axel might get angry at me... He might stop trusting me because I didn't tell him who my old pack was. I can't let that happen either! Why is this so hard?

'Celina, you ok? You got a lot of jumbled up thoughts running through your mind right now,' Axel informs me as he breaks the wall I'm currently trying to keep up.

'I'm fine,' I answer shortly and Axel glances at me with worry in his eyes. I don't say anything further, though, so he lets it drop.

Another few hours later and we are about to enter my old pack's territory. Given half an hour or so and we'll be there.

I wonder how my new pack will react to my old pack. I wonder how my old pack will react to my new pack. Will a war start? Oh god, I can't handle that! What if Axel lashes out and kills them all? What if I break down in front of them, and they see me for the weakling that I really am? What if anything bad happens?

I start to hyperventilate as thought after thought, worry after worry race through my head.

"Axel, stop the car," I tell him as I feel the car start to cave in around me.

He doesn't stop the car and just looks at me with furrowed brows.

"Celina—"

I cut him off as I scream at him in frustration. "Stop the car!" I yell.

He pulls on the gear stick and slams it to a stop. The other two cars behind us step on their brakes as I push my door open and run towards the trees surrounding the road.

"Celina!" I hear Callum yell, and two sets of heavy footsteps come running behind me. I stop at about a hundred metres and collapse to my knees. I wrap my arms around my stomach as I take deep breaths to calm myself down. I don't even hear the footsteps coming closer until they skid to a stop.

"Celina?" Callum asks. I don't acknowledge him. He squats down in front of me as he gently lifts my chin. I break down as he looks at me.

"Please don't cry," he whispers as he wipes the tears away. I don't know I'm already crying.

A hand rests on my shoulder, and I look to my right to see Axel looking at me with pained eyes. He also wipes a few stray tears away from my cheeks as he sits down next to me, wrapping an arm around my shoulders.

"Tell us what's wrong," Axel states softly, but it sounds more like a question. I shake my head silently as they both glance at each other.

"Celina, is it something to do with the pack we're helping?" Callum guesses, and again, I stay silent. He runs a hand through his hair before looking back at me. "Celina, if it's something to do with this pack, then let the Moon Goddess help me because I will rip them to shreds before they can even touch you," Callum growls fiercely, his voice full of power that can only come from a beta.

I'm suddenly hit by a giant gust of wind. Then right before my eyes appear my mother and father in their ghostly forms.

"Mum, Dad?" I whisper, and they both nod their ghostly heads. Their bodies seem to move with the slightest breeze, and you can see right through them.

"What are you doing here?" I whisper again as Axel and Callum look at each other, confused.

"Celina, sweetheart, who are you talking to?" I can faintly hear Axel asking me, but I focus solely on my parents.

I unconsciously lift myself up and out of Axel's arms and walk towards my parents. This is the second time I've seen them, and I just love them even more.

"You should tell them," my mother's gentle voice advises me, but I just shake my head.

"I can't. They'll hurt them," I argue back. She smiles softly at me. My mother places her transparent hand on my cheek, and I lean into her cool touch.

"Your mother's right, princess. Your mate and guardians should know about your past, present, and future. It's what's best for not only you, but for the world," my father states wisely, and I stare into his shining, golden eyes. He nods his head at me, and I know that the time for arguing is over.

"I don't know if I'm ready," I whisper with shame as my head drops. My mother once again cups my face in her hands and brings it up capturing my eyes with hers. Her beautiful hair flows around her like a waterfall and her eyes shine with love for the daughter she never got to raise.

"You are," is all she whispers as she kisses my forehead before they disappear into thin air. Their bodies travel with the wind and leave me with a sort of emptiness.

I stay standing there, just listening to the wind and the animals in the forest.

"Celina?" Axel timidly begins to ask, and I turn around to look into his beautiful, greyish, silver eyes.

"Are you ok?" Callum finishes his question, and I look into his worried brown eyes. I guess I have to tell them...

19

AXEL

Celina seems frozen to the spot as she stares into nothing. She finishes talking to herself, and I'm a bit worried that she's losing her mind. Still, I don't think that's the case, though. She just seems... shocked or stunned, I guess.

"Celina, sweetheart. Come on, snap out of it," I calmly say as I place my large hands on her slim shoulders. She jumps slightly and whirls around to look at me. Her golden eyes lock with my silver ones as they fill with worry.

She gently places her hand on my cheek and rubs it soothingly.

"You might want to take a seat," she tells me after taking a deep breath and backing away from my touch.

She gives Callum a look to do the same, so both he and I take a seat and lean against some trees while I watch Celina's face fill with uncertainty and worry.

"Um, how do I start this..." she asks herself as she trails off. Callum and I look at each other. We both shrug our shoulders.

"The beginning," Callum tells her, and she looks at him for a moment. It seems to be going through her mind, but she seems torn.

"I don't know where the beginning is..." she trails off again as she takes a seat on the green grass and crosses her legs, genie style. She takes a deep breath as she stares into the distance. "How about we start when you first told me about this pack," she tells us, still not making eye contact. "This pack, The Moonlight Pack, is my old pack."

An immediate growl comes from my lips, but Callum looks a bit confused. So this is the pack that broke her? She doesn't pay us any mind as she continues.

"When I ran away, I stumbled upon your pack, the Nightfall Pack. You took me in, and I couldn't have been happier, but what guided me to you wasn't the happiest thing," she mumbles as her eyes go distant.

She stops again as she looks at my pissed off face and Callum's still confused one. He never really found out anything about Celina's old pack. I'm just happy she felt the need to tell me at the time. Otherwise, this will be a very difficult situation for us.

"When I was seven, my parents died. Not my real parents but my fake parents. They loved me, though, and I loved them. Before they died, I was happy. I had a family, and I was surrounded by people who I thought loved me. How I was so wrong..."

"I was told by my ruthless alpha that my parents died. I cried for days, and when I came out of the comfort of my room, I was instantly turned into a pack maid and punching bag."

"The people who I thought loved me beat me regularly and made me do everything from cleaning to the cooking. I was never treated fairly, and they even went as far as to take me out of school after my parents died. I was heartbroken," she says as she chokes on a sob.

I want to wrap her in my arms and tell her everything's going to be ok, but I stay where I am and give her the space she needs and wants. Although I've already heard this, it's still hard to hear how her pack treated her. This is more for Callum's benefit anyway.

"The last time I saw them was when I was accused of liking the new alpha, the son of the alpha who told me my parents died. Alpha Damon is his name, a name that will always be engraved in my mind." Her voice becomes softer as she says that part and my heart breaks as I feel all her emotions rush through the mate bond. She's so hurt...

"That same night, I left. I ran and never looked back. Well, now I'm returning to the place that I thought would kill me. Now I'm returning to the place where I vowed I would never go again. Now I'm returning to the place that needs help because of my little act of running away. Now I'm returning... because of me," she tells us, but it sounds like she's talking to herself.

This time, I take her in my arms and stroke her hair as she bursts out crying. I can't believe that an alpha would actually treat one of his pack members like that. It's just... There's not even a word for it.

Callum looks torn and just doesn't seem to know what to do. He looks like he has failed and can't ever win back the honour. I wonder how Comrade would feel at this moment, probably the same.

"Shh, sweetheart. It's ok, you have me now. You have Callum and Comrade, too. No one's gonna hurt you," I tell her softly, and she sniffles.

"Really?" she asks softly as she buries her head further into my chest. I smile softly down at her.

"Really," I tell her. My wolf howls in my head at the hurt and anguish that my delicate little mate has gone through. All the anger I don't even know I have comes rushing to the surface and my body goes rigid.

"Callum, take Celina. Now!" I growl at him when he doesn't move. He scurries to his feet and takes Celina in his arms. I give him a stiff nod, and he returns it.

As soon as they're out of sight, I growl loudly and punch the nearest tree. It splits and goes crashing to the ground. My nails elongate, my eyes turn pitch black, my chest heaves up and down with heavy breaths, and fur starts to sprout out of my body.

I can't shift, though. Celina will not want that. If she's come all this way and makes the decision to still help her old pack, then I won't go barging in there in wolf form and tear them all to shreds.

Instead, I lash out at the tree. I scratch, kick, scream, and growl at it as I let out all of my pent up anger. When I deem myself acceptable enough to be in another's presence, I slowly make my way back towards where the cars are.

I angrily walk to my car and pull the door open with more force than necessary. I slam it shut with a growl and start the car.

As I speed down the road, I thought of how I absolutely love to kill Celina's old pack seep through, but I restrain myself from doing so. A small hand rests on my shoulder, and it seems to instantly calm me, pushing my anger to the side.

"Calm down, Axel. I've made my choice, and now you need to make yours." Celina's soft, yet stern voice filters through my ears.

I glance at her and my black eyes go back to their sterling silver.

"They hurt you, Celina, stripped you of your will. They deserve it," I mutter through clenched teeth.

"I know, each one of them deserves what's running through your head right now, but I won't let you. They're all living, breathing people and, even though they've done something bad, they deserve to live. A few beatings aren't the same as a hundred deaths." Her voice of reason seems to calm me even more, but I'm still pissed off at them.

"Always the voice of reason, aren't you?" I mutter, and she giggles. The sound is music to my ears.

"Always the one for action, aren't you?" she mocks me, and I let a grin slip onto my face.

"Tsk, mates," Callum mutters under his breath, but I just chuckle at him.

'Just you wait, Callum. One day you'll find her,' I taunt, and he growls at me in his head. I chuckle again and focus back on driving to where Celina once called home, also known as her own personal hell.

About an hour later and we pull up in front of the pack house. Celina's shaking slightly, but she takes deep breaths to calm her racing heartbeat.

"You can still turn them down, Celina," I tell her. She glances at me. "I would love to have the honours of killing every wolf here."

She rolls her eyes at me as she gently swats my arm.

"Yeah, yeah," she mutters as I jump out and come around to her side of the car. I help her out and wrap a possessive arm around her waist.

We walk to the front of our group, and we're met by the former Alpha and Luna and the current alpha, Damon. I restrain the growl that wants to rip through my throat and tighten my arm around Celina's waste while clenching my jaw.

Damon plasters an obviously fake smile on his face when he sees us. How can he smile when he knows what he's done to an innocent girl?

"Welcome, alpha Axel. We're so glad that you made it here safely," he announces formally.

"Likewise," I say gruffly, and that's when all eyes land on Celina. Gasps are heard from the Alphas and Luna and the crowd that came out when they heard the cars.

"Celina?" Damon asks. Celina holds her head up with confidence and power oozes from her. I grin down at her. That's my little mate.

Damon's face grows angry as he looks at her. My guard immediately goes up and everyone around us, fighters and all, get into defense position. No one will hurt their Luna, and as I sift through their minds, they certainly agree.

"What the hell are you doing under an alpha's arm? Asking for protection like the weakling you are? You're nothing to him," he snarls, and I snarl right back. Celina, however, keeps a blank face.

"It's nice to see you again, Damon. You too, Mr. and Mrs. Holler," Celina addresses formally, and they all stare at her in shock.

"Don't play that game with us, you little, worthless, excuse of a wolf!" Greg, Damon's dad, booms at her. I growl at him and step in front of Celina protectively.

A soft hand pushes me away, though, Celina's hand. She smiles reassuringly at me before strutting with the confidence of a Luna right up to Greg.

"Actually, Greg—" She spits his name. "—I'm a much stronger wolf than you'll ever be, and you can't do anything about it. You call me worthless when you, your wife, and your flipping son over there are the worthless ones!" Her voice rises as she continues and I feel my pride swell in me as power radiates off her, royal power. I never knew my mate could yell so loudly either.

"So, don't you dare go telling me that I'm worthless because that will be the last thing you ever do." Her voice lowers to a deathly silent one, and fear crosses Greg and his Luna's faces. Damon, on the other hand, doesn't get the message.

"How dare you speak to your former alpha that way?! He demands respect, and so do I. And, we will get it! You can't even shift!" he yells at her as his face fills with fury.

I growl at him, as does everyone, but no one interferes out of fear of what their Luna will do. She's a force to reckon with at the moment. All thoughts of helping her old pack are probably being thrown out the window.

Celina slowly turns to him and takes menacing steps towards him. She gets right up in his face, even though she's a heap smaller and thinner.

"Neither you, nor your parents, deserve any respect. Axel, my pack, and I are the ones that deserve respect. You are nothing but weaklings compared to us, and you don't even know the extent of what I can do," she states in a calm voice.

She turns her back on Damon and walks calmly back to me. Just as I'm about to take her in my arms, the shredding of clothing fills my ears, and the next thing I know, Celina is being tackled to the ground by a dark brown wolf.

Everyone seems to be frozen in shock, but before anyone can react, Celina shifts into her snow white wolf, throwing Damon's wolf off her without hesitation. Damon's wolf freezes, Greg and his Luna freeze, and the crowd that we've drawn from inside the house freezes. Everyone just freezes and stares at Celina's wolf. Her snow white colour, her shining gold eyes, the sheer size of her, and the way she radiates royal power... She's a true princess.

"That's impossible..." Greg's astonished voice trails off. Celina's wolf doesn't even glance at him as she leaps at Damon and gets a firm hold on his neck just like that.

His wolf whimpers and shows his submission. I can see in Celina's eyes, though, that she doesn't want to let go, she looks like she wants to clamp down harder. As much as I love to have the person who probably tortured her the most, killed, I won't let her because she'll regret it for the rest of her life.

"Celina, as much as I would love to see you rip Damon's head off, I know you'll regret it. Please, come back to me," I say softly as I cautiously approach her wolf. Her wolf gained control when Damon pounced. He brought it upon himself. I'm just helping her gain her control back, even though I really don't want to.

I stroke her beautiful white fur and look her in the eye.

"Come back to me, Celina," I whisper and just like that, her shining gold eyes turn back to their normal gold colour.

She whines as she releases Damon's neck and gently nudges me with her head. I smile down at her and pet her large wolf head. That's my girl.

'Um, Axel,' Celina's voice suddenly fills my mind, and I smile at how perfect it sounds.

'Yes, sweetheart?' I answer.

'I need clothes,' she mumbles, embarrassed. It takes a moment for her words to process in my mind, but when they do, a protective growl passes through my lips.

Without thinking, I strip off my shirt and hand it to her. She takes it in her mouth, after admiring my bare chest, and walks off into the forest, coming out a minute later with my black shirt covering her body to just above her knees.

I push her behind me when she reaches me, keeping peering eyes away from her long, tanned, luscious legs.

Greg clears his throat awkwardly.

"Well, why don't we all head inside?" he offers. My company glances at a very pissed off, bright red Celina and at me before looking back at me again.

I shake my head, and all of them head back to the cars without even a single glance at Greg and the others.

"We will continue this inside," I say gruffly as Greg eyes all the retreating fighters. He nods his head and his Luna, who I still don't know the name of, and Damon himself all head inside without even leading us in. I growl lowly at the lack of respect.

"Welcome to my life," Celina mutters into my back. I shake my head with a small chuckle. Even in the worst of times, Celina always seems to lighten the mood even if she doesn't know it.

I lead her to the porch when small, dainty hands land on my chest and pull me away from Celina.

"What the..." I mutter when a blonde haired bimbo suddenly comes into my line of sight. She honestly looks like a desperate, dyed-blonde, big-boobed, bitchy wannabe.

"Why, hello there," she says seductively, but it sounds more like a penguin call. A very unattractive one...

Before I can answer, a growl is heard behind me. I smirk when Celina comes stomping up and roughly removes the bimbo's hand from my chest.

"Hands off, Tina! He's not one of your little bangs. He's mine," Celina growls at her, but Tina just smirks.

"Please, everyone leaves you, Celina, everyone. I mean, your parents left you and now that hunk of a muscle over there is going to leave you, too." Her voice is like nails scratching down a chalkboard.

"Take it back," Celina snarls through clenched teeth.

"No," Tina bites back and the next thing she knows, she's being punched straight in the face. Her head jerks back as a scream escapes her lips. Celina draws her fist back as Tina's followers run to her aid.

"Like I said, Tina, he's mine," Celina all but growls. She then turns to me, grabs my shoulders, and brings me down for a rough kiss.

She pushes back and smirks at me. I like this feisty Celina. She's so confident and in control. I smirk back at her.

"Let's go inside," she tells me as she drags me through the door, ignoring the death glare from Tina.

We take a seat on the couch, and that's when we get down to business.

"Right, alpha Damon, what's your proposal?" I ask in my business voice. Damon glances at Celina then at me, then back to Celina.

"Well, actually, all our problems will be solved if you just give Celina back to us, where she belongs. Deal done," Damon states as he makes a move to grab Celina. Over my dead body.

I growl loudly at him and push Celina behind me while I stand up into a defensive position.

"Over my dead body," I repeat my thought with a snarl.

Damon smirks when he glances at his mother and father. "That can be arranged."

I growl loudly again at his smug voice, but this time, it's joined with Celina's as well.

"Unless you want a war, I would suggest that you take back what you just said," I snarl at him, but the smirk stays.

"Now, why would I do that? I'm not gonna start a war over that pathetic piece of shit. Just hand it over and this will all be resolved," Damon calmly states, reaching his hand out for Celina to take.

"First of all, she is not a pathetic piece of shit, you are. Second, Celina is not an 'it.' Celina is a living human being, and she's a better human being than you'll ever be," I snarl at him, barely keeping my anger together.

Damon scoffs while saying, "Please, you'll leave her once you discover just how worthless she really is. She isn't worth your time, and she's certainly not worth fussing over."

I start to shake with anger at his words. Worthless? Not worth fussing over? I know for a fact that Celina is not worthless, but a true gem. She has a heart of gold. She couldn't even sentence her own pack to death. She's perfect, and I'll fuss over her all I like. I'll fuss over her to the ends of the earth because she's mine. She's special and unique, and she's all mine.

I'm not gonna waste my time explaining that to this douchebag, though. What he said has just pushed me over the line, and there's no going back.

"This means war," I seethe then storm out of the pack house with Celina tucked safely in my arms.

I haul myself and Celina into the car and speed off Moonlight Pack territory. All that's running through my head is how much I'll go through to kill that son of a bitch, Damon. What he just did and what he's done to Celina is just cruel! No matter what Celina says, he doesn't deserve to live.

Speaking of Celina, she's been really quiet since Damon proposed that he take her back. I wearily glance at her from the driver's side. She's looking out her window with that adorable thinking face on, the one with her eyebrows furrowed and her lips puckered just that little bit.

"Celina?" I call, but she doesn't answer. "Celina?" I say a bit louder. She still doesn't answer. "Celina!" I exclaim, and she jumps in her seat.

She puts a hand on her heart as she tries to even out her breathing.

"Geez, Axel, don't do that! You scared the living daylights out of me!" she screams at me, and I smile sheepishly at her.

"Sorry. You ok? You seem a bit out of it," I question her. She just shrugs and looks out the window again.

"Celina, you're stuck in a car with me for another ten hours, you'll have to tell me sooner or later," I tell her and she sighs in defeat. Callum's in another car since he knows that I'm pissed off, so it's just Celina and me.

"Axel, it's just... I don't know. A lot of memories just sort of rose to the surface when Damon bluntly said he would take me back. He said it like he owned me like I was his possession that nobody could take away, not even you," she mumbles the last part, and all I can do is place a comforting hand on her thigh. She smiles softly at me as she places her hand over mine.

What Damon did to Celina, the pain and hurt she felt, he's gonna feel it ten times worse when I get my hands on him. He won't even know what hit him...

20

CELINA

I lie on my bed just looking up at the ceiling. We arrived home a few hours ago. Everyone's downstairs for dinner, but I told Axel I wasn't hungry. He left reluctantly, but I think he knew that I needed some space.

Being back there, I don't know... It just brought forward memories that I would rather have locked far away in my mind. All the beatings, orders, and dominance over me, it came back full force. That's why I acted like I did. On any normal day, I wouldn't have punched Tina, and I wouldn't have growled at not only one but two alphas as well as a Luna. That's definitely not me...

Then there was Damon, thinking he could take me back just like that. Just take me away from Axel, my pack, and my happy life. Axel wouldn't let him, though, and because of that, I've started a war. A war for dominance and power, just as the prophecy said would happen.

I close my eyes as I try to calm myself. Why does life have to be so hard? Why can't it just be simple? Just for one day, I don't want anything going on in my mind. I just want to relax.

'I can make that happen,' my wolf suddenly states. I raise an eyebrow at her.

'Really, now?' She nods her big wolf head at me. I sigh again, what have I got to lose? 'Ok, go ahead,' I tell her. I don't bother to ask her what she's gonna do. I just want to think of nothing.

She's silent for a few minutes before a feeling rushes through me, making me gasp. Want and need fill my whole body and all that's in my mind is Axel. How he speaks, how his laugh turns my stomach into a frenzy, how his beautiful silver eyes gaze into my gold ones, his soft white hair that I love to run my fingers through, everything. Everything Axel invades my mind.

'What did you do?' I ask my wolf as I try to keep myself on the bed and not run downstairs into Axel's arms.

'I've made you go into heat. You didn't want anything on your mind, so this is the best I could do. Have fun,' she says cheekily then disappears into the shadows of my mind.

I groan as pain washes over my body. I need him, I need Axel. I start to pant heavily as my stomach does twists and turns, and I thrash my head from side to side to try and ease the pain. A cool sweat rests all over my body, and my toes curl against the pain. How is this fun?

At least five minutes later, Axel comes waltzing into the room without a care in the world. When he catches sight of me, he goes rigid. His eyes turn from their sterling silver to a midnight black.

"A-Axel," I call weakly as the pain makes me arch my back. He leans against the door as a groan escapes his lips. 'God, I want him right now! I need him right now!'

"Celina, you've gone into heat. I need you to stay calm and try to control it," he advises me as he makes his way cautiously to me.

I'm still lying on the bed, so he timidly sits next to me and places a cool hand on my boiling head. Sparks shoot through me, and all I can do is gasp in pure pleasure.

Without giving time for Axel to react, I push him down on the bed at lightning speed and straddle him. I run my hands slowly up his shirt covered chest, earning a grunt from him, and tangle them in his hair as I lean my head down so my face is only millimetres from his.

"I want you, Axel," I tell him in a hoarse whisper, my voice thick with lust and want. "I need you so bad."

I rip Axel's shirt off his chest and watch as the shredded material falls to the floor. I pepper light kisses all over his chest, earning groans and grunts. I trace the rim of his jeans, and he stiffens.

"Please, Axel," I beg and the next thing I know, I'm flipped over with Axel hovering above me.

"Sweetheart, you are a very naughty girl," he growls then crashes his lips to mine in a brutal force that leaves me moaning.

I kiss him back with everything I've got as I run my fingers through his soft, white hair.

"Nah uh, sweetheart, it's my turn," Axel growls against my lips before pinning my hands above my head.

He sucks on my bottom lip asking for entrance, and I happily oblige. Our tongues battle for dominance, but I lose, of course.

Axel's hands travel down my sides and grip the hem of my shirt, yanking it up and breaking our kiss. I gasp for breath as Axel's lips attack my neck, and his hands gently massage my bra covered breasts.

He roughly bites my soft spot, and I moan loudly.

"Axel!" I gasp when I feel his teeth graze over the same spot.

"All in good time, sweetheart, all in good time," he teases me while sucking on the same place.

After totally assaulting my neck, his magic lips slowly make their way down my body. They go past my cleavage and down my stomach to the waistband of the skirt I'm wearing.

He hooks his fingers around the skirt and heatedly slides it down my long legs. He discards the skirt somewhere on the floor and kisses his way back up the inside of my legs. He sucks on my thigh as his hands trail slowly up and down my legs and sides.

He comes to my core but totally bypasses it as his lips travel back up my stomach. I whine loudly, and he chuckles at me.

Without saying a word, he unclips my bra and slides the straps off my arms, leaving my chest bare to him. My chest heaves up and down with the breaths I'm taking, and Axel's eyes become even darker.

Without warning, Axel's mouth latches onto one of my nipples. I groan loudly and arch my back into him as I grip his shoulders. It should be illegal to feel this good!

He licks, sucks, and plays with it until it feels raw then moves onto the other one. I'm just moaning and groaning the whole time and begging for more.

He pulls back to look at my flushed face and trails a finger over my jawline.

"So beautiful," he mutters, and I blush at his compliment.

I flip him over so he's the one on the bottom now. His eyes latch onto my breasts hanging from my chest and growls. I trail a teasing finger down his chest all the way to the hem of his jeans.

"My turn," I whisper then proceed to slowly peel his jeans off, leaving him only in his boxers.

His hard erection is very visible now. I can't wait any longer and rip his boxers to shreds. I hear a chuckle and lift my lust-filled eyes to look into Axel's.

"A little eager, are we?" he teases. I growl at his teasing tone and start to work my hands on his member to shut him up.

His head lolls back into the pillow with a groan as I slowly rub my hand over the length of him. When I have him where I want him, my hand ceases and my tongue takes its place. I torture Axel with pleasure that I don't even know I can give. When I'm done, his juices are all over me.

"Liked that, did ya?" I tease in his ear as I bite his earlobe hard. He growls and grips my hips, flipping us over once again.

He starts to grind against me, running himself on my core. I moan loudly and grip his shoulders.

"You're going to like this a lot more," he threatens then shreds my underwear into tiny, irretrievable bits. He grips a hold of my butt cheeks and yanks my hips high so that my core is lined up with his mouth. He growls at the sight before he ravages me with his mouth.

I moan loudly as my head lolls back and my eyes roll to the back of my head in pure pleasure.

"Axel!" I scream when I feel his fingers enter me as well as his tongue.

He continues with his pleasurable torture before moving away just before my climax. I whine loudly at him as I stare into his eyes.

"Axel, please," I beg in a whisper as an evil smirk makes its way onto his face.

"What was that, sweetheart? I couldn't hear you," he teases, and I growl. It's cut short though when he starts to stroke my core.

"Please, Axel, please," I beg louder this time, but his smirk just grows wider as his fingers start to work a whole lot faster.

"Axel, I'm begging you, please!" I scream at him, and he finally grants me my wish.

He lines himself up at my entrance, and without warning, he thrusts inside, breaking the barrier. A pain filled scream escapes my lips.

"Shh, sweetheart. The pain will be gone soon, it's ok," Axel coos in my ear. I take deep breaths, and sure enough, the pain subsides, and I'm filled with pleasure.

Axel starts to slowly thrust in and out until we both pick up our pace. My hips move with his as we come closer to our climax.

"I'm gonna mark you now, Celina," Axel tells me just before he sinks his teeth into my soft spot, and I come with a loud moan. Axel follows suit with a low growl.

Axel collapses next to me, pulling me into his arms. I can tell you right now, that there is no better feeling than being fully mated with the one person you're supposed to spend the rest of your life with.

"Wow..." is all I manage to say. I'm still trying to get over the amount of pleasure I've just experienced. Axel chuckles at me while brushing some stray hair away from my forehead.

I stare into his eyes as they seem to shine with a new emotion. Then Axel mutters three words I never expect to hear from my mate.

"I love you."

21

CELINA

"I love you."

My breath hitches in my throat at how those three little words just roll off Axel's tongue. I haven't heard those words for nine years! Do you know how amazing it is to finally hear them?

Without even hesitating or thinking it through, I just come straight out with it.

"I love you too," I whisper, and the smile that lights up Axel's face is so worth it.

"You have no clue how long I've been waiting to say that," he whispers then places a gentle kiss on my lips which leads to so much more.

For the rest of the week, while I'm in heat, we don't leave our room. Only when Axel goes to get food is when I actually get out of bed, that and to go to the bathroom.

As the week comes to an end and my heat settles down, I feel content. I look over to Axel and notice how the sun's rays from the early morning make his white hair shine to a new extent. I glance at the clock and realize that it's already seven in the morning.

I sigh. Axel has to be at the meeting by eight. I run my hand through his hair and gently tug at it.

"Axel, you need to get up," I say in his ear as I gently nibble his earlobe. He mumbles in his sleep and wraps his arms around me tighter. I roll my eyes at him.

"Axel, come on," I mutter in his ear again. I gently nudge him, but that doesn't seem to work either.

One last chance to wake him up, I press my lips softly to his. After a few moments, he responds and flips us so that I'm beneath him. He smirks at me as his lips connect with my neck.

"What a lovely wake-up call," he mumbles into my neck, making me giggle.

"Axel, come on," I whine. "You need to be at the meeting soon."

I involuntarily let my eyes close, and a breathy moan escapes me as he gently bites my neck, making me throb for him.

"The meeting can wait," he growls as he starts to tease me all over again. I must say, I'm happy my wolf sent me into heat. Even though it's over, Axel is still all over me.

We eventually get downstairs just after eight, Axel being fully dressed while I'm just wearing his oversized shirt.

I quickly scramble some eggs and make some toast. I place them in front of Axel, and he scoffs it down.

"You might want to go get dressed, you know," Axel mutters through a mouth full of eggs. Wonderful manners...

My eyebrows scrunch together when his words sink in.

"Why?" I ask as I hug his shirt closer to me. Axel finishes up eating and wraps his arms around my tiny waist, burying his head in my neck.

"Because, sweetheart, you're coming to the meeting too," he tells me softly, and I stare at him in surprise. He's letting me go to the meeting? "Of course, I'm letting you go to the meeting! You're officially the Luna now, after all" he says then runs his fingers over his mark, making my knees go weak.

Without hesitating, I bound up the stairs to our room and barge into the wardrobe. I sort through everything and sigh in frustration when I notice that none of the clothes will suit the occasion.

A small knocking sound is heard, and I turn from the wardrobe to see Chloe standing there with an amused look on her face.

"Do you need help, Luna?" she offers after a little giggle.

My face lights up at her words, and I nod my head vigorously. She giggles again and approaches the wardrobe to stand next to me.

"Hmm..." she mutters. She ventures deeper into the wardrobe, her eyes scanning all the clothing and shoes. "Well, since it's a proper meeting, I think you should wear something formal, but not too formal. Maybe a dress?" she advises, and I nod my head again.

She sorts through all my dresses till she pulls out a simple, emerald green, satin dress. It has spaghetti straps and a brown belt below the breast while the rest of the dress flows freely down to just below the knees. I smile at it and take it in my hands delicately.

"Thank you, Chloe. What would I ever do without you?" I say with a slight giggle. She rolls her eyes at me and shrugs.

"I have absolutely no clue, Luna." She then proceeds to tie my hair into a loose braid quickly and ushers me into the bathroom to get dressed. I do so and walk out to a squealing Chloe afterwards.

"Alright, you're ready for the meeting!" she exclaims excitedly like it's some high school dance.

I meet Axel just outside the pack's meeting room, and his eyes light up when he sees me.

"You look beautiful," he tells me, and I blush at the compliment.

He grips my hand, and we walk into the meeting exactly one hour late. All eyes turn to us. I squeeze Axel's hand for support as we take a seat at the head of the very long table.

Faces I recognize and don't, are all seated at the table. Callum, Matthew, and Comrade are the only faces I recognize.

"Celina, these are our best pack fighters, and this is former beta, Jason," Axel explains. I nod my head at Jason, and he respectfully nods back. "The fighters are Jacobs, Prince, Fred, Carl, and Leonard. You will be seeing a lot of them," Axel continues, and I also nod my head at them before the meeting commences. "Right, today we are here to discuss our situation with the Moonlight Pack," Axel announces. I immediately go stiff at his words. "We have declared war on them."

Everyone in the room goes into hushed whispers and starts to discuss the problem.

The former beta, Jason, clears his throat and asks, "Pardon me, alpha, but may I ask why we have declared war?"

Axel stays silent at the question and looks at me. I look back at him and quietly think to myself, 'They'll have to find out sooner or later and what is said in this room stays in this room, right?'

"Celina," Axel motions for me to speak up, so I take a deep breath and look at all the faces in the room.

"Before I say anything, I would like to make one thing clear. What is said in this room stays in this room. Agreed?" I begin, and there are mumbles of agreement. "The Moonlight Pack was once my old pack, and they did not treat me well. I was repeatedly beaten, forced to do things for them, and was disrespected by all. The alpha didn't even help to prevent it. He encouraged it," I tell them, surprised my voice comes out strong.

I stop for a moment to let this new information sink in. I glance at Comrade to see him gripping the table so hard that his knuckles have gone white. I never did tell him about my old pack. I now wish I did.

"When we went to help them out, the alpha had simply stated that he was taking me back, and their problems will be over. Of course, my mate didn't allow that to happen, and you could say that the Moonlight Pack's alpha seemingly challenged my mate and your alpha. Therefore, this resulted in war," I conclude and everyone looks at me in shock.

I feel shocked myself, one, for actually telling them all that and two, at how strongly I just spoke. I guess all that royal blood running through me is finally starting to come to the surface.

"As you could tell, I did not take this lightly," Axel continues on where I left off. "To prevent any of our wolves being severely injured or even facing death, training will be issued to all pack members who wish to fight and defend their Luna. Any questions?"

Comrade clears his throat and we all look at him. "Alpha, I believe that it would benefit our Luna's safety if she has, at least, two members with her at all times. Unless if she's with you, of course," he suggests. He glances at me during his speech and I instantly agree. I turn to Axel to see he is contemplating it.

"I agree," he finally mutters then looks at me.

"Who do you want to guard you, sweetheart?" he asks in my mind. I'm glad he's giving me a choice in the matter and not just issuing people I've never met before to be my guards.

I look at Callum and Comrade and instantly know who I want to be with me at all times.

"Callum and Comrade," I tell him without hesitation. Who else is better than your very own guardians?

He nods his head. "Very well," he says out loud, and everyone looks at him expectantly. "Callum and Comrade will be with the Luna at all times to help keep her safe," Axel announces to everyone. I see pride and joy swell in both Callum and Comrade's eyes, and I smile at the two of them.

The meeting continues with discussions about war tactics and how to approach the situation. Thinking about how much effort Axel is putting into this makes me wonder how my old pack reacted after we declared war. I bet they're just lounging around without a care in the world while a war is brewing right on their doorstep. Although, when the need arises, they have good tactics and one hell of a punch.

"Right, we will inform the pack tonight. Jacobs and Prince, inform the pack to be here in an hour. I want everyone to know as soon as possible. Meeting dismissed," Axel concludes. Everyone scurries out of the room while Axel plops into his chair from his recent standing position.

I move behind his chair and massage his temples soothingly. He sighs contentedly and let his eyes slip close.

"What's on your mind?" I ask.

"Everything," he grunts and brings my hands to a standstill by gently grabbing them. He kisses my knuckles, his thumb running over them afterwards.

"Why does everything have to be so difficult?" he asks me, but I think it's a rhetorical question.

Axel pulls me onto his lap and rests his head in the crook of my neck, his warm breath hitting his mark and making me shiver.

Without my permission, the thought of this upcoming war suddenly enters my mind. I want to help, I know that. What can I do, though? It's not as if I can just jump into the fight. Maybe I can use my powers... I haven't even given them a thought yet, maybe I can get Axel to help me practice!

"Axel, do you think—"

I'm cut off abruptly when Matthew comes through the door.

"Alpha, the pack is here and waiting for the announcement," he tells Axel. He keeps his head bowed while he sneaks a cheeky wink at me. I roll my eyes at his antics and push myself off Axel's lap.

"Very well," he sighs then we both follow Matthew out to the backyard.

He joins the crowd as Axel, and I walk up the steps where I fell down when I was first introduced to the pack. A blush rises to my cheeks at the thought, and Axel chuckles when he sees it in my mind.

We stand before the crowd as they all look at us, silently asking why they got called here on such short notice.

"Welcome, one and all. We are deeply sorry for having this meeting at such short notice, but it's urgent," Axel booms in his alpha voice. "We have declared war on the Moonlight Pack."

Well, that's a bit blunt. Couldn't he have eased it onto them?

Whispers erupt in the crowd as gasps are heard and a little girl starts crying.

"Silence!" Axel booms and everything goes silent. "Like most of you, I'm sure you'll want a reason for this sudden declaration. The reason is that the Moonlight Pack's alpha attempted to forcefully take my mate and your Luna from us while we were in his territory."

Growls, snarls, and protests erupt from the crowd, and pride swells in me knowing that my pack won't let anything happen to me.

"For those of you who wish to fight for your Luna, please stay afterwards and my beta will discuss the tactics with you. For those of you with families and mates, I will advise you to think very carefully about this and how it will affect you. Although the Moonlight Pack may be weak, they can still put up a fight," Axel warns as people hug their mates and children. "For those of you who do not decide to fight, be aware that you are not cowards, but are people who value their families and loved ones."

I look over each of the faces, and most of which are looking at either children or mates. Silent conversations are being said with their eyes as they come to their own conclusions and decisions.

"Axel?" I whisper in his ear. He turns his head to look at me. "Can I say something?"

His eyes widen for a moment before nodding. Axel clears his throat loudly, gaining everyone's attention. He takes a step back as he encourages me with a smile.

"I would just like to say something quickly that concerns all of you," I start off, and everyone focus their undivided attention on me. "Know that although this pack may seem weak and may not be able to keep itself up, it still has power. The Moonlight Pack has excellent fighters, and they will show no mercy; I have experienced it first-hand. So, for those who are willing to fight, please think it through thoroughly. This fight will not be for the faint-hearted."

Silence follows my little speech and they all glance at each other. I see in some people's eyes that they are really thinking about what they should do. Protect their Luna, or protect their family?

"How do you know?" a guy somewhere in the crowd cries out. I scan the faces trying to see who yelled it, but failed.

I answer the question anyway, though, "Because, like I've said, I've encountered their brutality and fierceness first-hand. No one, and I mean no one, wants to be a victim of that."

After that, a scene from one of my beatings appears in my mind, and it's as if I'm actually experiencing the pain. It was a year before my escape when I was fifteen. I was sick and couldn't do any work, so Damon and Tina barged into my room with a knife in one hand and ropes on the other.

Tina tied me down, but I was too weak to protest or fight back. She punched, kicked, and spat on me for who knows how long. Damon then came up with the knife and whispered a few cruel words in my ear, that I would much rather not repeat. He then stabbed me right in the stomach, but not deep enough to kill me. They kept on beating me with the knife still lodged in my stomach and only stopped when they deemed my punishment acceptable. That was the worst beating of my life.

I hear two loud groans come from the crowd, bringing me out of the memory, and snap my head up to see Callum and Comrade holding their stomachs in pain, the same place where I was stabbed. I grip my own stomach as the memory comes rushing back again, causing me more pain.

Next thing I know, Axel has dismissed the meeting and rushed me inside, Callum and Comrade following closely behind. We make it to our room, and Axel places me gently on the bed.

I shut my eyes tightly as I bear the pain and wait for it to pass. When it does, I see Callum and Comrade gripping the bedposts with blood-stained shirts.

"Oh my god!" I cry as I rush over to them. I lift Callum's shirt to see a stab wound. I rush to the bathroom and get two hand towels, soaking them with water.

"Lie down," I tell them both. They do as I say, and they both lay down as I hand one towel to Axel. I lift Comrade's shirt next, then decide to just tear it off because it seems to be causing him discomfort. I see Axel do the same to Callum's, leaving us with two tanned, well-toned werewolves, lying on our bed. I'm glad my heat's over...

I gently dab at the wound on Comrade's stomach as guilt hits me hard. If I didn't have that stupid memory, then none of this would've happened. I couldn't stop it, though. It was as if it just popped out of nowhere.

"It's not your fault, Snow," Comrade mutters and I gently touch his face. He leans into my touch as I continue to clean up his stomach.

After Callum's and Comrade's stomachs are clean, their wounds seem to heal quickly, and I breathe a sigh of relief. A thought strikes me then. Did they feel the pain of my mating Axel the other night? Oh god, that would be embarrassing.

"Um, Callum? Comrade?" I begin to say while biting my lip. Axel smirks at me as he knows exactly what I'm thinking. I glare at him, stupid alpha.

"Did you guys feel any... pain about a week back?" I ask shyly as a blush rushes to my cheeks in full force.

They glance at each other with a smirk as they look back at me.

"No, we didn't feel the pain while you were mating," Callum finally admits, and I breathe a sigh of relief. Thank the Goddess!

They all chuckle at me as Axel takes me in his arms.

"Alright guys, you're good now. Run along and do what you do. Callum, you need to go see the pack, though," Axel tells them, and they both jump off the bed and leave.

Axel puts me down onto the bed, and I squeal when I fall with a loud thump.

"Now that we're alone, I can finally have some release," Axel mutters as he kisses down my neck.

A soft moan slips from my lips as he bites his mark gently. I guess my powers can wait till tomorrow morning...

22

CELINA

"No, Axel, listen," I command as I back away from his really big, black wolf. His wolfish head tilts to the side, and his eyes fill with mischief.

"You take one more step, and I'm not sleeping with you for a month!" I warn, and he freezes. I don't mean that in a sexual way, I just mean not sharing the same bed.

'You're bluffing,' he says smugly in my mind, and I stare at him.

'Really? Try me,' I challenge, and he does. He takes one step towards me and my eyebrows shoot up.

"I can't believe you thought I was bluffing," I say, shocked, and worry fills Axel's eyes. Yeah, that's right, keep thinking that you've lost.

"Well, I'm not sleeping in the same bed with you for a month then," I grumble, then start walking back towards the pack house.

A growl erupts out of Axel's chest, and he lunges at me. I collapse to the ground as his wolf breathes heavily on top of me. He then gets that stupid look in his eyes like he's going to do something I won't like. My eyes widen when I realize what he's going to do.

"Axel, don't you da—" I'm cut off when his overly-sized tongue licks right up the side of my face, leaving a big stream of drool.

"Eww!" I squeal as I scramble to try and get out from under him.

Axel's laugh reverberates in my head, and I glare at him while attempting to wipe off the slobber. Keyword: attempting.

'You... You should've... Seen... Your face!' Axel laughs in my mind, and I growl playfully at him. He growls right back, and I roll my eyes at his challenging stance. Stupid Alpha...

I was going to ask him about my powers this morning, but then he suggested a run, and I thought why not? A run would do me good. So we went for a run, and Axel ended up stalking me like I was his next meal. I really need to talk to him about my powers, though...

"Axel, can you shift? I want to talk to you about something," I mumble, and all playfulness disappears as he shifts and walks up to me stark naked. I hand him the pants I'm carrying, and he slips them on before sitting down and cradling me in his lap.

"What is it, sweetheart?" Axel questions softly and I sigh. Will he even let me?

"Can you teach me about my powers?" I rush out, and Axel's body goes rigid beneath me. I look into his eyes to see them staring right back at me.

I gulp at his next words as he says, "Learning about powers, Celina, is not for those who will back out. It requires strength, endurance, and determination. The training is hard and brutal. Think hard about this first, because once you decide, there's no going back."

I let myself think about what Axel has just said. Am I ready for this? An image of my fake mother and father, and my real mother and father come to mind then. Even though my fake mother and father never told me the truth, they still raised me to be strong and go for what I believe. Even though my real mother and father weren't there for my upbringing, I still have their blood running through my veins, giving me power and determination.

So, am I ready? Yes, yes I am.

"I'm ready," I tell Axel without a waver in my voice. He looks at me for a moment before he nods and gets up.

He starts to speed walk back to the pack house, and I follow closely behind. He passes the kitchen, lounge room, study, and goes straight to the very back of the house.

He approaches a door hidden by a curtain that blends with the wall. It has no handle, but Axel punches in some code onto the keypad next to it. His eye gets scanned and then the thick, metal door opens.

Axel doesn't hesitate as he walks inside. I follow him again, but a bit of fear creeps in when I realize I have no clue where we're going.

The door opens straight to a set of stairs, we both walk down them. Axel opens another door, and we walk into what seems like a training room. Exercise bikes, exercise balls, treadmills, gymnastic rings, rowers, padded walls, everything, really. There's also no window, and the whole place is made of concrete, floors, and all.

"What is this place?" I ask with awe as I look around the room at all the new equipment. There's two of everything, one for the trainer and one for the trainee.

"This, my dear Celina, is the training room. This is where you will be trained until the war and after that. This is where you will learn to use and control your powers. This is where you will finally become a fully strengthened royal," Axel explains with pride in his voice.

I turn to look at him and notice he's holding pieces of clothing in one hand and shoes in the other.

I walk up to him and grab them as he points to a changing room that's tucked away in the far right corner of the room.

I quickly strip my clothes and put on the workout bra, mini shorts, and trainers. I tie my hair up in a ponytail and glance down at myself. Really?

I walk out of the room, and lust fills Axel's eyes almost instantly.

"Really?" I repeat my thoughts. "Do I really have to wear this?"

Axel nods his head at me, and I look at him expectantly for an explanation.

"You have to wear it because there's a greater chance that you will injure yourself when you are wearing more clothing than necessary. It's only for the time being. After you've learned to control your powers, you can wear whatever you like," he explains, and I nod my head with a slight frown on my face. He's so making that up.

"Right!" he suddenly exclaims, and I jump. "Let's get to work!"

We go into full blown training, spending half an hour on each set of equipment and doing hand to hand combat on the padded mats. Axel teaches me how to block, attack, and defend when needed and teaches me how to actually work all the equipment in here.

By lunch time, I'm stuffed. I collapse to the floor as sweat rolls off me and onto the concrete floor.

"Come on, Celina, that's the warm up! We haven't even gotten to the power part yet," Axel tells me, and I snap my head in his direction with wide eyes.

"What?" I snap and, if only I have the energy, I will be strangling him at the moment. He's got to be kidding me!

Axel laughs at me. He has just started sweating, and his breathing is only a little bit laboured. He seems unmoved by the workout while I'm looking pathetic on the floor.

"Come on, sweetheart, you couldn't have strangled me even if you tried." He laughs again then adds, "Yes, that isn't even the extreme stuff yet. We'll get some lunch then head back down here, and the real fun can begin." He smirks and hauls my sorry butt up the never ending stairs.

I stumble into the kitchen and sit tiredly on one of the stools. Chloe, Declan, Matthew, and Jasper decide to walk in at that point. I swear there isn't a time where I haven't seen them together!

"Wow, what happened to you, my dear Luna?" Matthew asks cheekily, and I growl at him, not in the mood for his antics.

"Calm down! He's only asking." Declan chuckles and I shoot him a glare. He puts his hands up in mock surrender as I let my head drop into my arms that are resting on the counter top.

"Come on, guys, she looks pooped out. Don't give her a hard time," Chloe scolds the two boys, and I stick my tongue out at them. Very childish, I know.

Their mouths drop open as Declan points an accusing finger at me.

"Did you just see what she did? She poked her tongue out at us!" he exclaims, and I chuckle at him.

"You gotta remember, guys, I'm no older than you are," I tell them tiredly, and Jasper, who has been suspiciously quiet, scoffs at me.

"Please, you couldn't be as young as us. We're like sixteen and seventeen. Matthew over there being the oldest," Jasper says, and I lock my eyes onto Matthew. He does seem a bit more... manly than the other two boys. That just might be because of his beta gene, though.

"Well then, that means Matthew's older than me. You gotta remember, I'm only sixteen," I tell them, smiling innocently as their jaws drop, except Chloe's. I guess her Mum told her.

I roll my eyes and spin my chair back round to the counter to see a chicken sandwich sitting there. I immediately tuck into it as Axel gets a thoughtful look on his face.

"When is your birthday anyway?" he suddenly asks, and I choke on a piece of chicken.

"W-why do you want to know?" I retort after a gulp of water. He looks at me like I'm crazy and shakes his head.

"So I will know when to buy my mate presents and bake a cake for her. Also, to know when she's getting older," Axel adds on as an afterthought, and I glare at him.

"I'll always be younger than you," I shoot back, and 'oohs' are heard around the room. Axel glares at me challengingly, and I glare right back.

"What if I tell you mine? Will you tell me yours?" he bargains, and I think about it for a moment.

"Maybe," I said, and Axel sighs.

"Well, even if you don't tell me, I want a present. Mine's the third of March," he tells me with a cheeky grin.

I look at his face to make sure he's not lying. I glance at Chloe, and she nods her head, accepting that it is the right answer.

"Third of March, hey? I'll make sure to remember that," I tell him and get back to eating my sandwich. March has already come and gone, it's about the start of October now.

Everyone continues to look at me expectantly. I sigh and put my half-eaten sandwich down.

"Do you really want to know that badly?" I ask, and they all nod their heads vigorously, except for Axel, who already knows I've given in.

"Fine! My birthday's on the eleventh of September!" I blurt out and they all high five each other as I stuff the rest of the sandwich in my mouth.

"Now that wasn't so hard, was it?" Axel teases from across the counter, but I just mumble something under my breath. "Right! Well, we better get back to our training," Axel announces, and I look to my four friends for help. They chuckle at me as I'm dragged away from them. So much for protecting their Luna...

Axel has to drag me all the way down to the training room, and when we get there, I huff in annoyance.

"Hey, this was what you wanted! If it were my choice, I would've made sure that you never knew this room existed," Axel complains with a frown. I just roll my eyes at him.

"Come on, teach me something!" I exclaim excitedly, and Axel rolls his eyes at me.

"Let's start off with something simple," he mumbles. He thinks for a moment with his eyebrows scrunching then clicks his fingers.

"Flying! Flying isn't so hard," he says with mischief in his voice. He then magically levitates into the air and hovers above me. I gape at him as he smirks down at me.

"H-how did you do that?" I ask, dumbfounded. He slowly comes back to the ground and his feet land on the cold concrete.

"Practice," is his simple explanation. "You're going to learn how to do it."

I blink at him as he grips my hands and slowly leads me to the center of the room.

"What I want you to do is focus on imagining that your body has no weight, nothing at all. Pretend you're a feather, but you're one that can be controlled," he explains and let go of my hands.

I close my eyes and think of myself as a feather that can't be carried by the wind. 'I am as light as a feather, I am as light as a feather,' I chant in my head.

"That's great, Celina! Keep going!" Axel applauds and I peek open an eye to see that I'm at least a metre above the floor.

My other eye snaps open as I gasp. I slightly drop towards the ground as I lose my concentration.

"Concentrate, Celina," Axel scolds and I focus my brain on concentrating again. Feather, Celina, you are a feather.

Soon enough, I can do it without thinking, and Axel joins me as we float around enjoying the feeling of being above ground.

"This is amazing," I whisper and let my eyes slip close. It truly is. Never in a million years do I think I'll be floating in the air alongside my mate.

"It is," Axel whispers. "When we're out in the open, we can reach the speed of up to 80 kilometres per hour. It's useful for when we want to take out enemies by surprise," he explains like he's reading off a script. He starts to slowly sink to the floor at that point.

"Come on, that's enough for today. You can get down now," he tells me, and I look at him unsurely. He seems to catch on what's wrong and chuckles while shaking his head.

"Just think of yourself gaining weight back slowly. Not too fast, though," he coaches. I do as he says, landing gracefully on the floor.

"You've done well. Not many Shaded Wolves can pick up their powers that fast. My mother's the Moon Goddess herself, and I had to attempt at least five times before I could properly fly," Axel grumbles, and I giggle at his face. He looks so cute.

Axel and I walk back upstairs, and I head straight for the shower. Once I'm clean, I jump straight into bed and don't even bother with dinner. Today's been a long day, and I seriously can't wait for what tomorrow's going to be like.

23

CELINA

My eyes flutter as I wake up. I stretch out my arms and legs and make a move to get up when strong arms squeeze me tighter to a solid chest. I look behind me and realize that Axel is the culprit.

I shake him awake lightly, making him bolt up with a start. Well, that's a different reaction compared to when I tried to wake him up the last time.

"What the..." he trails off when he notices no danger is around, silly, over-protective alpha.

I tap him on the shoulder, and his sleepy eyes land on my figure. He smiles at me while I put an innocent smile on my face.

"Axel..." I begin with a soft voice. He looks at me suspiciously, somehow knowing something's up. He's looking at me like that since he's forgotten a certain threat I made. "Do you remember what I told you yesterday about not sleeping with you for a month?" I ask in the same voice, and Axel's eyes widen the slightest fraction. "I meant it."

I push him off the bed, and he lands on the carpeted floor with a loud thud. He stares at me in shock as I stare back him innocently.

"I'm confused," he finally mutters and then it suddenly clicks in his head. He jumps up and brings me into his arms.

"Come on, sweetheart, you don't mean that. It was an empty threat, right?" he says, and I stare at him blankly. Oh, Axel...

"Right?" he urges with slight fear in his eyes.

I giggle. He won't last a night without being in the same bed as me. It's his fault, though, for not taking my threat seriously.

"Your fault, Axel," I repeat my thoughts to him, then jump off the bed and head to the wardrobe. I know that I'll probably break that threat tonight. But yeah, I'll have him thinking it so he doesn't do it again.

Axel growls and soon, I'm thrown back on the bed. I gasp as I bounce a few times before Axel firmly places himself on top of me. I heave a heavy sigh, knowing what's coming next.

"Axel, we don't have time for this," I say sternly. His grey eyes turn to bright silver as he runs his hands down my sides. "W-we need to keep practicing my powers," I mutter, losing all sternness as I lose myself in Axel.

He nibbles my ear as his fingers massage the sides of my hips. His lips leave my ear and travel down my neck, kissing around his mark, but not touching it. I squirm underneath him as he continues to torture me.

"Axel..." I whine when he still doesn't touch it. Then, when I least expect it, he jumps off me, leaving me all hot and flustered.

"Come on then, sweetheart, time for training," he says and smirks triumphantly at my flushed state.

I sigh as I head to the bathroom to clean myself up. Stupid alpha, teasing me... After cleaning myself up, I change into some loose fitting shorts, another sports bra, and the same trainers as yesterday.

I meet Axel down in the kitchen, and he places a plate full of bacon, eggs, and beans in front of me.

I look down at the food in front of me and make a face. I don't like bacon... Or eggs, or even beans really. Axel gives me a weird look before pointing at my food.

"Are you going to eat that?" he questions, but I shake my head. "Why?"

"I don't like anything that's on that plate," I tell him honestly and his jaw drops.

I ignore him as I grab a bowl, the milk, and some cereal. I sit back down to a still gaping Axel.

"What?" I ask as I start eating my cereal while secretly biting my lip to keep in my laughter.

"How do you not like bacon?" he suddenly bursts, and I giggle at his dumbfounded face. I shrug as he continues to mutter things about how everyone likes bacon while I sit there, happily watching him, and munching on my cereal, desperately trying not to burst out laughing.

When I'm done, I place the bowl in the dishwasher and tap Axel on the shoulder.

"Are you done with your mumbling?" I tease, and Axel shakes his head so he can focus. He clears his throat before answering.

"Right, um, in the backyard today. We're going to see if you can suck the life out of nature," he says casually, and I gape at him.

"What?" I ask disbelievingly. He ignores me and continues to walk outside while I follow him like a lost puppy.

"Since you can see visions like Queen Rosemary, I'm going to see if you can suck energy from nature like King Ronald," Axel explains. I feel myself swell with pride when I hear Axel speak of my parents so highly.

"First thing's first, though. Can you suck energy from a human?" he asks with a devious grin.

I stare at him in shock as Jasper and Declan come waltzing out of the pack house. They come to stand next to me as Axel continues.

"These two trouble makers are your guinea pigs," he tells me and I viciously shake my head.

"No way," I say, and Axel raises an eyebrow at me challengingly.

"These two have been getting into trouble lately at school, and this is their punishment. I told them the consequence, and they still chose to disobey me, so they can suffer the wrath of their Luna," Axel says with a smirk in their direction. The colour drains from both their faces at the sight of the smirk. He's not joking...

"I don't know, Axel..." I trail off. I've never used these powers before, so I don't know what I'll do. 'What if I kill them?'

"You won't kill them, sweetheart," Axel says with a chuckle.

I take a deep breath to calm myself. You know, sometimes I wish I knew how to block Axel out my mind so it would be a much quieter place.

"Fine, but I swear if I hurt them—" I start until...

"You won't," Axel cuts me off. I glance at the two boys, and Axel nods his head at them.

Declan's up first, and he's fidgeting madly. I feel so sorry for him, he's about to be a guinea pig for some crazy experiment. I really don't want to kill him...

"Um, Alpha? Do I have to do this?" he mumbles, a bit frightened. Axel growls at him, and he shrinks back, casting his eyes downward.

"I warned you that this would be your punishment, now you have to pay for it," Axel concludes. No room for argument. He walks over to me and looks Declan disapprovingly.

'I'm losing my edge, sweetheart,' he tells me. 'People are thinking of me as weak.'

I roll my eyes at his excuse, but I get ready to learn anyway.

"Right, now what I want you to do is envision that there's a current flowing between you and Declan. Think of sucking out his energy and transferring it to your body," he explains, and I nod. "Now, look into his eyes and let the magic take over."

I do as he says as I feel pins and needles start to prick at my hands. I imagine the current, and slowly but surely, Declan starts to look tired. I watch on as his eyes start to droop, and his limbs fall asleep.

"Whoa..." he mutters before he collapses to the ground in a heap.

"That was good, Celina! You're a quick learner," he mutters the last part as I run over to Declan and cradle his head in my lap.

"Is he okay?" I ask, not moving my eyes from Declan's seemingly peaceful face. Axel nods his head, and I relax a bit.

"He's fine. He'll wake up in a day or two. Possibly three," Axel says casually, walking up to me. I gasp in shock and slight outrage.

"A day!" I scream, and Axel nods his head like it's nothing.

"Possibly three," he reminds me while I glare at him. How is he so calm about this?

"Can Jasper at least take him to his room?" I ask, and Axel shakes his head.

"Nope, that's what Matthew's for."

As soon as he says it, Matthew comes strutting out the door. He takes one look at Declan and his eyes widen.

"Shit, is he okay?" he instantly rushes out. I nod and tell him to take him to his room. He throws Declan's arm around his shoulder and starts to walk away.

"Oh, and Matthew?" I call after him. He stops, and I whack him over the head once I reach him. "Don't swear," I say sweetly then walk back to a scared-looking Jasper and an amused-looking Axel.

"Right, this time, I want you to manoeuvre Jasper's body," Axel explains and looks at him in question.

"I don't get it," I admit.

"This is something I want you to do that's not in the book. It's quite simple actually. Just think of moving Jasper with your mind, as if you're in his body instead of your own," he tells me, and I nod my head doubtfully.

"You'll do fine," he encourages.

I take a deep breath then focus my undivided attention on Jasper. Slowly, his body begins to levitate, and I move his arms and legs so it looks like he's doing a dance in the air. It's quite funny actually.

"What the hell!" Jasper yells, and I giggle at his poor face. Poor thing, he must be freaked out.

"Good, now take the energy from him," Axel instructs, and I do as I'm told. I slowly start to suck the energy out of Jasper's body, imagining the current. He comes to a stop in the air as his eyes drop close.

Just as I set him back on the ground, Matthew comes back through the door and takes his other friend's arm and hauls him to his room.

"That was very well done, Celina," Axel praises and I smile at my mate. "Now try to do it with nature."

I nod my head and move to stand in the middle of the garden at the back of the pack house.

I put my hands out to each side of me and slowly breathe in through my nose and let it out through my mouth. I close my eyes as I feel the energy circulate through the air and imagine the current. Suddenly, my feet are off the ground.

My eyes snap open as I watch streaks of energy from flowers, trees, grass, and even the dirt make their way to me and absorb into my skin.

The energy runs through my body, and it feels like I've had a year's worth of sleep.

"This feels amazing," I say, but my voice sounds lighter and airier, as if it's being carried by the wind.

I see Axel out of the corner of my eye staring at me in disbelief, so I slowly float over to him and hover above him just that little bit. I place my hand on his cheek and notice that it's not my usual slightly tanned hand. Instead, my hand is covered with moving colours that represent nature. Browns, greens, and yellows are all swirling over my hands and up my arms.

Axel's eyes suddenly fill with fear, and I hastily float away from him. His mouth moves, but no sound comes out. I don't allow myself to panic, as I know that it's just the effect of nature playing with me... I hope. I don't want Axel to be scared of me, not now, not ever.

I close my eyes again and slowly return the energy to the now almost dead surroundings. As the energy goes from me, I gingerly land back on the ground. After the last of it leave, I peel my eyes open to see an amazed Axel. I look at my hands and notice they're back to normal, but they now have a kind of glow in them.

"Axel," I softly call out as I take a cautious step towards him. My voice is back to normal too, instead of the beautiful airy one I had when I was with nature.

"H-how did you do that?" he asks with the same awestruck look on his face. I shrug, and he shakes his head at me. "You don't understand, Celina. Only King Ronald has been able to do that, but the amazing thing is, you can return the energy back to the plants. Your father could never do that, and here you are, on your first try, sending the energy you just absorbed back to its rightful owner. How?" he continues to ask, baffled and awed.

The one-word question leaves Axel's awestruck voice, but I can't give him an answer. I don't know how I did it myself.

"I-I don't know," I tell him honestly. "It just came naturally."

I chuckle when I realize how my statement connects to what I've just done. Axel shakes his head to get out of his thoughts, clearing his throat at the same time.

"Something like this has never been recorded or predicted. Celina, do you know what this means?" he asks me, as a full blown smile lights up his face and his eyes widen with excitement.

Right at this moment, Axel looks more like a child at Christmas than an all-powerful alpha. Nevertheless, I shake my head slowly.

"You may have hidden powers that no Shaded Wolf has ever even dreamed. Powers that not even your parents possessed!" he bursts with joy, and I stare at him in shock.

Hidden powers? Me? How can I have hidden powers when I was practically hidden from this my whole life? On the other hand, how can I be more powerful than my parents? If what Axel is implying is true, then my parents, who did not think of or conjure these powers, intended that I have to be more powerful than them, right? This is too much to handle.

Axel's face is still a picture of joy, as theory after theory, power after power, races through his mind.

I grab his face firmly in my hands and make him look at me dead in the eye.

"Axel, we don't know that. I may just have a little something extra than the rest of the history bound Shaded Wolves. You never know, it may have just been a one-time thing," I try to convince him, but he's having none of that.

"Celina, don't you understand?" he says as he places his hands over my small ones that are still on his face. "This can change everything that the world knows about Shaded Wolves! This can change everything about what I've taught and told you. This can change the views of the Moon Goddess."

Axel's realization finally hits me once he said the last sentence. Changing the views of the Moon Goddess? Even I know that is not a good idea...

"This can change the views of the Moon Goddess," Axel repeats to himself again.

"Axel, Axel, look at me," I order, and he does with disbelief about what he's just discovered in his eyes. "You may be right, but none of that will matter if you don't focus here, right now, in the present. The future will come, but right now we need to deal with the prophecy and war that is unfolding right before our eyes."

I wait to see Axel's reaction and watch as the glint in his eyes fade and the grin he has plastered on his face drops into a scowl. I hate to see his happiness fade, but I don't want him going on false hopes that neither of us can prove.

"You're right," he says, pushing away from me to stand back in the middle of the backyard. "There's a war brewing, and we have no time to waste. We have to get back to training."

There's the Axel I know and love. The one that takes control over any situation, and the one that has a heart of stone around others, except with me.

I walk up to him and peck him on the lips.

"I love you," I whisper as I lean my forehead against his.

He smiles softly at me. "I love you too. Right, let's move onto the next power," Axel proclaims as he pecks me on the lips one last time. I giggle and step back, waiting for him to continue, "Manipulating the weather."

I gulp as I think about changing the weather patterns. That can't be good either... Isn't there a Mother Nature or something like that? I don't think she'll be too happy about me changing her weather. I don't voice my thoughts to Axel, though. I'm sure he knows what he's doing.

"I've never mastered this one before, and I don't think I ever will, but I have a feeling you'll get it the first few tries. Let's try to get some rain first, nice and simple," Axel states and I nod my head in agreement. That's before I remember something important.

"I thought only royals can fly and control the weather and do all these things. Why can you?" I ask, confused. Axel grins at me.

"Never one to miss a detail, are you?" he replies. I just shake my head and continue to stare at him. He hasn't answered my question. "Well, the Moon Goddess knew that one day you'd ask about your powers and want to be taught about them. Since your real parents didn't have the chance to show you, the Moon Goddess has graced me with the power to show you yours. Therefore, I can do everything a royal can," Axel explains while doing hand movements.

I accept what he says knowing the Moon Goddess has only the best interest in mind. I continue to stare at Axel, waiting for him to tell me what to do next.

"What do I do?" I ask, clueless when he doesn't continue. He shrugs his shoulders.

"Think of what we've done for the rest of your powers. It's like a big thinking game," he hints, and it clicks in my brain.

I look up to the sky and think of clouds forming, only over the pack house, though. When it doesn't work, I huff in annoyance.

"Try harder," Axel pushes. "Think of yourself as the base of the storm and harness it when you feel it's at its peak."

I try again, but it still doesn't work. I groan in frustration. How come I can get all my other powers in a snap and not this one?

"Why is this so hard?" I scream. Axel places his hands on my shoulders and looks me in the eye.

"I never told you it was going to be easy. Try this: think of the weather as your emotion. Assign an emotion to each type of season: summer, winter, autumn, and spring," Axel coaches. I do as he says and choose which emotion goes with which season.

Summer = happiness
Winter = anger or bitterness
Autumn = sadness
Spring = peacefulness

"Got them?" Axel asks, and I nod. "Good, now think of your sadness one. What is it?"

"Autumn," I immediately answer. Axel raises an eyebrow but doesn't question it. Most people would go for winter as sadness, but autumn was when my fake parents died. I will always dread the season for the rest of my life.

"Okay then. Now think of something that makes you so sad you just want to burst out crying," Axel tells me and my fake parents' faces instantly pop into my head.

"Now focus that emotion on the weather," he coaches, slightly starting to back away from me.

I harness the sadness I'm feeling, like Axel said before, and imagine I'm shooting a beam upwards into the sky. Storm clouds immediately start to brew, and rain comes plummeting down over the pack house. I don't believe it...

The occupants of the pack house glance outside in wonder, but once they see Axel and me, it flicks a switch in their brain, and they continue on with what they're doing.

As the memory of my parents starts to fade, so do the storm clouds. Once they've finally disappeared, Axel applauds me, and I giggle while doing a little curtsy. I'm giggling a lot today.

"That was amazing, Celina! I'm so proud of you!" he boasts while picking me up and spinning me around in the air.

I laugh again and suddenly have an idea. I take the happiness I'm feeling now and beam it up into the sky. The little clouds that are scattered around the sky disappear as the sky becomes bluer and the sun's light hits my face with the perfect amount of warmth.

Axel also looks up to the sky and smirks at me knowingly. I giggle again while nodding my head. Axel chuckles at me and shakes his head at my little show.

"Do you want to try spring and winter?" Axel questions just as a yawn escapes my mouth. He sets me down on my feet and wraps an arm around my waist. "You tired, sweetheart?" he asks, and I nod my head sleepily. I think I gave my energy back to the plants, not just their own.

He guides me through the pack house and up the stairs to our personal room. He tucks me into bed as I catch a glance at the clock. It's only two in the afternoon. Why am I so tired?

"Sweet dreams, Celina," Axel mutters as he plants a kiss on my forehead and I fall into the blackness of sleep.

24

CELINA

"Snow? Come on, Snow, you've been sleeping for ages. It's time to get up," a soft voice says as it travels through my sleep-filled mind.

I grumble under my breath and roll over so my face is buried in the pillows.

"I don't wanna get up," I complain. I hear a chuckle before light seeps through my closed eyelids. "What the..." I trail off as I open my eyes, and I'm met with the blinding sun.

"Come on, Snow, get up," the voice says again. Comrade comes into my line of view with a smirk on his face and a mischievous glint in his almost black eyes.

"No, let your Luna sleep for a bit longer," I say as I close my eyes again and get comfy.

"Celina, it's ten in the morning," Comrade tells me. I bolt upright upon hearing it, "Ten in the morning!"

"What?" I scream, and he chuckles. My hair's probably a mess, and I must look a sight from just waking up.

"Yeah, you've slept for like nineteen hours. Why are you so tired?" he asks, concerned, and I just look at him with furrowed eyebrows.

"I honestly don't know. Training wasn't that bad, so it can't be that," I mutter as I slowly get up from the bed. Comrade hands me a skirt and top, and I take them from him gratefully.

"Well, you're up now. Callum and I made you breakfast. So get dressed, get downstairs, and eat, woman!" he orders. I roll my eyes at him after doing a fake salute.

I quickly get changed and glance at myself in the mirror. Despite my nineteen hours of sleep, there are still bags under my eyes, and my skin looks a bit pale. I sigh and splash water on my face. My stomach suddenly squirms in discomfort, making me feel sick. I place my hand on it as I swallow back the bile that just rose into my throat. That's weird... Ugh, maybe food will help.

I slowly make my way downstairs and take a seat on one of the stools by the kitchen counter.

A plate of pancakes covered in whipped cream, maple syrup, ice cream, and a strawberry on top is placed right in front of me. A fork is also placed next to the pancakes as I stare at them in awe. My stomach squirms again but this time, in a good way. This leads me to think I should just get stuck right into these pancakes.

"Good morning, Celina," Callum chirps happily and leans against the counter with a smirk plastered on his face.

"Morning," I mumble as I continue to stare at the pancakes. They're calling to me, telling me to eat them.

"Enjoy your breakfast," he tells me and pushes my fork closer. I don't waste another second as I take a big chunk of the pancakes and stuff it into my mouth. Both Callum and Comrade chuckle at me while I just ignore them.

The fluffiness of the pancakes mixes amazingly with the syrup, ice cream, and whipped cream. I snatch the strawberry and pluck off the top as I stuff it into my mouth.

About halfway through devouring my pancakes, I ask, "Where's Axel?"

He wasn't there when I woke up, and he still isn't here now. So, where is he?

"He's training the people who stayed back at the meeting the other day. He wants them working to the fullest and reaching their maximum strength before the... war." Callum spits the word 'war' like it's a curse. I nod at him as another question pops into my head.

"Why aren't you two training?" I ask and they both smirk. They should be training if they're taking part in the war, too.

"We have to protect our little, defenceless Luna," Comrade taunts, and I growl at him, finishing off my pancakes. They both laugh at me.

"Seriously, though, why aren't you guys out there training when I know both of you are going to fight in the wretched war?" I implored with genuine curiosity. Comrade squirms uncomfortably as Callum sighs.

"Celina, we are assigned to protect you at all costs." He pauses before going on. "That means that we're not taking part in the war because if you get hurt, neither of us will be able to live it down. As your protectors and guardians, we aren't going to take the chance of you being injured or even worse, die."

I stare at them in shock. "Callum, you're still the beta. You have the responsibility to fight alongside your alpha. Think of the lives you could save," I exclaim, then turn my eyes to a still squirming Comrade.

"I know you want to fight because you want to prove yourself. I can see it in your eyes. I don't want to be holding either of you back because you think I can't defend myself," I say. My voice is full of confidence and power as they both bow their heads to me.

"It's not in our power, Celina, it's in our instinct. As your guardians, we just want to protect you and keep you safe. That's all," Comrade whispers. I sigh in defeat, not wanting to upset either of them even more and have their guts fill with guilt.

Silence fills the room, and all I want to do is hug them both. I don't though because that will probably lower their egos to have their friend and Luna cuddle them.

I clear my throat, and they both look at me, begging with their eyes to break the silence.

"So, what are we going to do today?" I ask, and they both look at each other before shrugging, obviously having no clue.

I sigh as I get up from the stool, the tense atmosphere slightly lifting, and make my way into the cooking area of the kitchen. I start to take out different sized mixing bowls, ingredients, utensils, and other stuff used to bake cakes.

'How are you feeling today?' my wolf suddenly asks. I halt in my movements for a moment before I continue on with my eyebrows drawn together.

'Fine...' I tell her wearily. 'Why do you ask?'

'Just curious,' is all she says before going back into the corners of my mind. Uh, that's weird. She never asked random questions like that before...

Comrade brings me out of my thoughts by looking over my shoulder and startling me slightly.

"Whatcha doing?" he asks curiously, eyeing all the stuff I've put on the bench.

"I'm cooking, what does it look like I'm doing?" I retort, and they both shrug. I roll my eyes and signal for both of them to come to where I am. "You're going to help me," I tell them. Their eyes widen, and their hands go up in a surrender kind of motion as they start to slowly back away.

"We would love to, Snow, but uh... We don't cook," Comrade admits, and I huff.

"Obviously," I mutter under my breath. I pull them back to where I'm standing by their shirts and give them each a mixing bowl.

"First step, watch and learn, boys," I tell them as I grab my own mixing bowl and start to mix up flour, eggs, milk, and other ingredients to make a cake.

They copy my actions, and pretty soon, I've got them making and baking all sorts of cakes ranging from plain vanilla to Black Forest cake. During the whole time I'm teaching them how to bake, I keep going to the fridge for some sort of snack, which is weird because I only had breakfast a few hours ago...

I bite my lip as Comrade accidentally spills some flour on Callum's shirt. Callum slowly looks up and glares at Comrade playfully, very beta-like.

"You did not just do that," he says, strangely calm. Comrade smirks and nods his head. Oh, definitely very beta-like.

"Oh, I think I did," Comrade admits, and that one playful sentence sends them into a flour fight. Flour goes everywhere, the floor, the counter, and the cupboards, everywhere!

I burst out laughing when I see Comrade's usually brown hair turn almost white from the flour and Callum's once dark blue shirt also become white from the flour.

Both boys turn to look at me as I laugh. They look at each other and grin. I immediately stop laughing and start to slowly back away from them as they advance to me. Oh dear...

"Group hug!" Comrade suddenly yells and they both lunge towards me.

I squeak and jump out of the way, running through the kitchen door and leaving the boys in their own cloud of flour. I laugh again as they burst through the door looking like a couple of SWAT agents ready to go on a top secret mission. I bolt around the corner just as they catch sight of me.

"Celina, come back! We only want to give you a hug!" I hear Callum yell. I laugh louder and run faster as I see the backyard in sight.

"Celina!" Callum taunts again and I turn my head to see that they're gaining on me.

I squeal and grip the door handle, yanking it open and slamming it in their faces. Just as I'm about to get off the patio, I'm being tackled by a sudden burst of white bodies.

I scream as my face is about to make contact with the ground, but Comrade goes under me before I can. He yanks me up as he and Callum join together in squishing me into a hug. I wriggle in their grasp as I laugh again.

"Callum! Comrade! Let go of me right now!" I exclaim, trying to be stern, but they both just laugh at me. I start laughing along with them when I realize I can't get out of the situation.

They eventually release me, and I back away from them looking at my once tidy clothes. Let's just say, they're now white. Callum and Comrade take one look at me before bursting out laughing again. I glare at them as I put my hands on my hips. They collapse to the ground, rolling around like a bunch of idiots.

"Well, Snow, you definitely look like snow now," Comrade lamely jokes as he and Callum go into another round of laughter.

A thought strikes me then, we're gonna have to clean this all up. Well, I'm gonna have to clean this all up because I doubt the laughing hyenas over there will help.

I sigh as I make my way back into the pack house unnoticed, my happy mood gone in an instant. I grab the cleaning supplies and start in the kitchen. I clean off the bench and the things we used for cooking, and take out the cakes we cooked before Callum and Comrade finally decide to make an appearance.

"Wow, Celina, did you clean all this?" Callum asks, shocked, but Comrade just stares blankly at me with a knowing glint in his eyes.

"Yeah," I mutter, "A lot easier than cleaning a whole pack house."

Nobody is meant to hear the last part, but Callum and Comrade both send me looks. Callum's one of sympathy, which I hate, and Comrade's one of understanding. I blink at the two different emotions. Callum's I understand, but Comrade's? Not so much.

I chuck a rug at each of them and point them out into the hall.

"Clean your white footprints off the floor and wherever you touched," I order, and they both raise their eyebrows at me, "Now!"

They both scurry into the hall, grumbling protests along the way.

I continue to clean the floor and cupboards in the kitchen until everything is sparkling clean. I wipe the sweat off my forehead and lean against the counter, mentally patting myself on the back for a job well done.

I close my eyes and rest my head on the counter top. I open them with a sigh and white assaults my vision. I gasp as I push myself off the counter and stare, dumbfounded at the ceiling. How the hell did they get flour on the ceiling?

I sigh heavily and grab a cloth to wipe it up with. Then I just float to the ceiling without any trouble and start wiping the areas with flour. I'm not going to even try to figure out how they got flour on the ceiling.

"Celina, we've finished the—" I hear Comrade's voice until he cuts himself off.

"Celina?" he calls again, and I look down from the ceiling to see both Callum and Comrade looking around the kitchen for me.

I laugh silently at them in my head and decide to freak them out a bit. Concentrating, I move the wooden spoon that's still sitting on the counter and watch as it floats towards Callum.

I keep in my laugh as it whacks him on the butt, then quickly shoots up to the ceiling before he can notice.

"Ow!" he yells and whips around to see the culprit. He's met with nothing as the spoon now goes behind Comrade.

"What?" Comrade asks before he's also hit. "Ow!"

This time, I can't keep in my laughter and both heads snap towards the ceiling as my laughter fills the room.

"Celina," they growl, and I laugh again as I gracefully float back down while grabbing the still floating wooden spoon and place it in the right drawer.

"Yes?" I ask innocently. They growl again while I just chuckle at them.

"Come on, let's go watch a movie," I suggest with a smile. They protest at first, saying they don't want to watch a movie, but I eventually convince them. Soon, we're all seated on the couch, I'm squished between the two of them, with a bowl of popcorn each. I let the boys choose since I swatted them with a floating wooden spoon. To my surprise, they don't choose horror as I thought they would. Instead, they choose a 'shoot 'em up, bang 'em up' type of movie. I think it's called *GI Joe*. I don't know.

About half way through the movie, my stomach starts to churn again, and a loud groaning noise is heard. I place a hand on my stomach and put the popcorn down on the coffee table in front of us. Neither of the boys seems to notice since they're so absorbed in the movie.

I continue to watch the movie until I feel bile rise in my throat, for the second time today, and a wave of nausea hits me hard. I place a hand over my mouth and sprint to the closest bathroom, ignoring the calls of Callum and Comrade.

I continue to run until I see the familiar door of the first-floor bathroom. I yank open the door and go straight to the toilet. I get down on my knees and puke my guts out without a second thought.

"Snow?" I hear a soft voice that's full of concern call from the doorway, but I'm too busy emptying my stomach.

I can feel my hair being pulled back from behind and a soothing hand rub over my back. I instantly know its Comrade because that's just what Comrade does.

"Deep breaths, Snow," he says softly as Callum waits near the door, looking worried.

I don't know how long it is, but I eventually take my head out of the toilet and lean against the cool tiles on the wall.

"Ugh..." I groan as Comrade flushes the toilet.

Callum rushes over and gently pulls me into his arms, bridal style. He picks me up effortlessly and places me down on the couch that I just ran from. He places the back of his hand on my forehead.

"She's a bit warm. Maybe she's got a fever," he says lowly to Comrade.

I suddenly feel my stomach churn again in pain and grip it. It doesn't die down for a while, and Callum and Comrade just sit there watching me the whole time. They also buckle over in pain, and guilt fills me as I know I'm the cause of it.

The pain soon ceases and I collapse onto the couch with a sweaty forehead and breathless.

"She needs a doctor," Callum speaks up after he's also recovered from the sudden pain. Comrade instantly rushes to the phone, regaining his breath back on the way.

"A-Axel... G-get Axel, please," I beg as exhaustion consumes me, and I welcome the darkness.

"Luna? Luna, I'm gonna need you to wake up," a distant voice says. I strain my ears to hear it, and I do. It's soft and full of concern. "Luna?" it asks again, but I can't seem to peel my eyes open.

"Move," an angry voice says. I feel sparks shoot up my arm from my hand and instantly know that it's Axel.

"Celina, sweetheart. Wake up. Come on, sweetheart, just open your eyes," Axel begs in my ear quietly.

I try my hardest to do what he says, and my eyes crack open the slightest bit. Axel's handsome face comes into view, and I smile softly up at him through half shut eyelids.

"Axel?" I say to him and place a weak hand on his cheek. Ugh, I hate feeling like this, all weak and helpless. It reminds me of... No. I stop my thoughts right there, not daring to let my mind wander any further.

Axel grips my hand, and his face is flooded with relief as audible sighs are heard around the room.

"Thank the Goddess," Axel mutters. "It's me, Celina. It's ok, I'm here."

I take this time to look around the room. I can't see any of the people because they all seem to be standing behind me. All I can see is Axel. I'm also definitely not in the lounge room where I was in before. It actually looks like I'm in a hospital room.

"Where am I?" I ask. A brown haired lady comes into view at my question.

"You're in the pack recovery room," the same lady says, and my eyebrows furrow.

"The recovery room? What am I recovering from?" I ask again and right after I've said it, a sharp pain travels through my stomach. I grimace and grip the fabric of my shirt in pain. I hear two sharp intakes of breath and instantly know that the people standing behind me are Comrade and Callum.

The pain slowly passes, and I let my tense muscles relax, guilt filling me again about causing my two guardians pain.

Axel growls.

"What the hell was that?" he booms. I wince from the loudness of his voice. The lady, who I still don't know the name of, seems to pick up on it.

"Alpha, please keep your voice down. The noise isn't good for the Luna," she says softly and bows her head to show respect to her alpha. He growls again, but it's low and not as loud.

"Answer the question, Doctor Aileen. What. Was. That?" Axel says, accentuating each word. I shrink back slightly from the intensity of his words.

The doctor glances at me before looking at Callum and Comrade.

"For the time being, this only concerns the Alpha and Luna, so I'm asking you all to leave," she says calmly, but her voice still sounds stern.

They both make their way out the door and when they're gone, my attention goes back to Doctor Aileen, as I now know her.

"Well?" Axel urges and the doctor sighs.

"You might want to take a seat, Alpha," she suggests, so Axel drags a chair next to my bed and takes a seat. He grips my hand in his and waits for the doctor to say something, anything, about what the hell is going on with me.

"I've noticed that you two have mated and let me say congratulations," the doctor starts as Axel growls in annoyance. I squeeze his hand to calm him down.

"Luna, have you been tired lately, eating large amounts of food, and maybe throwing up once or twice?" she inquires. I nod my head at each. Why does it all matter?

Doctor Aileen looks at me like it will all click in my brain. I think about it. I've been really tired lately, which isn't normal. I've been wolfing down all my meals, sometimes going for seconds. I've also been eating snacks in between all my meals. I threw up today, but my stomach's been feeling off since this morning. What does that all mean?

Sleeping more, eating more, throwing-up, the pains...

I gasp as I come to the realization. I stare at the doctor in disbelief as she nods her head at me. I shake my head furiously as I grip Axel's hand tighter.

"No! No, I'm 16! I can't... No! I won't believe it!" I cry in vain as tears slip from my eyes.

"I'm sorry, Luna, but there's nothing I can do. What's done is done," Doctor Aileen tells me.

"What's wrong? What's going on?" Axel asks in haste out of worry.

This can't be happening, not now! In the future, sure, but not now that a war's about to start. How could I be so careless? How could I let this happen? I can't be... I just can't. I start to hyperventilate as everything comes parading into my mind. This can't be happening. This can't be happening...

"It is happening, and you have to choose to accept it," my wolf tells me in my haste to figure out what's really happening. "It is meant to be."

I snap once she says that. "You knew," I whisper. "You knew that this would happen, didn't you?" I yell at her as she whimpers. "'ou knew from the very beginning, and you didn't even bother to tell me!" I continue to scream in my head.

"Celina!" Axel yells, snatching my attention from my encounter with my wolf. "What's going on?"

I stare at his loving, greyish silver eyes and watch the emotions swim around their depths. I have to tell him. I don't know how he'll react, but I have to tell him.

"I-I..." I stutter, my voice shaking. I clear my throat as I try to get the words out.

"I'm pregnant," I let it out in a hoarse whisper.

Just like that, my world comes crumbling apart.

25

AXEL

I'm so confused right now! I come home to a call from Callum, telling me Celina is throwing up and in major pain. Then I'm hauling her into the medic station at the pack house. And now Celina and Doctor Aileen seem to be having a conversation with their eyes, and they're ignoring my questions! What the hell!

Celina suddenly gasps, and my head snaps at her, giving her my full attention.

"Celina!" I yell, catching her attention. "What's going on?"

I stare into her beautiful golden eyes that seem to be swimming with uncertainty, pain, and most of all, remorse. Why?

"I-I..." she stutters, her voice shaking. She clears her throat as she tries to get the words out.

"I'm pregnant," she lets out in a hoarse whisper. I freeze. That's all I can do.

Tears brim Celina's eyes, and all I can do is stare at her. She's pregnant? My Celina, my beautiful and wonderful mate, is pregnant with my pup?

My gaze snaps to Doctor Aileen. I swear if this is some cruel joke, I'll have her turned rogue for it.

"Are you sure?" I ask her, and she nods her head, certainty in her eyes.

"If it helps to ease the shock, I can set up to do an ultrasound," she suggests, and I nod my head furiously. She immediately starts rushing around, setting everything up as I turn back to a still crying Celina.

"Celina, sweetheart, look at me," I tell her gently as I put a finger under her chin, forcing her to look at me. I look at her face and the emotions passing through her eyes, and my breath catches in my throat. She looks so torn and broken, not the usual her that I've grown to love.

"Oh, Celina," I whisper as I take her in my arms.

She just breaks apart as she cries onto my chest. She grips my shirt in her tiny hands and buries her head in my chest, soaking my shirt with her tears. I rub her back soothingly as I whisper sweet nothings in her ear to try to calm her down.

Knowing that Celina is carrying my pup is as much a shock as it is exciting. Right now, in Celina's womb, my pup is growing. A boy or girl, I don't care. It's my pup, and I'm gonna do everything in my power to keep him or her safe, as well as Celina.

Celina looks so torn about it. After all, she's only sixteen. Her birthday's coming up in less than a month, though, so when she actually gives birth, she'll be seventeen. I don't think that makes the situation any easier for her.

It's not rare for our kind to have pups at a young age. Some mates even have pups by the time they're eighteen. The youngest recorded is 16. She went on to be a wonderful mother with a caring mate. Again, I don't think this shines a light on the situation for Celina.

"Ok, the ultrasound is all set up, Alpha," Doctor Aileen announces, and Celina pulls away from me at the sound of her voice. I wipe the tears still falling down her cheeks and kiss her softly on the lips. She takes in a shaky breath as she tries to compose herself.

"It's ok, sweetheart. I'm right here. Always will be," I tell her with all the honesty in my heart. She takes a deep breath and nods her head, believing that I'm not leaving her.

Doctor Aileen squeezes the gel onto Celina's stomach. She winces from the coldness. She adjusts the screen so that both of us can see it. Celina squeezes my hand for comfort, and I squeeze right back.

"Are you ready?" Doctor Aileen asks, eyeing us both warily. Celina nods as I stay still and watch the screen.

Doctor Aileen places the machine wand thing on Celina's stomach, and we get a glimpse of what Celina is actually carrying.

I hold my breath, hearing Celina also take a sharp intake of breath and then she squeezes my hand harder.

The tiniest body pops up on the screen, and my eyes widen as I realize that it's my pup. That's my child, the future Alpha that my mate is carrying. I glance over at Celina to see her watching the screen in wonder and awe.

The pup's so tiny. If it isn't for Doctor Aileen pointing the body out, we can't see it. It's just our tiny bundle of joy.

"Well, there we go. It's too early to see what sex it is, but—" Doctor Aileen abruptly stops her sentence as she spots something else on the screen. She moves the wand a little more to the right to catch a glimpse.

Another small body pops up, and Celina becomes frozen beside me.

"Is... Is that another baby?" she whispers, and Doctor Aileen nods as she stares at the screen in shock.

She moves the wand around again, and another small body pops up. I gulp audibly as she continues to move the wand around and count how many pups my mate's carrying.

I squeeze Celina's hand in support as I notice she starts to tremble. She takes deep breaths to calm herself down as she closes her eyes. She opens them again when Doctor Aileen begins to speak.

"Well, um... this is very unexpected," she whispers as she checks over and over again to make sure what she's seeing is true. She stops her movement when we can clearly see three little bodies on the small screen. They're tiny, but they're there.

I gasp as I realize that my mate has three pups growing inside her. Three, we're going to have triplets.

"It... It seems like you're having triplets. Congratulations, Alpha, Luna," Doctor Aileen says with pride and bows her head to the both of us.

No thought travel through my mind. No reaction comes out of me. My wolf stays silent as he tries to absorb all this information. My mate has three pups growing inside her, and we didn't even know it.

"How far is she along?" I ask. Doctor Aileen lifts her head to stare at Celina, inspecting her almost.

"I'd say at least a month or two," she tells us, then bows her head again.

"Oh my gosh!" Celina whispers as she covers her mouth with her hand.

Doctor Aileen quickly snaps a picture of the screen and leaves it there for us to look at as she hastily leaves the room, giving us the privacy we need.

We both stay silent as we just stare at the screen in absolute shock. We're having three pups, triplets.

I look at Celina to see tears streaming down her face again as she stares at the screen in shock and awe at the same time. I quietly get a cloth, wipe away the gel from her stomach, pull her top down, and pull her onto my lap.

"Celina, it's going to be ok. You're going to get through this. We're going to get through this," I whisper in her ear as she chokes on a sob.

"I-I don't know, Axel. I'm c-carrying three babies, and I'm only sixteen. H-how in the world will I be able to c-cope with t-this?" she asks between her sobs.

I hold her tighter to me as I mumble in her ear, "You'll cope because you have me."

She chokes on a sob again and pulls away from my chest to look me in the eyes.

"What if I don't survive?" My eyes widen at her whispered question. I growl loudly, and she shrinks away from me, trying to get off my lap. I hold her to me as another growl erupts from my chest.

"Never, and I mean never, think that way, Celina!" I growl at her. "You will survive because if you don't, I certainly won't."

She starts to cry again and a loud sob escapes from her perfect lips. We just sit there, with me cuddling her and her holding onto me for dear life as she breaks down in my arms.

Her cries soon die down after a long while. When I look down at her, she's fast asleep, probably from exhaustion and shock of this whole situation.

I gently lift her up in my arms and walk out of the medic station. Callum and Comrade are still waiting outside. When they see Celina, they run to her in haste. Callum brushes back the hair from her tear- stained face as Comrade wipes away any abandoned tear.

"What happened?" Comrade whispers. I shake my head. They both back away as I start to walk up the stairs.

"Not now," is all I whisper. It leaves them knowing that I will eventually tell them but now's just not the time.

I carry Celina all the way to our room and gently place her down on the bed. Her face is the picture of peacefulness, apart from the tear stains, and her body is perfectly relaxed. I sigh as I take her hand in mine and gently kiss it.

The situation would have been different if Celina is just older, if we don't have a war coming up, and if we are certain that she will survive this birth.

'Callum, Comrade,' I call through the mind link. They immediately tune in to what I'm about to inform them, 'Head up here. I'm going to go talk to Doctor Aileen, and I need you guys to watch over Celina for me.'

In less than thirty seconds after I sent the message through the link, there is a soft knock at the door.

"Come in," I mutter. Callum and Comrade walk in with worried expressions. They can probably feel Celina's sadness since they are affected by her strongest emotions.

I kiss Celina on the forehead then make my way to the door.

"Just... stay with her. She needs comfort right now, and I think you two will be able to do the job," I tell them then make my way out the door and back downstairs to find Doctor Aileen.

Having all these suddenly put on both Celina's and my shoulders... is something to really think about. Celina is very mature for her age, and I know she'll be a perfect mother, but I'm not sure she's ready. Yes, she's strong, mature, and amazingly special, but three pups? I have no doubt in the future that we will have pups, but she's only sixteen. I'll do anything right now to see what's running through her head. She's finally figured out how to block me.

On top of that, we have a bloody war! Her old pack members are a couple of idiotic morons if they think they're going to win this war. Problem is, now that Celina's pregnant, she'll be a major target. She'll be hunted down whether she's part of the war or not. I can't let that happen.

I smell Doctor Aileen's scent when I pass by the medic station, so I open the door without knocking and walk straight in like I own the place.

Doctor Aileen looks up, instantly bowing her head in respect when she notices it's me.

"Alpha," she murmurs under her breath.

I simply nod at her and motion for her to take a seat. She does so, and I take one opposite her. I take a deep breath through my nose and let it out through my mouth. How do I approach this? Maybe bluntly is the way to do it.

"Will she die?" I ask, going for bluntness.

Doctor Aileen looks taken back for a second, then it registers in her mind, and she casts her eyes downward, not answering.

"Will. She. Die?" I repeat a bit more fiercely, this time, emphasizing each word.

Doctor Aileen whimpers slightly. My annoyance and irritation grow as she continues to look down and not answer the question.

"Answer me!" I order in my Alpha voice, and I feel her wolf instantly submit.

"There's a possibility," she whispers, and an almighty growl escapes my throat. She continues on, though, like she didn't hear me at all.

"Alpha, the Luna is only sixteen, and her body might not be able to handle the pain. Giving birth is painful enough with just one baby, add another two and you honestly have pure torture. The Luna is strong, and she will fight, but there's still that possibility that she won't make it after she gives birth. Having you there will help because you're her mate, but it will only help slightly," she says, tying it all up in an annoying bloody package.

I stay silent, my breath coming out in short pants as I fight to control my wolf.

"What are the chances?" I growl out as I try to rein in my wolf. He wants out.

"There's a 75% chance she won't make it," Doctor Aileen whispers, and I don't waste another second as I barge out of the pack house and shift into my midnight black wolf.

I take off into a sprint as a pain-filled howl escapes my lips. My wolf continues to run, and I pretty much give him full control. I just need a chance to think, and this is one way of doing it.

My mate has a 75% chance of dying after giving birth. How can any mate cope with that? How can any mate stay sane knowing that in a few months' time, their mate may not be alive anymore? How can anyone cope with that?

Another pain-filled howl escapes into the night sky as my wolf continues to run. We run until the early hours of the morning, seeing as we left in the late afternoon.

At about five in the morning as the sun starts to come up, I decide to head back, the pain of leaving Celina becoming too strong to ignore. I run all the way back to the pack house and shift on the doorstep.

I can tell everyone's still asleep by the sound of light snoring and even breathing I can hear, so I try not to make a sound as I quietly shut the door behind me.

I make my way up to my room, stark naked, to see Callum, Comrade, and Celina all asleep. Celina on the bed, Callum on the couch, and Comrade on a chair by the bed, I sigh as I look at them. They all look so peaceful, yet their lives are so full of drama that they can never take a break to just breathe.

I make my way to the bathroom and have a quick shower, washing off the dirt and grime that I picked up while on my run.

I walk out with a towel wrapped around my waist and make my way to the wardrobe. I pull on some jeans then stare out the window that is practically a wall. I let my thoughts consume me at this point.

I can't believe I was stupid enough to not even think of using protection! I was just so caught up in the feeling and mood that it just sort of slipped my mind. The only thing on my mind was Celina and that I was going to make her mine. I was being stupid, though and look where that's got me, with a mate who's 16 and pregnant with triplets.

Don't get me wrong, aside from all the negatives and the put downs of this pregnancy, I can't be happier. Celina, my mate, the love of my life, is carrying my pups in her womb right now. Having that one happy thought erases all the bad ones and shows me the light. Even though a war is brewing and we have no idea when it's going to hit, I'm still happy. Even though my mate is only 16 and pregnant, I'm still happy. Even though Celina may have a chance of dying, I'm still happy. Not so much for the last one, but I'm still happy.

"Axel?" a soft voice asks, tearing me from my thoughts. I spin on my heels to see Celina rubbing her eyes like a baby and looking at me tiredly, her hair dishevelled and her clothes from yesterday crinkled.

I instantly rush to her side and plant my lips softly on hers.

"Good morning, sweetheart," I whisper. We stare into each other's eyes for a moment before Celina's eyes widen.

"I'm pregnant," she whispers. I chuckle at the recognition in her voice. Oh, Celina...

"Oh my gosh! I'm pregnant with triplets!" she cries. I get ready to see the tears fall and to take her in my arms, but they don't. All that comes is a small smile.

"Celina, you feeling ok?" I ask wearily. She laughs lightly at me. She takes a hold of my wrist and places my hand on her slight baby bump I haven't noticed before.

She smiles at me.

"I'm fine, happy even. I'm carrying your babies," she whispers and places a soft kiss on my lips. As happy as I am to hear that, this is a major difference from yesterday and how she was feeling about it. What changed her mind?

"What about yesterday? I thought you—"

She silences me with a finger to my lips. She looks at me seriously and says in an equally serious voice, "I know how I reacted yesterday, but what's done is done. We can't change that fact. I've decided to embrace the fact that I'm pregnant and not neglect it, so please, just bear with me."

I take her in my arms as I skilfully manoeuvre us so that I'm now sitting comfortably on the bed with Celina on my lap. We sit there in silence for a few moments before Celina breaks it.

"You did want me to get pregnant with your babies, right?" she suddenly asks, and I chuckle at her worried tone.

I place my hand back on her stomach and rest my head on her shoulder.

"Of course, I did!" I tell her, then I decide to ask a question that's been nagging at me for a while. "Did you want pups?"

She stays silent for a moment. I start to think she didn't when she speaks.

"Why do you call them pups?" she asks, making me sigh at her obvious effort to try to avoid the question.

"That's what we're supposed to call them. Pups are a smaller version of wolves, so that's how we refer to them," I explain, and she nods her head.

"Back to the former question..." I trail off, hinting at her to answer my earlier question.

Celina stays quiet for a long time. She looks deep in thought, thinking really hard about what her answer must be. She seems a bit unsure, and I tense as I watch her slowly open her mouth to answer.

"I guess I did," she whispers, and I feel myself relax at her words. "I think I would've liked them in the future, though after I've turned 18 and after the war."

I sigh again and bury my head in her neck. I would've liked that too, but we're going through it now so we'll just have to deal with it.

"Unfortunately, fate didn't want to work that way," I mutter.

26

AXEL

We sit there for another hour or two before Comrade stirs in the chair. He opens his eyes and stretches out his arms, cracking his neck in the process. I feel Celina shudder in my arms after she hears the sound. I must admit, I've never liked the sound of cracking bones ever since my first shift...

"Ugh... Remind me never to sleep in a chair again," he mumbles, and Celina looks at him sheepishly.

"Sorry, you didn't have to stay, you know," she whispers. Comrade just smiles gently at her.

"Nah, all good. I would sleep in a chair for you any day," he tells her honestly as I roll my eyes at his cliché remark. To my surprise, though, a slight blush graces Celina's cheeks.

Callum decides to wake up at this point as well with a loud yawn. Geez, he's annoying when he's awake and half asleep.

"Morning," he mumbles as he slowly gets up and rubs the sleep from his eyes.

"Oh, don't tell me you slept on the couch all night, too!" Celina exclaims, appalled. Callum just shrugs and makes his way over to us.

He suddenly looks uncomfortable as he stands behind Comrade's chair. He clears his throat before asking, "So, uh... Did you figure out what was wrong with you?"

Comrade perks up at this question and stares at Celina intently.

Celina stiffens in my arms and swallows audibly. I pull her closer to my chest. She sniffles a little, and I notice tears once again pooling in her eyes. Wait, what? She was fine with this only a few hours ago, and now she's upset again? Maybe it's the hormones...

"Um, I..." she begins, but can't finish. This leads me to believe that she isn't ready to tell anyone about her pregnancy yet, so I quickly butt in before this situation can get out of hand.

"It was just stomach flu. Doctor Aileen gave her some pain killers, so she's all good now," I reassure them both, but they still look pretty uneasy about the whole thing.

"It seemed like a lot worse than the stomach flu from Doctor Aileen's eyes. It hurt a lot more than the stomach flu too," Callum mutters the last part. Comrade doesn't seem to pay mind to him as he stares at Celina curiously.

I growl warningly at him, but he ignores me as his eyebrows furrow and his eyes light with curiosity.

"Celina, is that true?" Comrade asks in a soft voice. Celina looks at him startled and immediately starts to stutter over her words.

"I... uh... Well, you know... We—" she stutters as she blinks furiously. Before she can embarrass herself any further, Comrade cuts in again.

"Are you sure you're not hiding something?" His voice is filled with curiosity and a little bit of hurt at the same time. He's always the one to persuade and convince people into saying or doing things. He even helped with some rogues a few years back because they weren't telling us the information we needed. He's always had a way with words and he used it to convince Celina to join the pack.

Celina immediately places a hand over her stomach and gulps again. Comrade follows the action, and it all suddenly clicks in his brain. I must say, he's a very smart pup when he wants to be.

His eyes widen as he says the next few words that has Celina in tears, "You're pregnant."

Callum looks to him in shock while I growl and glare furiously at him. Again, for a pup, he's pretty smart.

He takes Celina's hand in his, and Callum does the same with her other hand. She stays firmly in my lap as they both try to calm her cries. She eventually stops crying and collapses onto my chest, resting her head on my shoulder.

"Please, please, don't tell anyone," Celina begs in a whisper. Callum and Comrade seem torn for a second before they both nod in sync.

"We wouldn't dream of it," Callum states. I nod curtly at him, my best friend. For all the years I've known him, and that's a really long time, I've never known him to break a promise. What he just said is a silent promise that I know he will keep safe until he dies.

I look at Comrade to see him smiling gently at Celina.

"Don't worry. It's Axel's and your job to announce you're having a pup," Comrade says with a light smile.

Celina takes a breath before correcting him. "Pups," she whispers. "We're having pups."

I would've chuckled at their reaction if it wasn't the given situation. I can't believe she actually admitted that to them, although, they are her guardians, and they will never dream of hurting her.

"P-pups?" Comrade asks in surprise as he stutters over the one word. Callum just looks like he's about to jump over the moon. I can't blame him. After all, his Luna and his best friend, also his Alpha, are going to be having pups that will ensure this pack's survival. We'll probably make him a godparent knowing him and his antics.

'I am so going to be a godparent,' Callum tells me through the mind link and this time I do chuckle. My thoughts confirmed.

'So you guys are having twins?' Comrade asks again, but with a bit more excitement this time. Celina buries her head in my chest.

'Can you tell them?' she whispers to me through the bond. I nod silently at her and prepare to tell them what is going to probably make them go into shock, again.

"We're having triplets," I say firmly and, just like I thought, they go into complete and utter shock. That is until Callum breaks out into a full-blown grin and jumps up to fist pump the air.

"Hell yeah!" he screams, making Celina jump in my arms. "I'm going to be a godparent of three little kiddos!"

You know, sometimes I forget that Callum's 20 years old like me. He pretty much always acts like a teenager. He can shift into the role of a beta straight away, though, only if the need arises, of course.

Comrade stays silent before realization crosses over his face, and a look of horror replaces it.

"Are we going to feel the pain of you giving birth?" he yells, and Celina bursts out laughing. I smile broadly at her. That's the first time she laughed since the whole pregnancy thing.

"We'll have to wait and see," Celina says through her laughter. Both Callum and Comrade shudder. I actually kinda feel sorry for them. No bloke should have to feel the pain of birth, only a woman has that curse. The thought causes me to shudder.

"Holy crap! I'm supposed to be training the new fighters!" Callum exclaims and without even a goodbye, he races out the door. I chuckle at his awful memory and look to Comrade expectantly. He's got somewhere to be, doesn't he?

"Oh, um, I need to go do that... thing. Yeah, that thing. Uh, see ya later, Snow," he says in a rush as he makes a beeline for the door. He stops abruptly and turns to look at both of us with a small smile on his face.

"Congrats by the way," he says sincerely then he leaves, letting us be, finally...

Celina heaves a heavy sigh. I look at her questioningly.

"What's wrong, sweetheart, something on your mind?" I push. She silently nods her head and brings her mind wall down completely so I can see her thoughts.

She feels nervous about having the pups, not knowing if she'll live or not. She's also nervous about telling the pack. She doesn't want them to view her differently because she's 16 and pregnant with triplets. These thoughts continuously travel through her mind, torturing her and making her believe them.

"Hey..." I mumble as I put a finger under her chin and lift her head up, her beautiful golden eyes locking onto my silver ones in that moment. "You'll be fine. The pack won't view you differently, and you most certainly won't die on me because I'll be right there with you the whole way."

I wrap my arms around her thin waist and rest my hands on her stomach, rubbing it with my thumbs. Believe it or not, there's actually the slightest baby bump already forming.

"Promise?" she whispers as she places her hands on top of mine.

"Promise," I whisper back, and that's how we spend the next hour, sitting on the bed wrapped in each other's arms.

I think Celina will feel a lot more comfortable if she has a doctor's perspective on this whole situation. Maybe she'll find some closure and fully accept this situation because I can feel she doesn't truly want to believe it. She forgets to put her mind wall back up.

"Sweetheart, do you want to go see Doctor Aileen?" I ask. I don't specify why we must see her, but Celina nods furiously and jumps out of my arms to get changed. I chuckle at her while I pull on a shirt since I already got dressed earlier.

She comes back out with a simple pair of black leggings and one of my shirts on. She looks good in my clothes... she should wear them more often.

"Let's go!" she urges as she grabs my hand and starts to pull me to the medic station.

"Hold on there, sweetheart," I say as I pull her to a stop when we're about to pass the kitchen. I point a finger at her.

"Eat first, then the doctor," I order, leaving no room for argument. She reluctantly enters the kitchen, grumbling under her breath the whole time.

I chuckle as I go to the cupboards and get out some cereal, knowing that her stomach can only handle cereal for the time being.

I place a bowl of *Crunchy Nut* down in front of her, and she immediately gets stuck into it. I pour myself a bowl of it too and take a seat next to my mate.

I gave her three times as much as she would usually eat because she's eating for four now. I wonder if she really intended to get pregnant while she was in heat. She probably didn't, considering the reaction she had when she found out. A man can wish, though, right?

I wonder what would've happened if I waited to claim her until after the war, or even when she's at the actual legal age. Maybe then, she would've had a different reaction and welcomed the idea of pups with open arms. Could I really have waited two years, though? Could I really go through that many heats and had Celina go through so much pain because I just wouldn't claim her? I don't think so. If I did manage to, though, I would be a very happy wolf when I finally get to mate her.

"Axel, hurry up!" I hear Celina whine as she nudges my shoulder with her tiny hand. "I want to go see Doctor Aileen!"

I look down at her cereal bowl and notice she's finished eating. Damn, that girl can eat! I look down at my own bowl and notice I haven't even touched it.

I quickly eat the now soggy cereal as Celina watches on in anticipation, it's like she's watching a movie that's about to hit its climax. As soon as I take the last bite, Celina launches off her seat, taking me with her, and drags me to the medic station.

She doesn't even knock as she barges in there. Doctor Aileen looks up with a start but instantly relaxes once she sees it's us.

"Alpha, Luna," she says respectfully, bowing her head.

I nod back at her as Celina does so too, in her haste. She takes a hold of Doctor Aileen's wrist and drags her to the couch on the other side of the room. I follow them with an amused look on my face.

Once I reach them, I take a seat on a single chair and haul Celina's bouncing butt onto my lap. She comes down with a huff and looks at me with a pout. I softly kiss her lips, and she's smiling, all happy again. Wow, hormones have definitely kicked in, I think with a silent chuckle.

"What can I do for you both?" Doctor Aileen asks and before I can open my mouth, Celina beats me to it.

"We have some questions," she tells her as she places a hand on her stomach. I follow her action, putting mine on top of hers.

I speak up first. "As you probably know, I have absolutely no clue how this pregnancy thing works, so I'm gonna ask a simple question." I pause for a second, and both Doctor Aileen and Celina's eyes are on me curiously.

"How many months until she actually goes into labor?" I ask. Now, to some, this may seem like a stupid question, but werewolf pups can grow faster in the mother's womb. This means that instead of a normal nine months like humans, we have a shorter period of time for the pups to grow and for the mother to give birth.

"Well, the normal time frame for a single pup is about three months. For twins, it's about four so triplets will be about five or six months, maximum," Doctor Aileen explains.

"Ok, five to six months. I can deal with that," I mutter to myself, making sure to say it low enough so Celina won't hear.

"However, since they have alpha and royal blood in them, it may only take four months minimum and five months maximum," she adds, and I nod.

I glance at Celina's face to see it turn into one like that of a deer caught in headlights. She's scared, I can tell that much.

'Sweetheart?' I try to get her attention through the mind link, but I don't get an answer back.

'Sweetheart?' I try again and this time, I get a little mumble from her. 'You're going to be fine. I'll be here with you, just like I promised.'

She relaxes in my arms after that. I hate seeing her so stressed out. It can't be good for her and the pups. She needs to rest and leave all the worrying to her guardians and me. After all, that's our job.

"Do you have any suggestions to keep the pups healthy and not have any issues?" I continue on with the inquiry in a business toned voice. I feel Celina shudder in my arms and smirk at the effect I have on her. I should use that voice more often...

"All I would suggest is that you always give in to your cravings when they arise. You should eat more too since you're feeding for four now, and maybe let up on the training," she advises and pause when she sees Celina stiffen in my arms.

"You want me to stop training?" she asks in a hushed whisper, sounding broken. I kiss the back of her head to let her know I'm still with her. This may be a big blow to her... She's really enjoyed the training so far, even if it has only been two days. She's really getting into it, and now all of it has to halt.

"Only for a few months, Luna. You may continue with the light training but nothing too strenuous, like controlling the weather. It would be too much for you and the pups to handle," Doctor Aileen explains. Celina finally nods, coming to terms with what's been said.

"Anything else you would like to know?" Doctor Aileen questions. I shake my head, but Celina nods. I look at her curiously. She ignores me like she does when she's upset or doesn't want me to interfere with something.

She takes a deep breath, looking unsure whether to ask the question or not. She closes her eyes and bites her lip, thinking it through. With a little hesitation, she whispers, "I-is there a possibility th-that I might... die?"

I stiffen at her question as it seems to reverberate around the room. Doctor Aileen keeps a blank face while my eyes widen. She looks to me.

'Alpha, she deserves to know, but it's your call,' she tells me, and I shake my head. She may be right about Celina having a right to know, but I know it will just stress her out, and she'll probably go off and do something she'll regret.

"Luna, there is only a slight possibility, but it can be easily avoided if your mate is with you and you have prepared," Doctor Aileen lies straight through her teeth, but I guess only the first part's a lie. If I'm there with Celina, and we've prepared for the worst, then there's a 25% chance she'll live and stay with me and our pups.

I feel Celina relax in my arms. Guilt threatens to bubble up inside me, but I push it back down. It's for her own good and protection. I will do anything to protect her, even if it means keeping her own possible death from her.

"This isn't the way to go about it!" my wolf growls at me. I growl right back.

"How do you suppose we approach it then? Just go straight out and say it? Do you know how heartbroken she'll be! She'll be gloomy for the rest of her pregnancy!" I yell at him. I take a breath to calm myself down as my wolf glowers at me.

"If I were you, I would want to see her happy. If she does die when she gives birth, I want to remember her laugh, smile, giggle, and everything about her. Not a gloomy mate who knows her time has come." My voice is much calmer now, sadder. My wolf decides to retreat back into the corners of my mind after I say that. Maybe he understands.

I'm brought back to the scene before me when Celina mutters a small, "Thank you."

Doctor Aileen stays silent, just nodding her head at her with a tight smile. Her wolf is probably scolding her for lying to her Luna but doesn't know what to do about it because her wolf still has to obey her Alpha.

"Come on, Axel, let's go," Celina says as she pulls me up. I wrap an arm around her waist and lead her out of the medic station. I glance at Doctor Aileen over my shoulder to see her guilt-filled eyes. She lied to her Luna, and now she's feeling the consequence. I can't help her, though. I told her to do it, and that must stay as it is.

27

CELINA

Two months later, I wake up to the sun's early rays streaming in through the window that covers the wall. I sigh contentedly and turn to see that Axel is no longer in bed. I'm not surprised. Since about a month back, Axel has started to work long days, starting from when the sun rises to when the moon is high up in the sky.

He's been really stressed out about the war and what the outcome's going to be like. We sent in a spy to keep tabs on my old pack, and he's reported back some nerve-wracking things. Apparently, they've been training nonstop. They have all wolves fighting, including mothers, children, and those who have just shifted. Damon is showing no mercy for his pack, and it's quite clear he won't show mercy for ours. Honestly, this news doesn't surprise me. Damon has always been a cruel monster, maybe not to the pack, but I know his inner being.

On top of that, Axel is also stressed out about the pups and I. It's safe to say that I'm almost as big as a whale, and I'm only half way there! It's ridiculous! Axel's had me locked up in my room for the last month, not letting me downstairs, not letting anyone in the room without him. He won't even let me go to the toilet alone!

He's been overly protective at making sure that I'm not injured, that I'm safe, that I'm fed, that I'm clean, that I'm happy. It's so flipping annoying! I wanted to go outside yesterday, and when I asked Axel, he had a fit. Safe to say, I'm never asking that question again. I understand he's just being what his wolf is pushing him to be, but can he lay-off just a bit? It doesn't help that he's an Alpha either.

I sigh as I slowly get up and out of bed. The floor boards under the carpet groan as I put my weight on them. I huff. I'm not that fat...

I sleepily waddle my way to the bathroom and do my business. I splash water on my face to get rid of the sleep and head back into the room.

I'm still drying my hands on Axel's shirt — it's comfy to sleep in, and it's the only thing that fits me now — when I suddenly stumble into something that seems as hard as brick.

I stumble back a bit before warm hands land on my waist and steady me. I look up to see Axel with a disapproving look on his face. I smile sheepishly.

"Hi, Axel," I mutter. He sighs and picks me up in his arms, carrying me back to bed.

"Celina, I told you to stay in bed and call me when you're going to get up," Axel lightly scolds me. I roll my eyes, see what I mean? I can't even go to the bathroom by myself.

"It's ok, Axel. I was only going to the bathroom," I tell him softly, resting a hand on his cheek.

He growls, and my eyes widen in shock. Did he just growl at me?

"Did you just growl at me?" I ask, voicing my thoughts, slightly pissed off. Axel shakes his as he tries to rein in his wolf. His eyes soon go back to the normal greyish silver that I love.

"I'm sorry," he whispers while resting his forehead against mine. "It's just... my wolf's on edge, and he doesn't want you doing anything without us. Frankly, I feel the same way."

I slap him slightly on the shoulder. He chuckles at me and wraps his arms around my waist, placing his hands on my stomach and getting comfortable on the bed.

I suddenly feel a kick, then another, and another. I gasp as I place my hand on my stomach. The pups are kicking! This is the first time they've kicked! Tears pool in my eyes, but I blink them back. My pups are kicking, our pups are kicking.

"See, Axel, the pups are fine, happily kicking away," I tell him in an amused voice. He also chuckles as a pup kicks his hand.

We stay silent while we just savour the feeling of being in each other's arms. We haven't been able to do this for ages, and I can't be happier knowing that my mate is right here beside me.

"How's everything going?" I ask, breaking the comfortable silence that has surrounded us. Axel sighs and buries his head in my neck, inhaling my scent.

"I don't want to talk about it. It could stress you out, and that won't be good for you or the pups," he tells me honestly. I turn in his arms to look him in the eye.

"Axel, I'm your alpha female and Luna. I deserve to know what is going on within this pack," I say firmly, and

Axel's eyes darken with lust. I roll my eyes. Of course, he finds my being firm a turn on.

He slowly starts to kiss down my neck and to his mark, but not touching it. Why does he always do that?

"Axel... S-stay focused," I try to say, but it comes out as a muffled moan.

He chuckles before pulling back. It takes a moment for me to clear my lust-filled mind, and when I do, I slap his chest.

"You did that on purpose!" I exclaim with a pout. He just kisses me on the lips softly.

"You love me," he says cheekily, and I rest my head on his chest.

"I know," I sigh in defeat. He chuckles, wrapping his arms around my waist again.

"Don't change the subject, though. Tell me what's going on," I demand and Axel finally gives in.

"We just received news on your old pack," Axel murmurs as I freeze in his arms. I know I should be used to it by now, but I'm not. The Moonlight Pack will forever haunt me until the day I die.

"And?" I urge him on, doing hand movements for him to continue.

"We found out when they plan to attack. They plan to attack within the next two or three months. We're still not sure on the exact date," he finally says after pausing for a few moments.

I blink at him. He looks so gloomy, like the whole world is resting on his shoulders. Why?

"What's wrong? We know when we're getting attacked, we can use that to our advantage," I tell him, but he shakes his head.

"Celina, think what's gonna happen in the next two months onwards," Axel says. I dig my brain for answers, but nothing comes to mind. I shrug as Axel sighs and shakes his head.

"You have the worst memory," he mutters before telling me what I should've known. "You're having the pups."

Realization must show in my eyes because Axel rolls his. I clear my throat.

"I knew that... What does that have to do with anything?" I retort, confused again.

"It means that while the war's on, you'll either be in labor, nearing it, or have already given birth!" Axel suddenly snaps. I stare at him in shock as he breathes heavily. I can't be in labor during the war! Can I?

I stay silent as Axel stares at me in anticipation.

"Well?" he pushes, but I have nothing to say. Two months is only the minimum time period for me to give birth, though, right? I might have the pups after the war! Yeah, let's stick with that possibility.

"A-Axel, two months is the minimum for me. You never know, I may go into labor a month or two after the war," I try to convince him and lighten the tension by telling him my point of view, but it doesn't seem to work. He looks even more stressed.

"Celina, we have to assume the worst, and that is you going into labor during the war. I can't have that. I need to be with you," Axel says, broken.

"Oh, Axel," I whisper as I take him in my arms. I think most of you are wondering why at this point we haven't considered having a Caesarean section. The answer is because we werewolves give birth naturally, that's just how it's always been.

I feel a single tear slip down my cheek, but it's not mine. I pull back to stare at Axel in shock. He has tears in his eyes, and he looks so vulnerable that my heart just breaks for him. He's supposed to be the strong one, holding me while I cry. This is the first time I've seen Axel cry, and honestly, I never want to see it again.

I grip him close and don't let go. No mate should have to go through this. No wolf should have to go through a war. It's not fair for us, our pack, or the pups.

Axel pulls back after who knows how long and offers me a small smile. I smile back as I place my hand on his cheek and rub it soothingly. He closes his eyes and leans into my hand, turning his head to kiss it.

"I should go, I have some stuff to work out," Axel says quietly. I sigh and drop my hand, moving away from him. He's leaving me, again.

I nod my head silently as I feel sadness rise within my chest. I don't know why I feel sad. He's just doing his job as Alpha. I'm the Luna, though, I should be helping too.

"Celina?" Axel calls quietly. I lift my head to look at him. "Want to come down with me?"

I beam at him and furiously nod my head. He chuckles as I launch off the bed and pull on a pair of tracksuit pants, keeping on his shirt. I tie my black hair up into a messy bun as I walk out of the bathroom.

Axel and I make our way downstairs. Well, more like Axel carrying me downstairs. He goes to his office while I head to the kitchen.

"Snow?" a surprised voice comes from the kitchen doorway as I'm looking through the fridge for custard and fish fingers. Hey, don't knock it till you try it.

I turn around, with the custard and fish fingers in my hands, to see Comrade looking at me with an amused grin on his face. He's leaning lazily against the doorframe as he eyes the fish fingers and custard suspiciously.

"Are you going to eat those together?" he asks, not believing his eyes. I shrug. I've been craving it for ages, and Doctor Aileen told me to always give in to my cravings so I am, simple as that.

"I'm craving it," I tell him simply. He still looks stunned as I put the fish fingers in the oven and pour some of the custard in a bowl.

"Don't knock it till you try it," I say with a grin. A flicker of amusement crosses Comrade's face at my words.

I pull out the fish fingers from the oven and place all of them on a plate. I grab the bowl of custard and take a seat on one of the stools by the counter.

I motion for Comrade to sit beside me, and he does without complaint. I dip the first fish finger into the custard and sigh in satisfaction when I take a bite.

"Want one?" I offer to Comrade, holding out a fish finger. He shakes his head as a sideways grin spreads across his face. I shrug, more for me then.

"So, where's Callum?" I ask. Comrade's shoulders dropped, and his whole demeanour changes.

"He's helping Axel figure out battle plans and an approach," he says quietly, but with a scowl on his face. I guess he doesn't like the idea as much as me.

"Oh," is all I say as I continue to munch on the fish fingers. I don't know what to say. I know Callum and Comrade want to fight, but they can't because they both have to stay with me. I guess Callum's way of contributing to this fight is by helping out Axel with ways to approach it. He's Beta, though, so he has to do it anyway.

Comrade, on the other hand, can't do anything because he's just a pack member who happens to be one of my guardians. He should be able to help, though. Comrade has been a part of this pack since he was born, so I presume he should be able to fight.

"You know what, Comrade?" I suddenly ask, a new determination bubbling up inside me. Comrade turns to look at me and immediately gets a weary look on his face.

"I'm gonna go give Axel a piece of my mind! You deserve to help, and he's keeping you from that," I say deadpan.

I get up from my seat, but before I can make my way to Axel's office, Comrade grabs my wrist lightly and pulls me back.

"Snow, there's no need for that. I'm fine with just protecting you," he says sincerely, but I still feel guilty.

"Comrade, you've been a part of this pack since birth! You deserve to have a say," I state firmly, but Comrade's face drops and his eyes fill with guilt. He lets go of my wrist and walks into the living room. I follow him and see him collapse onto the couch with his head in his hands.

"Comrade?" I ask softly. "Are you ok?"

I lightly sit down next to him and place a hand on his shoulder. He turns his head so that he can see me.

"Celina, I haven't been in this pack since I was born," he suddenly admits, and my eyebrows furrow.

"What?"

28

CELINA

"What?" I ask, confused. What does Comrade mean that he hasn't been in this pack since birth? Everyone's been in their pack since birth! Except me and a few choice others, I guess...

Comrade motions for me to sit down next to him, which I do timidly.

"Now, Celina, until I'm finished with the story, don't speak, don't ask questions, and don't interrupt," he says in a serious tone and sad eyes. I raise an eyebrow at this. "Please," he quickly adds, and I nod.

He takes a deep breath before continuing, "I was originally born into the Shining Sun Pack. My parents and I were happily living there with no threats that would affect us."

I stare at Comrade, shocked while his eyes stare straight ahead, but they look like they're somewhere else.

"When I was twelve, my Mum and I were happily playing out in the woods, my Mum in wolf form and me human since I hadn't shifted yet," he continues. Tears start to gather in his eyes and slowly make their way down his cheeks. I pull him in for a hug, but he doesn't seem to notice. I've never seen Comrade cry before and after this, I don't intend to ever again.

"At least eight rogue wolves suddenly surrounded us," he says in a broken whisper. "My Dad popped up out of nowhere and started fighting them with my Mum. My Mum told me to run, so I shot up the nearest tree and watched as the rogues tore my parents apart. They didn't stand a chance."

Tears now stream down my cheeks as I hear Comrade's heart-pulling story. He's been through so much, yet he's still able to put a smile on his face.

"I ran back to the pack house and went straight to the Alpha. I told him what happened, and he was furious. I first thought it was because of the rogues, but only minutes later, I found out it was directed to me," he admits quietly. I gasp at Comrade's statement, covering my mouth with one hand.

"I was shunned by my pack because they all thought it was my fault my parents died. Everyone loved my parents, and it was like a knife in the gut to know that they died at the hands of rogues," he murmurs almost in a whisper.

He draws in a shaky breath before continuing on again in the same voice, "I couldn't stay there. I couldn't stay with a pack who shunned me. I couldn't stay at the place where I've seen my parents brutally murdered, so I left. I ran for days until I found this pack. Axel took me in, and I've been here ever since."

He wipes the tears that are still falling down his cheeks away and looks at me, waiting for me to say something. What do I say, though? Comrade just told me his life story, and I can't even say anything. What do you say when you find out that one of your friends and guardians saw his own parents being ripped apart and didn't get any sympathy or help from their pack?

"I'm sorry," I whisper. That's all I can say. I take him in my arms again, and he gladly accepts the hug. I don't know how long we stay like that, but Comrade pulls back first with a small smile.

"We can't change our past, but we can change our future, and I certainly have," he tells me in a whisper. I smile at him as a single tear slide down my cheek.

"I couldn't be happier that you maneuvered your way into my future, Comrade. I couldn't be happier," I tell him back.

We spend the rest of the day on the couch just talking about random stuff and watching the worst movies in history. We laugh, we sing, we snort. This is the happiest I've been in a long time, and it's all thanks to Comrade and his wild and mischievous ways.

When the sun starts to go down, Axel comes into the room. He announces that it's time for me to head back upstairs. I pout at him, but he gives me a look that says, "Don't argue with me." So I say goodnight to Comrade and head upstairs in Axel's arms.

I'm happy about today. I got to relax without the thought of the triplets and the war weighing on my shoulders. I just spend the day relaxing with Comrade, and that's something I haven't done in a very long time.

"How was your day, sweetheart?" Axel asks as he gently places me on the bed. I shrug my shoulders and grin. Axel raises a questioning eyebrow at me, but I just shake my head.

"Today was the most fun I've had in two months!" I exclaim. Axel laughs at me before kissing me on the forehead.

"Get some sleep. I have something special planned for us tomorrow, and I don't want you falling asleep half way through it," he tells me while pointing an accusing finger at me. I giggle at him. He's so childish at times.

"Where are we going?" I ask as a yawn escapes my lips. Axel brings the sheets up so that they sit just below my chin.

"It's a surprise," he whispers, but before I can continue to interrogate him, I fall into a dreamless sleep.

"Why can't you just tell me where we're going?" I complain for the hundredth time. When I woke up this morning, Axel told me to dress in something comfy then proceeded to blindfold me. I've been blindfolded for the past three hours!

"Celina, stop asking! You'll know when we get there," Axel snaps back at me. I huff and cross my arms on my chest. We stay silent after that.

It's nice to know that Axel is doing something special for me. I guess you can call this our first date. That's funny, I'm on my first date, and I'm pregnant. Nice.

It's also nice to just escape for a little while. With everything that's going on with training and the war, it'll be nice to relax for a bit.

Axel, in particular, has been really stressed out. The day before yesterday, he started work at five in the morning, and I know for a fact that he got to bed just after midnight. It's not healthy for him to be working hours like that! I guess the prospect of war and me giving birth are really getting to him...

"We're here!" Axel suddenly announces, bringing me out of my thoughts.

"Finally," I mutter as Axel gets out of the car, slamming his door behind him. A second later, my door's being opened and Axel's guiding me down what seems like a very uneven road.

I don't say anything as I know he will probably ignore me. I can't keep the excited smile off my face, though, and I'm guessing that Axel is grinning like the Cheshire cat in front of me.

Axel's hands suddenly let go of mine, and I panic slightly, that's before the blindfold is taken away from my eyes. Before I can properly look at my surroundings, Axel's hand covers my eyes. I groan, and Axel chuckles at my reaction.

"Keep your eyes closed for a second, sweetheart," Axel's voice speaks right next to my ear in a whisper. I shiver as his warm breath hits it and travels down my neck.

Axel removes his hand, and I obey like a good girl and keep my eyes shut. I hear some shuffling before Axel gives me the all clear to open my eyes.

I do and gasp at what's before me. A huge, clear, blue lake is the first thing I see. The water sparkles as the sun hits it and the black swans swim around gracefully, basking in the morning sun. My eyes then travel to the rest of my surroundings, and I see we're in a secluded part of the lake's edge. The area's surrounded by trees, but there's a clearing just before the lake, that's where we're standing right now. Birds chirp happily in the trees, and I can hear animals running on the forest floor. All in all, it's absolutely beautiful.

I look at Axel with wide eyes. At Axel's feet, a picnic blanket has been set up. Cakes, sandwiches, biscuits, and all sorts of drinks are all neatly placed on a certain part of the blanket, waiting to be eaten.

I look back to Axel with teary eyes. The grin that is on his face suddenly drops. He races over to me and engulfs me in a hug.

"What's wrong, sweetheart? Don't you like it?" he asks with nervousness lacing his voice.

I stare at him in shock. "Axel, it's beautiful. I can't believe you've done all this for me," I tell him honestly in a whisper. Axel breathes a sigh of relief at my news. I look at him questioningly. His shining, greyish silver eyes lock with mine.

"I thought you wouldn't like it," he whispers as he places his hands on my stomach. I roll my eyes at him.

"Of course, you would think that. You know, sometimes I think—" I'm abruptly cut off when Axel places a soft kiss on my lips, silencing me. He pulls away too soon, causing me to pout at him. He chuckles.

"Relax, sweetheart. You can have me all you like tonight," he whispers huskily in my ear. I shiver as different scenarios enter my mind. I shake my head to get rid of them, blushing.

Axel smirks at me, knowing full well what I'm thinking about. I lightly slap his chest and make my way to the blanket. Before I can sit down, Axel is behind me and helping me slowly lower onto the blanket. Once I'm safely sitting, Axel makes himself comfortable behind me, pulling me to his chest.

"I can sit down on my own," I grumble. Axel just laughs at me, the sound reverberating off his chest, causing the movement to also move me.

"I know pretty soon you won't be able to," Axel tells me while placing his hands on my ever growing stomach. I swear I'm bigger than I was yesterday!

"Why's that?" I ask with a small grin.

"You'll be too big to move," he says, and Axel's laugh soon fills the air. I turn my neck awkwardly to gape at him. Did he really just say that?

"You bet I did!" Axel says through his laughter after reading my mind.

I huff and cross my arms on my chest. Stupid Alpha...

Axel soon quiets down and wraps his arms around me again. I lean into his touch as he rubs soothing circles on my stomach with his thumbs.

"I can't wait till you have our pups. We're going to be parents," Axel tells me while resting his head on my shoulder.

"Great, I'm gonna be a mummy at seventeen, and you're gonna be a daddy at 20. What more could we want?" I ask sarcastically. Axel chuckles at me before going quiet. It's calming to know that Axel is relaxed and his mind is off the subject of war. It doesn't only put him at peace, but also me.

For the rest of the day, we joke around, laugh, and eat the food, with me devouring three-quarters of it. Just as the sun's setting over the lake, giving it a beautiful sparkle and a magical golden glow, Axel stands up and takes me with him. I smile up at him, and he smiles back.

"Celina, I love you with all my heart, and until the day I die, I will never leave you. You are my world and everything. Now, as a thank you gift, here's a little something. I hope you accept it." Axel's voice holds nothing but sincerity and love that it actually pulls at my heartstrings.

Axel suddenly gets down on one knee and presents a black velvet box. He opens it to reveal the most beautiful ring I have ever seen. I gasp in shock as the scene before me unfolds.

"Celina, will you do the honours of being my wife?" Axel asks with a wide smile.

He stares lovingly into my eyes, so much love that I'm rendered speechless. That and the fact he just asked me to marry him!

All my life, I never thought I would find my mate. All my life, I never thought I would escape the hellhole I called home. All my life, I never anticipated myself being pregnant at 16 and being asked to marry my mate at 17. So what do I say? Yes, of course!

I nod my head happily as the biggest smile I've ever worn blooms on my face. Axel gently takes a hold of my left hand and slips the ring on my ring finger. I stare at it in awe. It's beautiful, to say the least. It has a diamond shaped like a rhombus, with smaller black, blue, and violet gems surrounding it. It's all held together on a gold rose and white gold band that's been swirled to perfection.

Axel stands in front of me with a wide smile on his face. Nobody in the entire world can match my happiness right at this moment, not even if they tried.

"Celina Night," Axel whispers, my soon to be name rolling off his tongue. "You will be my wife soon."

Axel's lips soon capture mine in a passionate kiss that leads to a lot more.

As I lay down on the blanket in Axel's arms, staring up at the sky, I can't help wonder, how did I ever get so lucky?

29

CELINA

I'm happily sitting in the kitchen talking to Callum and Comrade when a ferocious growl is heard around the whole pack house. I freeze once I recognize it as Axel's.

I bolt up off my seat and race towards his office the fastest I can, looking like a running whale. Callum and Comrade are trailing behind me seemingly trying to get me to slow down.

I burst into Axel's office to see it destroyed to an extent where you can't even recognize it. I look at Axel with wide eyes. His chest is heaving evenly, his eyes are glowing silver, and his nails elongate. I slowly and cautiously walk up to him.

"Axel?" I ask softly while placing my hand on his cheek. His head snaps towards me, his eyes softening a bit before they go back to their hard, glowing state.

"The patrols that were running had an encounter with some Moonlight Pack members. Apparently, they've been monitoring our every move," he growls while moving from my touch and punching the wall, creating another of several holes.

"What happened to the patrols?" I ask quietly. Axel whips around to face me.

"They're fine, only minor injuries. They told Doctor Aileen that it was a warning," he growls again. I wrap my arms around his waist, trying to get him to calm down.

"What does this mean, Alpha?" Callum asks as well. Although he's the Beta and Axel's best friend, you always show respect by using the title given when a higher ranked in the pack is ticked off.

Axel's arms tighten around my waist as he breathes in my scent.

"It means that the war may be coming sooner than we think," he says, then hesitates before pulling back and looking me in the eye. "They also know that Celina's pregnant."

I freeze at his words and go into a state of shock. They know? This changes everything. What if they come after me? What if they try to kill me? Or worse, kill my pups?

In my shocked state, I don't hear Axel yelling out orders to Callum and Comrade. His voice is probably loud and clear, but all I can hear is my heart beating in my chest and my uneven breathing.

I feel someone shake my shoulders, and I place my shocked eyes on Axel's worried ones. His mouth moves, but no sound comes out. His face grows more worried by the second, but I can't do a thing about it. I'm in shock.

Without thinking, I rip out of his hold and bolt out of the room. I run all the way to the backyard without stopping. I continue to run towards the forest until I come to a clearing. I drop to my knees and will the tears to fall, but they don't. My body feels numb, and I don't care what happens to me at this moment. Not even the fact that I've just run at a fast pace bothers me right now.

I place my hand on my stomach and take calming breaths. Everything's going to be fine. Everything's going to be fine. I just repeat this over and over in my head, but no matter how many times I think it, I know everything's going to be the opposite.

The snapping of a twig brings me out of my calm state. My head snaps around, but I make no move to leave. Another twig snaps and the person finally decides to grace me with his presence.

To my utter relief, Callum steps out from the trees. He takes one look at me, and his whole body slumps with relief. I release the breath I don't know I've been holding as Callum rushes to my side. He embraces me and finally my tears start to fall.

"Celina, thank the Moon Goddess!" Callum exclaims happily. He continues to stroke my hair, soothing me.

"Shh, shh, Celina. Everything's fine, everything's going to be alright," he coos in my ear. I cry harder at his words because I know everything isn't going to be alright. Damon knows I'm pregnant, and he'll use it against Axel.

A few minutes later, I pull away from Callum. I smile weakly through my tears and wipe the remaining ones away. I have to be strong, crying won't help.

"Thanks," I whisper. Callum smiles at me while helping me up.

"Come on, we're way too close to the border. We're literally sitting on it," he says a little panicky.

As we make our way back, a voice that is all too familiar stops us in our tracks, speaking in a taunting voice, "Well, if it isn't little, pathetic Celina Heart."

I shiver as his cold voice is carried through the once peaceful air.

I slowly turn around and there, standing with only shorts on, is none other than Damon. A vicious growl escapes Callum as he pushes me behind him. Damon smirks at the action before looking Callum up and down.

"Well, you're certainly not her mate, so you must be one of her two guardians," he taunts, earning another growl from Callum. So, he really has been watching us.

'Celina, mind link Axel now!' Callum's powerful voice enters my head. I quickly obey and try to get into Axel's head. He's blocked. I start to bang on his wall, trying my hardest to get through to him, but it doesn't budge.

I groan internally then mind link the next best person: Comrade. He answers immediately.

'Snow? Thank the Moon Goddess! Where the hell are you?' he yells at me after having his little relief session.

'Callum, where are we?' I quickly ask since he's a little preoccupied watching Damon.

'West border,' is all he says before releasing a growl when Damon takes a step forward.

'West border, now hurry!' I scream through to Comrade. I hear some rustling and turn to my left to see a wolf growling and snarling at us.

Callum whips his head around and growls loudly at the wolf. He growls right back. I snap my head to Damon when I hear him chuckle.

"Seems like you're in a bit of a predicament," he says with another chuckle. Two more wolves come out of the woods, one behind, and one to my right. We're surrounded. I press myself closer to Callum's back, seeking comfort.

"It's ok, Celina. We're going to be fine," he says softly in my mind. I nod on his back.

"Here's what I'm going to propose: you hand over Celina, and we will stop this war. You don't hand over Celina, and we will strike in exactly two months," Damon bargains. I can sense Callum's wolf trying to break free, so I gently rub his back with my hand.

"I guess we'll see you in two months then!" an angry and totally pissed off voice sounds from behind me. I whip around to see Axel standing with only shorts on. I cry out for joy in my head, thinking it's not the best thing to do out loud at the moment.

"Now, you release my mate and Beta and go on your way with no harm done to you," Axel says in his alpha voice while squaring his shoulders out. Of course, Damon isn't affected by this, but the wolves surrounding us are, and they slowly start to back up.

"Your turn, Damon," Axel growls, spitting out his name like a curse.

"Two months, Axel, two months," he taunts the reminder with a smirk before disappearing into the darkness of the trees.

Next thing I know, I'm being ripped away from Callum and into Axel's chest.

"Mine," he growls lowly. He buries his head in my neck, lightly kissing my mark and breathing in my scent. I run my hands through his hair, trying to get him to relax.

"That's right, Axel. I'm yours and only yours," I coo him. He seems to visibly relax at my words. I glance at Callum, and he nods, already understanding without me having to say anything.

"Alpha, it's not safe for the Luna to be out here. You should return her to the pack house," Callum says in all seriousness and in his beta voice. I've never heard him use it, so it's a surprise when I do. It holds just as much power as Axel's, just a little less.

Axel carefully picks me up bridal style and takes off running to the pack house. He ignores the pack and runs up the stairs to our room. He plops me down on the bed before moving in next to me. He pulls my back against his chest and buries his head in my neck.

"Don't run like that ever again, Celina. You almost gave me a heart attack when I couldn't find you," Axel whispers on my neck. I sigh.

"I'm sorry. I was just so upset that we were being watched, and we didn't even know it," I reply in a whisper.

Axel growls again, pulling his face off my neck. His eyes shine with a new intensity as they start to glow.

"It will never happen again." His voice holds a promise in it, letting me know that it will never happen again as long as he's around.

"I've mind linked Callum to sort out a stricter patrol circuit, and starting tomorrow, all training is going up a few notches," he says firmly, his mouth forming into a frown and his eyebrows pulling together.

I smile at him before some of my alpha female side kicks in, and my smile turns into a frown. "Don't work the younger wolves too hard. We don't want them too tired to not be able to fight," I tell him firmly. Axel smirks at me before kissing me softly.

"Yes, Ma'am," he mocks. I roll my eyes at him before the urge to pee suddenly overtakes me.

I wriggle out of Axel's hold and waddle my way to the bathroom.

"Stay right there, Mister," I say while pointing a finger at him. He winks at me to which I chuckle and enter the bathroom.

Once I've done my business, I plop back down on the bed. Axel's hand immediately comes to my stomach, stroking it with his thumb.

"I swear, you were smaller when we went on our date a few days ago," Axel says, confused. I sigh, aggravated.

"I know! These pups of yours just don't want to stop growing! In a few days, I won't be able to even walk!" I exclaim with a bit of an attitude.

"Good, that means you can't wander off and get attacked in the woods," Axel replies cheekily, but with a sad glint in his eyes.

"Yeah, yeah," I joke, trying to lighten the now sad mood.

It's been about a month since my little encounter with Damon and a month less till he's going to attack.

I was right when I said I wouldn't be able to walk in a few days because exactly three days after saying that, I couldn't get out of bed! Now think about this, how embarrassing would it be for you if you needed help in going to the toilet every time? Pretty much embarrassing, huh?

The pups are kicking a lot more now, and the cravings haven't died down one bit. When these pups are born, they're going to be a lot to handle.

So anyway, for the past month I've been entertaining myself with movies, word searches, and other boring things. I've even done some colouring for goodness sake! Children's colouring to be exact.

I haven't seen Axel a lot in the past month either. He seems to be stressing and working way longer than usual with only minimal sleep. I worry about him. He's too stressed for my liking...

A knock on the door interrupts my thoughts. I glance up and notice Callum in the doorway with Comrade behind him. I beam at them.

"Hey!" I exclaim, happy to have some company. They beam back at me.

"Hey," they say simultaneously. They walk in, and that's when I notice that Callum is holding three massive bowls of popcorn while Comrade is holding a stack of movies, ranging from Disney to 'shoot em up, bang em up.'

I grin at them and move to the middle of the bed so that they can sit on the sides. It's a king size after all. Comrade lays all the movies out and tells me to close my eyes.

"Now point in a random direction," he tells me, which I do. I open my eyes to see that I pointed at *The Legend of Ron Burgundy*. I squeal and fist-pump the air, they both chuckle at me. Ron Burgundy is the best comedy movie in the world! If you haven't seen it, watch it!

Comrade puts the movie in, and we all sit back to watch with popcorn in hand and staring intently at the screen.

I laugh harder as Ron gets a panicked look on his face and starts screaming, "he's gonna die." I glance at Callum and Comrade to see that they're also laughing but seem a bit off.

After the scene ends, I paused the movie earning me questioning looks from the both of them.

"What's wrong? You guys seem off," I tell them, looking at them both curiously.

Comrade lies back, resting his head against the headboard and closing his eyes.

"Should we tell her?" he suddenly asks Callum. I whip my head around to look at Callum. "Tell me what?"

"I guess." Callum sighs. He lifts himself up from the headboard and gives Comrade a look, almost like he's asking him if he's sure about this. Comrade just nods and looks away.

"Celina, since the Moonlight Pack knows our weaknesses and our strengths, Axel has asked us to fight. The Moonlight Pack won't see it coming, and we're gonna use that to our advantage. Since becoming your guardians, Comrade and I have been upgraded, if you will. We're stronger, faster, stealthier, so we'll be major assets in the fight," Callum tells me with a soft voice, Comrade mumbling an agreement.

I stare at him in shock and sadness, but also, pride knowing that my guardians are not the only ones protecting me, but the pack, too.

"You guys are gonna fight?" I ask sadly, despite my pride. Two pairs of arms wrap around my waist at that moment, Callum's and Comrade's.

"We're sorry, Snow, but our pack needs us and, as much as we want to protect you, we have a duty to Axel, the pack, and even you, the Luna," Comrade tells me softly. I sniffle but accept what has to be done.

I press play, trying to avoid the conversation, and watch as the movie starts up again. We continue to watch, but the playful atmosphere is gone.

When it hits late afternoon, I say goodbye to Callum and Comrade since I feel a bit sleepy. At the exit, they both kiss me on the top of my head and say goodnight. Before they can close the door fully, though, a hand lands on it. I look at the door curiously to see Axel standing there with a small smile. I smile widely at him and open my arms as if to say 'hug me.' I haven't seen him in ages!

He doesn't waste a second as he crosses the room and takes me in his arms, hugging the life out of me. Without a word, he climbs on the bed and sits behind me while placing his hands on my absolutely massive stomach.

"I missed you," I whisper as my eyes start to get droopy.

"I missed you too, but now you need to sleep," he whispers in my ear. I obey like a good girl and fall into a sleep filled with what I imagine to be the upcoming war. I just hope that Axel, Comrade, and Callum stay safe...

30

AXEL

I wake up to someone kissing me softly on the lips. I immediately respond, knowing it's Celina. I pull back after a while and open my eyes and see her face.

"Hey, sweetheart," I murmur softly. She smiles at me and brushes some of my white hair off my face. I always wonder why I get the white hair and Celina gets the black hair. That's just how fate works, I guess...

We sleepily get ready for the day, with me taking extra time. I haven't had a good night's sleep in two months so cuddling up to my mate before three in the morning is a nice feeling.

I slowly carry Celina down the stairs and into my office. I place her down on the couch that is opposite my desk while she gives me a confused look. I can't blame her. I make her stay cooped up in our room for over a month since she can't walk, just to keep her safe.

"I need some advice on things and who better to ask than my beautiful, lovely mate," I say innocently. Celina just rolls her eyes, not saying anything.

I make my way to my desk and pull out the first matter at hand: the war.

The war is all I've been focusing on for the past two months. With the recent news that we've been watched, I've asked Callum and Comrade to join the fight. I'm confident since they've become stronger. They're sort of like our secret weapon. This may sound like I'm using them, but in a way, I am. They are essential to this pack's survival, and I will do anything to protect my pack and the ones I love.

I clear my throat to catch Celina's attention. Her head whips to me, a small smile on her face. I smile back.

"Celina, have Callum and Comrade told you the news about the war?" I ask calmly, trying hard not to raise suspicion.

Celina's face drops. I'm not sure if that's because of the mention of the war or if she already knows...

"Yes, I know," she states in a quiet whisper. She avoids eye contact after that, getting engrossed in her thoughts.

I know Celina loves Callum and Comrade, but they're also her guardians. They are alive to protect her and make sure she's safe at all possible times. Like a second mate, but without the lust.

I continue to look back at the paperwork in front of me.

- Members of the Moonlight Pack have been spotted on the borders of our territory but have not crossed over or came in within 100 metres.

- The Greenwood Pack has offered to support us.

- The Firelight Pack has offered to support us.

- The Harold's Pack has declined to help us.

- One Moonlight Pack member was spotted on our land.

All the rest are the same, what packs aren't and are helping and updates on the Moonlight Pack. I can't wait to get my hands on that son of a bitch Damon and tear him to shreds! He's what started all of this, and I'm gonna end it. Him and everyone else in his pathetic pack isn't gonna live to see another day once I'm through with them.

A growl escapes me, making Celina gasp from across the room. My head snaps to my frightened mate. I instinctively rein in my wolf so as not to frighten her anymore.

"Sorry, sweetheart, this is just so infuriating! The Moonlight Pack is causing trouble, and so far, only two packs are offering to help us. It's all Damon's bloody fault!" I roar as I throw a chair across the room.

My breathing comes out heavy, my hands ball into fists, and my eyes are glowing silver.

"Come here, Axel," the little voice of my mate orders. I stalk my way over to her, my wolf, and I still pissed off.

Her small hands land on my shoulders, massaging them and making the tension leave. My wolf slowly starts to relax at the feel of our mate comforting us.

I take Celina in my arms, breathing in her addicting scent. My hands trail up and down her back, sending a shiver down her spine.

"I'm sorry," I whisper as I softly kiss my mark, earning me a quiet moan. I love the effect I have on her, it makes me smile.

"That's ok, just control yourself," she whispers back, running her hand through my hair. I sigh in contentment at the feeling.

"We have a meeting with Doctor Aileen today," Celina informs me. I pull away from her in confusion. We do?

"We do?" I ask, voicing my thoughts. Celina nods her head giggling. I smile and scoop her into my arms.

"Well then, let's get to that appointment," I announce with a grin. It's something to get my mind off things anyway.

I run out my office with a laughing Celina in my arms and head straight to the medic room. I burst through the door with Celina laughing her head off and me almost doubling over from laughing so much. I don't even know what's funny... I guess that's what makes it funny. This is the most fun I've had in ages, all because of my little mate.

Doctor Aileen looks up at us with a start but relaxes once she realizes it's just us.

"Alpha, Luna. What can I do for you?" she asks politely.

I gently place Celina on the bed and turn to Doctor Aileen.

"We've come for our supposed appointment." I mimic Celina's words, making her whack me on the arm. I chuckle as I see her eyes sparkle.

"Oh! I thought that would be in another few hours," Doctor Aileen says in surprise. It's obviously directed towards Celina because she has a sheepish smile on her face and Doctor Aileen is staring right at her.

"Sorry," she mumbles, her cheeks going a soft pink. I smile at the colour, she's actually blushing. She looks adorable when she blushes.

"Nonsense, Luna! It's fine! I'll just do the testing now," Doctor Aileen says with a warm smile on her face.

As Doctor Aileen sets up, I make my way to a fidgeting Celina on the bed. About a week ago, she couldn't walk anymore so it's rare for her to be out of bed. I'm just happy that the reason she can't walk is because of our pups and not anything else...

"What's this appointment for anyway?" I ask Celina quietly. Her fidgeting halts as she stares at me in shock. What?

"Do you not listen to me at all?" she asks dumbfounded. Confusion passes over my face then a thinking expression. What has she told me over the past week? She's told me about how much she hates staying in bed, how much she hates not being able to walk, how much she hates not being able to spend time with me, and how much she hates not being able to do anything herself... She's pretty much whined for the past week. I smile sheepishly at her, having no clue what she's talking about.

She rolls her eyes at me and whacks my head.

"Ow! What was that for?" I yell as I feign hurt. She didn't have to hit me! She rolls her eyes again.

"If you had been listening, you would've known that today we are finding out the gender of our pups! I swear men never listen to a pregnant lady..." She trails off, but all I hear is gender and pups. I get to know if I'm having boys, girls, or both?

What about names? We haven't discussed names yet. Why didn't I know about this? Wow, I sound like a girl. I grin mentally. I'm losing my man pride without even knowing it.

Before my thoughts go on a rampage, Doctor Aileen pops up again. I notice that she's hooked up all the machines and has the wand and gel ready to scan Celina.

She pulls up Celina's top and places a fair amount of gel on her stomach. I grip Celina's hand as I feel her nerves travel through me from the mate bond.

"Everything is gonna be alright, sweetheart. Don't worry," I coo to her through our link. She merely nods at me, focusing all her attention on the screen.

I also turn my attention to the screen and beam at the image in front of me. Three healthy looking pups all growing in my beautiful mate's womb. There are two slightly bigger ones and a smaller one that seems to be cuddled between the two. I bet the small one is a girl, my baby girl. The thought makes my smile even bigger.

"Well, it seems like you're having a baby boy, another baby boy, and a little baby girl. Congratulations," Doctor Aileen says excitedly while beaming at us.

Doctor Aileen walks out the door, giving us some privacy. I continue to gaze at the screen in complete awe. Two baby boys and a baby girl, my baby girl.

Celina hasn't even given birth yet, and our little girl's already got me wrapped around her tiny little finger!

A soft hand lands on my chin, turning my head. I face Celina with glassy eyes.

"We're having a baby girl," I whisper, turning my head back to the screen. She chuckles at me.

"Two baby boys as well, Axel. Don't forget about your sons and future Alpha," Celina teases. I turn back to her with a smile on my face and kiss her softly.

"We're gonna be Mum and Dad," I whisper as the thought finally settles into my mind. "We're gonna be Mum and Dad," I repeat a bit louder. Celina's eyes widen, and she raises an eyebrow. "Hell, I'm gonna be a Dad!" I exclaim, pure joy radiating off me.

Celina bursts out laughing for the second time today next to me as I look down at her with happiness in my eyes. I'm gonna be a Dad...

"Yes, Axel, you're gonna be a Dad. You have been for three months," she says while giggling. I wrap my arms around her, placing my hands on her stomach.

"I can't wait for you to give birth to our pups," I whisper in Celina's ear, love, and adoration coursing through my veins. All we have to figure out now is how to win the war...

After I take Celina back to our room and place her in bed, I head straight back down to my office, calling Callum on the way.

Callum's sitting on the couch going through all the files we could find about the Moonlight Pack, trying to find something we can use against them.

I'm going through dates. About a month ago, we had a run-in with Damon. The prick had the guts to show up on my land! He must be absolutely desperate to get Celina back. It can't just be for the maid service. It has to be for more...

Going off from the topic a bit there... so, we had a run-in, and he stated that he would attack in exactly two months. That exact day is the estimated time for Celina to give birth. See my problem?

If the war and Celina giving birth happen on the same day, I honestly don't know what I will do. I don't know who will die and who will live. I don't know if Celina will live to see another day, but I do know that I have to be by her side no matter what, always and forever.

That's my first problem. My second is what Damon really wants with Celina.

I'm sure that he doesn't just want her for maid services. Maybe it could've started out like that, but thinking of a bigger picture, it can't be that simple. The only problem is, I don't know what he wants to do with Celina, and I intend to find out.

Callum has shined some possibilities on me that I never wanted to enter my brain. For example, he said that maybe Damon wanted Celina as a mate, for her power, and for her pups. I have to hold back a growl as the thoughts enter my mind once again. Let's just say that Callum didn't confront me for a few days after that. No one did.

I shake my head and look back to the dates. That's the only important thing right now, nothing else.

8th November, Friday, 2013

That's the day Damon confronted us. It's been a month since then. One more month and we'll have our war and our pups. Hopefully, one after the other...

A sudden loud growl brings me out of my thoughts. My head snaps up to Callum's frustrated eyes as he throws the papers in aggravation.

"This is hopeless! There's nothing in here that shows weakness, strengths, pack alliances, nothing! It's absolute shit!" Callum yells, throwing his hands up in the air. His eyes start to turn black as his wolf fights for control. I stand up and make my way to him calmly.

"Callum, calm down," I state in my alpha voice. Callum may be the beta, but my power ranks over him so it does affect him in a way.

"This is pointless, Axel," he says, a lot calmer this time. "We have nothing to go on for information. This war's in a month's time, we're getting nowhere, and Celina will be having your pups soon. On top of that, Christmas is coming up, and we always hold a big Christmas feast for the whole pack and we have to get presents for all the children. When did life get so hard?"

He falls back onto the couch, me joining him. We both stay silent as we stare at the wall in front of us. When did life get so hard? Before Celina came, we never had a war to worry about. Before Celina came, we never had to deal with other packs. Before Celina came, we were never stressed about Christmas, out of all the holidays to stress over. Plus, before Celina came, pups weren't even in the picture!

That's when it all clicks, like a switch going off inside of me. All this pain, stress, and heartache, is all because of Celina. Ever since she came, pups, wars, stress, and every other thing you can think of, just sort of fall into place because of her. She's the reason why I'm getting no sleep. She's the reason why my pack's in danger. She's the reason why I'm focusing more on family than on my alpha duties. She's the reason. Celina's the reason.

A loud growl erupts in my head as my thoughts start to spiral out of control.

"Don't you dare think of our mate that way! She's not the reason all of this has happened!" my wolf growls at me, baring his teeth in my mind.

"Then tell me why! Tell me why all of this has happened! Tell me why!" I growl back, frustrated with myself. Everything's just so complicated, and my mind just can't fathom it.

"Ask your mother," is all my wolf says, calmly I might add, before disappearing into the corners of my mind.

My mother? He wants me to ask my mother? Actually, she would know. She would know why everything's happening. She's the Moon Goddess, after all...

With that thought in mind, I launch myself off the couch. I don't register Callum calling me as I race through the pack house and out the front door, shifting as soon as I get to the tree line.

I run for a good half hour before I come to the place I'm looking for. Some people call it the *summoning field* while others call it the *calling valley*. Me? I call it my phone home.

I shift back to human form, pulling on a pair of shorts that are tucked behind a tree. I make my way to the middle of the small clearing that is scattered with four leaf clovers.

This small clearing is in the middle of my territory. This one place has four leaf clovers that are actually illegal to pick because they really do give you good luck. The last person who picked one was never heard of again. The clovers are said to be weaved by the Moon Goddess herself, but I don't even know if that's true.

As I stand in the clearing, I start to hum a little tune that I remember my mother singing to me when I was born all those years ago. A wind starts to whip around me as I continue to hum the tune. My eyes shoot open as silver swirls erupt from them, climbing to the point where I can't even see them. I start to slowly levitate off the ground until I'm above the highest tree in sight.

For me, this is normal. I would do this every time I was sent to help the Shaded Wolves.

After another few minutes, everything becomes quiet. I look around to find myself in a familiar room. The walls are made of crystal, the floor gold, the ceiling a never ending blue sky, and a throne high on a podium.

I slowly start to walk towards the throne, closer to someone I haven't seen in centuries.

A woman with hair as white as snow, skin as pale as ice, silver eyes as bright as the moon, and lips as red as a rose comes into view. She's wearing a crystal dress that seems to clutch at her body but fall around her at the same time.

When I'm in front of the throne, I get down on one knee with my head down.

"Moon Goddess," I say with pride, joy, and a tad of nervousness in my voice.

My mother slowly rises from her throne, a large crystal crown resting on her head with a multi-coloured gem smack bay in the middle. It represents all wolves that have existed.

She descends the stairs leading up to her throne and stands before me.

"Rise," her melodic voice echoes throughout the room, willing me to obey.

I do as she says and rises to come face to face with the woman I call my mother. She smiles warmly at me before pulling me into a hug.

"My son," she whispers in my ear. I sigh at the sound of her motherly voice, feeling myself relax.

"I haven't seen you in centuries. You must tell me what has occurred," she says. To some, her way of talking may seem strange, but to me it's normal, and that's how I talk around her as well.

"Much has happened over the past few centuries, mother. Pack feuds being something major..." I begin. I continue to tell her everything that has happened over the last few hundred years. She doesn't interrupt, just stays silent, and takes in everything I'm saying, absorbing it and engraving it into her mind.

"Well, it sounds as if there is more hate than love, sadness than happiness, grief than celebration. It's your job to fix that, my son. It always has been, so why are you not doing your job?" My mother's voice echoes through the grand room, but my voice does not answer.

This is the reason I've come here for, to ask for her help and guidance.

"Mother..." I trail off wearily. My mother's eyes light up when she realizes I called her mother. It's a very rare occurrence when I actually call her mother. I usually call her Moon Goddess out of respect.

"That is why I'm here. For the last two decades, I have been part of the Nightfall Pack. Starting out as a mere child since I'm able to regenerate. I was taken in by the Alpha and Luna because they could not bear a child. I grew up, and now I'm the Alpha of the pack," I explain, but stop for a moment to let it all sink in.

"I have heard rumours that you have become an Alpha, but I was not sure what to believe. I guess I do now, though." She smiles at me and places a hand on my cheek. I smile back at her before moving on.

"I met my mate a few months ago and—" I continue to say before my mother's hand leaves me and she steps back.

"I beg your pardon? Did you just say you met your mate?" she asks in disbelief. I silently nod.

"Who is she?" she demands to know.

I hesitate before answering, "Her name is Celina Goddess Heart. She is the daughter of King Ronald Heart and Queen Rosemary Heart."

My mother freezes for a fragment of a second, something only I will ever see: the Moon Goddess in shock.

"She's the little girl I saved all those many years ago?" my mother questions quietly. I nod again.

"Little Celina Heart is all grown up and my son's mate. Is it true that you are having pups, triplets?" she asks again with a bright smile on her face.

"Yes, mother, two boys and a girl," I say with pride as the image of my pups fill my mind. "May I continue?" I ask politely. She motions for me to continue with her small, delicate hand. "As I was saying, I met my mate, and since I have met her, many unplanned things have happened. A war has broken out between her old pack and her now new pack. We are expecting triplets and many other minor details. The reason I have come today is to ask you for help. What do I do?" I plead.

My mother just stares at me for a moment. Her moon-like eyes look calculating as she comes to a perfect conclusion.

"Let fate take its course," she says wisely. I stare at her with furrowed eyebrows and a deep frown.

"What is our fate, mother?" I question with a pleading tone.

Her voice is full of wisdom as she says, "It is what you make of it. Only you and little Celina Heart can control your fate. It is not her fault alone that this has happened. It is all your faults. Celina for allowing herself close to you, Callum for accepting his role as her guardian and being your Beta, Comrade for accepting his role as her guardian and as the actual person who first made her meet you and who first made her feel safe, comfortable, and happy. Then there's you and your faults. You fought for Celina. You fought for your mate just like any mate would do, but that simple action has led to a series of events that could never be changed.

"There are many paths to choose from, but only one path shall you take. You may be led by many directions, but only one direction shall you seek. My son, your fate is not sealed, nor is Celina's. You are both unique, different, and have found each other. You both have a past, present, and future. You both must lead the way."

As my mother's words start to sink in, the room starts to disappear. The gold floor begins to dim, the crystal walls lose their shine, and my mother slowly starts to fade. My time is up.

31

CELINA

Lying in bed all day is really boring when you have no company and nothing to do. I didn't know that? Well, I know now!

For the past few days, Axel has been acting really weird. He keeps mumbling things and always has his thinking face on whenever he's around me. He looks even more stressed, and he won't tell me why. I don't think it's about the war or anything like that. I'm not sure what it's about.

A soft knock sounds at the door. I look at it curiously, wondering who it is. Knowing it's probably Callum or Comrade, though, my curiosity dies.

"Come in," I call in a bored tone. The person's head that pops through surprises me to say the least.

Chloe's head of blonde hair peeks through the doorway with a small smile on her face.

"Hey..." she says nervously, not fully coming into the room.

My whole mood changes once I see her. I feel happy and excited that I'll have someone to talk to. Finally!

"Hey! Come in, come in," I say cheerfully, motioning with my hand. She shyly steps in with her hands behind her back. She makes her way to the foot of the bed, biting her lip nervously.

"So, how's it going?" she asks. I raise an eyebrow at her unsure tone. She bites her lip harder before literally vomiting out words. "Ok, so I went shopping the other day and felt really bad because you've been stuck in here for months on end with nothing to do, so I decided to get this for you because I think it's really neat and I think it'd be good for the pups and I think you'll really like it and so I bought it. Please like it!" she exclaims, her eyes going wide with anxiousness.

A half grin spreads across my face at her nervousness, she's so cute. That grin quickly drops when she brings her hands out from behind her back. I stare at the objects in shock. She actually got something special for the pups.

"Oh, Chloe," I whisper. She smiles as she takes a seat next to me on the bed, placing the gifts on my lap.

"Like I said, I thought they were neat, so I got them for you. That one is for the boy," she says and points to a light blue blanket with the words 'A Special Gift' sewn into it in dark blue.

"This one is for the other boy," she says again pointing to another blanket, but this one is dark blue and has the words 'Mummy's Boy' sewn into it in light blue. That makes me smile.

Before she can continue on with the gifts, I ask, "How do you even know what we're having?"

She grins at me with a knowing glint in her eye.

"News travels fast when your Luna of 17 is the last surviving white wolf, the strongest Shaded Wolf ever known and is pregnant with two boys and a girl," she explains in a duh tone. I roll my eyes at her playfulness, but let her continue.

"The last one's my favourite," she says quietly and picks up the last gift, directing my full attention to it.

It's absolutely beautiful. It's a gold chain with a locket on the end in the shape of a heart with the words 'Believe in Love' engraved on it. A baby doll with a pretty purple dress actually has the necklace clasped around her neck. It's so adorable and beautiful.

"I thought that your baby girl would want something special to call hers. I know it's a bit more extravagant than the blankets, but a girl has to feel like they're loved and what better way than to get her a doll and a necklace?" Chloe lightly jokes.

I stare at her in absolute shock and awe. I don't believe she spent all this money on my pups because she thought they looked neat.

"You're incredible, you know that?" I ask quietly as tears come to my eyes. She shrugs with a grin on her face.

"I know," she boasts. I laugh along with her at her lame excuse of a joke.

"So..." she says, trailing off as all playfulness leaves her face and is replaced by utter seriousness. "What's up with you and Axel? You guys seem a bit... off."

I sigh heavily. What is going on with Axel and me?

"I don't know," I tell her honestly. "He's been acting really weird, and he won't tell me what's wrong. I'm not sure if it's me, him, the war, or something else. He just won't tell me!"

Chloe places a comforting hand on my shoulder. This is what I love about Chloe. She's always there to just help out. You don't find many people like that these days.

"I'm sure he's on his man period or something. Don't beat yourself up to it. It's not your fault. Why don't you confront him about it?" she advises. I think about it. I've confronted Axel many times before, so I may as well do it again.

I nod my head in agreement and tell her with a determined look on my face, "Alright, yeah, I'll do that."

"Great! I'll go get him now," she announces, jumping up off the bed. Before I can protest, she's out the door and running down the stairs. I groan, I didn't mean now!

The next second, Axel is being shoved through the door, and he doesn't look very happy. Chloe stands in the doorway with a sheepish smile on her face before slamming the door shut, leaving Axel and me alone to talk.

Axel runs a hand over his face as a tired expression takes over. That's when I realize just how awful he looks. He has dark circles under his eyes, his hair is dishevelled, his lips are turned down into a frown, and his face just seems sunken a little bit.

"Celina, whatever you want to talk about, can't it wait? I'm really busy right now," Axel tells me as his hand goes for the door.

Hurt courses through me that my own mate will choose work over me. What have I done?

"So that's how it is now?" I ask quietly, making Axel freeze with his hand hovering over the doorknob. "Your work is more important than your mate? I'm glad to know I'm loved."

Axel's head whips around, his silver eyes locking with my gold ones. My gold ones hold hurt and rejection, but Axel's are guarded like he's hiding something from me.

He doesn't answer me nor does he move from his spot, he just stays frozen. My eyes narrow into slits. He's hiding something for sure.

"What are you hiding from me? Why can't you just tell me?" I scream with tears in my eyes. That seems to snap him out of it because he finally makes a move. One moment he's at the door, the next he's beside the bed and gripping my hand tightly in his.

"Celina, I would never choose work over you because you're my world. I love you with everything I have," Axel says sincerely with a broken look in his eyes. My breath catches in my throat once he says that. He hasn't said he loves me for a very long time, and it's nice to hear it.

"I love you too, but I'm not sure if I trust you anymore," I admit. Honestly, I'm not sure what or who to trust anymore. Since this war, everyone's been so careful and sneaky that it's hard to keep track of it all. I even feel a bit guarded around Chloe sometimes. I thought I can trust my mate, but I'm just not sure anymore.

"I promise, you can trust me with all your heart," Axel whispers with a pained look in his eyes.

"Then, what are you hiding? Tell me," I whisper back. He sighs, looking defeated. He gently moves me over so he can fit in next to me as he wraps an arm around my shoulders.

"Celina, I went to see my mother a few days ago, the Moon Goddess," he tells me hesitantly. I stare at him in shock. I remember he told me once that the last time he saw his mother was centuries ago. I guess he needed to tell her something of importance.

"Why?" I ask simply. He pinches the bridge of his nose before going on to explain.

"I somehow came to the conclusion that all the things that have been happening and are about to happen are your fault. I needed guidance, so I went to the best person I know. I asked her about our fates, mainly yours. I just don't know what to think anymore. She said that our fates aren't sealed, our paths aren't made, and that we have to make what we want to happen a reality. The problem is, I don't know how to do that, and I don't want to add stress to you and the pups, and I just can't take it anymore! I'm a wreck, and I don't want you to know," he confesses with all honesty in his eyes. I keep a blank face as I take his head and place it on my chest. Why didn't he tell me? I could've helped.

He buries his head in my neck and inhales my scent while I run my fingers through his hair.

"You know I'll support you in any way, and you're keeping it from me won't help," I say softly.

"I know," he groans. "I just didn't know what to do."

I sigh and lift his head so it's level with mine. He needs to know he can trust me, trust me with anything.

"You do what you feel's best. If that means keeping things from me, then I can understand that. If you're not sure, come tell me anyway, that's all I ask for," I say honestly. He nods his head with a small smile on his face before softly kissing me on the lips.

"Now, what's this about a Christmas feast I'm hearing about?" I ask with new eagerness. Chloe's right, news travels fast. Axel chuckles at my face.

"It's pretty much a big feast for all the pack, and we go out and buy little gifts for the children. It's like a tradition for us," he explains with a smile on his face.

Happiness overtakes me at the thought of Christmas. I never got to celebrate Christmas after my parents died. I did have to set everything up, though.

"When does it all happen?" I ask even more eagerly.

"Christmas Eve, so families can spend Christmas Day with each other," Axel tells me with the same smile while I break out into a grin.

"Maybe next year I can help out with the cooking," I say excitedly. I can't help cook when I'm the size of three whales now, can I? I'm not gonna let that ruin my mood, though, at least I'll be able to celebrate Christmas.

After Axel and I talk for a little longer, Chloe knocks on the door. Axel leaves after that while Chloe looks at the both of us triumphantly.

"Told ya so!" she squeals excitedly once Axel is out of earshot. She bounces on the bed, and I laugh at her as she continues to bounce, her blonde hair going with her.

For the rest of the day, Chloe and I just talk about random subjects, the war, and Axel never coming up.

When it's time for her to leave, we say our goodbyes, and I fall into a peaceful sleep with an eased mind.

32

DAMON

"I don't care if you've been sighted! I want to know Celina's every move, and it's your job to know that!" I yell furiously into the phone. How dare he say he lost track of her because he was sighted.

"I-I'm sorry, Alpha. I'll get r-right on it," the frightened voice says down the line.

I growl and seethe, "Good, now get back to your job."

I slam the phone down back onto the holder and growl loudly, punching the wall next to me and officially putting a hole in it.

This is ridiculous! All I ask is to know Celina's whereabouts, and what do I get? An idiot who thinks his job is over when he's sighted. Great! The only reason why that numbskull is on the job is because today's Christmas Eve, and he's pretty much a loner with no life.

I know for a fact that the Nightfall Pack always has a big feast on this day then spend Christmas with their friends and family. What absolute shit.

If you're wondering why I'm not celebrating Christmas, it's because I totally loathe the holiday and everything to do with it! This all started on my fourth Christmas when my Mum and Dad decided that every Christmas they'd go to Bali, leaving me alone. I don't really care anymore, though. It's just one of the many things that have made me what I am today.

The war is due to take place in less than a month, the same with Celina's giving birth. I've trained my men hard and trained my women harder. I want the Nightfall Pack to be taken down, and the only way to do that is to have as many wolves fighting as I possibly can, including the women and those who just shifted.

The wickedness of all of this is that Celina won't be able to use her powers. I did some research and found out that while she's pregnant, she's useless for the war. She has to wait at least a week before she can harness her powers again. So either way, everything works out. Well, for me at least.

That's what this war is all about, though, to have Celina all to myself. I will rule my pack with her by my side. She'll still be a maid when she has to be, but she'll be my personal slave that I can do anything and everything I wish to. Axel's whole pack is stupid if they think this whole war is because I want her back as a maid! Oh no, I want her for my own greed.

A loud knock brings me from my thoughts.

"What?" I yell as the door opens to reveal my Beta, John.

"Don't 'what' me. I have some powers too, you know," he jokes while I roll my eyes. He has no power over me. I am the Alpha, and I am the one in control.

"Sorry, John," I say sarcastically. He shakes his head at me, but I ignore his playful attitude. We have a war, and he's joking around, not very beta-like...

"Any updates?" he asks as he takes a seat opposite my desk. That's more like it, getting straight to business. I settle into my desk chair and grab a file off the desk with everything I need to know about the Nightfall Pack.

"Well, my spy was sighted, and he thought his job was over, so I yelled at him to get back to work. Then he hung up like the coward he is, so I punched a hole in the wall," I explain without looking up from the file, motioning behind me to the very obvious hole.

"I don't see why we don't just kidnap her. It'll be a lot easier, and you'll have her working again in no time," John shrugs.

I slam my hands down on the desk, creating a loud bang and scaring John half to death.

"That's not the reason I forged this war! She is power, she's a royal, and she's strong. The perfect qualities of an alpha female and the perfect material to create pups that will be invincible. So no, my objective is to not 'have her working again in no time,' but to have her for myself," I admit easily.

John stares at me in shock and slight fear at my confession.

"She's already pregnant, though... What are we gonna do with the pups?" he asks with curiosity and fear in his voice.

I smirk evilly.

"Easy, we make sure they disappear," I say menacingly. John catches on and smirks along with me. Celina and Axel will never know what hit them.

(20 days until the war)

We have twenty more days to prepare, and I'm not letting any slack get pass me. I begin training the newly shifted, with our newest fighter having only shifted five days ago. What I do is for my pack's survival. If that means putting more lives than necessary on the battlefield to keep the younger ones safe, then so be it.

"Go, go, go! You would all be dead if we were in the actual battle! Step up your game!" I growl out to the younger part of the group. They're lagging, and I don't like it.

We're doing surprise attacks, and I've treated it like a game, every wolf for himself, so to speak. The point is to pin as many wolves as possible to the ground without being pinned yourself. Everyone's getting the hang of it except for the ones that shifted less than a month ago.

"I said step up your game!" I growl louder as another young wolf gets tackled to the ground by one of the older ones. I growl loudly. This is hopeless!

"Ok, that's enough! Everyone shift and meet back here in five!" I order in my alpha voice.

Five minutes later and I got at least thirty young wolves in front of me, all panting, sweating, and looking just plain worn out. Too bad, training isn't over.

"That was our warm up," I admit to them with a devilish smirk. Groans and curses are heard throughout the group. I growl. Are they judging my teaching method?

"I wouldn't argue if I were you. I can make the rest of your training an absolute hell," I threaten with a low growl. That seems to shut them all up.

"Everyone, grab a partner," I order. They all immediately start to bustle around, trying to find someone they can fight. I watch as everyone finds a partner within a minute, silently judging who they've paired themselves with.

"In the unlikely event that you are attacked while still in human form, you need to build up strength. With only twenty days to go, I don't want any weaknesses to be spotted," I announce.

My eyes scan the crowd until I find a fairly larger boy out of the rest. I hear he's on the football team, and he was the first one to shift out of all of them, so he seems like a good opponent.

"You," I say as I point to him. All eyes snap to him, some of them showing pity.

He gulps visibly.

"Me?" he asks and points to himself with a shaky finger. I roll my eyes, nodding. I gesture with my hand for him to move towards me, and he does so slowly.

"What's your name?" I ask loudly. The boy flinches slightly from my harsh tone but answers nonetheless.

"Jarod, Alpha," he says meekly. Jarod? What a pathetic name.

"Well then, Jarod, you're going to be my dummy," I say bluntly, causing the young boy to freeze in fear. Good.

"What we're going to do is have one person try to pin the other. Whoever gets pinned three times first is out, and the person who wins has to find another partner. Jarod here is going to show you how to miserably fail because I doubt he can beat me," I say with a cocky voice, causing Jarod to gulp again.

A circle forms around us as I get into an attack stance while Jarod takes a deep breath and gets into a defensive one.

"Watch and learn, pups," I say before launching myself at Jarod.

Training went smoothly, and I have officially struck fear into their hearts. I'm now going over the Nightfall Pack's territory so that I'm familiar with my surroundings and not a sitting duck. With only twenty days left, who knows what could happen. Of course at that thought, John bursts through the door. Uninvited, I might add.

"What?" I growl, really not in the mood to deal with any more news for the day.

"It's about the Nightfall Pack, Alpha," John says in a rush. I roll my eyes, but motion him in anyway.

"This better be good," I warn. My Beta gulps and draws in a shaky breath. Whatever he's about to tell me, it is certainly not good.

"Celina has been put into a containment facility that can only be opened from the outside, and only Axel can open it. It is immobile to all weapons, liquids, chemicals, anything you can think of. Only Axel has the power to open it and even then, there are many levels of security. Celina is totally inaccessible to us," he finishes, then bolts out of the room after seeing my majorly pissed off expression.

Inaccessible? Inaccessible? No! She's our main target! She's the one we're going to capture! She's the one who will bring this pack to greatness! She's the one that bloody caused this war! She can't be inaccessible! I will find a way to her. I always find a way.

33

CELINA

"Celina, please, this is for your own good," Axel pleads with me. I shake my head in determination.

"No! I'm not being locked up in a box with only twenty days left until the war! You think a box will keep me safe? You know, sometimes I really think you don't have a brain in there, Axel," I snap at him.

Yes, you heard me right. Axel wants to lock me up in a box for twenty days until the war is over. Yeah, right! Hell no! No way! Keep dreaming!

"Celina, please, it's for your safety. I'll never forgive myself if something happens to you," Axel continues to plead. I glare at him.

"So what you're saying is that by locking me up in a box, I'll be safe while you, the pack, and everyone else outside of it will be in danger," I conclude in a disbelieving voice. Axel nods after my little wrap up of the whole thing. I feel my anger bubble at his plan. How dare he?

"May I remind you that this war is going to happen because of me, and let's not forget that I'm pretty much giving birth in twenty days too, to three pups, mind you! Axel, there is no way in hell that I'm being locked up in a box while a war is going on, and I may or may not be in labor. So, the answer to your question is no. I will not be locked up in a box, and that is final," I seethe, not caring that my anger has taken over me.

Axel looks at me stunned for a moment while I sport a triumphant grin. A knock on the door brings us out of our little moment.

"Come in!" I call, ignoring Axel's look. Comrade's head pops through with a sheepish smile on his face.

"Sorry to interrupt, but I couldn't help overhear," he admits shyly. "I have an idea, though. If it's for Celina's safety, why don't we trick the Moonlight Pack into thinking that we put Celina in the so-called box when we really don't? That way, Celina will still stay safe, and we will effectively piss off the Moonlight's Alpha."

I look at Axel with hopeful eyes while biting my lip. I hope he agrees to this, it's a pretty good plan.

"How will we do it?" he asks while putting his arms around my waist possessively and bringing me closer to him.

"Easy. Get a Celina look-a-like and bam!" He claps his hands together loudly, making me jump. "We have our so called Celina."

"Who will do it, though?" I ask. "Maybe a weak pack member that definitely won't be able to fight or something like that will do."

"Hmm, maybe. The question is who's willing to do it? It's a big thing to ask for. Being locked away from your friends and family for twenty days all by yourself can really change you," Axel says wisely. So now he gets it? Ugh!

I slap him on the head, making him wince. He glares down at me while rubbing where I hit him.

"Ow! What was that for?" he yells at me.

"That's for trying to lock me up in a box without a second thought! I swear men can be so stupid sometimes," I mutter the last part, but both Comrade and Axel hear it.

"Hey! I made up a new and better plan!" Comrade defends himself. I roll my eyes.

"Sometimes, I said sometimes," I tell him like I'm speaking to an idiot. Men! Well, in Comrade's case, since he's only 18, boys!

"Ok, ok, that's enough criticism for the male race in one day. Back to the task at hand, who has any ideas about who to send in?" Axel asks while rubbing his eyes. We all stay silent at Axel's question. Who will do it?

No one comes to mind. Except... No, no that wouldn't be fair. She doesn't deserve that. Axel notices my torn expression and kisses my temple.

"What? Do you have someone who will do it?" he asks in a hurry. I quickly shake my head.

"No, no, no one at all," I say nervously as I avoid eye contact will both males in the room.

"Yes you do, you just feel guilty about it. Who is it, Celina? We need to know," Axel pleads as Comrade takes a seat on the end of the bed.

I sigh. She's gonna absolutely hate me for this.

"Chloe," I whisper. They both look at me confused, opening their mouths to protest.

"Before you say anything, let me explain," I quickly rush out, holding up my finger to silence them. They look at each other before nodding at me. I sigh and take a deep breath through my nose. "Chloe is a sweet and happy girl with a lot of friends surrounding her. She has a mother and father and has her life set out in front of her."

I begin with Comrade and Axel listening intently to what I say. Comrade's eyes hold concern about what I'm saying. He's pretty close to Chloe. She obviously hasn't told him, though.

"Problem is, she's not happy at all. When she was young, I mean eight years old, she met her mate. Just shush!" I quickly say as Axel tries to talk. He grumbles something under his breath, but I just roll my eyes at him. "Her mate was already of age, so to speak. He was between the 16 and 18 mark, she never told me. Her mate didn't want her eight-year-old self for a mate, so he rejected her and left the pack. She was so torn and heartbroken that she couldn't bear to be around anyone that seemed to intimidate her. She stayed away from girls her age and older. She was fine with girls younger because they didn't pose a threat. Let me ask you a question, have you ever seen Chloe around other girls apart from her mother and myself?" I ask with a raised eyebrow. Both males shake their heads after putting on a thinking expression.

"My point exactly. Chloe is far from being happy. Yes, she has friends surrounding her, and yes, she has her mother and father, but she doesn't have the one thing that will bring her true love, true happiness, and true joy. She doesn't have her mate," I finish, my voice going to a whisper. I can't even imagine what my life would be like without Axel. It's heartbreaking.

Comrade stays silent as he thinks over everything I've said, but Axel doesn't seem to get it yet.

"Why would locking her in the box help her, though?" he asks, a little less confused than before.

I look at Comrade to see all the puzzle pieces click together in his mind. He knows why.

"It'll be her escape," he whispers, looking me directly in the eye. I nod.

"It will. It will be her way to finally end her torture and to finally have peace within herself. Locking her in that box for twenty days will give her time to do a great amount of thinking. She will see what she can finally do with her life. At the end of those twenty days, either a new Chloe will walk out... or no Chloe will walk out at all." I whisper the last part.

Comrade and Axel freeze in shock somewhat. They don't move, blink, or speak, I don't even know if they're breathing. They must know what I mean... it's a horrible thought to think, but it may just happen.

Don't ask me how I know this because I honestly can't explain it. Chloe and I have had many talks, and she's told me many things, including about her mate. She's never seen him since, and it's been eating away at her since the day he rejected her. He almost killed her because of it. Giving her this choice to escape from all her worries and all her pain may just bring her peace and contentment. It doesn't matter how, whether she ends her life or if she chooses to move on, she will be at peace.

"I guess it's up to Chloe then," Axel whispers in his shocked state. Comrade gives a stiff nod from behind him.

"It's all up to Chloe," I repeat. A single thought pops into my mind at that statement, I'm going to lose my best friend, my only proper girlfriend. My sweet and funny Chloe, I'm going to lose her. One way or another, I'm going to lose her.

A single tear slips from my eye, but I quickly wipe it away so no one can see.

"Right then, someone go and get her because I sure as hell can't get up." I try to joke, but it doesn't come out as one and no one laughs.

Comrade seems to bolt out the door at one moment then come barrelling back in with a stunned Chloe. A little bit angry Chloe, too.

"What the hell! Why did you drag me up here?" she asks with a confused look in her eyes. I purse my lips, patting the spot next to me. She timidly sits down while looking at the three of us strangely.

"What's going on?" she asks.

Callum should really be here for this, but it's too late to have him come strolling in without a care in the world. We'll explain it to him later.

I take a deep breath and look at Chloe. As soon as I begin, I know she'll catch on. The look in my eye will give it away, but I have to tell her. I have to get her to see reason.

"Chloe, we are giving you a choice," I begin, her eyes widening as she immediately catches on to what I'm saying. I know she will. She stands, shaking her head at me.

"Chloe, just listen—" I try to say.

"No," she cuts me off definitely. "No, no, no, no, no! You will not give me a choice! I have been suffering for eight years now, and I can't just throw that all away! I've made myself who I am today, and nothing can change that."

I nod at her, understanding.

"I know, Chloe, but please hear me out. I might have a way to help you be at peace," I whisper to her. She doesn't look convinced, but she sits down again and listens with all ears.

"Axel has devised a sort of ultimate box that can't be destroyed, attacked, broken, nothing. Only Axel has the power to open it and no one else. The choice is would you like to occupy it? For twenty days, you will be all by yourself, no one to hold on to and no one's shoulder to cry on. It will just be you and your thoughts. One way or another, you will come out of that box at peace with yourself, in whatever state you may be in," I tell her, trying to stay strong.

Chloe stays silent. She stays silent for a very long time. Her eyes don't move from mine as she goes over what I've said and what I've offered.

"So, you're telling me... I can escape the whole outside world and just be by myself for a whole twenty days? No interferences, no brothers, no Mums, no mates, nothing?" she whispers in astonishment. I nod with a neutral face.

Her answer now will impact herself and us greatly, whatever she chooses. She closes her eyes for another few moments before they snap open and stare straight into my own. They're bluer than I have ever seen them, seeming to shine with a new hope. In that millisecond, I know what her answer will be.

"Ok, I'll do it," she whispers in a voice I hardly recognize as Chloe's.

34

CELINA

(10 days until the war)

All I can think of is poor Chloe being cooped up in that box for the last ten days. I can't think of anything else! I don't even know if she's still alive! We give her food every day, well, Axel does. He won't tell me what her situation's like because we need to keep up the act that I'm actually the one in the box. If Axel stops bringing food, then the Moonlight Pack might get suspicious.

It was hard enough to get Chloe to look like me while I'm pregnant! Plus, my hair's black, hers is blonde. I have gold eyes, she has blue. I'm pregnant, she's not. Plus, we had to mask her scent somehow to smell like mine! We had to fix all of it! The hair was solved with a wig that was styled to look exactly like my hair, the eyes we fixed with contacts, much to Chloe's dislike, and for the scent, we just bought a perfume that

Axel claims smells exactly like me. Getting Chloe pregnant was a bit harder...

I don't mean that way! No, no! What I mean is, we couldn't just stuff a pillow up her shirt and call her pregnant. I'm so big that I can't even walk anymore, so if we had a walking Chloe that would be kinda weird. To solve it, we got the pack doctor to find a jelly substance and carve it to the shape of my super large belly. Surprisingly, it worked!

By the end of the transformation, Chloe was almost an exact replica of me. Gold eyes, black hair, the perfect scent, and she had a fake belly. When Axel scooped her up into his arms after we all said our goodbyes, he walked out the door, and that's the last I saw of Chloe.

Back to the present, I'm worried sick about her. Axel's gone to give her some food and should be back in about fifteen minutes. It takes a while to get there and then he has to go through all the security measures and so on and so forth. I honestly stopped listening to him after he said security. I did listen when he said that the box has an invisible force field around it that only he can get through, which means the Moonlight Pack won't be able to get through to Chloe. That put me at ease a bit.

Anyway, to pass the time over the past few days, I've decided to look into something that doesn't concern me in the slightest. What is it? Simple, I'm trying to find Chloe's mate.

All she gave me as a lead was his name and that he's eight years older than her. His name is very... posh, in a way. His name is Charles. I don't know what he looks like, what his scent is, where he lives, what pack he's in. I've only got his name, Charles, and age, which would be around the twenty-four or twenty-five mark right about now.

So here I am, sitting on my bed with all of Axel's files about packs and who they harbour. I swear, I've gone through at least fifty today and the pile doesn't look smaller at all! None of the packs I've gone through have the name Charles, and I don't even have a last name to work with! Do you know how hard this is? No, you don't. Ugh!

I take another file in my hands and instantly flip to the name section:

Fred

Bob

Tom

Greg

John

David

Kyle...

No Charles.

By this time, I hear the front door opening and closing and the sound of feet running up the stairs, taking three at a time. Seconds later, Axel calmly walks into the room and smiles at me. I quickly smile back then focus back on the files in front of me. Someone's got to have the name Charles...

"What are you doing?" Axel's confused voice fills the room. I barely glance at him before picking up another dreaded, pale yellow file.

"I'm looking through all the packs to try and find a flipping man by the name of Charles. I can't flipping find him, though, so I'm getting flipping frustrated and flipping annoyed!" I explain without looking up from the file I'm reading.

A warm hand is suddenly placed underneath my chin, lifting my head so that my eyes meet with Axel's beautiful, greyish silver ones.

"Celina, you need to relax. How long have you been doing this?" he asks, concerned, his voice showing nothing but worry.

I sigh.

"I've been doing it for a few days now. I kept on falling asleep, though, so I've only gotten through like 200 files, and it's just so—" My rising voice is cut off by a pair of soft lips landing on my dry ones.

I instantly melt into Axel, wrapping my hands around his neck and licking his lips for entrance. He chuckles at my actions before pulling away and resting his forehead on mine, his hands gently massaging my still growing stomach. How big can it get?

"You need to relax," he repeats softly. "Take a break from looking over these folders and just relax for a moment. Plus, I have a surprise for you that I know you're gonna love."

He lightly kisses my nose as he smiles at me.

I bite my lip. I really should have a break... The relaxation will do me good, right? No. I'm doing this for Chloe, I can't just stop.

"Don't be so stubborn! Go and see the surprise our mate has! I'm very intrigued..." My wolf tells me while purring lowly. I roll my eyes at what I know she's definitely thinking.

"Stop thinking dirty, you strange, strange thing that I call my wolf," I lightly scold in an amused tone, earning me a chuckle from my wolf. To my surprise, she doesn't move into the corners of my mind like she usually does. Instead, she stays exactly where she is and wills me to go with Axel and see what this grand surprise is. She must be excited...

"Fine," I sigh defeated, Axel grinning widely. I hear my wolf purr knowing that I've made our mate happy.

"Only for a little while, though, then I have to get back to work," I tell him sternly. He nods his head furiously while I chuckle at his childish behavior.

"Trust me, you'll love it," he assures before taking me in his arms and carrying me out the room.

He huffs before moving me around a bit to try and balance my weight.

"Geez, sweetheart, have you gained some weight lately?" he jokes, but I instantly feel self-conscious. Am I fat?

I wrap my arms around my belly and suck in a deep breath to make myself lighter.

"Sorry," I mumble. Axel chuckles lightly before placing a kiss on the top of my head.

"I'm just joking, sweetheart," he whispers in my ear before stopping in front of the door that's across from our room.

"Here we are!" he exclaims before opening the door to one of the most amazing surprises I have ever been given.

In front of my very wide eyes are my friends ranging from Declan, Jasper, Matthew, Callum, and Comrade, sadly no girlfriends, all wearing clothes that are covered in paint. Not only is the paint on their clothing, but on their faces, arms, legs, and even on their hair! They all have wide grins plastered on their faces, and their eyes seem to sparkle with excitement.

That's not what makes me gasp loudly and stare in shock, though. No. It's the beautiful nursery that has been set up in what used to seem like an empty, useless room.

One side of the room has pink walls with toys that little girls would play with, including the baby doll that Chloe gave me. A cot has also been set up with a cute little mattress and stuffed toys all over it. In fact, stuffed toys are all over what seems to be the girl's side of the room.

The walls are covered with crown stencils and gems that seem to sparkle in the afternoon sun. The only thing that seems to be out of place is the box filled with letters that are also pink and glittered. I wonder what they're for...

My eyes travel to the other side of the room. This half has light blue walls with rocket and dinosaur stencils. Two cots have been set up with another two adorable little mattresses and a mass of stuffed animals.

The two blankets that Chloe gave me rest nicely on the cot's edge, showing who will soon be sleeping in them. This side of the room also has a box full of blue letters, but with no glitter. All in all, it's absolutely stunning.

"A-Axel? What is all this?" I ask, bewildered. This has to be a dream...

"It's not like we helped or anything, you know," jokes a grinning Matthew, earning a slap on the head from Callum, brotherly love.

"I apologize for him, Celina. He was dropped on his head at birth," Callum says with fake sadness in his teasing tone.

"Are you sure it was him who was dropped on his head?" I ask innocently with wide eyes and a sweet smile. A series of 'ooohs' is heard around the room while Callum grins at me.

"It will remain a mystery to you, won't it?" he jokes again, earning an eye roll from me. That's when my mind snaps back to the task at hand. My pregnancy brain is all jumbled up!

"Anyway, you're way off the topic there. Did you guys do this?" My voice has a bewildered tone while all the guys nod with smiles on their shining faces.

"It's amazing," I whisper, my eyes glassing over with tears.

Axel slowly places me on the rocking chair that's off to the side as Declan continues to say, "It took a while, but we did it and once you get some photos, you can put them all over the walls. It was actually Chloe's idea."

A pang of sadness strikes my heart, but it's gone as soon as it came. No, I've worried about Chloe enough. I need to focus on the now. I'm still gonna find her mate, though...

"Well, it's beautiful. I can't believe you guys did this for me," I whisper to them. Lopsided smiles grace their faces as they all look at me with the same sparkling eyes.

"Oh!" Comrade suddenly exclaims. "Check this out."

He quickly rushes over to what looks like a miniature wardrobe. He grips the tiny handles before pulling open the doors to reveal a whole wardrobe for the three little pups.

I gasp again, putting a hand over my mouth and one to my chest.

"As unmanly as this sounds, I think it's really cute," he says in a boyish voice with a matching boyish grin. I laugh at his comment. It is pretty cute.

"Cute? It's adorable! Did you guys make that?" I ask as I now notice the very detailed carvings that go around the whole edge of it. They all nod as I shake my head.

"Unbelievable," I mutter to myself. The wonderful thing about that little wardrobe is that I can use it until the three pups have grown up. I think that wardrobe will be passed down through our generations.

"So, do you like it?" Axel asks nervously. I turn to him with a smile and pull his face towards mine only to place a soft kiss on his lips.

"I love it," I whisper, and I honestly do. It's absolutely the sweetest thing that's been done for me. A second later, a yawn escapes my mouth and that's when I realize how tired I actually am. Stupid pregnancy...

I'm suddenly being scooped up by a pair of strong arms, but they're not Axel's. I stiffen.

"Relax, it's only me," an amused voice whispers in my ear and I instantly recognize it as Callum's. I relax again as my eyes start to drop close.

"Callum, take her up to bed, will ya? I have a call to make," I hear Axel say, but it doesn't really register as I fall into a light sleep.

I awake as I feel myself being placed on our bed. Callum softly kisses my forehead before whispering, "Goodnight, Celina."

I quickly grip his hand as I feel him move away. I crack open my tired eyes and offer a small smile.

"Stay with me," I say tiredly. I feel safer when I know someone's in the room and who's better than my own guardian if Axel's not with me.

"Of course," he immediately answers, making himself comfy on the bed beside me. He softly strokes my hair and hums a soft lullaby that soon has me falling into another sleep once again.

35

CELINA

(5 days until the war)

I wake up to the sweet sound of birds chirping, the fresh sunlight streaming in, and the cool breeze coming in through the window.

Yeah, right!

Instead of the sweet chirping of birds, I can hear punches and kicks, growls and snarls. Instead of the fresh sunlight, I have the scorching sun. Instead of a cool breeze, I have the heat from the sun with no breeze or wind at all.

I guess that's what you get when it's five days until a life changing war.

Axel and Callum have been training everyone who volunteered at the start, and so far, no one has backed out. If anything, more people have joined, much to my dismay and horror.

The training of the pack starts at about seven in the morning and goes on until lunch time, which is about twelve or so. After that, everyone gets lunch and goes off to do their own thing; everyone except Axel, Callum, and Comrade. Yes, I said Comrade.

To my utter and complete horror, the three of them train for another two hours by themselves. Comrade and Callum have become stronger since they have truly become my guardians. This means that Axel is pushing them to their absolute limit.

For Callum, I guess it's just protocol because he's the Beta. I'm guessing, he had training that made him work harder than he did when he had the test to become Beta. That would've been some painful training...

Comrade, though... Comrade has never had this sort of training. After all, he was shunned from his pack and instead of fighting, he ran. Don't get me wrong, I'm not turning on Comrade and saying he's a weakling. No! Anything but that! I actually view him as brave for running. You never know, if he hadn't run he might have ended up with a worse fate than mine.

Anyway, back on track. Callum will be able to handle the intensity of the training, but Comrade won't be able to, or maybe not as well. From Axel's point of view, though, Comrade's doing really well.

Axel...

He's working way too hard! The only time he takes a break is when he has to take food to Chloe or when he sleeps. This is worse than a few weeks ago! Yes, the war is in five days and yes, Axel needs to be prepared. Working himself to the point of exhaustion, though, is certainly not the way to go.

I hardly get to spend any time with him anymore, and it's all because of this stupid, flipping war! Maybe if I hadn't run away, none of this would've happened... No! Stop right there, Celina Heart! You are put on this world for a reason, and it certainly isn't for burying yourself in sadness and uncertainty. It is to protect. Protect the ones you love and cherish the most.

A sudden pain erupts in my stomach, causing me to gasp in pain. I have to grip the bed sheets to keep from screaming. It stays for a while then passes again. This stupid pain has been happening to me all morning... It's super weird, but I haven't told anyone yet. I don't want anyone worrying more than they already are.

It's actually not morning anymore. It's about six in the evening or something like that. Everyone's down at dinner, including Axel, Callum, and Comrade, so I'm all alone in this massive room.

The pain suddenly hits me again, but with greater intensity. I bite my lip to keep myself from screaming, biting so hard that I draw blood. Oh god, this hurts! What the hell is happening? The pain passes again, leaving me absolutely baffled by the whole situation.

A few more hours pass and soon it's ten or so at night. Axel still hasn't come up, and I'm getting worried about him.

'Axel? Are you there?' I decide to call him through the mind link we share. He better answer.

'Yes, sweetheart, I'm here. You alright?' he asks, but he sounds really distracted. What is he doing?

'I was gonna ask you the same thing,' I mumble. Axel doesn't reply, my mind falling into silence.

'Uh, Axel? Are you still there?' I ask, thinking he's gone off into his own little world.

'Yeah, I'm here. Celina, can you hurry up? I'm in the middle of a phone conversation with another Alpha,' he quickly explains distractedly again.

'Oh, sorry. I, um—' I start to say until I'm cut off as the pain shoots through me again. I haven't had it in a few hours, so it hits me full force. I release a blood-curdling scream as I grip my stomach for dear life. What the hell is happening? I suddenly feel a warm liquid trickling down my leg, but I pay no mind to it. The pain is just too much!

Tears start to stream down my face as I sob loudly. The pain doesn't seem to pass this time, causing me to release another pain-filled scream. Oh god, this is hurting so freaking much!

The door suddenly bursts open to reveal three panicked-looking males. Axel, Callum, and Comrade. They take one look at me and inhale sharp breaths. Callum and Comrade seem to freeze as Axel rushes over and carefully picks me up.

"Shh, sweetheart, shh. Everything's gonna be ok, everything's gonna be fine." Axel tries to soothe me, but the pain just increases, and I scream once again.

My scream seems to pull Callum and Comrade from their shock as they race downstairs to what I presume is the medic station.

"A-Axel? What's happening?" I ask in a scared and pain-filled voice. Axel looks down at my shaking body and kisses me on the forehead.

"You're going into labor," he whispers hoarsely, causing me to freeze for a second before the pain fills me once more. Is childbirth supposed to be this painful?!

Axel bursts through the door of the medic station to find everything has been set up and ready for the birth of our pups. Axel sets me down gently on the made bed, then stays beside me holding my hand.

"I'm here, sweetheart. Just remember, I will always love you," Axel whispers with tears in his eyes.

"I love you too," I whisper back before the mayhem starts.

I'm stripped of my clothing and quickly dressed in scrub type things. I squeeze Axel's hand as the pain courses through me again.

A heart monitor is hooked to me, and an IV is hastily inserted in my arm. The pain it causes is nothing in comparison to the labor pains I'm currently experiencing.

Doctor Aileen suddenly comes into view. She looks frantic and very worried.

"Celina, I need you to listen to me. This is going to be very painful, and nothing you could've done will prepare you for what is to come. All I ask of you is to not fall asleep. Whatever you do, don't fall asleep while the pups are still inside you. The reasons are not important right now, just focus on staying awake and pushing. Understand?" she says hastily. I quickly nod in response to Doctor Aileen's strict and serious words.

A lower ranking wolf using my real name is a sign of disrespect, but in the circumstances, I don't care. I just want this to be over already!

"How long will this take?" Axel's strained voice flows through my ears. He sounds so scared and worried at the same time...

"At least three hours minimum," Doctor Aileen informs him as she positions the last of the machines.

Without any warning whatsoever, the strongest of pains courses through my entire body. I release one of my loudest screams and convulse on the bed. What's happening to me?

"Celina, come on! Stay strong, fight it!" I hear doctor Aileen's distant voice filter through my ears. Fight it? Fight what? Where are Callum and Comrade? I need them!

Another warm hand grips the one Axel isn't holding. I slowly look towards it to see Comrade looking at me with pained eyes and Callum standing next to him with equally pained eyes.

"Don't give up," they whisper at the same time.

Something inside me snaps at that moment. If I give up now, my pups may die. Axel will be left with no heirs, and the pack will hate me forever. I'll have to live with the fact that I was too weak to give birth. That's if... I even make it through this.

I turn my head to Axel. I need to know the truth. I need to know if I'm going to die.

"A-Axel, tell me the truth," I say painfully as I shut my eyes to try to block away the pain. It doesn't work. "Am I going to die?" I whisper in a strained voice.

The whole room goes silent, all movements ceasing. The only sound heard is my heavy breathing and the beeping of the heart monitor. Axel seems speechless.

"Axel, please," I beg quietly as my eyelids start to droop. Not even an hour has passed, and I'm already tired. Great, just great.

He suddenly snaps out of his speechless state and says determinedly, "Not if I can help it."

I smile at him before screaming out in pain again. This is going to be a long night...

After three pain-filled hours and absolute torture, Doctor Aileen finally gasps and says the words I've been dying to hear.

"Push, Celina, push! The first pup is ready to come out!" she exclaims as she gets into her position.

I scream as I push as hard as I can. I swear, these flipping pups better be worth it. Sweat covers my whole body, making my black hair stick to my forehead.

"I see the head!" Doctor Aileen exclaims before the sound of crying fills the room.

As I breathe heavily, I look up to see a little baby boy in the doctor's arms. He's so adorable...

The moment doesn't last long, though, as I suddenly feel really tired, and the beeping of the heart monitor starts to drop. Doctor Aileen looks over to me before hurriedly, but gently, placing our first born into the hands of an assistant doctor.

"Celina, stay with me. You still have two pups left. Come on, Celina, stay with me!" Doctor Aileen calls to me, her eyes looking crazed. I nod as the second pup's head is seen.

I push hard, but it seems more difficult than the first. I scream again as I give a final push before another crying baby emerges. I don't have time to see what he or she looks like as my eyelids slam closed. All I want to do is sleep...

"Celina? Celina, wake up! Come on, Celina, please!" a panicked voice yells directly into my ear. I groan as my eyes slowly open back up. I'm so tired... I just want to sleep.

I glance at Callum and Comrade, then to Axel. If I die tonight, I'm gonna miss these three people the most.

"I love you, guys," I whisper as the third pup starts to make its way out. I release scream after scream as I continue to push. Oh my freaking god!

Tears that started long ago continue to stream down my cheeks. I look to Axel in pain.

"Axel, it hurts so much!" I cry as I squeeze his hand harder. I swear I hear bones cracking. I hope I don't hurt him too much.

"Just hold on, Celina. You and the pups will be ok. You have to be," he whispers as tears slip from the corner of his eyes. I've never seen him cry, and the sight breaks my heart.

I weakly grab his head in my hands and bring his lips down for possibly the last kiss we will ever share together. I pull away as a scream bubbles up in my throat. I push painfully one last time, and for the third time, the cries of a newborn fill the room. Once again, I can't see what he or she looks like as my strength starts to rapidly leave my body. My vision starts to blur while I struggle to keep my eyes open.

I see Axel smile at the pup before looking down at me with the same smile. That smile instantly drops, though, once he sees me. He starts to scream at me, but as his lips move, no sound comes out. I look at Callum and Comrade to see that they're doing the same thing.

The only thing I can hear is the beeping of the heart monitor. It slowly gets slower and slower beats from my heart. Is this how it's gonna end? Me in a room surrounded by the people I love and knowing that my pups are safe? I don't think I could be happier to go any other way.

I weakly lift my hand and try to place it over Callum's or Comrade's, but I'm too weak. They catch on to what I want and place their much larger hands on top of mine. I painfully rotate my head towards Axel to see his tear-streaked face and sad eyes. I don't like him crying, it doesn't suit him.

I gently place my hand on his cheek, since he moved closer to meet me half way.

"Smile," I whisper. "All of you smile. I want to remember you with a smile on your face."

There's barely any sound to my voice, but they hear me loud and clear.

Callum and Comrade crack a smile, a genuine smile, but not Axel.

"You won't die, Celina. I won't let you!" he yells as more tears slip from his eyes.

"Just smile," I say again in my barely there voice. To help him, I send all the fun and happy times we spent together to all three of them, my true family.

To my surprise, Axel cracks a smile. It's small and barely there, but it's the smile I'll remember forever.

"I love you," I whisper as my eyelids begin to droop for the last time, and the beeping of the heart monitor becomes dangerously slow.

"I love you too," is the last thing I hear from Axel's mouth before I welcome the darkness.

I will never forget you, Axel Night.

36

AXEL

No. She isn't dead! She isn't dead! She won't even get to hold our pups. We won't be able to get married. She won't be with us anymore.

As soon as Celina's hand becomes limp in mine and the heart monitor gives a continuous, deafening beep, I know I lost her forever. I still can't believe it, though, never. She isn't dead, she can't be.

My eyes travel to the three sleeping angels in the three little beds. They're beautiful. Our first born, I'm proud to say, is a boy. He has Celina's pitch black hair, but you can easily tell he has the build of an Alpha. He's going to be a strong leader when he grows up.

Our second born is another boy. He's only slightly smaller than our first born, with pitch black hair also. He has a leaner build but looks just as strong. You never know, maybe he'll become Beta if Callum never finds his mate.

Our third born is a beautiful baby girl. She's got a much smaller build than the boys, the same as Celina's. Instead of Celina's pitch black hair, she has my snow white hair that looks as soft as a pillow.

I haven't been able to see any of their eyes yet since they just cried and cried then fell asleep after being placed in their little beds. As much as I want to hold my pups, I just can't do that to Celina. I want her to be the first to hold them, and if she's gone, she can't do that.

My head snaps at a grim-looking Doctor Aileen. She's as pale as a ghost, her hands shaking slightly.

"Do something," I whisper while looking her in the eye. She doesn't move but continues to stare at Celina's motionless body.

"Do something!" I yell furiously. She has to be able to do something! Anything!

Her head drops out of submission, her shoulders slumping in defeat.

"I'm sorry, Alpha. There's nothing I can do," she whispers while I see a single tear slip from her eye. Celina's death will affect all the pack, but knowing that Doctor Aileen could've done something to prevent it will burden her for the rest of her life.

I shut my eyes, desperately trying not to show weakness in front of her.

"Get out," I say roughly. Doctor Aileen quickly scrambles out of the room, leaving Callum, Comrade, myself, and of course, the pups too.

I go back to Celina's side and grip her hand in mine. I won't accept it. This isn't her fate, this isn't her destiny! This is not how it's supposed to work!

"Is she really gone?" I hear someone whisper. I look up into the sad and teary eyes of Comrade. I gulp, but don't answer. I won't believe it. She isn't dead! She isn't dead! She can't just leave me!

"What do we do?" Callum asks this time since Comrade looks like he's trying to hold back his waterworks. I turn to him with a stone look and shielded eyes.

"We wait. Remember, Celina is a strong fighter. She has royal and alpha blood in her. She can't just die because of childbirth. She can't. She just can't," I say determinedly, my voice cracking every few seconds.

The Moon Goddess has to save her. She can't just die! I know, though, no matter how many times I tell myself that, reality will hit me soon like a ton of bricks. I just can't believe it right now. Celina is my love, my mate, my Luna, and my rock. She's my everything! If she goes now, I don't know what I'll do with myself! Plus, she's only seventeen. She's not even an adult yet. She's too young to die!

"Please, Celina, please wake up. I need you. I need you here with me. The pups need you to raise them. I certainly can't. You need to be by my side and living, holding the pups in your small arms. Please, Celina, wake up," I whisper in her ear, leaving a soft kiss under her earlobe.

She doesn't react. Not even a flinch or anything. Maybe she really is gone...

"Axel, we can't just sit and wait. She's gone, and that's that. We need to tell the pack and organize a service for her. She needs to be remembered for who she was," Callum says wisely while he looks down at Celina like he's lost a piece of his heart.

I swallow the lump in my throat. Should I? I don't think the pack can handle it...

"No, we will not tell the pack. Not yet. Give it a few days, tell them Celina's healing. The pack won't be able to handle it," I reply, not taking my eyes off Celina.

"They deserve to know, Axel," Callum insists. My head snaps up at him in anger.

"I said no!" I yell with power. He immediately submits by dropping his head and looking back at Celina. He may be the Beta, but he does not run the pack. I'll tell my pack when I want to. He has no say in the situation.

"I'm gonna miss her so much," Comrade whispers suddenly, after a few moments of silence. I feel for the young boy. He is only 18 after all and treats Celina like a sister. He spent a lot of time with her and told her his past, which took a lot of willpower from him.

"We all will," I whisper back.

Hours pass. It must be nine in the morning by now, and we all just stay by Celina's side. "She. Isn't. Dead. Please mother, if you can hear me, save her. Bring her back. Please, I'll do anything! If you can't do it for me, do it for the pups. Do it for Callum and Comrade. Do it for this pack."

The pups woke up a few times, but I quickly shushed them and rocked them back to sleep. Not by holding them, just by rocking their little beds sideways. They just sleep so peacefully. Celina will be the first to hold them, though. She will. That's one unspoken promise that I will most certainly not break.

A soft knock sounds at the door, interrupting all of our thoughts.

"Come in," Callum calls weakly, certainly not beta-like, but I can't blame him. For all I know, I'm probably worse.

To my surprise, Doctor Aileen walks in. She silently closes the door behind her before making her way towards me.

"Pardon me, Alpha, but I need to check on the newborns. I'm just making sure that they're healthy and well, nothing more," she assures me while also explaining why she's here. I silently nod to show I understand.

She makes her way over to the pups but abruptly stops. I look towards her, and a confused look overcomes my face.

"Is everything alright, doc?" I asked, confused. She turns to me, equally confused.

"Yes, Alpha, I'm fine. But I can't get close to the pups, though," she explains, frowning.

I raise an eyebrow, my expression becoming serious.

"Now is not the time to mess around. What's really wrong?" I ask, hiding my irritation. I don't have time for all this nonsense. I just want her to do her job and get out.

"I'm sorry, Alpha, but I'm not messing around. I physically can't get further than where I am standing right now," she explains, frazzled.

With my anger rising, I march over to where she's standing and put out my hand. It seems to hit an invisible wall that certainly wasn't there before.

"What the hell..." I mutter, baffled. This can't be possible.

"What is it?" Callum asks as he makes his way over to us. Comrade stays by Celina, seeming to be in a trance and not noticing anything around him. He's been like this ever since Celina... well, you know. He only speaks when completely necessary. He's completely shut down.

Callum puts his hands up on the invisible wall, a confused expression taking over his face like the rest of us.

"I don't understand. There's nothing there," he states the obvious in a strange voice.

"It's as if there's an invisible wall surrounding the pups so no one can go near them. Why, though?" I ask as my mind tries to grasp any sensible reason as to why this invisible wall is blocking our path. Of course, there's none. Nothing seems sensible anymore.

"Is it magic?" Doctor Aileen asks. I shrug along with Callum. It could be...

"I don't know. Maybe it's a prank by one of the younger pack members," Callum offers.

"Uh, guys?"

I shake my head.

"No, there's no way they could've gotten into the room. It has to be something else," I mumble as my mind tries to think of a reason.

"They could've climbed in through the window," Callum suggests. I look at him like he's an idiot while Doctor Aileen releases an exasperated sigh.

"Guys?"

"No," is all I say. I highly doubt that anyone will have the nerve or indecency to actually keep me from my pups. If they do, however, I will personally detach their heads from their shoulders.

"I don't think they would be that desperate to piss off their Alpha by blocking him from his pups," I explain in a low voice to Callum, like you would use when speaking to a toddler. I swear if they did, they better be ready to expect the worse.

"What if—" Doctor Aileen starts to say something that will probably make sense before she's cut off by someone yelling.

"Guys! For goodness sake, Celina!" Comrade yells, finally getting our attention. We all whip around to a sight that is unimaginable and in the history of sensibleness is not possible.

There's Celina, wrapped in a kind of blanket made of gold and shining. She's hovering above the bed she was once dead on, with a new gold dress that splits down one end, instead of the scrubs we changed her into. The dress hugs her figure nicely, and it seems to be floor length, but that's not what I'm focusing on. Oh no. I'm more interested in the fact that Celina is magically floating in the air and is somehow waking up.

My eyes don't leave her as her light grows more and more intense. I keep my gaze on her until I have to look away in case I blind myself. The windows suddenly burst open as an almighty breeze rushes into the room. It all seems to be centered on Celina.

"What's going on?" I yell as I shield my eyes, and of course, no one knows the answer. We all continue to watch in awe as Celina shines in her gold dress with the air whizzing around her.

Just as everything begins to die down, the tap on the other side of the room starts to shake violently. The next second, water bursts out of it heading straight for Celina. I panic a little at this point. Is it gonna hurt her? Just before it's about to hit her, though, the water turns into mist and surrounds her like a fog. Seriously, what the hell is going on?

"Water and air are two of the most calming elements in the world," Comrade suddenly says as he takes a step towards Celina. There came an ear-piercing scream as soon as he makes that move. I instinctively cover my ears against the awful noise. Shit, that's loud!

"What the hell is that?" I yell. It sounds like a cat trying to sing on Halloween!

Comrade takes a step back again, and the screaming suddenly stops. I hesitantly uncover my ears and look at the others to make sure they're ok.

"Is everyone alright?" I ask and they all nod. Simultaneously, we all turn to Celina. Only thing is she isn't there anymore.

Crying fills the room, and it snaps me out of my shocked state. I spin around, thinking of checking on my pups, but abruptly stop. There, standing by the beds of my pups is none other than a very awake Celina.

My mouth drops open in shock, and my eyes widen to the size of saucers. No, that's not possible! She was dead! She should be dead!

I stand there in shock as Celina softly pets the top of our baby girl's head. She instantly stops crying and falls back into her peaceful sleeping state. Celina kisses her on the forehead before turning around and shocking me even more.

Nothing else and nobody else registers in my brain as my undivided awe and attention go directly to Celina.

The first thing I notice is her eyes. Yes, they're gold, but that's it. No white, no pupil, just beautiful, shining gold. I will myself not to get lost in them, but trust me, it's the hardest thing I've ever done. I can stare into those eyes for the rest of my life.

Then I also notice that her dress is actually a cover of glitter of sorts. The fabric looks as if it's moving from top to bottom, and continues into the floor without stopping. It looks absolutely stunning on her.

The last thing I notice is that she's staring right at me. Her gold eyes never blinking, her form never moving from beside the three little beds. She stays completely still, just staring into my greyish silver eyes.

"Celina?" I call to her in disbelief. This can't be possible. She... she's dead. I just didn't want to believe it, and now that the unbelievable has happened, that's the only thing I'm sticking on to.

At the sound of my voice, the air and mist stop flowing around her. The gold shrinks away from the whites to reveal a pupil. Her dress stops moving and becomes a normal one with a slit. Everything returns to normal. All in the time span of a few seconds.

As soon as her eyes return to their beautiful golden colour, she starts to wobble on her legs, gripping her head and shutting her eyes tightly. Without even thinking, I lunge towards her, the invisible wall no longer there.

I catch her before she falls to the ground, her body going limp in my arms. Instead of panicking and yelling at Doctor Aileen to do something, I wait. I just hold my wonderful mate in my arms and wait.

It could've been a few seconds, minutes, or maybe even hours, but the waiting pays off. Just as the last thread of hope is about to break and I'm about to accept what I've been willing myself not to, Celina opens her beautiful golden eyes slowly and whispers, "Axel?"

Her voice puts all my tense muscles at ease, calms my racing heart, and makes me release a thankful sigh.

At this moment, I can't be any happier to hear someone say my name.

37

CELINA

"Oh thank the Moon Goddess! Celina, you're alive!" Axel exclaims happily as he hugs me close to his chest. I sigh in contentment as I wrap my weak arms around his broad shoulders.

Axel peppers kisses all over my face, nose, chin, cheeks, and forehead, everywhere! He finally comes to my lips and places a soft kiss there, making sparks erupt from my heart.

"I missed you so much," I whisper as a few tears slip out my eye. Not only him, but I missed Callum and Comrade as well. I mean, who wouldn't?

"I don't understand," a feminine voice mutters. I look to my left to see Doctor Aileen standing there with a confused expression. "This isn't possible. All your vital organs, your heart, everything just stopped within you. You were dead. How in the world..." She trails off again while my mind starts to go back to the previous events.

"If I may, Doctor Aileen, this is a personal matter, and it would be greatly appreciated if you left the room so we can discuss it," Callum says politely. I must say, I'm shocked. I've never heard Callum being so polite before, it's like a miracle. Axel nods in agreement to Callum's suggestion. Doctor Aileen looks a little disappointed but leaves nonetheless.

"Celina, are you ok? You have this faraway look in your eye," Axel says as he cups my face lovingly. I blink a few times to focus on him then nod stiffly.

"Would you like to know how it's all possible?" I ask no one in particular. They must be curious. A series of murmurs is heard around the room. I sigh, letting my head drop.

"Then so be it," I say quietly before telling Axel to place me back on the bed. He does so without question. "So, this is what happened..."

As soon as my world goes black, everything becomes bright and white. I shield my eyes with my hands for a moment, it's so bright.

I look down at myself and notice I'm no longer in the scrubs I was changed into. Instead, I'm wearing a pristine white top and jeans. I have no clue how that happened...

"Celina," a voice whispers. I whip around to find the source of the voice, but come up with nothing.

"Celina," it whispers again, seemingly being carried by the breeze.

"Celina," it whispers a third time.

"Who are you?" I ask loudly. Whoever it is is freaking me out. This isn't some sick game.

"Celina, come to me," the voice whispers again. I start to feel scared and walk backwards in the direction I think is further away from the voice.

"Who are you?" I ask again as my eyes search the whiteness. There's nothing, I don't even know what I'm standing on.

"Where are you?" I mutter, but I receive no answer, nothing. Not even a whisper in return.

I keep my eyes ahead of me for as long as possible, but it seems like an endless nothingness. There are no walls, no floors, no ceiling, just nothing.

A hand suddenly rests on my shoulder, making me freeze and tense up. My eyes widen, and I literally stop breathing, thinking the mystery person will somehow hurt me.

"Relax, my dear Celina. Nothing will hurt you here," the voice says again, but this time not in a whisper. It seems more like a breeze wafting around me as the voice resembles beautiful, classical music. It soothes my muscles and makes my breathing resume normally.

"Who are you?" I ask for the third time in less than five minutes. I will myself to turn around, but I can't. It's like my feet are glued to the floor, and my eyes are stuck facing forward. Nothing I do can make me move or even blink.

The hand slips off my shoulder, making my wolf restless. Funny, I haven't spoken to her in ages, and now that a mysterious hand leaves my shoulder, she suddenly feels restless? I must have the weirdest wolf in the world.

A soft swooshing noise is heard before a stunningly beautiful woman shows herself: her hair as white as snow, skin as pale as ice, silver eyes as bright as the moon, and lips as red as a rose. She's wearing a crystal dress that seems to clutch at her body but fall around her at the same time. Like I said before, she's stunning.

There's only one person I know who looks like her, and that's Axel, so I'm guessing she's the Moon Goddess. I gasp loudly at my realization and quickly bow my head to her.

"Moon Goddess, it is my greatest pleasure to be in your presence," I tell her with pride in my voice knowing I've met the Moon Goddess.

"Lift your head, my child," she orders softly. I immediately do as she says, raising my head ever so slowly. My golden eyes lock onto her shining silver ones. She smiles. She actually smiles at me.

A confused expression takes over my face. What she does next, though, is something I really don't expect. She engulfs me in a hug, just as a mother would give her daughter, or sisters would give each other. A hug anyone would give to show love. The Moon Goddess, Axel's mother, the creator of all wolves, is hugging me as if she's known me my whole life. I'm in shock, pure shock.

She pulls back with a smile on her face while I stare at her with a gaping mouth and eyes as wide as saucers.

"It is an absolute pleasure to meet you. I just wish it is under better circumstances," she says sadly. Her words don't register for a long time since I'm still in a state of shock.

A few moments pass and her face starts to show worry. Her perfectly shaped eyebrows draw together slightly, her plump lips form a small frown, and her silver eyes are coated with doubt.

"Celina, darling, are you alright?" she asks, her voice sounding like the wind. She places a comforting hand on my shoulder which causes me to jump out of my shocked trance.

"Huh? Oh, yes! I'm fine," I say with a small forced smile then her earlier words register. Better circumstances?

"What do you mean under better circumstances?" I ask voicing out my thoughts as my mind fills with confusion. She smiles down at me sadly.

"Celina, you have died. Giving birth to your three pups was just too much for your young body to handle and you gave out," she informs me sadly.

Dead? I'm dead? Just like that? All I feel is sadness, loneliness, and worst of all, emptiness. No...

I'm dead? I can't be. Axel, the pups, and the pack need me. I can't just die, not like that.

"There has to be something I can do! I can't just die! Not like that!" I scream at her. "I want to die old and wrinkly with Axel by my side! I want to die with my three pups by my bedside! I want to die knowing that I've done everything I possibly can to help Axel, the pack, and the pups! I can't just die!"

A small smile makes its way onto her face. I look at her like she's gone crazy. Is she smiling about my death?

"Celina, dear, have you realized you have only seen one of your pups? You never got to see the other two, you do not even know their genders," she suddenly informs me. Tears well up in my eyes at the thought that I'll never be able to see or hold my pups ever. The thought breaks my heart.

"Can't you do something?" I whisper desperately. She has to be able to! I-I just can't die, not now.

"You're the Moon Goddess for goodness sake! Can't you just magically bring me back to life?" I scream at her with mixed emotions. Please, I can't die. I can't die...

Tears start to pour down my cheeks as I know she can't do anything to help me.

She shakes her perfectly formed head and sighs before saying, "I am sorry my dear, but that is not how it works. You are the only one who can bring yourself back to life."

I give her a confused look while a small smile still graces her face.

"Let me tell you something that doesn't seem important at the moment, Celina. The time span here is not the same as there on earth. One hour on earth is equivalent to one minute here, so let me ask you these: How long are you going to cry? How long are you going to blame yourself for everything? How long are you going to let your mate and guardians suffer? Simple questions need simple answers. How long, Princess Celina Heart?" she asks, her silver eyes full of wisdom and her smile genuine.

My breath stops short, and my mind goes blank at her wise and humble words. How long?

Axel needs me there with him so he can run his pack. Callum needs my help in finding his mate someday. Comrade needs me with him so he can have a friend that will allow him a shoulder to cry on. And most of all, my pups need me so that they can live a life with both a mother and a father.

"How do I do it?" I ask determinedly. No more tears shall fall. The Moon Goddess raises her suddenly glowing hand and places it on my head. A sudden burst of power surges through me, right to my core. I scream as the power engulfs my body and light rays burst out of my eyes, fingers, toes, everywhere.

"What's happening to me?" I cry out in pain. The Moon Goddess' hand doesn't move from its position, not even when I start to levitate in the air. She just goes with me, levitating herself.

"I am unlocking your powers to the fullest degree. You will be able to use your powers within two days at the most. You will be the most powerful being on earth," she says in a calm voice. It feels like hours have passed when actually, it's only a few minutes. That is hours on earth, though...

The Moon Goddess removes her hand, and I drop to the floor in a heap. I take a minute to catch my breath and try to comprehend what just happened. I slowly pull myself up, shaking, and look at the Moon Goddess through strands of my black hair.

"What now?" I ask. She stays silent as she watches me get up onto shaky legs.

"Understand this, Princess Celina Heart. Your powers and beauty come with a price," she says as her eyes start to glow even brighter than the moon itself while she stares straight into my widened gold ones.

A price? What kind of price? How big of a price?

"Once your time on earth has come to end, your reign will not. Once you die and cease to exist, you will live again. Instead of your human body, you shall be a guardian spirit. You will lead those below you. Everything comes with a price, and this is yours. Once you have completed what has to be done on earth, you shall start anew. Do you understand?" she asks in her airy voice.

I shake my head with furrowed brows. Is that a riddle?

"No, I don't understand what you're saying? I shall die, but live again? I don't understand!" I yell at her, my confusion getting the better of me.

She levitates off the ground once again and hovers above me like an angel.

She looks down at me, her silver eyes still shining. All I want is to be wrapped in Axel's arms and be told that everything will be alright.

Then, her melodic voice finally says, "Princess Celina Heart, you shall be the next Moon Goddess."

I don't know what emotion explodes within me, but whatever it is, it's strong. Water and air start to wrap around me, but I don't notice. My pristine white clothes are replaced by a beautiful golden gown with a slit down the side, but still I don't notice. I feel my eyes start to burn and turn gold, but I don't notice. All I can think is that I'm the next Moon Goddess. I'm the next spirit that's going to look over the whole werewolf race. That thought, that simple yet complicated thought, is the one thing that brings me out of death.

Everyone in the room stays silent, not even the pups are crying, just pure and utter silence. I look at Axel to see him with a blank expression. I look at Callum to see an awestruck expression as he looks at me with adoration. Finally, I look at Comrade. I don't really know what to expect when I look at him, but one thing's for sure, I don't expect him to have a smile on his face and a twinkle in his eye.

"What are you smiling about?" I ask in an almost sarcastic manner. As soon as Comrade's almost black eyes lock onto my gold ones, his smile gets wider, and the twinkle in his eyes becomes a full blown sparkle.

"I'm smiling because I'm honoured to be protecting the next Moon Goddess. Honestly, how excited can you be to be protecting the most important person in our world?" he asks with a grin. His enthusiastic words make some sense, but still.

A sudden idea enters my mind. If Comrade is so enthusiastic about protecting me, would he be just as enthusiastic about protecting my pups?

"Comrade..." I ask slowly, drawing out his name. "How would you feel if you were protecting the future Moon Goddess' pups?"

His eyes widen at my words, and he goes into a state of shock. I'd giggle at his face if it weren't for the seriousness of the situation.

"W-what?" he stutters as his eyes go wide and his jaw drops. I then turn to Axel.

"Do I have the power to pass Comrade's guardianship onto our pups instead of me?" I ask him with a hopeful look in my eyes.

He stares at me for a long moment while I stare back. His eyes look calculating like he's considering the idea, but rejecting it anyway.

"Celina, you just came back from the dead, you're going to be the future Moon Goddess, and you're asking to reassign one of your guardians to our pups?" he asks like it doesn't make sense in his brain. I nod my head once.

"Yes, that's exactly what I'm saying," I tell him bluntly. He shakes his head at me, staring at me as if I'm crazy.

"I don't know, Celina... I want you to have the utmost protection during this war that, might I remind, is going to take place in three days. I can't have you reassigning your guardians. I'm sorry," he apologizes, and his decision seems final. I'm not giving up, though.

"Won't you feel better though if you know your pups are safe as well as me? Axel, please! I couldn't live with myself knowing my pups could get hurt. Please, Axel, please," I whisper the last part as tears come to my eyes. He has to! He just has to!

"Celina, I—" he begins, but I cut him off.

"Please, Axel, think of the pups. Think of what we went through for them. Think of what we're going to go through for them. Are we just gonna throw that all away?" I ask sincerely, looking my mate directly in the eye.

He stays silent for a long while, not diverting our eye contact at all.

"Celina, you are my main priority. I love you so much, and I love our pups just as equally, but I know the pups will be safe in the safe room. You, on the other hand, since you have full capacity for powers, you'll probably be on the battlefield whether I like it or not. So, Celina, think about this: if you had to choose between your mate or pups, who would you choose?" he asks in a deadly tone as he gets all up in my face.

I gulp, staying silent while I think it over. I love Axel. I love my pups. Is there anything else to it?

"I couldn't, I wouldn't," I say honestly in a small voice.

"Then why are you asking me to?" he asks, I'm not sure with what emotion.

With that final question, Axel storms out of the room with steam almost bursting out of his ears.

I look down and let my hair cover my face. I've made Axel upset, and now he's angry with me. Not really the way I thought coming back from the dead would do.

Two comforting hands touch my shoulders. I lift my head to look at Callum and Comrade, both sporting encouraging smiles.

"It's ok, Celina, everything's gonna be ok," Callum reassures me with a small nudge.

"Yeah. Plus, the pups will be getting their own guardians pretty soon. Just you wait, Snow, just you wait," Comrade tells me with a smile. I smile back slightly. A mind-shattering thought suddenly enters my brain. I haven't even seen my pups yet!

I quickly rush over to the three little beds against the wall that hold all three of my little angels. My breath hitches in my throat once I see them. Two baby boys and a baby girl.

All I register are the three little angels sleeping soundly in their beds. I totally forget that Callum and Comrade are still in the same room and probably looking at me with smiles on their faces.

I gently pick up the baby girl, cradling her to my chest as she sleeps peacefully.

"You're so beautiful," I whisper to her as I hear the door open and close softly, probably Callum and Comrade leaving the room.

I look at my other two angels and smile softly. My two baby boys. One's slightly bigger than the other, but they both have the potential to be alphas.

I hear the door open and close again then footsteps making their way towards me. Without even turning around, I know its Axel. His strong arms wrap around my waist as he stares adoringly down at our baby girl. He must have felt my emotions through the mind link we share.

"She's so small," I whisper as her little hand takes one of my fingers, her eyes still closed.

"Yeah, I know," Axel whispers back. We stay silent after that, no thoughts about the mild fight we had only minutes ago enter our heads.

I turn around in Axel's arms as I look down at my baby girl. I'm sure he wants to hold her.

"Hold her," I tell him quietly as I look up. Axel's eyes widen as he holds his hands up in a defensive position while shaking his head.

"Please?" I ask softly while gazing down at the little girl. He sighs and closes his eyes, giving into my begging easily.

"Fine," he grumbles while I giggle at his face.

I carefully manoeuvre the baby in my arms and is about to give her to Axel, when he suddenly moves away. I look at him questioningly while he looks at me nervously.

"What if I drop her?" he asks, looking anywhere but my eyes. I smile and shake my head at him.

"You won't," I say simply. Before he can comprehend what I'm doing, I place our baby girl in his arms.

He stiffens for a moment and doesn't move. Once he looks down at her, though, he relaxes and smiles. His eyes fill with adoration as he looks down at his daughter. She's already got him wrapped around her little finger.

"She's so small," he whispers as he lovingly strokes her cheek with his finger.

I smile at the picture in front of me as I suddenly wish I have a camera in my hands.

I turn towards the other two little beds and gingerly pick up what I assume to be my second born since he's a bit smaller. I do what I did to the baby girl and cradle the baby boy to my chest.

"What do we name them?" Axel asks quietly as not to wake the baby girl in his arms.

I look at him confused. He hasn't named them yet?

"Haven't you already named them?" I ask, voicing my thoughts. He shakes his head at my question, his eyes not moving from the angel in his arms.

"Why?" I ask in confusion as his eyes meet mine.

He pauses for a moment before explaining in a calm voice, "I had hope that you weren't dead. I just couldn't believe you were gone forever, so I held onto hope."

I stare at him with shock, awe, and love shining in my eyes. He waited for me even though I was dead. He couldn't believe it, just like I couldn't accept it.

"Carissa," I say after a few minutes of silence. "Carissa Rosemary Night."

Axel smiles at the name and nods.

"What about this little angel here, what's his name gonna be?" I ask Axel as I motion to the sleeping baby boy in my arms.

"Dylan's a good name, how about that?" Axel asks after putting on a thoughtful expression. I nod smiling.

"Dylan Ronald Night," I tell him, giving both the younger pups my parents' names. I guess it's because I want to remember them in my own way.

"Why give them the name Night? Why not Heart?" Axel asks. I look at him in disbelief. He's forgotten already?

I hold my left hand up to him so he can see the engagement ring that I'm still wearing on my ring finger.

"We're getting married," I say in a duh tone. Axel's eyes widen before he nods his head with a nervous smile and a chuckle.

"That's right, we are getting married," he says as he averts his eyes back to Carissa. I roll my eyes at him. He has a horrible memory.

I hand Dylan to Axel as well, so he's now holding Carissa on his right arm and Dylan on his left. It's actually a funny sight with Axel holding two newborns with an expression that screams, 'Don't you dare drop them!' I won't have it any other way.

I carefully pull our first born to my chest and kiss the top of his head. He's heavier and bigger than the other two, but he is an Alpha.

"I think we should name our Editing "Unique, Different, Found" firstborn Jett. Do you like that?" I ask Axel without looking away from the baby boy in my arms.

One thing's for sure, though. Carissa is going to have two overprotective brothers by her side.

"I like that name, and it suits a soon-to-be Alpha," Axel says while looking at Jett and me. I smile at him for who knows what time today, but life's too short not to smile.

38

CELINA

Have you ever had a feeling when you know something's gonna happen but don't know when? Have you ever had a feeling when your stomach just drops, and you're consumed with fear? Have you ever had a feeling that tells you to run and never look back, but you stay and fight it anyway? That's exactly what I'm feeling right at this moment.

Standing in the middle of a massive clearing that runs across the whole pack border, fear, adrenaline, hope, and faith well up inside me. Axel stands by my side in all his bare-chested glory, only wearing a pair of shorts, much like the other males. He holds his head up as his eyes are on full alert, looking and searching for any signs of the Moonlight Pack, our enemy.

The argument between Axel and I, about if I should fight in the war was certainly something. He kept saying that if I die, he would be too sad to go on and would leave the pups all by themselves and *yadda yadda yadda*. I didn't budge, of course. I love my pups and my pack, and that's why I'm doing this. I'm fighting to protect them in my own way, and no one can stop me from doing that. Not even Axel. So here we are standing at the front of all the pack and trying to look brave when I know both of us are scared, scared for ourselves, for our pack, and for our pups.

Callum and Comrade are by our side, also holding their heads up high and trying to look brave. I can see it in their eyes, though. They're just as scared as the rest of us.

The pups are safely tucked away in the safe house, along with everyone else who isn't fighting. The safe house is a little house that has been stacked up with food and other essentials. People can't get in or out unless a code is entered, which Axel and I know, along with Callum, Comrade, and now Matthew. Matthew is in the safe house with everyone else because if Callum dies today, someone has to take over his place. As much as I hate the idea, it must be done.

Anyway, the safe house is invisible, thanks to Axel, so everyone in there is safe and secure. No way out. No way in. It's actually quite smart when you think about it. The only flaw to the safe house is that the only way to communicate is through the mind link. The pack won't mind link us though because they know it will disturb us and potentially kill us. I don't know about you, but I can't live with knowing I accidentally killed someone. It's also sound proof, so nothing can be heard from the outside or the inside.

Using this moment, I look back on what has happened to me so far. For most of my life, I've been beaten and tortured until I was begging for mercy. Then I ran away and got captured here. I was scared and didn't know what to expect, but having Callum and Comrade with me helped greatly. By this time, Axel had made his way into my life. He built up my confidence and strength, letting me gain control of my life which I so desperately needed. Now look at me, standing in front of the most powerful pack as their Luna and about to lead them into battle. Oh, how my life has changed...

The sun rests high in the sky. It has to be at least midday. I look behind me to see the determined and proud faces of the fighters defending me, their Alpha, and their pack. Their determination shows that they will not back down no matter what, and their pride means that they're brave to be fighting for the future.

Remember, the prophecy states that this war will change or seal the future of every living and soon to be living werewolf. If we lose this war, the world will become a dark place. If we win, however, the world just may change into something of greatness, possibly of peace and harmony. It all depends on what happens today.

A rustling in the bushes on the other side of the border suddenly grasps my attention, along with everyone else's. Guess who emerges, the devil himself, Damon. He has his award winning smirk plastered on his face while his eyes hold an evil glint in them that makes me want to run for the hills and hide. I don't though. I stand my ground, as do all the other wolves behind me.

"Well, well, well, if it isn't little Celina Heart," Damon says in that annoying and aggravating voice of his. "I thought you were locked up in a magic box."

I tense as I realize I'm supposed to be, but that's actually Chloe. Either dead or alive, I don't know. Now's not the time to be thinking about it. I'm sure I'll find out soon. Hopefully, she'll be alive and well. I know that there's a low possibility of that, but I know Chloe, and she'll choose the best for herself.

I quickly focus back on Damon, not wanting to think about Chloe at this moment.

"Well, change of plans," I bite back, adding a low growl in the end. Damon chuckles at me then his eyes dart down to my stomach. His smile grows wider, and the glint in his eyes becomes that of pure evil.

"I see you're not pregnant anymore. Tell me, did you name one after me?" he teases, releasing a booming laugh like it's the funniest thing in the world.

I growl loudly at the mention of my pups. He will not speak of them!

He chuckles at my reaction until he becomes serious for the first time. His eyes narrow and his smirk becomes a thin line.

"Let me promise you this, both of you. After this day has ended, all of your loved ones will be dead. Your pups, your guardians, your mate, everything you cherish and desire will be dead," he spits, cutting to the point.

I guess you can call it an explosion of some sorts. Well, that's what I think when I see what unfolds next...

At the mention of his loved ones dying, Axel lets out a ferocious growl and shifts into his huge, midnight black wolf. He releases a howl that signals everyone to shift and they do in anger. Damon smirks at him and shifts into his dark brown wolf, almost black, also releasing a 'charge' howl.

This, everyone, is how the worst war in werewolf history... begun.

As wolves charge at each other, Damon's wolves bursting through the confinements of the trees, I immediately levitate into the air. I watch as a sea of blondes and browns growl and snarl and go for any opening possible. Desperately trying to kill the opponent before the opponent kills them. War is a thing that should never occur, yet it's happening right in front of my eyes.

For the first few minutes, I don't interfere since I'm so caught up with watching the battle. I just look on as the weaker wolves die and the stronger ones battle it out with each other, never being able to tell which one will win. Looking down on it is absolute hell. As the sound of ripping flesh enters my ears, I finally snap out of it and release my power.

I let the energy flow through me as I concentrate on all the trees surrounding me. I haven't tried this one out yet though I've wanted to do it for a while. Being locked up in a room for some very long months, it gives you time to think. Time to think about all the things you would love to do with your powers. This is one of them. It's called... experimenting.

As I concentrate really hard, the trees around me start to shake. My own body starts to shake as I try not to focus on the agonizing screams and howls around me.

"Come on, come on," I say to myself. Never think talking to yourself doesn't work because as I continue to talk to myself, the trees seem to come alive. Their bark contorts into faces and their roots into hands and feet. High pitched sound waves are heard, momentarily shocking me, but not the ones fighting for their lives.

I drop my arms as I watch at least two dozen trees all start to move and make their way to the battlefield. Surprised yelps are heard from the Moonlight Pack as they slowly start to back away. Maybe we've made some progress... That is until Damon barks at them and they charge once again, running for the trees and going for their roots.

I levitate back to the ground and shift into my snow white wolf. I'll be able to help more if I'm actually fighting off the enemy. I've done all I can from the sky, it's time to do all I can from the ground.

I charge at the first wolf I see, which happens to be a muddy brown colour and male. He doesn't see me coming, so I swiftly jump on his back and clasp my teeth around his neck, snapping it. I didn't even think before I did it.

The lifeless body drops to the ground and shifts back into a boy who doesn't look older than 17. My eyes widen and a whimper escapes my throat as I realize I just killed someone who will never get to live his life again. He'll never be able to meet his mate. He'll never be able to do what he wants with his life. I just killed someone.

A nudge on my right snaps me back to the present and where I actually am. I whip around with my teeth bared and my body down in the attack position. A pitch black wolf stands before me and I instantly relax my stance knowing it's just Axel.

'You ok, sweetheart? You seem pretty torn,' he asks, concerned, glancing down at the dead body of the one I killed. Now, I know this moment isn't the right time to be having a heart filled speech, but who knows when we'll get another chance?

'I killed someone, Axel,' I tell him. If I was human, I'm sure I'd be crying.

'In this case, though, it was the right thing to do. Come on, sweetheart, fight with me. Stand by my side and fight for our future,' Axel tells me proudly. The sudden cries, howls, snarls, and growls fill my ears once again. Determination, anger, and adrenaline build up within me as I let out a loud howl. Axel howls along with me and we charge back into the battlefield.

We don't get very far as I'm tackled to the ground by what seems like a sandy coloured wolf. Axel doesn't notice as he's preoccupied with his own wolf.

She growls fiercely in my ear and snaps her jaws at me. I growl straight back and make a move to get out from under her. I hitch kick her off and jump to my feet, getting down in the attack position. The female wolf follows my motions but doesn't waste a second before she lunges again. Attacking without thinking is the worst mistake you can make.

I quickly calculate my chance of winning and sees that her neck is wide open and easily accessible, an easy target.

Just as I'm about to lunge for her neck and end it, another sandy wolf comes from the side and snaps her neck. The wolf's body drops to the ground, but I look away before I can see who she really is, was.

I stare at the wolf until his eyes make contact with mine. The familiar colour of its warm brown instantly has me knowing who it is, Callum. He nods his head at me before running back into the battle and disappearing from my sight.

Hours passed, and the war's still in full swing. I've lost count of how many wolves I've killed, and I can't be more disgusted with myself. These are innocent lives going to waste. I bet Damon's pack didn't even have a choice. He probably trained them from those who just shifted to those who have been fighting for years. You can tell the difference. The just trained are either dying or running, and the trained are either killing or defending others. I don't know how Damon thought this would help him in the long run, but he certainly has a sick and twisted mind to be putting innocent children in this war to die.

The trees that I made come alive are still holding back a lot of the wolves with a few leaking through here and there. The only injuries I've managed to get are a few scratches and small bites, nothing major. That's more than what I can say for some of our other pack members. I don't know how many we've lost, but you can easily tell the difference, same with Damon's pack. Lives are being taken in the blink of an eye, and I can't do a thing about it.

I snarl at the wolf in front of me and don't wait for her to growl back before I lunge and snap her neck with ease. Her lifeless body drops to the floor and shifts into a girl who can't be older than 16. I look away, shameful. Unfortunately, she's not the first teenager I've killed.

I've turned into a monster...

Not being able to stay in my wolf form that's covered in the blood of the lives I've taken, I sprint behind a tree and shift. I levitate back up into the air and assess the situation, totally ignoring my nakedness.

It's worse than I first thought.

The trees are easily holding off at least a hundred wolves from Damon's pack, but they're slowly slipping through and once they take charge, I know my pack will stand little chance.

I use the wind to push me over to where the trees are, a simple trick Axel told me about. I hover above the trees as no one seems to notice me. They're all too engrossed trying to kill their next opponent.

I look down and tears come to my eyes. So many innocent lives will be, have been, and are being lost. No one deserves that kind of fate.

I see a sandy wolf barrelling his way through the war and immediately know it's Callum. I watch, horrified, as he snaps neck after neck after neck without even a glance at who he just killed. His eyes are guarded and his body is stiff. He's nothing like the Callum I've come to love. I can see, though, he's trying not to let this all affect him.

I then focus my attention on trying to find a light brown wolf, Comrade. I search the whole grounds and can't find him. I start to panic until he bursts out from behind a tree and tackles a wolf to the ground. He snaps his neck and doesn't even look back, moving onto the next wolf just like Callum did. I never thought Comrade would be a killer. I love him just as much, though.

Looking for my mate is the easiest out of them all because he's the only pitch black wolf. I watch as he moves at lightning speed through the mesh of wolves. What catches my eye though is that he's only killing the ones that challenge him. All the rest he just ignores. It's like he's going for a target...

It hits me like a brick wall when I realize what he's hunting down. He's hunting down Damon, the person who started it all.

I search the crowd looking for his dark brown, almost black, coat. I don't find him anywhere, but Axel seems to have a lock on him. I hope he doesn't get hurt...

I shake my head off those thoughts. Axel is older and stronger than Damon. He'll take him down without a problem.

I avert my attention back to the task at hand and notice almost instantly that another few of Damon's wolves have escaped past the trees. That can't be good...

"Right, let's show these wolves what a Shaded Wolf can do," I say to myself once again.

I bring my hands up in front of me, my arms straight and my fingers stretched out with my palms down.

This is another little trick I want to try. What better time than when it counts most? Basically, what I'm trying to conjure is a massive amount of wind that picks up large amounts of mass and drops them so... Well, you know. It's cruel, but who would you rather: your own pack dead or the pack who's tortured you all your life?

I close my eyes as a light breeze starts to swirl my already matted hair around my face, but it soon picks up to an amazing speed. I whip my eyes open to see that a cyclone has started to form on the side of the trees where Damon's pack is.

A tingling sensation starts in my fingers and travels to my hands and arms. I slowly move my eyes down to see why and gasp loudly at what I see. Just like when I controlled nature, my skin changed. Instead of swirling natural colours though, white, pink, and yellow swirls appear on my skin.

"Whoa..." I mutter, but my voice comes out in a whisper. I think if I try to yell, it won't make a difference. Even though it's such an inappropriate time, this is pretty cool.

I shake my head and focus back on the cyclone I've created. Wolves that haven't noticed get sucked up into it, then it shoots them back out again. The only thing is there's no way they'd survive that fall. Not unless they have alpha or royal blood in them, they have no hope.

Tears streak down my face as I kill dozens and dozens of wolves at a time without them knowing. Half of them don't even know what's hitting them. That's war, though, where people fight and die. That's just what it is.

After about twenty minutes of me controlling the wind, I stop and watch as the cyclone ceases to exist. The dead bodies of wolves in their human form greet my already blurry eyes. I can't help the sob that escapes my lips as I levitate off the ground again, hidden behind the trees.

How can I do this? How can I kill so many innocent lives? This isn't me! This isn't me! So why am I doing this?

Slow clapping makes my tear-streaked face snap up and meet the eyes of none other than the infamous Damon. I growl lowly at him in warning as he just chuckles at me.

"Oh, little Celina. I never thought I would see the day that you willingly kill someone. Here you are, though, killing wolves by the dozen. I must say, it's certainly a sight to watch," he tells me with a smirk, making my anger rise.

"Axel will kill you. You won't make it out of this alive," I snarl at him as I stand up and stand my ground. He actually has the nerve to laugh at my statement.

"Just remember, Celina, I warned you that your loved ones will be dead. If I can't have that, one of them will. You better watch their back," he says darkly before shifting again into his dark brown wolf and running back into the fight. I shift also, not wanting to dwell on that fact.

I honestly say that I run straight into absolute hell, wolves baring their teeth at each other while others snarl and growl. So many dead bodies lay lifeless on the now blood red forest floor. More quickly join them as everyone lunges for their opponent's necks.

I quickly catch sight of Comrade being tackled to the ground by a wolf much bigger and stronger than him. He struggles to get back up, but he's trapped. As the wolf makes a move to snap his neck, I'm over there in lightning speed knocking him off. He goes flying!

No one, and I mean no one, will kill my loved ones tonight.

Comrade gets up and nudges my side in a thankful gesture. I nod my head in return then split ways with him to hunt down anyone who threatens to hurt the ones I love.

The war's still going strong, but the sun is down and the moon is up. Only a small number remain, with my pack being the one on top. Thankfully...

Axel, Callum, Comrade, and myself all fight together as we attack in a wall, bringing down at least five or six wolves at a time. Teamwork is the key. Only little numbers remain, under fifty for Damon's pack. All I hope is that we're the ones that triumph.

After bringing down another six or so wolves, I spot a wolf trying to run away from the fight. I bark and start to run after the light brown wolf, but Comrade beats me to it. He charges towards the forest, but not before giving me a wolfy grin and a wink. I shake my head at him. Of course, he decides to be funny near the end of a history-changing war. That's Comrade for you, always trying to impress.

A howl is suddenly released as all of Damon's remaining wolves suddenly dart off in the direction to where Comrade just ran, Damon going with them. Axel growls loudly and is about to follow them, but I block his path before he can. He's in no shape to go after them with his injuries.

'Axel, you're seriously battered and injured. You're in no shape to be chasing after them. Let them go,' I tell him sternly through the mind link. He growls at me in warning, but I stand my ground. He eventually shifts and starts to bark out orders.

"Callum! Get the safe house unlocked pronto and get the pack doctors here stat! We have a lot injured, and I am not losing any more wolves tonight!" he booms in Callum's direction. Callum quickly nods, still in his wolf form, and darts off towards the safe house.

"To all of those who aren't currently dying or seriously injured, attend to a pack member! Keep asking them questions, whatever it takes to keep their eyes open!" he orders to the remaining pack members that are still standing on their feet. They all rush to the nearest pack member they see, whether they're in wolf or human form.

I immediately attend to a nearby pack member who isn't awake, but still breathing. I place my ear to her chest and sigh in relief when I realize she's still alive and well. I think she's just knocked out...

I bring my head back to look at her face and gasp at what I see. She can't be older than 14! She hasn't even shifted!

"Axel!" I scream in panic. What is she doing here?

Axel bolts to my side and takes my astonished and frightened face in his hands.

"What is it, sweetheart? What's wrong?" he asks hurriedly.

I point to the girl in utter disbelief. I still can't believe she's here. How did she get here anyway? Isn't she supposed to be in the safe house? Who is she?

"Axel, she's a girl. She looks like she hasn't even shifted. No older than 14 probably. How did she get here?" I ask, totally freaked out. It's impossible...

"I don't know, but we need to get her back to the pack house to be checked," he tells me calmly while kissing my forehead. I nod, feeling relaxed at his touch.

"Comrade, get over here!" he calls Comrade as he places his hand on the girl's forehead, probably checking for her temperature.

Instead of Comrade appearing straight away, he doesn't come at all. I look up from the girl's face and towards where I last saw him run off into the forest.

"Comrade!" I call him as I get up and walk towards the place where he took off in his wolf form. "Comrade!" I call again in panic. Where is he? Did he ever come back from chasing that wolf? Oh please Goddess, no!

"Comrade!" I screech before shifting and bolting into the woods, ignoring Axel's cries for me to come back. I try to pick up on his scent, which I do. Yes! But it's really faint, though, so that dampens my mood. If his scent is still here, then that means he can't be far! I know I'm holding onto false hope, but it's all I've got.

Please, Comrade, be alive for me.

I run for what seems like hours, when in reality, it's only a few minutes. The strong smell of blood and death fills my sensitive nose, and I presume the worst. Have they killed him? Please, no! Moon Goddess, I swear, if you can hear me, please keep Comrade safe! Please! Let him be alive!

I follow the scent for another few agonizing minutes until I come across a dead corpse. I gulp after skidding to a halt behind the dead body. I draw in a deep breath, the smell of death washing over me. Please don't be Comrade, please don't be Comrade... Then I flip the body over.

I release the breath I'm holding as I realize it's the body of who Comrade was chasing. He must've finished them off. Question is, where's Comrade? I shift back into human form and look around. He's nowhere to be found, not even a scent.

"Comrade!" I call loudly. I can hear the scattering of the forest animals, but no Comrade. "Comrade!" I call even louder this time, almost yelling. I get no answer in return as I start to run through the forest in my human form. He can't be dead! He just can't...

"Comrade!" I cry out as tears stream down my face. I don't even try to stop them. I don't know where Comrade is, and it's freaking me out.

'Please don't be dead. Please don't be dead. Please don't be dead.' That's all I say over and over in my head. Even if I don't find him, I want him to be safe and alive. I won't know that, though, now will I?

'Comrade!' I try calling him through the mind link. I wait for a reply, with my panic bolting higher by the second. I don't get one. Not a whisper, not a mumble, nothing.

A rustling in the bushes suddenly stops all my movements. My eyes widen and my mouth slightly opens. I spin around slowly, hopefully.

"Comrade," I call in a whisper, knowing he will be able to hear me if it is him.

The rustling becomes louder and a figure pops out of the bushes with worried eyes and a frown on his face.

I stay frozen in my position, not knowing what to say or do. You know the moment when you think all your dreams are about to come true but are completely shattered at the last minute leaving you helpless? That's exactly what I'm feeling now.

The person who emerges from the bushes takes one look at me and engulfs me in a tight hug. I don't hug back, though. Mainly because the person hugging me isn't the person I want to be hugging me. I remain stiff as a log.

"Celina! Thank the Moon Goddess! You can't just run off like that, especially not after a war," Axel scolds with a heavy frown on his face. It's not Comrade scolding me with a heavy frown on his face. No. Instead, it's Axel.

"He's gone, Axel," I whisper as my dams break and tears flood down my face. I don't sob or shake or do anything like that, though. I just stand there and let the feeling of absolute disappointment and dread wash over me. No one in the whole world can match my pain right now.

"Shh, Celina, shh. It's ok. We'll find him. I promise," Axel coos in my ear while rubbing my back soothingly. I nod into his chest and he carefully picks me up as he starts to carry me back to the pack house.

Comrade will never be forgotten, ever. He will be found, and whoever has taken him will have to deal with my wrath. Whoever touches my loved ones, is a dead man.

END OF BOOK ONE

Can't get enough of Celina and Axel?
Make sure you sign up for the author's blog
to find out more about them!

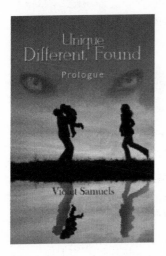 

Get these two bonus chapters and
more freebies when you sign up at
violet-samuels.awesomeauthors.org!

Here is a sample from the second book:

FORGOTTEN
SAVED
LOVED

VIOLET SAMUELS

Remember the guardian who always made people laugh? Remember the guardian who always tried to help? Remember the guardian who had a backstory? Do you remember the guardian who ran into the forest and never returned? That guardian was forgotten, or so he thought.

Did he escape?

No one knew other than the ones he loved the most.

Was he loved back? Everyone knew the answer to that.

Do you?

This is a story of the guardian who was forgotten, saved, and loved...

1

In a world of war, hate, and love, I stand alone. In a world of sadness, happiness, anger, and forgiveness, I struggle alone. In a world of selfishness, honour, generosity, and empathy, I feel alone. I stand alone. I struggle alone. I feel alone.

Alone, never again will I feel complete without knowing what's going to happen to me. Never again will I feel like my life has meaning.

How do people cope with a situation like this? Three years. It's been three years since I was captured, without even a clue if they're coming for me. These three years have caused so much pain and many fallen tears. Three years have passed and my hope is slowly slipping away. Three years... and I'm still not found. I guess you can say I'm forgotten.

Have you ever been forgotten? It's a horrible situation to be in. It makes you feel like you're not loved anymore, like no one cares. Being forgotten for so long can change a person. It can change a person so much... that he can't even remember himself. He can't remember the person he used to be. He can't remember the person who used to smile and joke around. He just can't remember.

How will you feel counting the days that you've been forgotten? How will you feel counting the times you've been beaten? How will you feel counting the wishes you've made that never came true? How will that make you feel? Sad? Angry? Annoyed? For some, it may be happy. In all honesty, it makes me feel like a total and utter crap. It makes me feel like I'm not loved and that I never was.

You know, for the past three years, all I've thought about was when they're going to come for me. When are they going to magically pop-up in front of me and say 'surprise'? When are they finally going to help me escape?

Everyday though, I wake up to the same sight. Instead of their smiling faces, I'm met with my guards' stony faces. Instead of their twinkling eyes, I'm met with the dull light of the bummed light bulb. Instead of their warm embraces, I'm met with the cold feeling that always surrounds me. I'm always met with the total opposite of what I wish, want, and need. Again, I'm all alone.

For the first year, I wished upon a star every night. I thought if all the fairytales were true, it would work and I'd magically beam back home. Believe it or not, I even tried The Wizard of Oz trick and clicked my heels together like Dorothy, while chanting: "There's no place like home. There's no place like home. There's no place like home." It never worked.

During the second year, I stopped crying and tried to grasp a hold on things. I put up with the beatings and trained my brain to help protect me against it. I trained my wolf to stay away in the shadows of my mind. I just stopped being a baby and took hold of myself. That helped.

Finally on the third year, after holding onto hope for so long... I let go of my last grip. My fingers uncurled from the thin strand and let it broke. I let my hope go. I became numb during the third year. I thought, "What the hell? No one cares anyway! What's hope gonna do, bring back my life?"

So, I became a heartless piece of nothing that rotted away in a tiny cell. My sanity, love, and happiness decayed ever so slowly. I willed my life to come to an end quicker. I just wanted this nightmare to be over. As I sit on my poor excuse of a bed, a rag on the cold cement floor, I bury my face in my hands and think. I think about what my life would've been like if I didn't end up here. I could've met my mate. I could've gotten married and had pups with her. I could've made my way up the ladder to finally become a general in training. I could've had a life. I stand up and grip my hands on the metal bars that cover the small window of my cell. It's so high up that my eyes can only see through it ever so slightly.

A beautiful sight greets me. Lush green grass is displayed on the ground, graceful butterflies are flapping their wings, wind is blowing lightly on my fingers, trees are swaying, and all I ever want is to rid myself of this confinement and get out into the world. This little window is the only way I'll know how many days have gone and passed. How many days I've been alone. I let go of the bars with a sigh and plonk back down onto the floor. Why is my life miserable? Oh yeah! Because I decided to help the ones I loved without thinking it through. I just acted on what my bloody instinct told me to do. The sound of the heavy, soundproof, metal door opening draws my attention away from my depressing thoughts. It's about five o'clock in the morning, so no guards should start their shift until at least another hour or so.

That only leaves one more person... Kate.

"Comrade?" I hear her faint whisper through the dim lighting. "Comrade, are you awake?" Yep, that's right. It's me, the little second choice for everything. The guardian that's forgotten, I'm Comrade Hollow.

I hurriedly scatter to the bars of my cell and stick my hand out into the darkness. "I'm here, Kate, follow my voice," I tell her in a hushed tone. The door may be soundproof, but it's still good to take precautions. Soon, I feel a small hand grasp my own. I slowly pull her to the bars and my eyes glimmer when I see her adorable face. Kate's a very pretty girl with waist-length dark blonde hair, and hazel eyes. She's short, about 5 ft. and 2 in. That's what you expect from a thirteen-year-old girl, though.

"Why are you up so early? You might be caught!" I scold lightly. She giggles and rolls her eyes at my lame excuse. She's always up this early to talk to me, I should know better. "Comrade, you know I always come early on a Saturday 'coz everyone's still asleep," she tells me back as she lightly smacks me through the bars. I roll my eyes "Yeah, yeah."

Kate was only ten when the war between the Nightfall and Moonlight packs happened. She was too young to fight but her parents weren't. Sadly, she lost both in the battle. She's still haunted by dreams of how they could've been killed. Since her parents died when she was at such a young age, even though it wasn't meant to be, she was put up for adoption. Here's a bit of a background story...

Remember Damon? Yeah, I'm sure you all remember him.

Well, the bastard got away and survived that bloody war. He survived the war so many other wolves didn't. He took what little pack members he had left with him and set himself up deep inside the woods of his territory. At least, that's where I think I am. As I chased and killed the runaway wolf, I was ambushed by his remaining pack members and got knocked out. I honestly wasn't in any condition to fight. I woke up in this cell and I haven't been out since.

About two years ago, Damon met his mate, Phyre (pronounced fear-e). She's Spanish, if you didn't get that. From what I've gathered, she's weird, funny, shy and when she first met me, she was a bit awkward. Also, for some odd reason, she wears combat boots every day. Honestly, I think she's a good mate for Damon because she can keep him in check against his harsh, cruel, and angry ways. Phyre is much smarter and more controlled.

On the other hand, that doesn't mean good news for me.

Unfortunately, they found out they couldn't produce pups. Phyre, of course, was heartbroken. Then you had Damon. He went on a total rampage. And guess who got the wrath of his fists? Yep, it was little weak me. I got all the hits and kicks and just dealt with it. That's when my hope started to slip away slowly.

Since there were many orphaned pups left from the war, Damon adopted one. That one is Kate. Kate was thrilled that she now had a family again, an alpha family at that. Phyre was also thrilled, but you could still see the sadness that lingered behind her eyes.

Overall, Damon found his mate and they adopted Kate. Since then, she's been coming to see me every single chance she gets. The stupid girl... I've never asked her why, though. I've never wondered why she's so intrigued with me.

"So, my pretty little girl," I begin, earning a small giggle from Kate. "What's been happening up above? I haven't seen you for at least four days!" I exclaim with mock outrage. Kate breaks out into a full on laughter and a ghost of a smile graces my face. I love her laugh. It gives me peace and makes me believe that there are still good people in this horrid and cruel world. Kate's the only one that can make me smile like this. If it wasn't for her, I don't know if I'd be coping.

"Well," she begins after her little laughing fit. "Mum has been trying to get Dad be happier and not angry all the time. You know, for certain reasons they can't help. Of course, he isn't angry around Mum and I. Um... Dad's been training all the newly shifted wolves. And apart from that, nothing much changed." For certain reasons, one of that is Damon still being angry about the baby situation.

Yes, she addresses Damon and Phyre as dad and mum. Don't ask me why, 'coz I will never do that. I think it gives her closure, knowing that she has replacement parents. I know her real parents can't be replaced though, never in a million years. No child should have to live through the pain of losing both parents in one day. I nod at her and rub my sore eyes. I sigh as I bury my face in my hands.

"Has there been any word?" I whispered. Kate knows exactly what I'm talking about. I want to know if there's been any word from Celina, Axel, or even Callum. I want to know if they're coming for me.

She puts on a sad smile as her eyes fill with sympathy. I instantly know the answer. No. "I'm sorry, Comrade, but nothing's been heard. If there is, then Dad's doing really well to keep it from everyone. I'm sorry," she repeats.

I close my eyes and sigh heavily. Life just isn't fair. "You should go," I whisper, my face still in my hands. I don't want her getting caught down here, who knows what Damon will do to her. "Comrade..." she trails off with tears in her eyes. She hates it when I ask her to leave. It breaks her tiny, little heart.

"Please, Kate. Just leave," I whisper again as I bring down my face from my hands. The truth is, I don't want her to see me like this, like the broken man I know I am. She takes one look at my eyes and her bottom lip quivers, her head nodding. "I'll be back soon," she promises, then darts out of the room. She locks the door behind her, letting me wallow in my self-pity once again.

No word from Celina. The one person who I thought I could trust. She's had three years to look for me and still, she hasn't found me. Yet, it was me who found her. I wonder how the triplets are doing. I've missed their first step, first word, first everything. I wanted to be there, to be uncle Comrade. I guess my fantasies will never become a reality. Axel is the man who has power, strength, and courage. In all honesty, I wanted to be like him. Key word: WANTED.

Now, all I want is to know why he hasn't found me yet. As I've said, he has power no one else in this world has. He's the Moon Goddess' son for Christ sake! He could've done something! He can do something. Then you have Callum, the first choice guardian, the first choice beta, the first choice friend, the first choice in everything. He even made Celina laugh first. He's seen the triplets' first step and heard their first word. He's the first uncle. Uncle Callum is always there to make someone laugh, always there to make Celina happy.

What did I do? I made her feel pain. I made her worry. I made her cry and cry and cry. There's one thing I did though that's good. That one little thing... was making her feel loved when nobody else did. Axel abandoned her when they first met. Callum just tagged along for the ride and wanted to see where it ended. Me? I cared for her. I loved her. I made her feel safe. I helped make who she is today, the confident and kind Celina Heart.

Again, I hear the doors unlocking and opening. This time though, it's not Kate. A buff man over six feet tall with greying brown hair, cold black eyes, and clothes to match his whole demeanour. Everyone, I like to introduce you to Mr. Crusher. That's all I know of his name, the nickname that was given to him for a very good reason. I learned that the first day I met him. Never again, never again...

I bolt into a standing position and clench my fists. Mr. Crusher catches onto this and chuckles darkly at me. "You know what today is, boy? Workout time," he booms in his almighty voice while unlocking my cell and grabbing me around the neck.

Four times a week, I'm forced to do workouts by fighting against the most, well-trained wolves and push my limits to the max. As torturous as that sounds, I find it as a way to vent my pent-up anger, to let everything out when I feel the need to. For me, it's a way of mentally fixing myself. It's also made me a lot buffer than I was before. I have biceps, an eight pack, calf muscles, and most importantly, I have the strength to carry on. Something I needed for a very long time. Mr. Crusher drags me to the workout station that's only a few metres away from my cell. He throws me straight into the wall that's adjacent to the weights. I look at them with an emotionless expression. Here comes the pain.

"Get to work, boy!" Mr. Crusher snarls. The vein in his head starts to make an appearance and his muscles flex with annoyance. Hey, I would be annoyed too if I had to wake up at six o'clock on a Saturday to supervise a prisoner. It'll probably be better if I just do what he says and get this over with, but where's the fun in that?

I take my sweet time while getting up just to aggravate him more and make my way over to the weights. I lower myself onto the bench press and physically prepare myself for the 250 kilograms I know I have to lift. "Don't test my temper, boy. I have power over you," Mr. Crusher threatens. To add to his threat, he of course, adds another 50 kilograms to the weights, forcing me to bench press 300 kilograms. That bloody bastard. On top of having werewolf strength, I also have my guardian strength added to that, making me extra strong and mighty helpful in these circumstances.

"One!" Mr. Crusher booms and I lift the weights with determination, just to prove the bastard wrong. He will not overpower me! "Two!" he continues and I lift it again. The muscles in my arms work with all their might as I strain and push them to the limit. "Three!" he booms again.

I lift the weights again and all that's going through my mind is: 'I hate that bloody son-of-a-bitch.' He continues until I've done 100 bench presses with a 300 kilogram weight. Yet, this is just the beginning. Mr. Crusher smirks at me. "Tired?" he asks curiously, his smirk still evident on his face and his eyes twinkling with hate towards me. I'm sure mine are burning with the hate I feel towards him too.

I smirk right back with a challenge in my eyes. "Not even the slightest." The smug smirk drops from his face and a deathly glare replaces it. Bring it on, Mr. Crusher.

Hours and hours of gruesome workout and I'm just about ready to collapse. I won't though, because that will mean giving in and I don't do that. I won't even mention the stuff Mr. Crusher got me to do. It's too painful to think about. "Had enough now, boy? Huh? All tired out and ready to give in?" Mr. Crusher mocks me. I shakily rise from the floor where I just had a defense and offence game with the one and only Mr. Crusher. Guess who won? Not me.

All my muscles are burning, my joints are aching, and I just want to fall to the floor and sleep. I don't answer his question, just breathe heavily. For what seems like forever, we just stare at each other and see whose stare is first to break.

We do this at the end of every workout, when I know I've had enough and when Mr. Crusher knows he's won. Neither of us admits it though because sometimes the outcome is different, and I'm the one who wins.

His smug smirk that I've become accustomed to shows on his face. "I do believe that this workout is over." His voice smugly states and all I want to do is punch that already crooked nose of his. I don't answer him. I just follow him back to my cell. He gives me a rough shove to which I growl at. He just laughs and proceeds to lock my cell then walks away.

As soon as I hear the heavy door closing, I collapse to the ground. This is what I had to live with for the last three years. This is the torture I had to go through... and it's only lunch time.

If you enjoyed this sample then look for **<u>Forgotten, Saved, Loved</u> on Amazon!**

Other books you might enjoy:

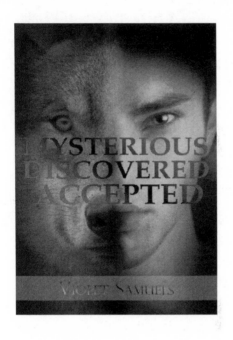

Mysterious Discoveries Accepted
Violet Samuels

Available on Amazon!

Break Me, Mate
Nique Joaquin
Available on Amazon!

Introducing the Characters Magazine App

Download the app to get the free issues of interviews from famous fiction characters and find your next favorite book!

iTunes: bit.ly/CharactersApple
Google Play: bit.ly/CharactersAndroid

Acknowledgements

This story is a work of fiction. Everything from the plot to the characters have all been created by my imagination and solely that. I thought one day, why not write down one of the stories going through my head? So I did and look where that got me.

Firstly, I would like to thank my friends. They were there for me when I first started writing this book and they were there when I finished it. They have been my rock and I'll be forever grateful to them for it. They never gave up on me and when I gave up on myself, they hauled me back up and pushed me to go on.

I would like to thank my parents and older brother. They supported me every step of the way with enthusiasm and happiness. I'm glad they were with me on the journey that I didn't even know I was walking down. They halted their plans to encourage me and motivate me to get this book published and I will always love them with all my heart for that. So, to my parents and brother, thank you so so much because without you, I wouldn't be here.

I would also like to thank my dedicated and amazing readers on Wattpad. If it wasn't for them, my book never would've hit one million reads and it probably would've never been published. They helped me to continue writing and not give up when writers block got in the way. They were always there with their amazing encouragements and awesome attitudes. Thanks Wattpad and I hope you guys continue to achieve the max.

One of the most important people in the process of publishing this story though, was my agent Le-an Lacaba. She's been a wonderful agent, always being there to help me through the process and actually giving me the unimaginable opportunity to have my story published. She helped me overcome fears and uncertainties along the way. I will always hold her close to my heart for everything she's done for me. Thank you Le-an and

I wish for you to have unmeasurable success in the future.

Everyone in my life has helped me write, create and publish this story and I couldn't be happier. It makes me cry knowing that all these people have given me the opportunity to do something I never believed I could do.

So, I don't have one specific person to thank for everything, but I have an immense amount of wonderful, inspiring and thoughtful people to thank because without all the people involved, I never would've achieved what I have today.

I love you all and you will always be close to my heart. Thank you so much and please, never forget the amazing fortune you have given me to be able to publish. For everything everyone has done, I am eternally grateful.

Thank you and I love you,
Violet

Special thanks to these awesome people:

Lisa Mak
Francesca Sanchez
Geydi Orozco
Martha McKinney-Perry
Madeline Bush
Stephanie Alcor
Melinda Cardona
Maddie Moudy
Maddie Moudy
Lesley collis
Hope

Author's Note

Hey there!

Thank you so much for reading Unique, Different, Found! I can't express how grateful I am for reading something that was once just a thought inside my head.

I'd love to hear from you! Please feel free to email me at violet_samuels@awesomeauthors.org and sign up at violet-samuels.awesomeauthors.org for freebies!

One last thing: I'd love to hear your thoughts on the book. Please leave a review on Amazon or Goodreads because I just love reading your comments and getting to know YOU!

Whether that review is good or bad, I'd still love to hear it!

Can't wait to hear from you!

Violet Samuels

About the Author

Violet Samuels lives in Australia, being half Australian and half Portuguese, and is a young girl/woman that is still in her youth. Even for being young, she's never lived in one place for more than two years.

However, the favourite place she has lived was on the Whitsunday's. Violet loved the Whitsunday's because it's where Unique Different Found all began and it's where her friends convinced her to go for it and have a go. Look at where that's brought her.

Violet Samuels is a bubbly and energetic girl/woman who is kind, caring and has a big heart. She loves to dance, sing and act and can't wait for so many people to read her book to let them escape from the rest of the world, even just for a little while.

Sign up to her blog for more freebies and updates! violet_samuels.awesomeauthors.org

Made in the USA
Middletown, DE
30 March 2018